OURS to LOSE

LACEY BURKE

Print ISBN: 978-1-964973-01-2

Cover Designer: Kari March
Editor: Emerald Edits
Copyeditor: Editing4Indies

For anyone who's had to say goodbye, and for everyone who never got the chance.

Content Note

While *Ours to Lose* is a light contemporary romance, it does contain mention of heavier topics, including death of a parent due to pancreatic cancer (off page) and themes of loss and grief. Please take care of yourself while reading.

Prologue

Three Years Ago

GABE

He tried to warn me. I'm surprised your friendship has survived the slaughter

AUBREY

He's used to it by now. Plus, it's his own fault for letting your family teach me how to play. I was an innocent child when I moved next door until Evan dragged me to a game night.

GABE

And now you're a cold-blooded killer. Too bad I'm leaving tomorrow or I'd demand a rematch

AUBREY

Does that mean you won't be home for Christmas?

GABE

Afraid so. Now that I've got the High Hitter fight to get ready for, I probably won't make it home again until next year

AUBREY

I'm so excited for you! I thought your mom was going to jump on the table when you got the call from your coach 😂. It sounds like an incredible opportunity.

GABE

We'll see. This style of tournament hasn't really worked for boxing on a global scale outside of the Olympics. But it sounds like the guys putting it together have enough money that it could be big

AUBREY

Well, I'm going to cook the hell out of the food for the watch party your mom and Evan will no doubt throw. And your dad's "no professional chefs in the kitchen on holidays" rule won't be able to stop me.

GABE

Only problem with that plan is I fully intend on having them with me for it in Japan. Sounds like you'll just have to join them

AUBREY

That depends…will there be merch I can wear?

GABE

I'll make sure you have a shirt with my name on it

AUBREY

Your face too?

GABE

Whatever you want

AUBREY

Deal 😄

I should probably get some sleep. I'm in charge of the kitchen tomorrow, which means I have to get to the restaurant early even though the day after Thanksgiving is usually dead. But thanks for texting. Having you home always makes the holidays feel right.

GABE

I was thinking the same about you. And I wanted to give you a proper goodbye, given how chaotic things still were when you left. With training for the tournament, I probably won't be great at staying in touch

AUBREY

Then I'll wish you luck now and see you in Japan. Go kick ass.

GABE

You too, killer. And I still want that rematch

AUBREY

Anytime, Hardt. Next time you're in town, give me a call.

GABE

Count on it. Don't make my baby bro cry too hard in the meantime

AUBREY

No promises

Thirteen Months Later

SATURDAY, DEC 25 · 5:14 P.M.

AUBREY

Hey. I'm thinking of you today. Evan said he hasn't heard from you, and I know how hard holidays can be, especially this soon after the funeral.

I've been thinking about your mom's gingerbread cookies and how she'd have us help decorate them when we were all home. The nonstop Christmas music she'd play while your dad cooked. How she bought us new mugs each year specifically for his eggnog. She's who I think of when I think of Christmas. It doesn't feel right that she's gone.

I know you may not want to talk, and if you don't, that's okay. But if you ever do, know that I'm here.

THURSDAY, FEB 24 · 3:31 P.M.

AUBREY

Just checking in. Hope you're doing okay.

WEDNESDAY, APR 27 · 11:27 A.M.

AUBREY

Saw you have a fight coming up. Glad you're back in the ring. Good luck.

SUNDAY, MAY 8 · 1:06 A.M.
GABE

I miss her

AUBREY

I know. I do too

Chapter One
Aubrey

Two Years Later

My boss was out of her fucking mind.

What else explained her marching backward up the stairs to the thirtieth-floor lobby of Matice Enterprises in a Hugo Boss dress and Louboutin stilettos while she cooed words of encouragement to the dozen burly men who trailed her, carrying what had to be over a thousand pounds of steel, glass, and wires?

"That's it, gentlemen. Almost there. Easy. Easy. There you go. Very nice."

Jillian crested the stairs to the landing and guided the movers to the center of the room, where they set down what looked like something between a disco and golf ball on steroids attached to a jumbo flagpole.

"Isn't it marvelous?" she said as she joined me along the wall while the men got to work attaching wires and arranging pieces.

"Definitely," I agreed. "What is it?" I didn't need to know to see it was pretty.

"A replica of the Millennium Times Square ball complete with 504 crystal panels and over 600 halogen bulbs."

"And it's going to…?"

"Drop tomorrow at midnight to bring in the New Year." She said it as if it was as simple as whipping together a cheese plate.

I glanced toward the sparkling globe again, where the workers seemed to be constructing some platform near the towering wall of windows. Through them, the glass skyscrapers of Philadelphia's Center City gleamed. "You mean…inside the building?"

"That's right. The drop will be shorter, naturally, so they'll adjust the speed of descent, and the fireworks will remain outside, but with the confetti cannons and light show, the overall impact should be about the same."

Filthy rich and out of her fucking mind. I hoped to be even half as delusional when I reached her age.

She turned her full attention to me, her auburn bangs swooping perfectly across her forehead. "How's the kitchen looking? Do you have everything you need for the party?"

I snapped into work mode and handed her the printout. "Just need you to approve the timing for the courses." It was all appetizers and desserts that would be served cocktail style, but I'd planned a progression for the dishes that would offer both the variety and excitement of a sit-down chef tasting. "The kitchen's all set, and I'm finishing prep this afternoon."

She nodded along as she read over the page, then handed it back. "Perfect. You're going to shine." Pride already gleamed in her eyes, and I could tell it was pride in *me* as much as the catering division of her restaurant we were launching tomorrow night.

Arden Catering, offshoot of Ardena Restaurant. All mine to lead, run, and grow.

I wished I shared Jillian's overflowing confidence it would be a hit. As it stood, my insides bubbled like caramel just thinking about it, and it was too soon to say if it would turn out silky and amber or a clump of charred rock.

It wasn't that I doubted my skill. Shove me in a room full of strangers, and I might be the last to speak, but that was the beauty of being a chef—my food spoke for itself. It deserved Jillian's pride. I wanted to soak it up and let it saturate the parts of me that hadn't had a grandma to praise my home-made cookies in six years or a mother figure to brag to her friends about me in two.

But this other part kept getting in the way—the one that felt as if a loaded food pallet had been set on my shoulders and was slowly crushing me to the ground. I wasn't sure when in the past few months it had arrived or what the problem was. Only that a heaviness I couldn't shake kept the smile I returned from feeling all the way real.

It had to be nerves. After all, I had a mountain of prep work to tackle and a catering debut for three hundred people to pull off. That would put anyone on edge. Except for maybe Jillian.

Back in the kitchen, Evan hauled in the last box of food and set it on the stainless steel prep table. Between his fitted jacket, styled blond hair, and dimpled chin, he made it look more like a Gap photo shoot than manual labor.

He glanced around and whistled. "I was worried all this food wouldn't fit, but that was before I knew you'd be cooking in a kitchen the size of my dad's house."

A house might have been a stretch, but my one-bedroom apartment would fit with square feet to spare. "Perks of the boss owning a near-billion-dollar company," I said.

He took in the vast space filled with boxes of raw ingredients. "Is Jase swinging by to help?"

"No, he's at the restaurant with the guys getting ready for tonight." I would have loved to have my old crew with me—not just Jase, but Zach and Luis too.

But it was both a Saturday night and the day before New Year's Eve, which meant Ardena would be slammed, and Zach and Luis would be needed there as line cooks as much as Jase would be needed as its head chef. One of those nights when the ticket machine never stopped printing and the flow of the kitchen took on a life of its own.

Based on the reservations, Jase anticipated it being one of the restaurant's busiest nights in the little over a year since it opened.

A wave of longing passed through me at missing out. A few months ago, I would have been at Ardena alongside the others, prepping for the onslaught.

Zach with his heavy-metal playlist burning out his speaker while Luis tried to sneak in a Taylor Swift song. Jase grumbling about not knowing how they could stand the noise despite secretly liking it. The four of us talking and laughing at jokes as we crossed off each item of the mise en place, building the energy that would take us through the night.

I hadn't been a part of it since taking on the role of head caterer three months ago. There was no time with a new prep kitchen to set up, menus to plan, and staff to hire. All tasks I'd done in some capacity as Jase's sous chef, but never ones I'd been in charge of on my own.

Now, I was in charge of it all: the planning, the prep, the execution. Since I had yet to find any staff, I was also in charge of getting it all done in time.

I would. I was good at my job.

I just wished I had my team to do it with me.

"He'll be at the party tomorrow night," I reminded myself as much as Evan. "And I'll have Zach helping me in the kitchen for most of it." I wished I could bring him over to the catering side full-time, but Zach was happy where he was as a line cook.

I'd been happy where I was as Jase's sous chef, but the time had come to move on. I'd known it would at some point. I just hadn't expected it to be so soon.

When Jillian and Jase approached me with the catering idea at the end of summer, there was no question it was the right move for Ardena. We'd just catered a hugely successful symposium that had garnered more than a little interest, and a dedicated catering team was the perfect way to capitalize on it.

Then they'd asked me to head it up, and I couldn't tell them no.

I hadn't *wanted* to say no. I'd enjoyed catering the symposium, and it meant the world that Jillian and Jase trusted me to do this.

Just nerves, I assured myself. That was all the weight glued to the pit of my stomach was.

"Speaking of tomorrow," Evan said, "I came up with a plan." He wore the same look as when he'd decided we should run for senior class office so we could change our high school's official mascot to a sponge.

"No," I said, grabbing a box of produce to load into the walk-in.

Evan grabbed one too. "You don't even know what I was going to say."

"Yet I still know my answer is no."

"You might actually like this one," he said as we placed the boxes on a shelf.

"Will I?"

"Probably not, but you should hear me out anyway."

I sighed.

Evan grinned. "Okay, I figure since you'll be working all night, you won't have time to scout out a kiss for midnight."

I pushed past him for the door. "No way."

"But I'm already going to be scouting for a kiss of my own. I can easily keep an eye out for a guy for you."

"And what? You'll drag him back here thirty seconds before midnight and ask him to smoosh faces with me?" That landed solidly in my "nightmare scenario" column.

Evan shrugged as if that was a perfectly normal expectation. "Yeah."

He was as delusional as Jillian.

"Absolutely not." I rounded the prep table to grab another box, bringing this one to the counter with the cutting board I'd set out earlier.

"I'd pick a good one," he said, trailing me. "And it'd be healthy for you. It's been forever since Patrick, and this is the perfect opportunity to try something new without any pressure."

Three years was hardly forever, though I could see how it might feel that way to Evan. He rarely went more than a week between hookups.

I set out my phone and pulled up my prep list. "I'm not kissing some random dude you pick out for me in a crowd just to have a New Year's kiss. I'm not that desperate."

"I never said you were desperate."

"Your plan kind of did that for you." I peeled an onion as my phone buzzed on the counter.

"No, my plan—"

His sudden silence had me glancing up to find him staring at my phone. Gabe's name filled the notification pop-up with the first part of his message visible.

Gabe: You would love it. Next time I'll...

I lowered the onion and took a deep breath before meeting Evan's stare.

His nostrils flared as he held his voice steady. "You're still texting him? After he bailed again?"

"He didn't bail on Christmas," I said, careful to keep my tone neutral. "His flight got canceled because of a storm." And he'd apologized to his dad and me about fifty times for missing it despite there being nothing he could have done short of gaining the ability to control the weather.

He'd have apologized to Evan too if Evan would have bothered to read the message.

Evan's jaw tensed. "Doesn't mean you have to keep texting him."

"Someone should."

I'd been that someone for the better part of two years. The only consistent thread of connection Gabe had to his home after everything shattered.

I hadn't planned to be. Hadn't expected him to respond after the first couple of times I'd checked in, never mind keep responding.

But he'd been a thread of connection for me too. An unexpected source of comfort that could make me laugh or feel seen with a few simple words through my phone screen. One I saw no reason to give up just because Evan had taken a pair of kitchen shears to his own relationship with Gabe.

"You think *I* should, is that it?" His gaze lowered to the counter, hands squeezed into fists, every part of him drawn tight.

We were both adults, nearly twenty-nine, but all I saw in front of me was the boy I'd grown up with. The one who loved so big and hurt even bigger. Who did everything he could to protect himself from pain for fear it would be too much.

I kept my voice gentle. "Do I think you should reconcile your estranged relationship with your brother who, for most of your life, was your best friend? Yes. I do."

"I don't need him as a best friend," he insisted. "I've got you."

My heart squeezed at the depth of that simple truth. He did have me, just like I had him. Just like we'd always had each other. There wasn't a day I wasn't grateful.

I grazed his fist with my pinky, and he uncurled his own to hook with mine.

"What about as a brother? Do you not need that either?"

I asked, knowing how much he did. No one else could fill the void of all Gabe was to him.

His voice was hollow. "He made that choice for me when he left."

"And now he's coming back. You get to decide what that means for you, but I won't shun him just because you are."

He finally met my gaze, his eyes red. "He still might bail."

"He might," I agreed. I didn't believe he would, but there were no guarantees.

"And even if he doesn't, that won't mean he'll stay."

"You're right."

He sighed through his nose, not liking where that left him but too tired to fight it. He rocked our linked hands. "You've got work to do. I'll finish unpacking the boxes."

"FIFTEEN MINUTES TO MIDNIGHT," I called to Zach as I finished plating a tray of lamb and pear meatballs with a pomegranate-balsamic reduction. "I want the last of the dishes ready to go out in ten. You almost done with the wild mushrooms?"

I patted my hands on the towel tucked into my apron, then reached for the linen napkin to wipe the rims of the plates. The adrenaline rush from the start of the night redoubled as the ball drop drew near, perspiration gathering beneath my chef coat and along the bandanna I wore to keep loose hair off my face.

"Bringing them to you now. Behind." Zach approached my prep table, his tattoos, piercings, and shaved mohawk as punk rock as you could get in a pristine white chef jacket, and placed the hot frying pan of perfectly glazed wild mushrooms to my right. The earthy aroma of black garlic infused the air.

"Looks good, Chef. Thank you."

The night was going well so far. Food flowed out of the kitchen on schedule, and empty trays came back in record time. Zach and I had slid into the zone, communication coming easily from having worked hundreds of dinner services together at Ardena.

Once we got through this push, there'd be only desserts and cleanup to handle. With the desserts waiting to be garnished in the blast chiller and two industrial dishwasher machines at our disposal, the rest of the night would be a breeze.

My phone buzzed as I sent out the final round of savory food. I smiled when I saw Gabe's name, the first I'd heard from him today. It was just before five a.m. in London, which meant either he was up early or he'd had one hell of a New Year's celebration of his own.

I'd filled him in last night on Evan's plan to find me a stranger to kiss. A plan Evan had determinedly tried to convince me to accept. He'd popped into the kitchen three times tonight to describe potential candidates he'd spotted at the party in case I'd changed my mind.

I hadn't. But I did explain to Gabe the reasoning behind Evan's plan, including that I'd never had a New Year's kiss, despite Patrick and I being together for three years.

Where I loved any excuse to dress in something sparkly and dance in a crowded room, Patrick had embraced the accountant stereotype of preferring to be in bed by eleven. He'd encouraged me to go out and have fun, which I did. It just meant I'd gotten New Year's Day kisses, but never one at midnight.

I should have known when I'd mentioned it to Evan months ago that he'd take it on as his personal mission. The only thing as fun for him as prowling through his own love life was meddling in mine.

I smirked at Gabe's text. They might not be talking, but he and Evan were definitely still brothers.

Gabe: I could help you with that

A handful of butterflies kicked up their wings at the thought, a holdover from the childhood crush I'd buried around the time I left for culinary school. Not that it took a crush to see how attractive Gabe was. Half the people at this party would easily jump on his kiss.

Me: Ha. You'd have to be on the same continent as me first.

"Can we head out for the ball drop, Chef?" Zach asked after starting a load of dishes.

I pocketed my phone. "Definitely. In fact, enjoy the rest of the party. I have dessert covered."

His face lit up. "Really?"

"You earned it."

"I can still help with cleanup."

I waved him off. "Let's go say hi to everyone."

We weaved through the crowd of expensive suits and glittering dresses until we found Jase and the group on the edge of the dance floor. They cheered as we approached. Jase's girlfriend, Dani, was wrapped in his arms while his brother, Alec, and sister-in-law, Steph, raised glasses of champagne.

"The food's been incredible!" Dani said with a warm smile, her brown hair and fair skin popping against the deep purple of her dress. With Jase in dark trousers and a navy sweater, his own dark hair intentionally ruffled, they looked absurdly attractive together. Not to mention ridiculously happy.

"For real, I can't stop eating that cheesy onion thing," Alec said. The sweet onion galette with truffle fonduta. It was basically French onion soup in fancy bite-size form and was always a crowd-pleaser.

Jase flashed me a look that said he'd never expected different. "You're crushing it, Chef."

That uncomfortable slurry of pride and melancholy swirled around my chest at the compliment, intensifying when Jase turned to Zach and asked, "You looking for your boyfriend?"

My gaze swung to Zach, who was taking advantage of his wiry height to peer over me into the crowd. "Boyfriend?" I asked. "Since when?"

His gauged ears went pink as he failed to hold back a smile. "That guy from the concert last month. We sort of made it official a few days ago."

Had I heard about the guy from the concert? I had no clue which concert, so probably not.

"Luis brought a date too," Zach added, eager to shift the attention from himself. "He finally asked out that girl who's been coming into the restaurant."

"Which girl?" I asked.

"The short one with bangs? Always orders the maitake steak? She started coming in a few weeks ago."

I managed a smile, forcing it wider as he and Jase joked about the look of pure terror Luis had worn before making his move. A pit opened in my stomach the longer I listened.

How much had I missed in the past three months? What else was I out of the loop on when it came to these boys I practically counted as little brothers?

Not nearly as much as I'd miss from now on.

I may have still been a part of the Ardena family, but not in the same way as before. We were no longer a single unit. They weren't here celebrating our achievement; they were here celebrating mine.

I was crushing it. *I* was shining. Yet somehow, it felt like *I* was being left behind.

The pit in my stomach gaped wider as it fed on itself like a black hole.

An arm draped around my shoulders, and Evan pulled me into a side hug. "The badass of the hour." He nodded toward the stunning Asian woman at his side with silky dark hair and cheekbones any social-media model would envy. "Emily here said she hates collards, and even she couldn't get enough of the fried rolls."

"They were really good," she agreed about the collard spanakopita cigars with mint oil. She turned a flirtatious grin toward Evan. "I can't wait for dessert."

His arm fell from my shoulders as he pulled her close, his voice dropping low. "Oh yeah?"

I averted my eyes. As glad for him as I was he'd found his kiss for the night, I didn't need to see it up close.

Only, one look around, and I found myself surrounded by couples.

Boyfriend and girlfriend. Boyfriend and boyfriend. Husband and wife. Special someones, if only for tonight. It hadn't felt significant before this moment, standing amid the cluster of them…alone.

Everyone paired off with me as the odd one out.

"One minute to go!" Jillian announced from the stage, turning the party's attention to the crystal-studded ball at the far end of the room.

In less than sixty seconds, it would reach the stage in a whirlwind of lights and confetti, and every person here would turn to their partner to share the moment with while I floated adrift, not forgotten but not chosen either. The background extra in someone else's movie.

My neck went hot as an uncomfortable feeling took root in my stomach, its vines growing and twisting around my organs and squeezing too tight.

"I'll be right back," I blurted. My voice got swallowed by the swell of music as I ducked away while everyone's attention stayed fixed on the display.

The live band started a drumroll, and claps picked up in time to the countdown—all of it drowned out by the pulse in my ears as I pushed my way to the kitchen. Even as I reached the solitude of tiled floors and stainless steel appliances, my breaths refused to slow, my eyes burning for reasons I didn't understand as I dug through my pocket for my phone.

What was happening? Nothing about tonight should have upset me. The people I loved showing up for me shouldn't have made me feel worse. My throat shouldn't have been tightening with held-back tears while everything around me seemed to stretch and fold into a cavern of empty space with me stranded in the middle.

I wasn't new to being alone, yet here it was swallowing me up like a snake with its jaw stretched wide.

Maybe I should have said yes to one of the guys Evan picked for me. Maybe something shallow and meaningless would have been enough to prevent whatever crack this was inside me from forming.

Something told me it would have made everything worse.

Throat thick, I unlocked my screen and opened Gabe's messages, seeking the buzz of connection I got any time his texts came through.

My fingers stalled over the keyboard with no clue how to put into words what I wanted. Then I remembered I'd either be waking him or interrupting whatever he'd gotten up so early for before.

A blast of percussion and cheers flooded the kitchen as the door behind me opened, the countdown from ten carrying in the background. I tucked my phone away and adjusted my headband, not wanting to turn around. Except it was probably a drunk couple who had wandered off, and the one thing sure to make this moment worse was hearing strangers have sex in my kitchen.

I blew out a breath and drew on my customer-service face, then spun and froze as I registered the person in front of me.

Not a stranger.

Gabe.

He towered before me like a Greek sculpture, all power and beauty captured in sharp lines and tan skin with broad muscles Zeus himself would probably find some envy for.

Somehow not in London at all but standing beside my prep bench mere feet away.

His soft blue eyes landed on me, made softer by his growing smile, the kitchen's fluorescent lights shining off his silky blond hair and comfy-looking sweats.

Seeing him, the twisted vines inside me loosened, and the frenzied energy of the night—every spike of adrenaline and emotion from the past six hours—narrowed to a single burning impulse.

I didn't ask what he was doing here when his flight wasn't supposed to arrive until tomorrow night. I didn't ask how he'd known where to find me or if he was hungry. I didn't ask if he wanted to see the ball drop.

I didn't ask him anything.

I closed the five steps between us and kissed him.

Chapter Two
Gabe

I'D ONLY BEEN KNOCKED out once in my boxing career, the first year I'd gone pro. One second, I was on my feet getting ready to swing, and the next, I woke flat on my back with the world spinning around me, no clue who I was or how I got there, trying to remember how to speak.

That was how it felt to have Aubrey's lips pressed to mine.

One second, I was taking her in from across the room for the first time since my mom's funeral, and the next, I was dizzy with that coconut scent of hers in my head, the sweet taste of her on my tongue, her hands clasped around my neck to tug my mouth to hers.

Letting her wasn't a decision so much as a calling.

I followed it, letting my fingers graze her cheek as I met her halfway. My palm settled against the soft skin below her jaw, and I hurried to obey the demand of her lips, both gentle but determined as her fingers scraped the base of my neck, trying to thread through my short strands.

It awoke every cell in my body. Her scent invaded my senses, my skin buzzing where we touched, and her arm tightened around me, spurring me to tug her hips forward to eliminate the space between us.

She let out a soft noise as our bodies connected, then rose on her toes and pressed closer, and all thought flew from my mind. There was nothing except me and her, my tongue finding hers as she opened for me on a moan and yanked my shoulders lower.

Holy shit, she felt good. Her warmth radiated through my hoodie, and I slid my hands over her chef jacket to palm her ass, my fingers flexing in a gentle squeeze. Her sound of pleasure echoed off the stainless steel appliances, driving my body hotter until I had her pressed against the wall with my thigh between her legs, nearly lifting her off the ground.

When I'd offered a New Year's kiss, this wasn't what I'd pictured. My mind had played out something quiet and sweet, the way Aubrey so often had been around me growing up. But the urgent roll of her hips as she practically climbed my torso to take what she wanted was something else entirely.

It had me one second from lifting her for real—wrapping her thighs around my hips and grinding my stiff cock right against her heat.

I would have if the sound of glass shattering didn't jerk me from the moment. My head snapped up as I shifted to block her body from view despite us being fully clothed.

Drunken taunts came from the hallway beyond the kitchen door as whoever dropped the glass laughed it off with their friends and moved on. My heart rate eased to normal.

At least, until I looked at Aubrey.

Fuck, she was beautiful.

Her blond hair was pulled into a bun, a navy bandanna keeping the wisps from her face so all I could see were her big hazel eyes staring up at me as she caught her breath. Her pink lips were swollen, the skin around her mouth red from the scrape of my stubble—there'd been no time to shave after the eight-hour flight from London. Seeing it gave me a sick satisfaction.

I hadn't originally planned to get here by midnight. The goal had been to surprise her by coming home a day early so I could make her big catering debut, but then she told me how she'd never had a New Year's kiss, and my plans had changed again.

I'd been more eager than I probably should have to make the offer. It turned out, she'd beat me to it. I wasn't complaining.

I flashed her an easy smile. "Happy New Year."

She ran two fingers over her lips, her gaze falling to my mouth.

My smile widened. It was a good fucking kiss.

One I wouldn't be against repeating, though I doubted she'd want that. Aubrey was more someone who settled down, and I didn't have much to offer long-term.

The reminder helped calm my body a few more notches.

"Thanks," she mumbled, then shook herself from her daze. "I mean, Happy New Year. Well, and also thanks. I mean—" A flush rose to her cheeks. "For letting me kiss you."

My skin flashed hot at the memory, and I shifted my weight to get my blood pumping a direction other than south. "My pleasure. Did it meet expectations?"

Her brows rose. "Hmm?"

I fought a grin. "Your first New Year's kiss."

"Oh, right. Yes. Yes, it definitely did." She rolled her lips together and pushed from the wall, heading to what looked like a mini fridge on the other side of the room. She pulled out a tray lined with light purple domes the size of hockey pucks and placed it on the nearest counter before crossing to the big walk-in fridge and asking over her shoulder, "How are you even here right now? I thought your flight got in tomorrow?"

I leaned against the wall and watched her work. "I caught an earlier flight on standby. Wanted to surprise you and the family." Mostly her. I wasn't as confident my family would be so glad to see me. Not all of them, anyway.

Back at the counter, she intently drizzled dark brown sauce onto the hockey pucks and topped each one with some sort of crumb. "Your dad's going to be ecstatic. He's been holding out on making eggnog all week so the holidays will only be official once you're here."

Yup. He was the one who'd be glad to see me.

"Evan around?" I asked. No sense avoiding the elephant in the room. She knew its size, shape, and emotional weight better than anyone.

"He's here somewhere. Probably won't get home until way later if you want some one-on-one time with your dad."

"Dad won't be asleep by now?"

"Evan says he's usually up late."

I tensed. "Since when?" My entire life, Dad had gone to bed by nine and been up at five. No alarm, no grumbling. Snores sailed down the hallway five minutes after he said good night, and he'd be well into his second mug of tea, morning paper read front to back, before anyone else stumbled out of bed. I couldn't remember him staying up this late, even for New Year's Eve. Not in the past decade.

Her shoulders were stiff in their shrug. "The past year. Maybe two. Sometimes he goes to bed earlier and gets up for a few hours during the night."

The words struck like a sucker punch, filling my mouth with the bitter taste of guilt. A reminder of the reality I'd soon have to face—the reason Evan knew our dad was having trouble sleeping and I didn't. That our dad was having trouble sleeping at all.

That there was nothing I could do about it because there was no way to bring back the wife he'd slept beside for thirty-five years and lost.

I swallowed it down. "I'll text him. Let him know I'm getting in tonight."

"You didn't tell him yet? Where were you planning on sleeping?"

My lips tipped up. "I hadn't planned that far ahead. I had a kiss to make happen."

She blushed again before turning all her focus to the desserts.

A minute later, two servers in white shirts and black ties came through with empty trays. Aubrey loaded them with the finished hockey pucks, which turned out to be concord grape semifreddo with peanut caramel and French toast crumble. I only had a loose grasp of what that meant, but I'd sure as hell eat it.

After the servers left, desserts in tow, I stood from the wall. "I'll get out of your hair. Don't want to interrupt the flow any more than I already have."

She gave another shy smile, a reminder we hadn't spoken

much in person as adults. Not like we had over texts. There was a familiarity to our messages that our body language and mannerisms hadn't had the chance to gain.

Maybe that would change now that I was back.

I hoped so. Just standing here in the same room as her brought a similar relief to seeing her name on my phone. A reprieve from the bone-deep weariness that had haunted me the past two years to the point it sometimes took everything I had just to make it through the day. A weariness that being home both eased and made infinitely worse.

I wanted more of that ease. For both of us.

I turned for the door, the familiar weight of exhaustion already heavying my steps.

"Hey, Gabe."

Aubrey rounded the counter and headed for me, no hesitation in her movements, soft understanding in her eyes. Understanding that came from her own acquaintance with grief as much as her big heart.

My chest lightened as I opened my arms and pulled her in for a hug. She tucked herself against me, her ear pressing to where my heart pounded too quickly, sending warmth throughout my body.

I let the scent of her coconut shampoo comfort me as I inhaled slow and deep, then brushed a soft kiss to her head.

"Welcome home," she said.

My shoulders dropped at the sincerity of her words. A weight somewhere inside me lifted for a moment I knew wouldn't last but that I was grateful for all the same.

I squeezed her shoulders before releasing her. "See you around?"

It wasn't what I wanted to say. But putting into words the

enormity of the gratitude and tenderness I felt for her wasn't something I knew how to do. And even if it was, sharing those words with her didn't seem fair. Not coming from a liability like me.

She nodded once, her hazel eyes wide with compassion, and I left her to her work before I did something stupid like kiss her for an entirely different reason.

Back in the hallway, boisterous cheers and laughter from the party rose above the live music, flavoring the air with a contagious sort of high. One I nearly caught until my gaze reached the end of the hall.

I let out a resigned sigh.

I'd hoped to walk out of here without having to face the one person who now despised me. The person whose disdain hurt nearly as much as Mom's death. It figured I wasn't that lucky.

Down the corridor, stopped short at the sight of me, stood my brother.

He was still a few inches shorter than me, several pounds leaner, and a hundred times more handsome with his buttoned suit and polished sideswept hair the same blond as mine.

I almost strode to him and pulled him in for a hug the way I would have three years ago. The way I had every time I first saw him after being away for long stretches since I turned pro at eighteen and he was thirteen.

He was my baby brother. My best friend.

I missed him.

But then I saw the clench of his jaw and cold bitterness in his eyes and remembered.

He wouldn't accept my hug if I tried. I didn't blame him.

"Hey," I said instead.

He turned to the elegant brunette on his arm and tipped his chin toward the stairs. "I'll meet you by the coats. Just going to say goodbye to Aubrey and grab you a dessert, okay?"

She flashed a curious glance my way as she strode down the hall.

Evan squared his shoulders to me as if stepping into the ring. "What the hell are you doing here?"

Fair. He didn't owe me pleasantries.

I assumed he meant what was I doing at the party since, according to Aubrey, he'd known since Thanksgiving I planned to come home for the holidays. So that was what I answered. "I wanted to be here for Aubrey."

"Yeah?" he snapped back. "The way you were there for Mom?"

I flinched but didn't argue. That was fair too. "I know it's been a long time. I'm hoping to make up for it."

"You mean you're actually staying this time? There's not going to be a plane you have to catch two weeks from now for an opportunity that's just too good to pass up?"

I swallowed. "Training camp for one of my fighters starts in a week. Selection for the Olympics. I'll be gone for a month or two, but then I'll be back."

He laughed humorlessly and strode for the kitchen door. "Sure you will."

"Evan." I reached for him as he passed.

He snatched his arm away and rounded on me. "You know what? Don't bother coming back from camp. Dad and I don't need you here, and Aubrey doesn't either."

The truth of his words hit harder than any punch could,

the sting lingering longest around her name. The one person to make me feel something like hope in the aftermath of our world going dark.

"I'm allowed to be friends with her," I defended.

"No, you're not. The last thing she needs is another person in her life who bails on her. She's better off without you, and so am I. Stay the fuck away from us both."

He shoved through the kitchen door, leaving it swinging in his wake as my chest tightened around my lungs. More servers rushed by with trays, jostling me to the side and trailing confetti on the carpet from the party where hundreds of people celebrated a new start.

Two minutes into the new year, and I'd already managed to fuck it up.

THE FRONT DOOR to the house opened, and Dad emerged onto the steps before the cab even reached a full stop. I paid the driver and grabbed the strap of my large duffel, adjusting my grip a few times as I waited for my pulse to slow.

Two years, one month, and fourteen days.

That was how long it had been since I'd last seen my dad in person. The same amount of time since I'd last been home. I'd spent the ride counting the number, right after texting Dad to let him know I was coming.

He'd responded right away.

So many times, I'd come home like this after being gone three, eight, twelve months straight. Enough that I held a picture of it in my mind, exactly how it would look when I turned around and stepped from the cab.

The large maple tree standing watch out front, its branches bare, the fallen leaves long since raked and removed from the yard. Mom's trimmed rose bushes that lined the walkway to the door where the porch light shone to welcome me home. The tidy brick exterior with its large bay window and slanted gray roof Evan and I tried to climb onto from his bedroom window more than once growing up, like the fools we'd been. It was a miracle we hadn't broken more bones.

I knew what waited for me, and still, I was terrified to face it. Because all of those things could be the same, but nothing about home would be.

The smack of the storm door rang through the quiet street, telling me my dad was walking down the steps. I took a last deep breath and flung open the cab door.

The cold air seized me a second before my dad did. His arms were around me almost before I was out of the cab, crushing me to him like he worried I'd disappear if he let go. I couldn't really blame him for it.

I hugged him back as fiercely, dropping my chin to his shoulder with my eyes kept shut, too afraid to open them. Too afraid to do anything else. I strained to keep my breathing normal as emotion constricted my chest.

"Welcome home, son," Dad whispered with a squeeze. His voice cracked as he said it, and I pinched my eyes shut harder.

I didn't deserve his welcome. Didn't know what to say in response. My throat was too hoarse to speak anyway, so I kept hugging him, letting him be the one to pull away.

When he finally did, the cab was gone, and my ears stung from the cold. I would have rather frozen out here the rest of the night than face what came next.

I started with just facing Dad.

He grinned up at me, tall as ever but still a few inches shorter than my six-two, his eyes the same blue Evan and I shared. His shone with joy as he assessed me the way I assessed him, and my immediate thought was just *Dad.*

The fierceness of how much I'd missed him almost took me to the ground. Unlike Evan, Dad had taken my calls when I finally sucked up the courage to make them too many months after Mom's funeral, but it wasn't the same. Not even close.

It was part of why I'd avoided coming home in the first place. This overwhelming wave of emotion there'd be no getting around that I had no idea how to deal with.

Maybe my dad felt the same. If he did, he didn't seem to expect us to figure it out now.

He clapped me on the shoulder and bent for my bag. "Let's get inside. Is it this cold in London?"

"Nearly," I said as I followed him up the walkway. Not that I could really tell. My body had gone numb beneath my hoodie with each step we took toward the house.

It looked exactly as I'd pictured.

I almost wished it looked different. Like in a dream when what was supposed to be one thing was another. You were "home," but it resembled your high school cafeteria or the set of a Disney ride you went on when you were twelve.

I wanted this house to look as foreign as I felt.

Dad reached for the door handle, and I rolled my hands into fists to stop them from shaking. He swung the door open, and my heart pounded in my throat as I stepped inside, my muscles bracing as if the floor had been laid with hidden traps.

None sprang. It was just the house I'd grown up in, exactly as I remembered it.

The same family photos on the walls. Same welcome mat on the floor. Same couch and loveseat in front of the TV. Dad's chair still in the corner beside the lamp that spilled warm light into the room.

The TV tray next to Dad's chair was the only new addition. That and the missing floral scent. Even in the cold months, Mom had some sort of candle or spray to imitate pine or a winter bouquet. Now it smelled like nothing.

"I'll go put this in your room," Dad said, hauling my duffel up the stairs. "Want me to grab you some slippers?"

I unglued my feet from the entryway and shut the door behind me, swallowing the dryness from my mouth. "No, I'm good. Thanks."

While he disappeared to the second floor, I toed off my shoes and wandered inside.

For as similar as it appeared, nothing about the house felt the same. Like it was an aquarium drained of its water; the life it once contained drained with it. All that remained were empty shells, and every one of them, from the couch and curtains to the dining furniture and kitchen clock, seemed to turn their accusing eyes on me.

I felt like a stranger. Unsure of my place, not wanting to touch anything I shouldn't.

Not wanting to be here.

The floor creaked as Dad descended the stairs. "I changed your sheets when you texted. They're the flannel ones. They should keep you plenty warm. Are you hungry?"

"I can wait until morning. It's late."

He waved me off. "That doesn't matter. You had a long flight, and I'm not sending you to bed on an empty stomach."

I followed him into the kitchen, where he rooted through the fridge.

"I don't have much in the way of leftovers, but we've got bread if you want a sandwich. Or I could make eggs. Oh, and I'll heat some eggnog."

I almost argued but decided not to. He clearly needed this, and I was as glad for his company, even if it meant he didn't sleep.

There was no question Aubrey had been right about him staying up late. In the bright light of the kitchen, his changes were painfully obvious.

He'd lost weight. Looked older.

He'd had white hair for years, so that wasn't it, and the lines in his face weren't any deeper. Somehow, he was just… frail. Wilted. A tired version of the sixty-something retiree who used to be bounding with energy. Energy he still seemed to lack even with the huge smile on his face.

Or maybe that was due to the bags under his eyes. They shouted at me like an accusation, stabbing at my guilt.

As much as I'd known when I left the way I did how fucked up it was—to stay away and not text, to rarely call, to all but disappear—a part of me had believed my dad and Evan would be okay. That they would be there for each other the way I couldn't be there for anyone. That together, they would find the path toward healing I didn't get to find after the shitty son I'd been.

It wasn't like there was anything I could offer. Not hope. Not strength. Not solace. I was a toxin it was better for everyone to be far away from, and believing it was how I'd stayed gone for so long. But even as I let myself live inside the delusion, a part of me had known it wasn't true.

None of us were okay. My dad least of all.

And I hadn't been here for him any more than I'd been there for Mom.

He placed a mug of eggnog in front of me at the small breakfast table, the steam warming my nose. "So are you back for a while?" he asked as he sat across from me with his own mug. The hope in his voice was impossible to miss.

"I think so." I tried to make my voice light. "I've been training this kid, Noah—I think I told you about him."

"The kid from Allentown?"

"Him. He's got selection camp for the Olympics starting next week, so I'll fly out for that. But then, I'll be back. Coach Lou is looking for someone to sell his gym to, and I'm going to see if I can make it work."

"Your own gym?" Dad's whole face lifted with delight. "Son, that's incredible. Tell me more about what Coach Lou said—wait, first..." He hopped up and grabbed the bread off the counter. "Sandwich or eggs? We could even have some real fun and go for French toast. What'll it be?"

The rocks that had filled my stomach compressed into one massive lump between my ribs, even as my mouth watered. Dad's French toast was the best. His sandwiches and eggs too. Anything he cooked.

Here he was, wanting to cook for *me*, to spoil and take care of me. To treat me like I hadn't been MIA for two years. Like I hadn't abandoned him. Like I still deserved his love despite the holidays I'd missed and excuses I'd made.

Like loving me was as easy for him as it had always been.

Of all the ways tonight had been painful, that might have been the worst.

Chapter Three

TUESDAY, JAN 9 · 8:21 P.M.
GABE

Just landed

AUBREY LIKED A MESSAGE.

AUBREY

How's the altitude? Dizzy yet?

GABE

No, but I could put it to the test. Maybe go for a run, hit the booze?

AUBREY

Definitely the run. If you end up puking, you don't want to waste all that good Colorado beer.

GABE

See, these are the important considerations I count on you for

AUBREY

You're welcome

. . .

FRIDAY, JAN 12 · 6:31 P.M.
GABE

Noah's completely in his element. He's going to crush this selection

AUBREY

Woo-hoo! He's doing well so far?

GABE

The best I've seen him

AUBREY

I'm wishing him luck

THURSDAY, JAN 18 · 4:12 P.M.

AUBREY

Welp, I'm 0 for 4 on sous chef interviews. I didn't think it'd be so hard to find someone.

GABE

The ones you met with didn't have enough experience?

AUBREY

Some did on paper, but they weren't good fits.

GABE

You'll find the right one

SUNDAY, JAN 28 · 8:28 P.M.
GABE

Went with Noah and his parents today to see some sculptures his mom heard about. They reminded me of your tattoos

[Image 1]

[Image 2]

AUBREY

Ooh, pretty! I should get Evan to design me something like the bird in the first pic

GABE

That one was my favorite

AUBREY

I have a space on my back where it might look cool. Or maybe my thigh.

GABE

What'd you do today? Another event?

AUBREY

Not today. Catered a rehearsal dinner yesterday, so today was cleanup and getting ready for a few consultations next week.

Now I'm watching Nana's favorite movie in honor of her birthday.

GABE LOVED A MESSAGE.
GABE

Which movie?

AUBREY

A true Christmas classic

GABE

It's a Wonderful Life?

AUBREY

Close. Die Hard

GABE

Are you serious?

AUBREY

Swear to God

GABE

Your grandma's favorite movie was Die Hard?

AUBREY

She had good taste.

GABE

Apparently. I wish I'd hung out with her more. Think she would have watched boxing with me?

AUBREY

Strong, shirtless men punching each other and getting all sweaty for entertainment? It wouldn't have been a hard sell.

GABE

Is that all I am to you? A strong, shirtless man?

AUBREY

Of course not

You give good TV suggestions too. Ted Lasso was *chef's kiss*

GABE

I see how it is

Better go find another show to recommend since that's all I'm good for

Although you still haven't taken my word on
The Bear

AUBREY

I believe it's good! I'd just rather not watch a
show that'll shove the most stressful parts of
restaurant life in my face.

GABE

Fair enough

I guess if I want to honor your nana, I'm left
with taking strong, shirtless selfies

AUBREY

I'm sure her spirit wouldn't complain.

GABE

I'll wait till I'm in the gym with Noah so I can
be nice and sweaty too

AUBREY

Very considerate of you

MONDAY, JAN 29 · 2:07 P.M.
GABE

[Image]

For Nana

AUBREY LIKED AN IMAGE.

AUBREY

She would have loved it.

GABE

As much as Die Hard?

AUBREY

Too close to say

THURSDAY, FEB 1 · 5:49 P.M.

AUBREY

I have 2 chef interviews lined up this week!
Fingers crossed one of them is a fit.

GABE

It's gonna happen. I can feel it

TUESDAY, FEB 6 · 12:33 P.M.
GABE

How'd the interviews go?

AUBREY

0 for 7

GABE

Shit. Sorry

AUBREY

It is what it is. Dani's birthday's tomorrow, so
a group of us are going out to dinner, which
should be a fun distraction.

GABE

She was at Thanksgiving at my dad's house
this year, right?

AUBREY

Yeah, Jase's girlfriend.

GABE

Have fun

AUBREY

Thanks. If I was still working at the restaurant, I wouldn't be able to go, so that's a plus side to catering.

GABE

Who else is going?

AUBREY

A few of Dani's friends she works with and Neela from the restaurant. It'll be a girls' night since Jase is working.

GABE

How many of those have you had?

AUBREY

Ha, none. My wardrobe's excited to see some action.

GABE

Do I get to see the outfit?

AUBREY

Depends on whether I need help picking out shoes.

GABE

I think you should run it by me either way, just to be sure. For completely selfless reasons.

AUBREY

Hmm. Maybe if you ask nicely.

GABE

I'll say please as many times as you want

. . .

WEDNESDAY, FEB 7 · 6:42 P.M.

AUBREY

What do you think?

[Image]

GABE

Yes

AUBREY

So it meets your discerning fashion standards?

GABE

If by fashion standards, you mean I think you look incredible, then yes

Do me a favor?

AUBREY

Sure

GABE

Let me know when you get home?

AUBREY

Will do

THURSDAY, FEB 8 · 1:04 AM

AUBREY

Home

GABE LOVED A MESSAGE.
GABE

Did you have fun?

AUBREY

Yeah 😊 Dani has cool friends.

I'm tired, though. I hardly stay up this late anymore.

GABE

Go get some sleep

AUBREY

On my way. Noah still doing well?

GABE

He's been on fire. No way he doesn't make the team

AUBREY

Good. I'll keep sending him luck.

Good night

GABE

Night

SATURDAY, FEB 10 · 5:06 P.M.

AUBREY

Note to self, never announce I'm pregnant at a friend's bridal shower.

GABE

Lmao no way. Who did that?

AUBREY

A bridesmaid at the bridal shower I catered today. She gave a surprise "toast" to tell everyone she's pregnant. The bride looked like her head was going to explode.

GABE

😄 Why would the bridesmaid think that was a good idea?

AUBREY

Right?? I don't even think she was related to the bride, so it's not like it was her family there. Everyone looked so confused, and the bride stormed out. It was wild.

GABE

I feel like we could find a way to get Evan to storm out of his own wedding shower if we tried hard enough

AUBREY

Not if he sticks to his "never getting married" plan.

GABE

Since when is that his plan?

AUBREY

Idk, some point in the past few years. He says he'd rather be a professional wedding guest than a groom.

GABE

Oh

How's my dad doing?

AUBREY

He seems good. Well, aside from the Eagles not making the Super Bowl.

GABE

An understandable tragedy

He's thinner than he was

AUBREY

Yeah. If it helps, he's been pretty steady at his current weight for about a year.

GABE

You've been tracking it?

AUBREY

Evan has. He got a scale that connects to an app so he can track it on his phone. He was worried too.

GABE

Oh. Good

AUBREY

You know, you can ask me how Evan is doing too if you want.

9:34 P.M.
GABE

How is he?

AUBREY

Evan?

GABE

Yeah

AUBREY

He's okay.

GABE

Still pissed at me, I take it

AUBREY

He won't talk about it, so it's a safe bet.

Have you tried texting him?

GABE

A couple weeks ago. No response

AUBREY

Give him time.

GABE

Yeah

SATURDAY, FEB 17 · 5:38 P.M.
GABE

Guess who's officially going to the Summer Olympics

AUBREY LOVED A MESSAGE.

AUBREY

Woo-hoo!

[Celebration GIF]

How does it feel?

GABE

I don't even know. I'm so proud

The really fucked-up thing is I think I'm a little envious too

AUBREY

Makes sense you would be. It's okay to miss it.

GABE

I know. It's just not always this bad

AUBREY

THURSDAY, FEB 22 · 12:57 P.M.

AUBREY

0 for 10

GABE

WEDNESDAY, FEB 28 · 9:22 P.M.

AUBREY

This bar has a beer from Colorado Springs.

[Image]

GABE

Which bar?

AUBREY

Blue Amber. Dani's friend Kelly picked it.

GABE

Another girls' night?

AUBREY

Sort of

I probably won't stay much longer.

GABE

Why? Something happen?

AUBREY

No, it's nothing. Just tired

GABE

You sure?

AUBREY

Yeah. Promise

GABE

Text me when you get home?

AUBREY

Yeah

WEDNESDAY, FEB 28 · 10:11 P.M.

AUBREY

Home

GABE LIKED A MESSAGE.
GABE

How was the rest of your night?

AUBREY

It was fine. Kind of a bust, but that's probably for the best.

GABE

Want to talk about it?

AUBREY

I'm good. Just gonna go to bed.

GABE

Let me know if you change your mind

AUBREY

I will. Thanks

GABE

Any time

Chapter Four
Aubrey

March

TEN SECONDS. That was how long I'd allow for self-pity before I dragged my forehead off the counter and resanitized the kitchen. You'd think the concept of a wipe-down rag and a sanitizing rag wouldn't be difficult for a grown chef to manage, but it sure had been for the chef who'd just finished his trial shift.

He was not getting the job.

And not merely because after three detailed explanations, including a visual demonstration, he'd continued to dunk the dirty wipe-down rag into the sanitizing solution until it was filthier than the counters it was supposed to be cleaning. It was because every other task I'd asked him to do throughout the day had gone the same.

I wasn't looking to hire perfection. I was more than willing to train someone still a bit green. I didn't even care if they'd gone to culinary school. But I couldn't have someone on my team who couldn't follow basic instructions. That was the bare minimum.

Twelve interviews in two months, and no prospective chef had hit it.

Which meant I'd be working tomorrow's event alone. Again.

Six events Arden Catering had done since New Year's, and all but one of them I'd worked by myself. The exception had been the first and only time I'd conducted a trial shift at the event instead of during prep the day before—a mistake I'd quickly learned from.

But the longer I went without a team, the longer Arden Catering would go without turning a profit. Three events a month wasn't enough to cover overhead now that we were renting a separate prep kitchen, and I wasn't willing to risk taking on much more on my own. Not when establishing a strong reputation was Jillian's top concern.

She didn't care about the money yet. Especially with how well the restaurant was doing. First and foremost, this catering operation's mission was to amplify the impression Ardena had made, which meant doing things right.

But we couldn't go on not making money forever. I refused for Arden Catering to become a burden for Ardena to carry. So if I had to suffer through a thousand more failed interviews, that was what I'd do.

Ugh.

I hauled myself to standing and filled a new sanitizing bucket while I tried to decide which was worse: hiring staff or my attempt at finding a hookup the other night. Another first and only to add to the list.

The going-out part hadn't been bad. I loved going to clubs, dancing and singing in a sway of bodies until my voice was hoarse and my feet were ready to fall off. I usually went with Evan, who kept an eye I was safe while finding his own dance partner to take home at the end of the night. Or sometimes I tagged along with Zach at a gay club where our tattooed, dancing duo would sweat through our clothes and laugh as hard as we sang.

This time had been different. I'd been on a mission: get laid.

Much as Evan tried, he didn't really work as my wingman. Guys either assumed we were together or secretly in love because apparently the concept of male-female platonic friendship was as baffling to some as a sanitation rag. That or the guys would get hypercompetitive with him in a macho, walking-red-flag kind of way, which was helpful to weed out in the long run but didn't solve my current problem of being very, very horny.

Like clockwork, another flashback to Gabe's New Year's kiss gripped me as fiercely as he had my waist. The warm heat of his body pinning mine to the wall, the round muscles of his shoulders and biceps flexing under my palms, our mouths locked in a perfect rhythm my hips had no choice but to chase.

"Did it meet expectations?"

Ha.

It had been good, all right. More like better than any kiss I'd had, ever. It didn't help I'd dreamed about kissing Gabe since I was nine.

Except the Gabe of my teenage dreams had kissed me like I was sweet and innocent, a fragile thing to be careful with.

Gabe in real life had kissed me like he wanted to ravish me. Like it took everything in him not to rip off my clothes and fuck me over the counter.

Heat rushed between my legs as the image of him fucking me over *this* counter filled my head, and I squeezed my thighs together, swallowing a moan of frustration as I scrubbed the prep table harder.

This was the problem. This constant *ache* I couldn't get rid of, no matter how many times I wore out the battery on my vibrator.

It used to be I'd power the thing up once a week and be set. Now, I was whipping it out morning and night and still had the urge to slip into the bathroom at work to rub one out.

I was going crazy with horniness. Craving the experience of being with another person that a vibrator could never give. The skin-on-skin, feeding off each other's arousal, having the weight of their body on you, hearing them groan kind of experience. The sensory high of it all.

Something *physical.*

It was what I'd imagined sex would be like until I'd had it, and the all-consuming whirlwind of pleasure turned out to be more of a light breeze.

Let's just say my vibrator had been more than enough in comparison.

Apparently not anymore. At least not with Gabe sending me shirtless pictures of himself all sweaty and toned from a workout.

That had been the straw that led me to reach out to Dani

and her friend Kelly, who I'd learned liked to socialize with the opposite sex as frequently as Evan did.

The plan had been simple enough. Go to a bar, meet a few guys…

I hadn't thought beyond that, seeing as I figured I'd be ready to jump on the first thing with two legs and a penis. But evidently, even supercharged horniness had its limits.

While Kelly had been in a lip-lock with her catch for the night within twenty minutes of arriving, I'd sat awkwardly at the bar with the guy's friend, two seconds from flashing Dani our "Get me the hell out of here" signal.

It wasn't an appearance issue so much as the way he kept eyeing my tattoos and asking me questions like, "So you're into pain?"

I really wasn't. I just liked tattoos. Liked how they could capture even a fraction of nature's beauty in my skin. How with each new flower or herb or creature, my body became that much closer to looking like a real-life fairy garden.

At one point, he followed me to the bathroom as if he assumed "I have to pee" was code for "come have sex with me in the corner stall." Which, why would that be a thing? What about public bathrooms made anyone go, "Hell yes, I for sure want to have sex beside this well-used toilet"?

But seeing as sex had been my goal, I let him lean in for a kiss. Maybe there was something to it I just hadn't discovered yet. Only the second he got close enough for me to smell his sour breath, I'd recoiled.

I didn't get it. How come Evan and Kelly had no problem making out with strangers, but I couldn't? It was like I was turned on by the idea of sex but not the reality of it.

My relationship with Patrick had pretty much checked

that box. I'd wanted to have sex with him, but every time I did felt like me hoping this would be the time that felt good. That I would finally understand what everyone else was so excited about.

I still didn't, despite being a straight woman who'd spent most of my life surrounded by men.

My social life growing up had been whichever of Evan's guy friends we hung out with at the time, since I'd been too shy to initiate my own friendships. I'd gotten along with some girls in school, but never to the point of real connection.

Then I went to culinary school and entered a male-dominated industry where every kitchen I worked in was a boy's club. According to mainstream television, that scenario should have landed me enough sexual partners to fill an advent calendar.

Meanwhile, I hadn't had sex for the first time until I was twenty-four, had slept with a grand total of one man, and hadn't seen a penis in real life since we broke up three years ago. If I was on a sitcom, my vagina would have shriveled up and died by now. I might have thought it had if it weren't for that kiss with Gabe.

It had been so easy with him. Automatic, almost. Like my body knew how to move and respond to his touch to the point I just sort of sank into it. I wasn't trapped in my head worrying whether I used too much tongue or if I should use more, or where to put my hands and what sort of noise I should make.

I hadn't been in my head at all. My body had been in charge, and for once, it hadn't tensed like a rabbit that spotted a hawk.

I wanted to see what else my body could do. What else came naturally when my defenses fell away.

But it wasn't like I could waltz up and ask Gabe to have sex with me. He didn't view me that way. The kiss on New Year's had just been him helping me out. One of what had to be a dozen New Year's kisses he'd likely had that meant nothing to him. The fact that it hadn't come up in any of our texts during the past two months essentially confirmed as much.

And really, I didn't have time for sex anyway. Until Arden Catering was on its feet, the only thing I needed to score was a competent sous chef.

And maybe a second vibrator.

I fed my frustration into my cleaning, polishing the counters until my reflection shone back at me. Ten minutes later as I was putting on my coat, Jillian walked through the door.

She was the same height as me, a mighty five-two, yet with how her presence filled the prep kitchen, you'd think her head scraped the ceiling.

"Oh good, I caught you," she said, placing her purse on the spotless counter and removing her leather gloves. "I thought you might have left."

It was a little after five, the time service started at Ardena. I was still adjusting to the fact that, except for the nights I had events, my evenings were now free.

"I just finished prep for the Cimorelli bridal shower tomorrow," I said. "We're all set."

"Excellent. There's something I need to discuss with you."

I nodded for the door. "Should we go to Ardena?" The catering prep kitchen was a short walk to the restaurant, and we'd had a few quick-brainstorming-turned-long-planning sessions there already.

"No need." She retrieved a folded pile of papers from her purse and slid them across the counter.

I pulled them apart and read the top page: *Pennsylvania Dining & Hospitality Association (PDHA) Flavor of Philadelphia Catering Competition.*

Arden Catering's information had been filled in, and at the bottom of the application, the status read: ACCEPTED.

My stomach tightened as the rest of my body braced as if sensing an oncoming train. I glanced at Jillian. "You entered us into a catering competition?"

A mischievous glint filled her eye.

Oh boy.

Chapter Five
Gabe

THE BANK'S front door felt heavier on the way out than it had walking in, as if the weight of rejection had been added over the course of my meeting with the loan officer.

Loan denied.

This was the fifth bank I'd tried since returning to Philly two weeks ago. A month and a half at selection camp had passed in a blink, and Noah was officially on the USA Olympic boxing team. I wasn't sure I'd ever felt so proud.

Or as solid in my decision to open my own gym. I wasn't competing anymore, but I still had plenty to offer this sport. Achievements I could strive for as a coach—like fostering a new generation of fighters and building the foundation for them to carve their own paths in the ring.

Now, it was a matter of finding a bank that would give me the loan to buy Coach Lou's gym. The same gym where I'd first learned to fight. Where boxing became more than a sport for me but a way of life.

I'd known going into the loan process that it might be a challenge, given I'd never owned a business. Hell, I'd never owned a car. Before retiring from fighting, I'd only spent money on things directly related to boxing—training gear, equipment, housing, my team. I didn't even have my own suit to wear to the loan interview—I'd borrowed my dad's.

Today's bank, at least, hadn't rejected me outright. They were willing to give me the loan despite my lack of business credit if I paid 40 percent down instead of the usual twenty. It was great news, except that I didn't have that much saved. I had a fair amount—a little more than half—but without the rest, it did me no good. Since I couldn't start training clients until I had a gym and the only other way I'd ever made money was by fighting, I had no clue how I was going to get it.

I'd figure something out. Time was one thing I had plenty of.

Halfway to the bus stop, my phone rang.

"No way," I joked when I answered, smiling against the cold breeze. "Is *the* Diego Bosques really calling me?"

Diego laughed. "The one and only. It's been a long time, man. How've you been?"

"Oh, you know." I hadn't heard from him in five years at least. We'd trained together as kids, the two of us giving Coach Lou more than one headache. While I went pro, Diego went into the business side of the sport, getting his promoter license and putting together events.

"I heard you're back, slumming it in Philly," he said.

"Yeah, well, I figured it was time you and Charlie had someone to keep you in line. You still revolutionizing the sport for the better?" He was the youngest boxing promoter in the US, and he and his business partner's company, RedGloves, had singlehandedly revived the local boxing scene in Philadelphia and throughout the Northeast.

"Sure trying. We're actually putting together an event a few months from now I thought your boy Noah might be good for. It's a tournament—all fighters with some tie to Philly. Winner gets a hefty prize, and it'll be televised across the East Coast. It'd be good promo for him if he's thinking of going pro."

"Sounds like it. If he weren't about to be too tied up training for the Olympics, I'd be all for it."

"Hold up, really?"

I grinned ear to ear. "We just got back from selection."

"Dude, congrats! Good for him."

"Thanks. And hey, when he does go pro, you'll be the first I let know."

"I better be. I call dibs. Do me a favor and let me know if you hear of anyone else who might want into the tournament. I've still got a few open spots."

"Sure thing."

We hung up, and my resolve to figure out this loan solidified. Not only was the gym a part of my history, but I already had close ties to the area. Any fighters I trained interested in going pro would have my connections to give them a leg up in finding the right opportunities.

It *was* my gym as far as I was concerned. Now, I needed to find a way to make it official.

Located in an up-and-coming area of Fishtown, the gym sat on a corner of Girard Ave across from both a light rail station and bus stop. The building had seen better days—its sand colored paint was faded and chipped, its broken windows boarded behind rusted metal bars. Coach Lou had a hard time maintaining it after his second heart attack forced him to close its doors and retire. It'd been sitting here since, a missing piece of the community waiting to be brought back to its former glory.

I got off the bus and made my way inside, surprised to find Coach Lou already in the office. Still bundled in his jacket, thin white hair peeking out the bottom of his cap, he sat hunched against the edge of the desk as if the chair behind it wasn't his place anymore. I tossed the gym's keys on the desk beside him and threw my suit jacket on the cot in the corner.

Coach watched it land and shook his head as if just looking at the cot made his back hurt. "I can't believe you choose to sleep here," he said.

"I like it. It's familiar."

"What about the home you grew up in? It's got an actual bed you can sleep in."

I flashed a grin. "I don't need a bed. I'm not an old man like you."

He blew out a hoarse laugh. "It's coming for you sooner than you think."

What I didn't say was this cold, abandoned building felt more like home to me than the home I grew up in. That when I'd slept there after New Year's, everything that had once felt familiar and comforting now brought nothing but shame. Like the walls themselves judged me.

"It's helpful being here," I told him. "Gives me inspiration for how I'll set it up when it's mine."

"How'd it go with the latest bank?" he asked. "Any luck?"

"Not exactly. It wasn't a hard no, but I'll need more cash

before they give me the loan. It might take me a bit to come up with, but I'll keep you posted."

We'd been meeting for lunch most of the past two weeks to talk out my business plan and break down the numbers. In fact, he was pretty much the only person I'd spent any real time with since returning from camp. I still hadn't even told Aubrey I was back.

That I hadn't ate at me. I *wanted* to see her. To tell her my every wild dream for this place so she could imagine it with me in the way only she could. She'd become one of my closest friends over the past two years. Someone I shared things with first and opened up to the easiest.

But that had all been over messages. Building that friendship in person felt bigger somehow, more permanent. And permanent wasn't something I had a lot of experience with.

Evan's words from the party still swam in my head, telling me the last thing she needed was another person who bailed.

I didn't want to be that person.

I'd been telling myself I would reach out to her as soon as I got the loan. That it would be an official sign I was here for good. But it wasn't looking like that'd be an option for a while, so I'd have to figure something else out.

Or maybe I didn't. I was probably overthinking this. Aubrey had never been the one who cared whether I was here or how long I stayed. She wouldn't hold it against me if I left.

"That's actually why I stopped by," Coach said.

I tucked away thoughts of Aubrey. "The loan?" I asked. "Did you have an idea?" He'd already agreed to sell to me for a steal, so going any lower on the price wasn't an option. He had a long retirement ahead to pay for.

"No. It's…well." He rubbed his forehead, almost nervous, the blue veins in his hand pronounced through his pale and thinning skin. "A developer approached me yesterday."

My heart dropped.

"They made me an offer on the building. A big one."

I hid the initial panic from my voice. "Did they tell you their plans for it?"

"Said they wanted to tear it down and put up some new apartments. Something to bring in a younger crowd."

Outside, I'd gone perfectly still. My body had dropped into boxing mode, composure on and adrenaline pumping as my pulse ran sprints through my veins.

"Did you accept?" I wouldn't blame him if he had. The kind of money they were probably offering meant he'd never have to worry about finances again. His medical bills would be handled, and his wife could stop stressing. He could take her on vacation. Take her on a few.

"I told them I needed to think about it. Look into it more, make sure it was legit. They gave me a few months before they'll make their offer final."

I blew out a breath and clasped my hands on my head, the rigid material of Dad's dress shirt pulling tight beneath my arms.

"I don't want this place to become some fancy apartments," Coach said. "You know that. I want you to have it. But I've got Cynthia to think about, and if you can't get the loan…I don't know if I can pass up this kind of offer."

"I know. I wouldn't want you to."

His voice went hopeful. "We've got three months. You get the loan by then, you have my word this place is yours. If not…I'm sorry, Gabe." The regret in his words reached his eyes, the weight of it hunching his shoulders.

He looked old. Tired like my dad. Worn from the world as much as age. From keeping this place going so long for kids like me. I didn't want to be one more load he tried to carry.

"I get it, Coach. Really. I appreciate the three months." I stepped forward and gave him a hug.

He slapped my back. "You can do this. I know you can." If I didn't find the money for the down payment, he'd have to say goodbye for good to what had once been his whole life. To what was still mine.

I couldn't lose boxing. Couldn't lose this chance to keep it a part of me, to solidify a new place for myself in this community. Already, it was slipping away from me, and I wouldn't let it. Not after everything I'd lost to get here.

I walked Coach to his car, then returned to the office and sat in the desk chair. Before I could overthink it, I pulled up Diego's number and dialed.

"How much is the purse for the tournament?" I asked when he answered.

He told me. It wasn't world-champion money, but it was enough to get me my loan.

"I have a fighter for you," I said.

"Really? Who?"

The only option I had left. "Me."

Chapter Six
Aubrey

"THE PRIZES ARE GREAT, and I can see why she thought it'd be a good opportunity, but there's no way I can maintain the current event load and come up with a strong enough concept when I don't even have a team yet," I said as I loaded the last supply crate into the catering van.

"What are the prizes?" Jase asked through my earbuds. The bridal shower ended thirty minutes ago, and this was the first chance since yesterday's meeting with Jillian I'd been able to talk to him about it.

I swung the van door shut and climbed into the driver's seat. "A featured spread in *Philadelphia Food Journal*, a hundred thousand dollars, and the opportunity to cater the art museum's seventy-fifth-anniversary celebration."

"And the submission deadline is in eight weeks?"

"Yeah." I pulled the van out of the driveway and onto the road that would take me from Cherry Hill back to Philly.

"You got Jillianed," he said.

I studied the pavement in front of me as if the solutions I needed would magically appear on the asphalt. "What does that even mean?"

"It's that thing where she signs us up for stuff she knows we'll object to without giving us any sort of notice or prior discussion so we have no choice but to pull it off."

I huffed. "You mean like committing Ardena to catering a massive fundraiser for a local nonprofit when we'd been open less than a year?"

"With an extremely limited team and almost no resources? That's exactly what I mean."

Jillian had sprung that one on Jase over the summer, much to his displeasure. I guess the event being wildly successful and the catalyst to the launch of Arden Catering wasn't exactly a deterrent for her.

And I could see where she was coming from with the competition. If I pulled this off and managed to win, we'd get all the recognition Jillian was eager for and more. It would solidify both Arden Catering and Ardena restaurant as staples in the Philly food scene.

The hundred grand for the business wouldn't hurt either. If I survived that long.

"I can't decide if she's lost it or is an actual genius," I said.

He snorted. "Welcome to the club. And it's probably both."

I half sighed, half chuckled, already fortifying myself for the next two months: work enough events to keep us somewhere near the black, hire at least one other chef to serve as my second, and conceptualize a one-of-a-kind catering concept to put us on the map.

Easy.

"At least the museum's anniversary party isn't for another year. If I can't find a halfway decent team by then, I'll know the problem is me." The rest I could handle on my own. I didn't *want* to do it on my own, but I'd find a way.

"You know what I'm going to say," Jase replied. "If you need help in the meantime, one of the guys can split their time—"

"No way. You've been packed every night of the week. You need them more than I do."

"We'll manage. The new prep cook's been working out okay."

"How the hell did you find someone so quickly?" I asked, squeezing the wheel to channel my frustration. "No one I've interviewed has even come close." Maybe I really was the problem.

"You're looking for a sous chef, not a prep cook. That's way different. I'd still be looking too if I was trying to replace you."

The words pinched my chest, and I forced a deep breath to shake it free. He wasn't trying to replace me. Not in the way it felt when he said it. I was moving up, not being left behind.

But a part of me wished I could do both—run the catering side and stay his sous chef.

"Have you promoted one of the guys yet?" I asked. It would be Zach. He deserved it.

"Not yet. Zach's almost ready, and he's hungry for it. I'm easing him in."

Good. That would be good.

My earbuds beeped, and I glanced at my phone. "Evan's calling me. I should take it."

"No problem. I need to get back to prep anyway."

"Have a good service. Tell the guys I say hi."

"I will."

Jase hung up, and I tapped my earbud to switch calls. "Hey."

"What are you doing tonight?" Evan asked. It sounded like he was outside, but it was hard to tell over the rumble of the van's tires. If it was a weekday, I'd assume he was in the city for work, but he didn't usually go in on the weekends. Not unless his boss called with a graphic design emergency.

"I have to unload the catering truck, then nothing. I'll probably get food somewhere."

"Let's do something. I need to get out of the house."

"What? Why?" He'd been living at his dad's house the past two years—ever since his mom's funeral—and so far, the two of them hadn't had a single problem. Half the time we hung out, we did it at his dad's house so Mr. Hardt could hang out with us.

"Gabe's coming over later, and I don't feel like dealing with him."

My attention snapped from the rearview mirror to the road as excitement kicked up in my belly. "He's home? When did he get back from camp?" It must not have been long if Gabe hadn't texted me. He usually did after a flight.

"A week or two ago? I don't know; he hasn't been staying here. But he came by yesterday to borrow a suit, and he and Dad made plans for dinner tonight."

The excitement in my gut soured like skunked beer.

A week or two.

The words stuck to the edges of my brain like flour along the sides of a bowl, refusing to fully incorporate.

Gabe had been back in Philly at least seven days and hadn't told me.

We'd texted like normal three nights ago. I'd sent him a picture of a coaster with a Colorado Springs brewery on it, thinking that was where he was, and he'd said nothing to indicate otherwise.

But why?

Could he think I already knew? Maybe he assumed Evan or his dad had told me, and the whole coaster thing was me referencing where he'd recently been?

Except we'd never used his family as proxies before. If anything, he usually told me this kind of thing first, and *I* communicated it to *them*.

And a suit? What would he need a suit for? And where was he staying that wasn't their dad's house?

Why wouldn't he tell me he was back?

Maybe because the last time he got to town, you jumped him the second he walked through the door like a rabid squirrel and assaulted him with your mouth.

Even knowing it was true, it didn't make sense. It wasn't like I'd chased him down after the kiss and demanded he define what we were.

I knew what we were. At least, I'd thought I did.

"So what do you think?" Evan asked, cutting into my spiral. "Want to grab dinner and watch a movie or something?"

I swallowed the hardened lump from my throat. "Yeah, that sounds good. Meet at my place at seven? We can order from Pho Dinh."

"Sure. Text me your order, and I'll grab it on my way."

Fifteen minutes later, I pulled in front of the prep kitchen and texted Evan what I wanted. Then I typed out a message to Gabe and deleted it twice before staring at it with my thumb hovering over the Send button.

Me: I heard you're back.

That was neutral enough, right? I didn't want him to think I was angry with him for not telling me.

I didn't want *to be* angry. It wasn't like we'd made plans to do something once he got back. If he'd been in any other city and forgot to tell me when he got there, it would have been no big deal because that was our dynamic.

No pressure. No expectations. No overthinking.

Yes, we were in the same city now, but that didn't automatically change things.

He'd probably been busy. He hadn't been home for long stretches since turning pro after high school, and there had to be a dozen old friends and boxing colleagues he was keen to catch up with who he hadn't seen over New Year's like he had me.

He'd always been popular. He and Evan both. And not in the obnoxious way jocks sometimes were when they were kind of mean but everyone idolized them anyway because of their good looks and athletic ability. The two of them had just always gotten along with everyone and made them feel accepted. No matter how shy or socially awkward.

Especially when that shy and socially awkward kid had just moved in next door and had no other friends.

At this point, I cared less about why Gabe hadn't told me

and more about making sure things between us were still okay.

I hit Send and threw the phone into my bag, willing my nerves to settle. He'd reply to me when he got the chance. Until then, I wouldn't worry about it.

It took me another half hour to unload the catering van and get everything cleaned and put away. When I checked my phone on my way out, something behind my ribs gave an annoying flutter.

Two new messages.

Gabe: Sorry I didn't tell you sooner. I've been working on something

Gabe: Can I show you?

My heart raced, relief at his response warring with a nagging sting I hadn't managed to bury. One mostly comprised of aggravation at myself for being this affected in the first place.

I wanted to cut off the source of the eagerness humming along my skin at the thought of seeing him again. To smother the thrill he sparked in me without even trying. To not slip back into my adolescent crush on him after all these years of finally building a true friendship.

More than that, I wanted to know what he had to show me. To peek under the steel cover he kept so tightly in place for everyone else.

Curiosity won out.

Me: I'd like that.

Thirty seconds later, a message came through with an address in Fishtown. I could take the subway, but it'd be tight to make it there and back to my place by seven. Driving would get me there in half the time, giving me an hour to see whatever it was and still make it home in time to shower.

Or I could ask Gabe to show me whatever it was tomorrow instead.

I grabbed the keys to the catering van and headed for the door.

It took three shoves to get the boarded-up door to the old building in Fishtown to budge free. I let it swing inward to allow as much fading daylight in as possible before I walked into what appeared to be a top-notch murder site.

Dark, deserted. Someplace no one would think to look for a body. There weren't any cars out front, but Gabe didn't have a car, so that didn't mean anything.

The glimpse of a punching bag reassured me. If boxing was involved, Gabe would be too.

I stepped inside, the heavy door latching behind me, and breathed in the musty air. It felt a little like stepping into a time capsule. All around were tokens of the past, little pieces of history that told the story of what this place once was.

Rows of faded punching bags with duct tape wrapped around their middles hung from chains hooked to the ceiling. Faded banners printed with different names and logos lined the brick walls. A weight rack sat off to the side, a few of the dumbbells missing, with a frayed jump rope looped over one corner.

Straight ahead, raised on a platform beneath a cluster of all but one burned-out lights, was a boxing ring. It rose from the concrete floor like a crown waiting for its king to claim it. I wandered its perimeter, running my hand along one of the ropes. My fingers came away with dust.

Footsteps across the room echoed off the shadowed walls. Gabe stopped next to one of the pillars that lined the space, standing nearly as tall and just as solid, watching me take in the surroundings.

Being in the same room as him again had my pulse humming. To see him with my own eyes, here instead of halfway across the country.

"What is this place?" I asked. My voice carried in the silence of the room.

"My old gym," he replied somewhat measured. Almost as if he was nervous of what I might think. "My first one, actually."

I swept another glance, taking in the space through the eyes of a fourteen-year-old Gabe. It was big, the room stretching in a long line away from the street, the air still crackling with energy accumulated from all the young boxers who must have trained here.

"It's amazing," I said.

"I'm going to buy it." His expression held the same determination he'd worn during his boxing matches in high school. The ones I would go to with Evan and his mom as an infatuated twelve-year-old and watch with wide eyes, amazed one person could carry so much power.

He'd been a giant to me then. A superhero. Immovable and unbreakable.

He'd since been broken.

Both physically and mentally, more than he let most people see. I wasn't sure why I was the one he'd chosen to show his wounds to, but he had, just like he'd invited me here.

Based on the resolve in his voice, this was how he intended to put himself back together.

"Is that why you needed a suit?"

He seemed surprised I knew about that but recovered quickly. "Yeah. I tried to get a loan, but I don't have enough cash for the bank to give me one yet. And I only have three months to get it before Coach Lou sells to someone else."

I blew out a breath and took a seat on the edge of the ring. This probably wasn't the kind of thing we could organize a few bake sales for and call it a day. He could try to crowdfund, but unless it went viral, that seemed like a long shot with only three months.

I wanted him to get this, though. Wanted him to have a win after all the hits he'd endured the past two years. He deserved a new purpose now that his time in the ring was over. Something that brought him just as much meaning and joy.

And if there was a secret part of me that hoped he'd find that purpose *here* so he would stay, I made sure to bury it deep enough not to notice.

He joined me to sit on the edge of the mat, his bent knees rising several inches above mine. "My buddy agreed to let me fight in a local tournament he's putting together. The prize is enough to get me the loan."

My pulse sped up as I realized what he was saying. From excitement at the possibility as much as concern at the risk. "Are you sure you want that?" I asked. "To fight again?"

He lowered his gaze to the floor, and texts from two years

ago floated to the surface of my mind. Heartbroken texts from a heartbroken son who'd lost not one but two of the things most important to him in the span of a few months.

"It's my shot at holding on to this," he said, resolved. He gazed out at the gym as he said it, but I didn't think it was only the gym he meant.

I swung my knee into his. "Then you got this."

He swung his knee back, mouth lifting. "What makes you so sure? You become a boxing expert while I was away or something? Going to train my ass back into shape?"

"No," I said with a laugh, though my ears went hot from how much boxing I *had* watched the past few years. Not enough to make me an expert but enough to be embarrassing. "I just know how hard you go after the things you want."

His smile softened, his eyes taking in my chef clothes before lifting to the bandanna still in my hair and drifting over my face. The tenderness in his gaze took my breath.

"What?" I asked with a laugh, my neck growing warm.

He shook his head. "Nothing." Before I could press, he asked, "Today was that bridal shower, right? The Italian one?"

"Yeah." Three generations of extended family had attended. As someone whose parents were only children and never had a big family reunion, all the hollering, laughter, and physical embraces had brought a sweet kind of longing to my chest. It was nice to see love that big celebrated out loud.

"Was it as hectic as you thought it'd be?"

I chuckled. "Not as bad as the one last month." That bridesmaid's pregnancy announcement had been a whole other level of drama. I'd texted Gabe in Colorado about it the second I got back to the kitchen.

Well. As far as I knew. He may have already been back in Philly by then.

He shifted beside me, seeming to track my thoughts. "I'm sorry I didn't tell you I was back."

Deep shadows cast across the tense line of his brows, dulling his aqua-blue eyes. He had a scar I'd never noticed at the end of one eyebrow, the small indented line probably left behind by stitches he'd gotten after a match.

"I wanted to," he went on. "Not just text you, but see you. I had my phone out at the airport. I just…" He stared off at a pillar as if the words he was looking for were hidden behind it.

"Just what?" I asked softly.

He kept staring forward. "I guess I wasn't sure what came next. I didn't want to start randomly dropping into your life, messing up your routine and complicating things with Evan. It seemed simpler to keep it how things were until I had more of a plan. Especially since Evan said some stuff on New Year's that made me think it might be simpler for you too." He finally glanced at me, seeking if I understood.

I did. Gabe didn't do relationships. Not just girlfriends, which as far as I knew, he hadn't had since high school. He didn't do real friendships either. Not the kind Evan and I had. The lifelong, knows every part of you, is your go-to person kind of friendship.

Gabe had situational acquaintances. Sparring partners he was close with at the gym but rarely hung out with outside of training. Coaches and managers he was close with as coworkers but didn't let into other parts of his life. Physical therapists and nutritionists whose partners and kids Gabe knew all the names of but whose houses he'd never stay at for holidays.

People whose company he enjoyed but who he wouldn't have to miss when his career took him to a different gym, city, or part of the world.

Evan was the only one who had crossed all lines. Gabe had let his brother into every part of himself right up until he'd shut Evan out altogether. And now as he was opening the door again, Evan had barricaded it from the other side.

Letting someone else in wasn't something Gabe was used to. And especially now, when his heart was already tender with so much grief, doing it through texts probably felt safer. He was right that it kept things simpler.

It didn't stop my mini flare-up of frustration toward both brothers. At Gabe for shutting himself off and at Evan for being part of the reason why.

"Evan tries to protect me, sometimes from things I don't need protecting from," I said, realizing it was true for both of them. "But he doesn't decide things for me. I choose my own friendships. And I happen to be fine with a little complication as long as we can be open about it. But if *you'd* rather stick to texting, we can do that too."

I wasn't looking to push him. And I especially didn't want to lose what we had. Even if it was just over texts, his presence in my life had come to mean too much to let go of completely.

But he shook his head firmly. "I don't want that. I like being around you in person. And I really like the sound of being open with each other. It's why I wanted to show you this place."

The zip tie around my stomach released, and for the first time since I learned he was back, I took a full breath. Whatever flittering my heart did was only more relief. Me being grateful our friendship was intact. I ignored it as we gazed out at the gym.

"Have you told anyone else about it?" I asked.

"My dad. He hasn't seen it yet, but he knows it's why I'm back."

"I bet he's losing his mind with happiness."

Gabe's eyes crinkled at the corners with his grin. "He's definitely all for it." His voice took on a sad note. "Mom would have been excited too."

My smile softened as I pictured it. "She'd already have this place polished. Would probably have her favorite boxing photos of yours printed and framed for you to hang on the walls."

He snorted. "Only most of them would have been from before I even went pro. Me as a fifteen-year-old about to get clocked in the face because my hands weren't up."

"Being able to see your face is what she would have loved about it."

He shook his head, a wistful smile on his lips. "It sucks not having her here to see it."

The sorrow in his eyes was the same shade of longing as when Nana wasn't there to attend Ardena's soft opening or see me as the head chef of a new catering venture. That deep yearning to have the people you loved most there for special moments, and the bottomless gap that opened in your heart at knowing they couldn't be.

I leaned into him, offering a hug. "I know." Nothing I said

could fill that gap. It'd been six years since my grandma died, and I still felt it every day.

He circled his arm around me, drawing me against him so my cheek rested on his shoulder. It happened naturally, as if we'd done it dozens of times before. I let my weight sink into him, and his other hand came up to brush a stray hair from my forehead.

Being in his arms felt safe. Simple. Like whatever heartaches or toils the real world had for me couldn't touch me within the warmth of his embrace. Like for this moment, I could let it all go.

It was the feeling of safety my grandma had provided me. One that was harder to find now that she was gone.

I breathed through the ache of missing her and focused on the coziness of Gabe's clean scent. "I'm glad you're home," I said.

His arm tightened around me. "Me too."

"Thank you for showing me this place."

My voice must have given me away because he squeezed my side again. "You okay?" he asked softly.

I nodded.

We sat in silence, wrapped together on the edge of the mat, giving and taking comfort. Comfort I hadn't let myself admit I needed before now. The same was probably true for him.

"I miss them," I finally whispered, thinking of his mom and Nana.

Three minuscule words attempting to convey a galaxy's worth of emptiness.

They were the only words I had.

"I do too," he said.

We held each other a few minutes longer, remembering.

Chapter Seven
Gabe

IT WAS EASIER to be at my parents' house during the day as if the memories it carried only sharpened their edges enough to pierce my skin at night. Right now, with the sun out and shining through the kitchen windows as I filled a glass from the faucet, it almost felt like any other house. Just a countertop and cabinets instead of where my mom had made me early dinners as a kid on weekdays before practices. Always something simple, like frozen chicken tenders with broccoli or mac and cheese with hot dogs, because she'd never been as good a cook as my dad, but she'd wanted me to have home-cooked meals, and practice started before he got home.

I was glad Dad had gone with takeout last night after I'd shown Aubrey the gym. Seeing him in the kitchen without Mom peeking around his arm and asking what he was doing would have stabbed deep.

Maybe for him too. More frozen meals filled the freezer

than fresh ingredients did the fridge. I knew he still cooked on holidays, but maybe more than that was too painful.

"What are you doing here?"

I held in my sigh and turned off the tap. Maybe one day, that wouldn't be the first thing my brother said to me.

He glared at me from the doorway.

"Dad invited me over."

"What for?"

"Game night!" Dad called from the stairs. He clapped Evan on the shoulders as he joined us in the kitchen. "We needed a fourth."

Game "night" was a loose term, given it was eleven thirty in the morning. They'd been in the actual evening growing up until Aubrey got her first job at a restaurant, and then Saturday game nights had turned into to Sunday game afternoons. I'd already gone pro by then, so I hadn't been here for as many, but Aubrey still came every week.

My skin buzzed as if I'd downed two energy drinks, just knowing she'd be here soon. Somehow, it also grounded me.

Being around her calmed the restlessness of being home, made it easier to sit in the here and now instead of drowning in the past. Especially now that our friendship had taken a new step. Yesterday's conversation had solidified it into something I could grip almost as fully as the cool glass in my hands.

It hadn't been that way before. She and Evan had been inseparable since the day they first met, not just like brother and sister but more like twins. The kind of connection that didn't need words. She sat right next to him in my childhood memories, a flash of blond hair and big teeth whose bubbly laughter followed wherever they ran.

She'd always been a little shy around me as a kid and had definitely had a crush on me at one point. I'd found it cute. Had liked having her around, brightening the room with her smile.

But I'd never seen her as my sister. Maybe because I'd always associated her as Evan's. Not like she belonged to him, but like they belonged to each other. He was her family, so she became mine—all of ours. And the role I took on was looking after them both. Making sure no one picked on them. Helping her open up by making her laugh. Making sure she knew she had a place with us.

Now it was like I was finally getting a piece of her that was mine. Not one that relied on Evan tying it together. As much as we'd already had that from our texts, getting to have it in person made it feel real.

"We play with three all the time," Evan challenged, not sharing Dad's enthusiasm at my presence.

Dad waved him away. "It's always better with four."

Evan's face told a different story, but he didn't bother arguing.

I gestured to Dad. "Before I forget, Diego will have tickets for me this week. Let me know how many you want."

Diego had agreed to let me into the tournament, but my spot wouldn't be final unless I sold fifty tickets for the event. Not all the fighters had to do it, but my name wasn't as big a pull now that I'd been out of the game for a while. They needed to know I could still put butts in seats, even if it meant me hunting them down myself.

"I'll tell Rudy and the guys. They'll probably all want one."

"Tickets for what?" Evan asked.

Out in the hallway, the front door clicked, and I caught a flash of dark blond hair. My pulse stuttered before taking off at a run.

"Gabe's fighting in a local tournament," Dad replied, all enthusiasm.

My eyes were glued to the hallway behind them.

"Wait. Like a boxing tournament?" Evan said. "I thought you retired?"

Aubrey stepped into the kitchen, and the rest of the room shrank away to nothing. She squeezed behind Evan, a plastic container of cookies in hand.

Sable cookies. I knew without seeing them. Probably filled with chocolate, like the ones Mom used to make. Pretty much the only recipe Mom could pull off since it was one her own mom had taught her. She'd bake them every game night, with chocolate filling instead of jam, specifically for Aubrey, who'd eat more than her nine-year-old frame should have been able to fit in her stomach.

Her eyes brightened when she saw me, and she lifted her hand in a small wave.

All I could think of was that hand gripping my sweatshirt, her head on my shoulder, while I breathed in the scent of her coconut shampoo, feeling more at home with her in the silence of my old gym than I had at any point in the past two years.

"I did retire," I answered Evan, keeping my scattered pulse hidden behind an easy tone. "The tournament is a one-time thing."

"And you think jumping back in after two years away is smart? What about your shoulder?"

Aubrey's smile faded as she picked up on the tension from Evan. I shifted my gaze to my brother.

"It'll be fine as long as I'm careful. I have eight weeks to train. That's plenty of time to get ready." I'd stayed in decent shape during retirement, still running most days and regularly serving as a sparring partner for Noah and some other fighters while I was an assistant trainer for Coach Peters. I had a lot of work to put in the next couple of months, but I wasn't starting at zero.

Evan didn't seem to think so. He shook his head. "Whatever. I'm going to set up the cards." He marched out the door to the dining room.

Aubrey shot me a sympathetic look. I wanted to pull her in for another hug and stay there for the next hour.

"What do you say, Aubrey?" my dad asked. "Been a while since you and I were partners. Will you do me the honor?"

She flashed him a warm smile. "Sure."

"We'll have our work cut out for us. Evan and Gabe were always a dangerous combination."

I almost laughed. Right now, the only one in danger was me.

Evan threw his last card—a three of clubs—on the pile, which Aubrey quickly collected to her side of the table along with her other tricks.

"Dude, you're not even trying," I said. He'd bid four tricks and hadn't gotten a single one. He had the cards for it too. Just played them in the worst possible combination like he had every other hand so far. Which he knew because he'd been a Spades shark since he was ten.

He shrugged. "Thought you had a higher card."

"When I only bid one and already played an ace?"

He shrugged again and pushed from the table. "I'm getting a drink."

I slid my own seat back and followed him to the kitchen. "I'm trying here."

"No need," he said, grabbing a seltzer from the fridge. "It's just a card game."

"You know that's not what I'm talking about."

He popped the lid of the can. "What I know is the only reason you're here right now is because of a boxing tournament. It's the only thing you've ever cared about. We may as well all stop pretending otherwise."

"That's not true."

"It's not? You mean you didn't pick boxing over Mom when she got sick? I somehow missed you sitting next to me in the hospital room when she died?"

I clenched my teeth. It did nothing against the burn in my stomach.

"Yeah," he said in response to my silence. "Then you picked it again the second the funeral was over. Screw what Dad needed. You couldn't get out of here fast enough. Not when there was a fight to win."

"I didn't know about this tournament when I decided to come back," I said. "It's not why I'm here."

Nothing I said could justify what happened with Mom. No words could get him to forgive me when I didn't forgive myself. When I racked my brain every day about the different choices I could have made, asked "what if?" about a thousand variables, and wondered if any one of them would have gotten me back in time. When I still struggled to breathe through the guilt of knowing she'd died without her whole family around her—that having us all together meant more to her than anything in the world—and I'd robbed her of it in her last moments with my selfishness.

I hadn't known how to face it after the funeral. I could hardly face it now. So I'd run. Retreated into boxing the way I knew how and let it take me as far away as it could.

But I was trying to be here now.

"So drop out," he challenged.

"I can't."

He looked ready to punch me. I almost wished he would. Get it all out so maybe we'd both feel better.

"You can," he insisted. "You choose not to. Even though it's reckless and fucking stupid, and you're going to put yourself in the hospital. But if it brings you glory, go for it, I guess."

"It has nothing to do with glory. I'm trying to win the money to buy Coach Lou's gym."

He raised his hands in retreat. "Whatever, man. Do what you want. I'm done trying to keep up."

Aubrey stepped into the kitchen. "We still playing?"

Evan set his mostly full seltzer on the counter. "I just remembered I have something I need to do for work. You want a ride back to the city?" he asked her.

Her shoulders sank. "Evan."

He raised his brows like a child challenging his babysitter.

"I really think you should stay," Aubrey said.

"Going alone it is." He made for the door.

"But I'm the one who bails?" I called after him.

"Guess we know who I learned it from."

Aubrey's gaze caught mine, indecision warring across her features. She waited another beat before letting out a growl and spinning on her heel. "Evan, wait up."

It was the decision I knew she'd make. The one I wanted her to. Their friendship would always be important to me because it was important to her. To both of them.

I was just glad she thought me worth considering at all.

Chapter Eight
Aubrey

"You know you're being a dick, right?" I asked as Evan pulled his car out of his dad's neighborhood. We had a thirty-minute drive back to Philly, and I planned to use every one of them to call him out on his shit.

"He deserves it."

"No, he doesn't. He lost your mom too. We all did."

She'd been more of a mom to me than my mom ever was. Both my parents had been all too eager to offload me to my grandma rather than deal with me as they moved from one air force base to another. From the day they dropped me off and a boy named Evan wandered next door to make friends with the new girl, Mrs. Hardt had welcomed me into her home—into her family—like I was her own daughter.

She'd bought me presents for my birthday and Christmas. Not just gifts from Evan, but from her and Mr. Hardt too. She'd baked me cookies on game nights. She went prom dress shopping with me and taught me how to put on makeup. She was in the front row of my graduation from culinary school, right next to my grandma. She was warm and loving and fun and whip smart, and when she died, she took a piece of me with her that could never be replaced.

I knew the same was as true for Evan as it was for Gabe.

"He wasn't even there," Evan said.

"You know that wasn't his fault."

"He chose to stay for that fight."

"He thought she had more time."

The cancer diagnosis had been a shock. Aside from the occasional stomach pain, she'd seemed the picture of health. By the time they realized it was pancreatic cancer, it had advanced to stage 4. Her doctors came up with an aggressive treatment plan and were confident with her age and overall health that she'd have at least another year. They did one surgery to remove what they could of the tumors, and a week later, she was gone.

Gabe made it back in time for her funeral but not to say goodbye.

I'd never seen him so hollow. The funeral was the first time since I'd known him he'd ever looked small. Like an empty candy bar wrapper that could as easily be blown away by the breeze as it could be crumpled into a ball and discarded.

I would have been the same had I not been there with Nana for her final moments. The hours spent with her by her bed, even when she'd no longer been aware I was there, brought peace for me in her passing—a closure Gabe would never have.

"Then he should have been here for Dad," Evan insisted, his grip tight on the steering wheel. "He didn't even stick around a week after the funeral to be here for Thanksgiving. Two days after the burial, he's gone. You know how hard that Thanksgiving was for Dad? That Christmas?"

I did. Holidays were a big deal for the Hardt family. Mr. and Mrs. Hardt cherished nothing more than celebrating life with the people they loved, most of all their sons. Mr. Hardt cooked, Mrs. Hardt decorated, and together, their home transformed into the kind of scene you'd want depicted in a Norman Rockwell painting. A moment you could capture in time and keep with you forever. No holiday since had been the same, though Mr. Hardt did his best to honor his wife.

"He was grieving too," I said.

"Not here. Not with us. Then he comes back two years later, and I'm supposed to welcome him with open arms?"

"I'm not saying to pretend everything is okay or not to be hurt. I get how much it sucks to be left behind." Evan had distracted me from enough birthdays without so much as a phone call from my mom or dad to know how true that was. "But your brother is here, and he's trying, which is more than I ever got from my parents. I'm afraid if you keep pushing him away for dealing with his pain in his own way, you'll push him away for good. And if that happens, the only person you'll have to blame for him not being in your life is *you*."

I caught my breath and realized how tense I'd become. Enough that I'd almost been yelling. I peered out the passenger window and let the blur of passing buildings settle the pounding in my chest.

"Have you heard from them lately?" Evan asked. "Your parents?" The anger had softened from his voice.

"Nothing since their lawyer informed me they were dropping the case."

Nana had left me everything when she died, which hadn't amounted to much aside from her house. She and my grandpa had bought it in the seventies, a few years before my mom was born, and Nana had maintained it as well as my grandpa had before he'd died. The resale value was high, and my parents thought they should be the ones who got to cash in on it. It turned out Nana hadn't agreed.

I'd offered to sell the house to my parents, but it wasn't the house they wanted. They hired a lawyer to contest the will, but Nana had changed it to make me her beneficiary almost ten years before she died, when I'd been twelve and she'd been of perfectly sound mind. They eventually gave up, at which point I sold it myself. It wasn't home without Nana, and she'd want me to use the money to build my own future.

Unlike Gabe with his mom, my parents hadn't made it to my grandma's funeral. Hadn't even tried to get leave. Last I heard, they were stationed in Hawaii.

"I'm sorry your parents are shitty," Evan said.

I blew a bitter laugh through my nose. "Me too. Gabe's not, though."

Evan shot me a look before returning his eyes to the road. "You still have a crush on him or something?"

My stomach flipped, but I forced my voice even. "That ended when we were still in high school."

A few resurfacing butterflies didn't make it any less true. All the heated skin and restless energy I'd had in response to Gabe recently was just a holdover from the kiss, and the kiss had meant nothing. A simple favor between friends. I didn't imagine him as Prince Charming and dream of marrying him anymore. And thoughts of anything else, I flung from my mind.

"He is my friend, though," I added, "and even if you say different, I think you need him. I think you need each other. He's your brother, and he loves you."

I'd always wished for that sibling love—a built-in best friend who would stand by you no matter what and keep you from ever truly being alone. To a military brat who had no friends because I'd moved every two years when my parents got assigned to a new base, it was all I ever wanted.

Then my parents left me with my grandma, and I got Evan. He was my brother in all the ways that counted. And even still, what we had didn't compare to the innate closeness he and Gabe shared throughout our childhood.

He could be pissed at Gabe all he wanted, but I wasn't sure I could forgive him if he threw that kind of bond away.

I pulled out my phone and sent a message to Gabe.

Me: You okay?

He responded right away.

Gabe: All good

I doubted that, but then again, most of us hadn't been all the way good for at least two years. Some days, good didn't feel attainable anymore. Not when the people we loved most were missing.

Gabe didn't have to deal with it alone anymore. I may have left with Evan, but I wanted him to know I was here for him too. Especially now that we'd gone all in on our friendship.

Me: Want to grab coffee tomorrow morning?

Another immediate response.

Gabe: Yes

Gabe: Where should I meet you? I can head there after my run

He'd start training for the tournament soon. More than the workouts he already did most weeks. I couldn't be the one to whip him into shape, but I could support him in other ways.

Me: I'll bring the drinks to you.

Chapter Nine
Gabe

My legs screamed as I sprinted the last few meters to the base of the museum steps, the brisk morning air burning my nose and throat on the way to my lungs and back out. As I crossed the invisible finish line, the rush of endorphins coated my muscles in relief. I slowed to a walk, my hands finding the top of my head, sweat dripping off my face, and cooled down in big circles.

It was still early enough that while plenty of cars were out, only a few other pedestrians dotted the museum's courtyard. I liked to get here even earlier when I could. Just in time for the sun to crest the horizon and bathe the museum's stone in orange light. I missed it this morning, in part because I'd gone to bed late.

After Evan and Aubrey had left game night early, I'd hung out with my dad until well past dark and caught the last bus back to the city.

Growing up, I hadn't had much time with him, just the

two of us. Either Evan, my mom, or both were with us, or I was popping in and out to see friends while home for short visits between training. I'd never felt like our relationship had been missing anything; it was just how we were.

But being with him now felt like we'd hung out that way for years. Without trying, we'd settled into a mode where we could just be—watch a game or something on TV—no conversation necessary. It was like he was content just to have me near despite my presence driving Evan away.

No way that didn't hurt Dad. No way it didn't press directly on the wounds I'd poured salt into by ghosting. The same way my refusing to sleep at the house probably did.

Yet he hadn't asked me to. Or pressured me to stay last night even though it was late. He'd just given me a hug and told me he loved me.

He should hate me. Should struggle to look at me. He should have slammed the door in my face on New Year's and made me sleep on the steps.

I was grateful he was stronger than I was.

It probably helped he hadn't seen the state of the gym or the size of the cot I was sleeping on.

Aubrey was the only one it felt right to give that glimpse to yet. She'd seen enough of the other broken parts of me without criticism that I knew she wouldn't judge.

In some ways, it felt like she and I had hung out this way for years too. Like we grabbed coffee every week at our usual spot and knew each other's orders when, in truth, this was the first time besides the other night we'd be together just the two of us. Before now, it had always been Hardt family gatherings or, at the very least, something with Evan.

It made getting coffee kind of a big step for our friendship. One I was surprisingly nervous about. The fun kind of nerves—like the ones that kept my blood pumping before a fight—but still nerves.

Boxing used to be the only thing that sparked them.

Across the street, a flash of blond hair caught the breeze from beneath the purple beanie containing it, drawing my eye to Aubrey as she made her way through the crosswalk. She was bundled in a leather jacket and gloves, all black, including her leggings and boots, like the world's most adorable burglar.

Halfway across the intersection, she spotted me and beamed. My heart gave a kick in my chest that had nothing to do with the three miles I'd just run.

Since retiring, my routine had been two miles in the morning, four days a week. Now that I was back in training for real, the first step was to dial that distance up and add two more days. Nothing else I did would matter if my cardio couldn't keep up.

That was why I'd suggested we meet here. It was a route I liked to run, and the museum was a closer trek for her than the gym. Not to mention, the gym was practically this cold anyway, but without the sun to warm our skin.

Plus, this had always been one of my favorite spots in the city: The view straight down the Parkway to city hall where William Penn's statue stood tall among the skyline. The subtle peace of the Schuylkill River beside us. The way it felt like its own little bubble, both plugged in enough to still feel the charge of the city but on the outskirts enough to have space to breathe.

I needed that space more than ever with the strain of being home a constant pressure on my chest.

"Hi," Aubrey said as she reached me at the base of the museum's steps. She hadn't been running, but she sounded a little out of breath. She thrust one of the two green cardboard cups she held at me like she'd rehearsed how to do it and didn't want to forget.

My mouth ticked up, my own nerves settling at the sight of hers.

This was Aubrey. Always a little flustered around me, but still sharp and observant. I'd known since we were kids how to get her to open up, to crack a warm smile and share a genuine laugh. Just like she knew how to prod me over texts to dig a little deeper and share a little more.

This might have been a new step for our friendship, but we were still us.

I accepted the drink, the cup warm against my cold hands. "Thank you." The first sip of green tea was scorching hot. I drank coffee sometimes, but I wasn't a fan of too much caffeine during a training session. I nodded at her cup. "What'd you get?"

"A mocha."

I grinned. "Should have known." If chocolate was an option, Aubrey was all over it.

"Hey, sometimes I get a plain latte," she said, her nose pink from the wind. "But today felt like a special occasion."

My smile softened. It did feel special. I liked that she thought so too. I raised my cup for a toast, and she tapped hers to it.

"So is this usually when you go to work?" I asked as we headed to sit on the steps. I steered us toward a sunny spot.

"Sometimes. It depends on the day. Morning events mean

getting to the kitchen at four a.m. Evening events, I can usually wait until noon."

"Do you have a preference?"

She tilted her head and gazed out at the city. "Probably evening events, but that may just be because the schedule is easier for me to manage."

"What, you're not a morning person?"

She cringed. "God, no. Sometimes I wish I was, especially in the summer when it's sunny and bright. It can be a bummer to feel like I missed so much of the day."

I almost never had that problem. Over a decade of early training sessions meant I couldn't sleep in if I tried. "I could start giving you wake-up calls every morning before my run," I joked. "How does five o'clock sound?"

Her laughter warmed me better than the tea. "Like a good way to get me to block your number."

"Come on. Think of all those early hours you could take advantage of. The sun would be thrilled to see you."

"Somehow, I think the sun will manage."

I knew firsthand what the sun would be missing by not experiencing her in person. "In that case, I'm flattered you met me this early. The coffee must be worth it."

"It's worth it without the coffee," she said. Her expression grew more serious. "It gives me a chance to apologize for everything with Evan yesterday."

I shook my head before she finished the sentence, my smile gone. "Don't. It's not your job to fix our relationship. And it definitely isn't your fault it's broken." That responsibility didn't belong anywhere near her shoulders.

"No, I know," she said, glancing at the cup in her hands. Her gloved thumbs ran along the rim of the lid. "I just felt bad leaving like that. I didn't want you to think I agreed with what he said."

I knew she didn't. *I* might have agreed with it, but that was my own shit to figure out. She was the last person I wanted carrying it. "Trust me, you being here for me the way you have is more than enough." Way more. It was everything.

I never would have reached out to someone to talk about the stuff with Mom if Aubrey hadn't reached out first. All the anger and confusion and pain still clinging to my ribs, to my lungs and heart, would have taken me all the way over and eaten me from the inside out like a toxic mold. I didn't know where I would have ended up, but it wouldn't have been back in Philly. I doubted I would even be me anymore.

A smile touched her cheeks. "Okay, good. Because I also want to be there for you at the tournament." She set down her drink and presented me her cupped hands, her eyes alight. "One ticket, please."

My mouth twitched. She'd learned those puppy dog eyes from Evan. "No," I said lightly.

"What, you don't want me there?"

I held back a scoff. "Of course I do, but you don't have to buy a ticket. You can come as my guest."

"But I *want* to pay for it. I want to contribute to you getting your gym." Her bottom lip jutted out. "Please?"

More laughter stirred in my chest. I ignored it and tried to look stern. Then she blinked her long lashes at me, her big hazel eyes brighter than ever against her purple hat, and I crumbled. "Fine. I'll bring you one tomorrow."

Her grin overtook her face as she bounced her knees in a seated victory dance that was equal parts ridiculous and utterly cute. As much as I'd rather not take her money, a softness filled my chest at how happy she was to support me. That I could make her this happy by letting her.

"You'll be the first person to officially buy one," I said. Dad wouldn't know how many tickets he needed for at least a few days, so she may as well embrace it fully.

"*Yes*," she quietly exclaimed.

I shook my head, amused.

"Oh, come on, this is an honor. And if it helps, I can find a way for you to do something for me in exchange. That way, you'd be contributing to my business too."

I slid her my gaze. "I'm listening."

"Come to dinner with me this week. I was planning on checking out one of the other restaurants doing the catering competition to get a feel for what I'm up against."

I suppressed the thrill that shot through me and pretended to consider. "I *am* experienced with opponent research." Watching hours of film before a fight to try to get a read on the other guy had been as much a part of my training as bag work.

"See, and I'm brand new at it. You could be the difference between me winning and losing."

"Now that, I highly doubt. But I'd be honored to join you."

"Good." She smirked like she'd just landed a triple word score. "Then we're both honored."

"Looks like it."

She raised her mostly empty coffee cup for another toast. I tapped mine against hers and watched her lips rise. Her eyes lowered as they did, like she wanted to keep the extent of her joy a secret, but I saw.

Honored was right.

Chapter Ten
Aubrey

Ursa Minor was like the cooler younger sister of some of the more established fine-dining restaurants in Philly. Instead of a stripped-down modern aesthetic, splashes of color greeted you in every direction, from the mosaic tile flooring to the graffiti-stained glass windows and the mismatched velvet chairs at every table. Upbeat music spilled from the speakers, and the rest of the decor gave off a retro feel that made me want to dance.

The Midtown Village spot was busy for a Wednesday, which made it perfect for subtle reconnaissance. Jillian had learned who a handful of the other catering competition applicants were, and I figured getting a feel for their food might be helpful.

Plus, eating incredible food from other chefs was the best inspiration out there. Not just by learning from what they did well but by imagining what I might do differently.

It was part of what I missed about working in the same kitchen as Jase—working alongside him made me better.

Cool air kissed my spine as I slid off my leather jacket and placed it in the circular booth. My dress was long-sleeved with a low back that showed off the tattoos along my spine and hugged my hips before ending mid-thigh. It was pink and shimmery too, which made it a favorite for nights like this. I wore loose black pants and a boxy white jacket as a uniform sixty hours a week; any opportunity to glamour out and feel like Barbie, I took full advantage of.

As I turned to sit, Gabe emerged from the crowd with our drinks. His gaze locked on me, roaming the full length of my body, down my bare legs to my heels, his throat moving on a swallow.

My skin heated, but not with self-consciousness. I liked the way he looked at me.

I liked looking at him too.

His usual sweats and workout clothes were gone, replaced with the sexiest-fitting Henley I'd ever seen and a snug pair of black jeans to match. Add to that the scent he brought with him as he slid into the booth, and it was enough to make goose bumps erupt along my body. The smell of something clean layered with something masculine. Sandalwood maybe.

Whatever it was, I breathed it in, and my tongue went heavy with the urge to lick. I forced down a groan.

I wasn't supposed to want to lick him. We were here as friends and friends only. A mutual exchange of helpful contributions to each other's business ventures.

This was not the time for my horniness meter to skyrocket into the red.

"What's the verdict on the food?" he asked, stretching one

arm across the back of the booth and taking his drink with the other. It shouldn't have been attractive, but it was.

Everything about the way he moved was. Like he was swimming through air, effortless and confident yet smooth and controlled. I wanted to curl up with a pillow and watch him do it naked.

Which was another temptation I needed to rein in. No licking and *no* naked thoughts. *Just focus on the food.*

I turned my attention to the card stock, skimming over the words I'd already studied on the website. "The menu looks fun. Some of their flavor combinations will be interesting."

"What should we order?" He shifted closer to look at the menu, and his hand brushed my leg.

I stiffened.

"Shit, sorry," he said, snatching it away.

"No, I—" I swallowed against the sparks still firing through my body from the touch. "It's fine."

My voice was too tight. Too strained. I tried to relax, but it was as if someone had turned me into a wind-up doll and cranked me to my limit.

Being here with Gabe felt different, and not just because of our clothes. The restaurant itself was sexy: the lighting dim but warm, the music sensual with a steady bass, and the booth small enough to feel private. All of it charged me to the point of shocking anything I touched.

I'd never felt this electric with anyone. Definitely not Patrick, who had been as timid at initiating sex as I was. So much so we'd waited a whole year into our relationship before actually fucking.

Not that the word "fucking" really fit. The sex between

Patrick and me had been as measured and predictable as the rest of our relationship. Which, in fairness, was exactly what I'd liked about it.

Patrick had come into my life right after my grandma had died when my world had become untethered. He'd been the accountant in charge of Nana's finances and helped me manage it all in the months after she was gone. When he'd expressed an interest in more, I'd clung to it. Moving through life back then had felt like sitting in a spinning teacup that kept going faster and faster, and for three years, he was the stable fixture I held on to.

I felt untethered in a different way now, craving the experience of a fuller kind of sex. As if for years, I'd been buckled into a skydiving plane, and I was finally ready to jump. What I still needed was someone to jump with.

Trying a random hookup hadn't worked. The bar Kelly had chosen for our night out was sexy too, but talking to that guy had left me the opposite of charged.

I ran my fingers along the smooth edge of my glass as my mind spun, letting my metallic press-ons catch the light. I never wore nail polish in the kitchen for risk of it chipping into the food, but my nails deserved to feel pretty during my off hours too.

I cleared my throat. "Can I ask you something?"

"Sure," Gabe said, setting aside his drink. "Anything."

"Have you ever had sex in a public bathroom?"

His brows jumped before his lips curved with amusement. "Yes."

I didn't imagine it. Didn't picture him locked in a tight space, rushing to undo his fly as legs wrapped around his waist and pulled him closer. Didn't see his hands shove up a skirt and tug panties aside, his every movement frantic with need and the risk of being caught. I definitely didn't imagine it was *my* legs around his waist or *my* skirt he bunched.

"I've never understood what's sexy about it," I said, though that might not have been true anymore.

He nodded in understanding, then studied the table as if deciding how to respond. After a moment, he leaned in close. "It's not the bathroom itself that's sexy," he explained, voice low and full in my ear. "It's the urgency. The being so consumed by another person that you can't wait long enough to get somewhere more comfortable or private. The feeling you'll die if you don't have them then and there, on the nearest surface, and knowing they need it just as bad. It's not caring that everyone else in the building will probably know you're fucking, because fucking each other is the only thing that matters."

I tried to breathe and couldn't. My body had drawn so tight there was no room for air in my lungs. I waited for him to continue, to give me more glimpses at the type of sex I wasn't sure really existed, but he didn't. His eyes caught mine in their snare.

"I've never felt that way before," I managed shakily.

His gaze flashed to my lips so quickly I might have imagined it. "What about with your exes?"

"There's only one. We weren't big on PDA." No way Patrick *or* I would have gone for bathroom sex when we were together.

A corner of Gabe's mouth tipped up. "No bathroom sex. No New Year's kisses. What was he big on?"

I stared at his lips as *our* New Year's kiss flashed through my mind. I could hardly remember who Patrick was, though

I still felt a need to defend him. "It wasn't all him. I didn't push for more either."

"Did you ever want to?" Gabe asked as if it wasn't completely bizarre we were talking about this. More bizarre was how easy it felt.

Sex wasn't something I talked about much, even with Evan. He and I discussed our love lives plenty, but not to this degree. I could see myself eventually trying with Dani or even Kelly, but not yet. Sharing it with Gabe was a relief.

"Maybe," I answered but knew in my gut it wasn't right. "Yes," I corrected. "Or I would have, except…I didn't really like sex with him much." Guilt bubbled up at admitting it out loud.

"Why not?" There was no judgment in Gabe's voice, only curiosity.

I studied the coral-pink color of my drink. "I'm not sure. I think I didn't *know* what I liked and was never fully comfortable to figure it out."

"Seems like you two didn't have much of a physical connection, huh," he asked gently, as if I might be sad over it.

Maybe I was. Sad that Patrick and I had been closer to friends than anything else. We'd cared about each other deeply, but I wasn't sure we'd ever truly desired one another.

But also sad we hadn't. Sad we'd spent so long together despite missing something so obvious.

"He gave me a lot of what I needed back then, which I'm grateful for," I said. "But I think I'm realizing how much I need something different now." Something I'd only become aware of after Gabe walked into my kitchen on New Year's Eve.

I found his gaze. The blue of his eyes caught me off

guard every time, as clear and crisp as the sky. They contained something else at the moment, an intensity I couldn't look away from, making that same something grow and expand inside me until it had wrapped me up completely and sent my body spinning.

This time, I let myself imagine what it would be like if his hand shifted to graze my knee.

How the touch would shoot sparks up my leg. How his fingers would tighten a fraction, maybe intentionally, maybe a reflex, before he trailed them up my thigh. I could hear my own gasp slip through my lips as I shifted in my seat, hitching my skirt an inch higher. His pinky would tease the newly exposed skin, then pass below my skirt, drawing my nipples tight.

He'd notice, his eyes heating. Then he'd tease me again, letting his hand travel higher, his fingers edging closer to where I was desperate for them. My lace panties would be drenched, and no matter how I shifted, I wouldn't be able to ease the ache that bloomed between my thighs.

I could feel my breathing shallow, see my legs part in invitation, his eyes still holding mine like we were the only two in the room as his fingers grazed my panties—

I sprang from my seat and scrambled out of the booth.

The fantasy hadn't been real, but my heavy breathing was. Gabe was half out of the booth with me, an alarmed look on his face.

"I need to use the bathroom." I spun from the table before he could respond and weaved into the shuffle of people, grateful for their cover. Gabe seeing me get turned on while I imagined him fingering me under the table was bad enough. I did *not* need him asking concerned questions while

I tried to compose myself enough to come up with an excuse that didn't mortify us both.

"*Oof!*" My shoulder connected with someone in front of me, and I reached out to steady us both. "I'm sorry! Are you all right?"

The man lifted his head, and the fevered mess of nerves and arousal burning through my body instantly snuffed out.

He drew himself straight and smirked. "If it isn't Aubrey Witter."

"Christian."

My ex-coworker looked half a tube of hair gel away from earning his supervillain badge. His brown hair was slicked back enough to withstand a hurricane as he stood in a stiff leather jacket he couldn't quite fill, his skin extra pale in the restaurant's low lighting.

I was surprised to see him here. Pépère, where Jase and I used to work, was open on Wednesdays, and since Jase had left, Christian was the head chef.

Then again, Christian had never had half of Jase's work ethic. He probably had whoever the new sous chefs were running things all but two nights a week.

"What are you doing here?" he asked, making a show of looking over my shoulder. "Is Jase here too? That's all you do, right? Follow him around wherever he goes?"

I smiled back, well-practiced at not reacting to his bullshit. He would have jumped at the chance to slap me with a "hysterical woman" label at the first sign of frustration, and earning respect as a woman in a professional kitchen was tough enough without the sexist stereotypes. "Just here to enjoy the food. I'll let Jase know you miss him, though."

He gave a sharp laugh. "You do that. Be sure to let him know I won a James Beard Award too."

Ah yes, Pépère's Outstanding Restaurant award. It was honestly a miracle he'd held that in this long.

"I saw the article. Congrats."

His eyes narrowed with skepticism.

"I mean it," I said. "You must have done a great job cooking Jase's menu."

His smirk dropped. He didn't deny it, which told me everything I needed to know.

In more than a full year since Jase and I had left Pépère, Christian had yet to improve upon Jase's menu or find a way to make it his own. Any success he might claim was still only a result of Jase's actions. First, the menu Jase had created, and then, Jase's decision to leave. Christian would still be a sous chef if he hadn't.

I was all too aware Arden Catering was my opportunity to do what Christian hadn't. To step out from Jase's influence and contribute something of my own.

I wanted it, and I didn't. Wanted to make something impactful, to uplevel my craft, but I had no interest in notoriety if it meant standing on a pedestal alone.

All Christian cared about was the pedestal.

"It won't be Jase's menu I submit to the Flavor of Philadelphia Catering Competition," he threw back. "I heard your little Arden whatever applied too. You don't stand a chance."

It made sense that Pépère had entered. Most of the names on Jillian's list were heavy hitters—well-established restaurants run by big groups with multiple locations or celebrity chefs partnered with five-star hotels. Pépère fell in among that crowd more than Ardena did.

Not that it would stop me from wiping the floor with him. "We'll see," I replied.

His lips thinned when I didn't take the bait. "Let me guess," he said, sweeping his gaze over of my appearance. It made me want to jump into a bath of sanitizing solution. "You're here to get Chef Garis to help you with the menu. You really think he'll give you tips if you bat your lashes and put on a slutty dress? Or is it that Jase won't screw you, so you're after any chef who will?"

I laughed. I shouldn't have, but I did.

Not only because the idea of me pining after Jase was hilarious but also because no chef in this city would believe I slept my way anywhere. The fact that Christian had gone there showed how desperate he was to get under my skin.

"Enjoy your meal, Christian." I made to step past him, but he blocked my path.

"No, answer me." His voice sharpened at the edges. "At least admit to throwing yourself at Jase so he'd make you his little pet."

I leaned away, trapped in the sea of bodies. He opened his mouth—

"There you are, babe," Gabe said, emerging beside me, a wall of sex and muscle. He handed me my glass from earlier and dropped a kiss to my neck, his free hand settling on the small of my back. "I got your drink."

A delicious thrill shot up my spine, made sweeter by watching the smirk fall from Christian's face. Painting me as a pathetic man chaser was a little hard when I was here with who could easily be argued was the best-looking guy in the bar. The satisfaction was yummier than the sugar that rimmed my drink.

"Who's this?" Gabe asked, turning his attention to Christian. Gabe towered over him by a good five inches, and it brought to mind the image of a shoe crushing a bug.

Christian puffed out his chest and extended his hand. "Christian Grady. I used to be Aubrey's boss."

"He means equal. We were both sous chefs," I clarified for Gabe. And Christian, apparently. Not that "equals" was a concept he'd ever fully grasped.

I expected Gabe to do that intimidating handshake thing where he gripped Christian's hand tight enough to crush it, but he didn't bother. He didn't move to shake Christian's hand at all. He just stared at it like he had no idea why it was hovering there until Christian finally lowered it.

Gabe glanced at me. "Ready to eat?"

I beamed up at him. "Yup."

"See you around, Kevin."

"It's Christian," Christian said, but Gabe showed no sign of hearing him. He guided me by the waist, putting his body between Christian and me as we made our way back to our table, both protective and possessive at once.

I liked it way too much. His confidence as we walked. His hand resting on my lower back, solid and warm against my skin. The way he supported me, strong but not macho, like we were on the same team.

It made me feel bold. Like I could channel his confidence, turn around, and kiss him. And after that, I didn't even know.

Except I did know. I knew exactly what I wanted to happen next.

I wanted to slide into our dimly lit booth and guide his

hand under my skirt. To go somewhere more private and crawl onto his lap. To wrap my legs around his waist, grind over his hardness, and relish in the impressive bulge I felt briefly on New Year's.

I wanted to have sex with him. Just to know what it was like.

To explore all my body's sensations when I was around him and maybe experience a sliver of the kind of sex I'd missed out on with Patrick. To hear the filthy words Gabe might whisper in my ear as he bent me over my kitchen counter and drove my body to new heights of pleasure. To know what it was like to experience the kind of sex that came from being so turned on your brain stopped working.

To know what it was like for sex to feel good.

To not still feel like a virgin at twenty-eight even though a) I'd already had sex and b) virginity as a concept held as much basis in reality as Christian being my boss.

And Gabe had kissed me back.

I'd jumped him on New Year's Eve, and he'd let me. He'd pressed me against the wall and pulled my body against his with his hands on my ass, urging me on. I'd told myself it hadn't meant anything, but maybe it did.

Maybe it meant he'd *liked* kissing me. That there was a chance he was attracted to me the way I was attracted to him. That he'd let me kiss him again.

Maybe he'd let me have sex with him too.

It'd be like the New Year's kiss—him helping me with something that was no big deal to him. He probably had sex all the time. It wouldn't have to mean anything.

If he didn't get the money for the gym in time, he'd likely end up leaving again anyway, to whatever new adventure in boxing awaited him. We'd go back to texting, and I'd be better equipped to navigate the world of sex on my own.

And if he did get the money and ended up staying, we'd just be friends who'd slept together a few times. Nothing two mature adults couldn't handle.

We reached our booth, where Gabe waited for me to sit before rounding to the other side. That mouthwatering scent of his hit the back of my nose as he slid close, and I decided.

Tonight, I would ask Gabe to have sex with me.

Chapter Eleven
Gabe

I DRAPED my leather jacket over Aubrey's shoulders as we walked the final two blocks from the subway to her apartment. It swallowed her up as she pulled it around her and flashed me a grateful smile. The night wasn't too cold for early March, but it was chilly enough to have her shivering beneath her own leather jacket in the best and worst dress to ever happen to me.

The best because I'd never seen a woman look so fucking sexy, and the worst because the longer I stared, the more certain I was it would kill me.

Despite her small size, her legs were endless in it, her heels only adding to the illusion, while the short skirt hugged her ass and revealed the tattoos along her legs and back. Somehow her arms and chest being fully covered made the whole thing sexier.

It had taken every shred of discipline I'd honed as a professional athlete not to offer to thread her hand with mine, lead her to the back of the restaurant, and show her just how good bathroom sex could be. Especially after hearing about her experience with her ex.

She had no idea how fucking sexy she was. How sensual and desirable without fucking trying. How I'd been hard throughout most of dinner just from her sweet scent and the accidental grazes of our skin, and from those shaky breaths she took whenever I said something that turned her on.

She deserved to feel all that from sex and more. To come a hundred times in a hundred different ways and locations and positions. She deserved to have fun with sex. To feel freedom in it. To fall in love with it. Not to feel like something was wrong with her for not knowing what was possible.

Not that I'd been much better as a sexual partner. I wouldn't say I'd been with a lot of women, but I'd certainly been with enough, and I probably hadn't given half of them the attention they deserved.

When I'd been pro, boxing had been my life. I hadn't cared about girlfriends or getting laid. If an opportunity came to have a night of fun, I took it, but it was never about more than what felt good to *me*. At the time, I'd have told you I rocked their world, but that was because I'd been too single-minded in my own world to pay attention.

With Aubrey, I paid attention to everything. Like the little hops she did on her toes when she was excited but tried to play it cool, or how dilated her eyes grew just from kissing me on New Year's. Little things I never got to witness through texts.

It was how I knew that Christian guy was more than some stranger she'd bumped into. Her shoulders had tensed, and her ankles had locked like she was reinforcing her body for a fight.

I didn't know what he said, but I'd been around enough competition to recognize something friendly versus a personal grudge. And while I had no doubt Aubrey could handle herself, as long as I was around, she'd never have to fight alone. The second Christian had blocked her with his body, I'd wanted them both to know she had backup. If Christian wanted to mess with her, he could mess with me too. Letting him believe I was her boyfriend was simply the easiest way to make that message clear.

I tried not to focus on how good it had felt for her to go along with it. Or how much I wished he was still around so I'd have an excuse to hold her hand the rest of the walk home.

When we reached Aubrey's building a few minutes later, I couldn't help but laugh. "How did you manage to find a pink apartment building in Philly?"

She grinned as she stepped onto the marble stoop leading to the sole pale-pink stone building on a street lined with red brick. "Haven't you heard of manifestation?"

"I've heard of luck." I joined her on the stoop with my hands in my pockets.

"There was some of that too." She peered fondly at the building. "I found it after my grandma died, right when I was putting her house on the market. I've always thought of it as something she put in my path. Like her way of looking out for me after she was gone."

She dropped her chin, her smile fading with a longing I recognized. One for the past. For a person in it. Her grandma, who filled so many of her stories and whose absence would always be an ache that never fully went away.

My own ache throbbed in my chest.

"Anyway." Her smile grew shy. "Thanks for coming with me tonight. I had a lot of fun."

"Me too."

She lifted her gaze to mine, those hazel eyes stealing my breath.

Goddamn, I wanted to kiss her. To fall back into the softness of her lips I still recalled from New Year's.

I recalled it way more often than I should—every one of her touches and sounds, the press of her softness against me.

None of it was mine to ask for more of. My only move was to say good night, turn around, and pour this restless energy into training. I was about to do just that when she cleared her throat.

"There's, um, something I want to ask you," she said as she played with her keys. It was hard to tell in the dimness of the porch light, but her neck looked flushed. "I just think maybe it's the sort of thing that would be better to ask you upstairs so we could talk about it—I mean, if you're even open to it. But it's also the kind of thing that might make you uncomfortable, and I don't want you to feel trapped or something, so it might be better for me to just ask you here—"

"Hey." I tucked my finger under her chin and, with a graze of her skin, nudged her to look at me. "Whatever it is, it's okay. Go ahead and ask."

Her eyes remained hesitant, so I gave an encouraging nod. If I wasn't so curious, I might have been worried.

She forced out a breath. "Well...you know that stuff about my ex and how I didn't like having sex?"

"Yeah."

She rolled her lips together as if still not sure she should let the words out. Then she released them in a rush. "I was thinking I might be able to figure out what I like with *you*."

It took me a second to process her meaning. "You want to have sex with me?"

She gave a faint nod.

My mind went fuzzy as if I'd been jabbed in the head, the ground no longer solid. That wasn't where I'd expected this to go. Despite my head spinning, my body had no problem keeping up. My cock was half hard and getting harder each second she stared at me with that hopeful gaze.

There was uncertainty too, as if she was trying to figure out a way to undo saying it and pretend this never happened.

Which was the absolute last thing I wanted.

The first involved any of a dozen scenarios that had been playing through my head since I saw her in that dress.

"Would you…be open to it?" she asked, timid.

My answer would have been the same even if it weren't for the vulnerability in her eyes. Seeing it just made me want this more.

I plucked the keys from her grasp and took her hand in mine. "You're right. We should go upstairs."

***

AUBREY LED the way to the second floor and unlocked the door to her own little fairy garden. More kinds of plants than I could name filled the space, hanging from tall curtain rods and perched on her shelves. There were overhead lights that would flood the small apartment, but she flicked on a few lamps instead, adding to the glow of the white Christmas lights lining the high ceilings.

Anything not plants was color. The green velvet of her couch, the deep reds and purples of her rug, the warm amber of her furniture and bright fabrics of her throw pillows. Where the gym I slept in was faded and dull, this space overflowed with vibrance.

None of it was more breathtaking than the woman in front of me.

She took off my jacket then hers underneath, and hung them in the narrow closet off the kitchen. "Do you want something to drink?" she offered. "I have wine or beer."

"Water's good."

Tomorrow, I would have to get strict about my diet again. No more alcohol or rich restaurant meals. Not if I wanted a real shot at winning this tournament.

She avoided my gaze as she filled two gold-rimmed glasses from a pitcher and handed me one. Her own, she took to the coffee table and placed beside a vase of wildflowers before dropping onto the couch and tucking her legs under her. A fuzzy white pillow landed in her lap.

I wanted to join her on the couch, tug her to the cushions, and lick my way beneath her dress.

If I were honest with myself, I'd wanted it since long before tonight. Not even just since New Year's.

Since all the way back to the last time I was home before my mom's funeral, one year before she died. It'd been my first Thanksgiving home in four years, and in had walked a gorgeous woman with flowing blond hair and a smile that lit up the room, wearing a long-sleeved dress that hugged soft curves, and holding an arrangement of flowers that looked lifeless compared to her. I'd stared for a full minute before realizing it was Aubrey, all grown up.

The whole day, I'd been drawn to her, my gaze following her like a compass seeking true north, my smile matching hers as she schooled me in Hardt-style Clue. It was like the world somehow lifted with the edges of her mouth, and every time our eyes met, I became aware of the growing heat of my skin and the way my muscles tightened as if holding their breath.

I'd texted her after, not wanting to release that breath, knowing I'd have to in order to give my all to the High Hitter event, but holding onto the possibility of maybe.

Maybe she'd come to Japan. Maybe we'd connect. Maybe this tug in my body would reveal a chance for something more.

Then my mom got sick, and "maybe" disintegrated with the rest of reality as I knew it.

Now here Aubrey was, carrying that same quiet authority I couldn't look away from while asking me to help her enjoy sex, and knowing she felt safe enough with me to ask for it brought me right to the edge.

I'd do whatever she wanted me to. Would let her do whatever she wanted to *me*. As far as I was concerned, my body was hers to use. She could chain me up and whip me raw if it brought her pleasure.

The thought sent heat racing to my groin. Through force of will I didn't know I had, I stayed where I was on the edge of her kitchen.

Talk first.

"Okay," I said, setting my glass aside and gripping the counter. "Tell me exactly what you want this to be."

Coming upstairs must have eased some of her anxiety because she answered right away. "I want to know what good sex feels like. And maybe try some things I've never done before. To actually see what I like and don't like instead of guessing or never finding out."

"You want to explore."

"Yes."

"So this would be more than a one-time thing? You're picturing something ongoing?"

She squirmed on the cushion. "If you're open to it." Anticipation pulsed through my body, only curbing when she added, "I mean, not forever. We could set a limit upfront if you want, or just see how it goes. Either way, I'm not expecting anything long-term."

If she was, I'd be the last person she'd turn to, rightfully so. No matter how much it stung that she knew it.

"And whenever it ends, you still want to be friends?"

"Yes." Her eyes snapped to mine. "That's really important to me. I don't want to do this if you think that won't be possible."

It was just as important to me. Over the past two years, she'd become the person I could talk to about anything. The only person I wanted to talk to about most things. Given my current relationship status with my family, she was pretty much the most important person in my life right now.

Which made our friendship the one thing in all of this that made me nervous. "I've never done something like this with a friend," I admitted.

Sex had never carried stakes for me before. Not just because I'd been too selfish to think past what felt good in the moment but because there had never been a relationship beyond it I cared about losing.

Maybe that meant I shouldn't risk my relationship with Aubrey by bringing sex into the mix, but I wanted it too much to turn her away when she was the one asking.

"Do you think it's a bad idea?" she asked.

I knew what I wanted the answer to be. "No. But I think if we're going to do this, we need ground rules."

Her shoulders eased. "I think so too."

Our stares met across the room, and something passed between us in the brief silence. An acknowledgment that we were actually discussing this. Her mouth lifted at the corners.

I swallowed. "Then for starters, no being with anyone else while we do this. For either of us." Even putting aside the added health risks, I wouldn't be able to handle the thought of another man's hands on her while we were together. I could hardly stand the thought of it happening after we were back to just friends, but that would be a problem for my future self to deal with.

Her eyes flashed with a similar spark of possession that made me want to say fuck it and bury my head between her legs right now. "Agreed."

"I got tested last year," I continued. "Everything was negative, and I haven't been with anyone since."

"I got tested after Patrick and I broke up, and same. And I still have an IUD, but I'd rather use condoms anyway if that's all right with you."

"Of course." Whatever would make her most comfortable. God knew I wasn't qualified to be a father.

"Also, maybe we don't tell Evan," she added. "There's

enough going on between you two as is, and I don't want this to make everything worse."

"You sure?" It wasn't like he gave me many opportunities to talk to him. This would affect her relationship with him more than mine.

But she nodded. "I'm sure."

"Then we won't tell him."

"Anything else?" she asked.

"Yeah."

I abandoned the safety of the counter and rounded the coffee table to join her on the couch, leaving a good six inches between us. I did it partly for my own control and partly to make sure she didn't feel pressured now that we'd agreed to do this.

"Tell me what wasn't good for you about sex with your ex."

She dropped her chin, fingers running through the fibers of the pillow as if she wasn't sure how to answer. "It wasn't anything specific," she said. "He did all the right things and touched all the right places. We used lube so there wasn't friction. It just never really *felt* like anything. Not in a numb way. I mean, I could feel stuff. It just didn't feel particularly good. Sometimes it hurt."

I tensed.

"Not because of Patrick," she hurried to clarify. "He was never careless or rough or anything. He did his best to help me enjoy it."

My muscles relaxed a little. "Did you tell him when it hurt?"

Her cheeks went red. "Not after the first couple of times. Mostly because it wasn't anything he did wrong. I just could never…get ready enough. And that made me nervous about the next time, which pretty much made it impossible to relax…"

"Which didn't help it feel any better."

She released a frustrated breath. "Yeah."

No wonder she'd never tried sleeping with anyone else. She wasn't just nervous about pain; she probably expected it. A concern I'd never had to worry about as a guy. Even the worst sex I'd had still felt good. I couldn't imagine what it'd be like to carry around not just the possibility but the likelihood it wouldn't.

The need to give her everything she wanted from this solidified in me like a steel fucking wall. At the very least, she'd know sex didn't have to hurt.

Hopefully, that we were having this conversation right now meant she was comfortable enough with me for that not to be an issue. And if getting aroused was the problem, our New Year's kiss sure suggested I turned her on just fine.

What we needed was to get her out of her head.

"Was there anything you liked?" I asked. "Anything that always felt good for you?" Starting in her comfort zone seemed like the best way to ease her into more.

She glanced at my lips. "I…liked kissing."

"Yeah?" I liked kissing her too. A lot. Enough to have me stiffening against my zipper just remembering it. "What about oral?"

Her blush returned as she looked away, and I knew what was coming before she even said it. "Patrick did it once."

"Only once?"

She nodded at the pillow. "I could tell he didn't like it, so I felt weird asking again."

My nostrils flared at the self-consciousness in her tone, the embarrassment that told me she believed it was her fault, like she'd somehow done something wrong.

"Did he ask you to go down on him?"

"I volunteered a few times, but we mostly skipped oral altogether."

Right. *That* wouldn't be happening here. Her ex might have hated giving oral, or maybe he'd been nervous about it. Either way, I didn't have that problem. I'd be more than happy to give her what she'd missed.

In fact, my new mission was to take every disappointing experience she'd had with sex and replace it with one a hundred times better.

"You want to find out if you like it?"

An edge of excitement lit her eyes. She tried to contain it as she nodded.

"Good, because I fucking love giving oral." I wanted no question in her mind when I went down on her that it was exactly where I wanted to be. Just thinking of giving her a taste of it, of getting *my* first taste of *her*, had my skin going hot beneath my shirt. "What else do you like?"

She swallowed, her eyes going hazy like she was remembering something. "I like when you touch me."

Had I touched her? Barely. Light nudges and accidental grazes. The occasional hug.

New Year's.

My hands had been all over her then.

I wanted them all over her now. My voice came out low. "You want me to touch you?"

She bit her bottom lip and nodded.

Something shifted in the energy around us, the air

growing thick. My eyes traveled the length of her, along the ink flowers winding up her legs and disappearing under the short hem of that goddamn dress. Her chest rose on a deep breath, drawing my stare to the swell of her breasts and the faint points of her nipples peeking through.

"Gabe?"

I lifted my gaze, breath catching at how fucking gorgeous she was.

"Can we start tonight?"

I was fully hard again. My hands nearly shot across the couch of their own free will. I blew out a slow, steadying breath. "One more thing first."

Her gaze held mine, her hazel eyes dark pools reflecting the glowing lights. My skin buzzed, and I shifted in my seat, not used to her seeing so much. To her being able to read my body in addition to my words.

I might not have liked it, except I got to see as much of her. To catch the lift of her lips as she studied me. To witness rather than imagine if I made her blush or laugh. It helped me voice my last condition.

"You're the one in control," I said. "You take the lead and set the pace. You tell me what you want, what you like, what you don't. You tell me when you're done. No hard feelings, no awkwardness after. Just be open with me. I need that."

It wasn't that I didn't *want* to take the lead. It was that with her, I knew I'd take too much. There was no way for me not to be selfish with her or to not always want more when I shouldn't have even taken what she'd already given me. I needed the scales to stay in her favor if I had any hope of not hating myself when this was over.

More than I already did.

Instead of saying anything, she moved the pillow from her lap and scooted my way, her initiative easing my own tight nerves. Her thigh brushed along mine, and we both seemed to still at the contact.

Not accidental. Not fleeting.

A precursor to every touch that would follow, and neither of us had to pretend we didn't want it.

She released a shaky breath as she met my gaze. "Now what?"

My pulse picked up the way it had sitting beside her in the restaurant booth. Like we were in high school, and I was about to have my first kiss.

"That's up to you. What do you want to happen?"

Her face grew shy, that flush climbing her neck. "I don't know where to start."

She was willing to take the lead, but she needed me to guide her. I could do that. I licked my lips. "I could tell you what I wanted to do to you at the restaurant."

Her eyes widened. "You were thinking about it then?"

"I couldn't stop thinking about it." Torturing myself, more like. "You do this thing where you bite your lip when you're deciding something, like which dish to try next. Every single time, I wanted to take that lip between my teeth and tug."

I imagined doing it between bites too. Tasting the dishes off her lips instead of the plate. Letting her enjoy the food while I enjoyed her.

Her words came out breathless. "I was thinking about stuff too."

"Yeah?"

She nodded, her hazel eyes glued to mine like she

couldn't move them away. As if she was as hypnotized by me as I was by her.

"Tell me," I rasped.

"Mostly you touching me. Your hand on my leg."

As if being pulled by a string, I bent to skim my hand along her calf. "You mean here?"

She bit back her smile and shook her head. "Higher."

The tips of my fingers burned on their way up her leg. I flexed my hand over her knee before trailing it to the hem of her dress. "Here?"

She squirmed the tiniest bit as if trying to stay still. "Higher."

My body pounded with my pulse as I dipped my hand below her skirt. Just an inch. Just so I could watch it disappear and feel the heat of her skin beneath the material. And when that wasn't enough, I slid higher, fitting my fingers over the curve of her thigh, following the soft bend to where her legs met. Her breath sawed in and out as I traced the crease of her hip.

I angled my lips to her ear, letting my chest press against her side, her warmth flush with mine. "What else?" I whispered. My voice was gravel along stone.

Her head fell against the back of the couch as she shifted her thighs apart, enough for me to feather a touch directly between her legs. Soft lace grazed my skin as a shiver rippled through her.

"I straddled your lap," she moaned.

With the sound still on her lips, I scooped her up by the thighs and set her on top of me, her knees on either side of my hips. "How's this?"

She rocked experimentally, a purely instinctual motion,

and I watched the groan break across her face at how hard I was between her legs. Her hooded gaze found mine as she bit her bottom lip.

"You're killing me," I murmured, drawing her lip free.

A smirk raised the corners of her mouth as I let my thumb linger over the soft skin. Inches separated us. I could see the flutter of her pulse in her throat, her pupils already dilated.

"Do something about it," she taunted.

My lips rose. "You want me to?"

She stared at my mouth and nodded. Every muscle in my body hardened to iron as my heart tried to pound through my chest.

There'd been more than one moment tonight when I'd imagined she wanted to kiss me; when my head had gotten away from me, and I'd imagined kissing her. But it was different knowing it was about to happen. Different lowering my stare to her lips and letting myself dip forward until our noses brushed and her scent made my head go dizzy.

I pulled away for a second, smiling as she leaned in to follow. Then I took her bottom lip between my teeth and gave a light tug, drawing a moan from her throat.

Another tug, slightly harder, and her fingers curled over my shoulders.

My patience finally snapped. I captured her mouth with mine, and the feel of her washed over and through me as she sighed against my lips.

It was different from our first kiss. Slower. As if we were meeting for the first time, learning each other from scratch.

I held myself in place, only my head and lips moving, as she kissed me in return. Kisses so gentle, they were barely there, yet every one cranked my body higher, setting my need on edge.

Her tongue grazed my lips, and I opened for her, responding with teasing licks. The instant I did, her own need seemed to burst. Her body melted against mine, like all her tension had released. She gripped my face to angle me just the way she wanted, and I had to force down my smile so I could keep kissing her.

"Touch me," she ordered between swipes of her tongue.

I held in a groan as my fingers twitched. "Where?"

"Anywhere."

I found the soft dip above her hip and trailed my fingers along the exposed skin of her back.

"*Oh*," she moaned, her kisses growing harder. "I love when you touch me."

Fucking same. I traced my way up her spine, drawing a shiver from her, and all at once, it was like her body took over. She spread her knees wider and rocked forward, our tongues finding each other in a maddening rush.

"Keep touching me," she demanded as her hips rolled on a wave.

My dick was rock solid. Seeing her lose herself in pleasure, knowing I was the reason, was more erotic than any porn I could remember.

I trailed my hands down her back and gave her ass a light squeeze, drawing another moan from her.

"You like that?" I breathed.

A helpless sound escaped her before she dragged her fingers through my hair and rocked against me, finding her rhythm. "Keep going."

I slid my hands under the stretchy material of her skirt

and below her panties to palm her bare ass. Her hips jerked in a frantic rut.

"Gabe—" She cut off with a groan, squeezing my hips between her knees. "Oh my God."

"That's it. Find what you're looking for." I urged her over my cock, twisting the lace of her panties into my fist, fucking dying to rip them off and stretch her over my length, to drive into her until she gushed all over my lap and was too weak to move.

She pushed higher onto her knees, wrapping her arms around my shoulders and grinding over the head of my cock through my jeans. "Oh," she sighed, grinding faster. "*Oh.*"

"Jesus, fuck yes," I groaned. "Let me have it."

The front of her skirt was around her waist, the back pushed below my hands that squeezed her ass hard enough to leave palm prints for a week. Her breasts thrust into my face as she threw back her head, and if I died right now, I'd be okay with it as long as I got to see her come first.

A moment later, I did.

"I'm coming," she panted, her voice going up at the end like it had caught her off guard and she feared it would be too much.

"I know, baby. I know. Ride it out."

She gasped into a cry as her muscles locked up, and her hands strangled my shirt. Her legs squeezed my hips in a death grip so she could bear down on my cock, which was leaking through my boxers to add to the mess on my jeans. Her hips circled a few more times before she collapsed onto my chest, her face buried in the crook of my neck.

Our panting echoed off her tall ceilings, her warm breath

tickling below my ear. Something wet brushed my neck, and a moment later, she sighed. "Mmm."

I trailed my fingers up her spine and chuckled. "Did you just lick me?" My cock was still hard and straining against my zipper, but I couldn't care less with her boneless and sated in my arms.

She mumbled against my neck, "Is that okay?"

"Hell yes. Lick away."

I could feel the rise of her lips against my skin. The urge to hold her like this all night brought my hand to the back of her head. I carefully ran my fingers through her silky strands.

"How are you feeling?" I asked. That had been a bit more than the make-out session I'd envisioned. "More" being one of the hottest things I'd ever fucking experienced. But only if it had been as hot for her.

She shifted her weight. "I don't know."

I pulled back to see her eyes. "Too rough?" She'd been grinding near the button of my jeans. Sometimes things that felt good in the moment didn't so much after. Or maybe it had all been too fast.

She denied it with a shake of her head, her gaze the most radiant I'd seen it—no embarrassment or reluctance in sight. Pride ballooned in my chest.

"I just—" She circled her hips again. "I think I want more."

Fuck. I clamped my hands over her thighs and squeezed my eyes shut as pleasure tightened my groin. "Yeah?" I strained to calm my suddenly harsh breaths. "You have something in mind?" 'Cause I had several. Playing across my eyelids like the only movie I ever wanted to watch again.

Did this count as manifestation?

My grip on her tensed as she continued to squirm, my body almost back under my control.

"Not really," she said. "I'm usually too sensitive to keep going when I try to use my vibrator back to back."

I squeezed my eyes shut harder and exhaled through my nose. Imagining her using her vibrator was not helpful with the heat of her pussy radiating through my pants.

"What kind of vibrator do you use?" I asked. For fact-finding purposes. It didn't count as torturing myself if it was for a good cause.

"The suction kind."

My hands flexed. I tucked that information away for later.

She squirmed again, and I finally opened my eyes.

"I could do something about this," she offered, rolling herself against my erection. Her lips quirked in a devious smile, even as she dropped her gaze.

"Is that what you want to do?"

She opened her mouth to respond, then paused to think about it.

Good. Nervous was fine if it came from excitement, but her leading from a place of "should" instead of "want" was my one dealbreaker.

"I want to," she ended up saying, "but I'm nervous about it right now."

"Then we'll do it another time," I said easily. "Let's let tonight be about you."

Her expression softened as her nails scraped lightly at the nape of my neck, drawing tingles all along my skin. She leaned in for another kiss.

Our tongues met, and her hips grew restless before she breathed against my lips, "I can keep going?"

I shifted my hands under her skirt so it bunched completely at her waist, revealing a flash of light purple underneath. Her soaked panties. I could smell her arousal from here, a musky sweetness that went straight to my head and drove me out of my mind.

She sat on my lap, a garden nymph in my hold, her dress rucked up and nothing but trust in her eyes. My heart cradled that trust as its prized possession.

I urged her hips forward and back in consent. "Take what feels good, Aubrey. You set the pace."

She licked her lips and watched me with heavy lids as she rode away on her pleasure.

I was the luckiest bastard in the world to be the one to see it.

Chapter Twelve
Aubrey

I STARED at the dandelion greens that mocked me from the plate as their bitter aftertaste continued to burn off the walls of my mouth. In less than forty-eight hours, I'd managed to go from the ultimate sex high to the worst creative funk of my life.

Menu planning for the catering competition was off to a great start.

I was beginning to wonder if it was possible to have the groove fucked *out* of you instead of the other way around because the two orgasms I'd had two nights ago were clearly doing nothing for me now. This was my third new dish concept that had turned out practically inedible.

Then again, Gabe and I hadn't had *sex* sex, so maybe there was fine print somewhere that stipulated my mystical inspiration wasn't allowed to strike until the dick that made me come did it inside me. As if that was the most likely way for a woman to orgasm.

In truth, the orgasms weren't the problem. Everything about my evening with Gabe had been perfect—from our flirting at the restaurant to him not only considering but also agreeing to my outlandish proposal. Then the way he'd kissed my lips swollen and hiked my skirt over my waist so I could grind myself to bliss.

Already, Gabe had given me the best sexual encounter of my life, and we hadn't even taken our clothes off.

My body still rang at the fact that he'd said yes. And took it seriously enough to have *rules*. Including that I be the one to set the pace. Just the idea of asking for what I wanted and telling him what I didn't sparked embers in my belly instead of stiffness down my spine. And as long as we stayed honest with each other, I trusted there would be no hard feelings in the end.

No, the arrangement with Gabe wasn't the problem.

The problem was yesterday's interview that showed thirty minutes late without any attempt at letting me know. She hadn't even given an excuse—no "my alarm didn't go off" or "my car didn't start." Just meandered in like this was the principal's office and she'd rather be smoking a joint behind the bleachers. Then she asked if she could skip chopping the onions I asked her to prep because "the skin gives her the creeps."

In other words, I'd worked this morning's corporate brunch alone.

Then I came back to the silence of the prep kitchen and cooked three dishes in a row that made me question whether I'd actually attended culinary school or had hallucinated the whole thing.

I *hated* how quiet it was in here. Not even the rumble of

the walk-in fridge was loud enough to count as white noise. Every chop of my knife on the cutting board and tap of my spoon against the pan ricocheted around the room like an echo chamber designed to drive me insane.

I felt like I was being watched, my every move scrutinized. Like everyone was silently waiting on the sidelines to witness me pull this off or fail trying.

Earlier, I'd played Zach's heavy-metal playlist to drown out the silence, but it had overwhelmed the small kitchen in a way it never had at Ardena with Zach and Luis laughing in the background and Jase's stoic presence by my side.

Alone in this kitchen, everything I cooked tasted flat. Sterile. Less like what I'd grown up knowing food to be from the love my grandma poured into hers and more like something I imagined would come out of one of those futuristic microwaves in sci-fi shows that materialized food from thin air.

Being here any longer tonight wouldn't help that feeling. I needed to be around people. My people.

I tossed the dandelion greens into the compost bin and cleaned the rest of the kitchen, then walked the four minutes to Ardena.

It wasn't even seven, and the bar was standing room only with people waiting for a table. I weaved my way through the crowd to the side closest to the kitchen.

"Hey!" Dani greeted. She was in the end stool that had unofficially become hers during the months leading up to the symposium Ardena had catered. Dani was the event planner for the nonprofit that hosted it and had spent more than a little time here with her laptop, fine-tuning every event detail. Their office had gone remote on Fridays, so she'd probably worked from here today too, which was how she'd snagged the spot before the rush.

"Has it been like this for a while?" I asked as I squeezed in beside her.

"Since about five thirty. If it's anything like last weekend, they won't catch a break until midnight."

I caught a glimpse into the kitchen of Zach and Luis on the sauté line, shuffling pans as they kept up with tickets. A young man with dark brown skin and a head of curls who must have been the new prep cook emerged from the walk-in, two full prep pans in hand, and hurried back to the cold station. Jase stood inside the food window, firing orders and putting up plates, completely in the zone.

"You okay?" Dani asked, watching me watch them. The sudden crush of sadness must have shown on my face.

I forced my lips to rise. "I'm good. Just a long day."

"Want to talk about it?"

I wasn't sure I knew *how* to talk about it. What—the incredible job opportunity I'd been given was a little bit hard? I missed the comfort and ease of my old job? It felt trivial to say out loud.

This wasn't anything I couldn't handle. I knew it wasn't, so why did my throat tighten when I tried to say no to Dani's question?

It felt like the chaotic rhythm of my life had flipped, and everything usually under my control had left me in the dark. Cooking was a struggle. My composure was breaking. I wanted to curl into myself like a roly-poly until my world went back to spinning normally, but I couldn't do that here. I refused. I didn't cause drama at work, and I didn't let my emotions get the best of me in front of my team.

Even if they didn't feel like my team anymore.

I could go upstairs to the staff room or Jillian's office, but then I'd be alone again because, as compassionate and understanding as Dani was, she wasn't the person I wanted to be with right now.

"I'm actually going to head out," I said as I realized where I wanted to be. I flashed another forced smile.

"Okay." She didn't sound convinced. "If you ever change your mind…"

My expression softened into something more genuine. "Thank you." I didn't know Dani that well yet, but she continued to make an effort to include me in her life as much as Jase's, and I appreciated it. Not every girlfriend accepted their boyfriend's female friends.

Her lips lifted with a nod.

I glanced one more time at the kitchen that still felt like home, the team I used to belong to moving just as smoothly without me, and left.

THE GYM DOOR blew shut behind me, cutting off the wind's sharp chill with a bang of the latch. I was glad I'd changed into jeans before leaving the prep kitchen. Chef pants sucked at blocking the cold.

It wasn't much warmer in here. A space heater in the center of the room was trying its best but coming up short against the draft through the broken windows. I adjusted my knit beanie and followed the clanging of metal plates to the far corner of the space.

Gabe stepped to the middle of the weighted bar and

tucked his shoulders under, adjusting his grip before lifting the bar off the rack. I watched from the shadow of a pillar as he started a set of squats.

I couldn't tell you how much weight was on the bar or whether his form was correct, but to me, the steady up-and-down tempo of his movement screamed *power*.

Muscles contracted all along the back of his body, carving lines through his arms and shoulders beneath his sweat-darkened tee. His calves bulged with definition, disappearing under the shadow of his ass as he bent his legs and lowered toward the ground.

His ass was…I lost track as his glutes contracted when he stood, and the thought of those glutes contracting as he thrust inside *me* paralyzed me with lust.

This was a problem.

The way I craved him couldn't be okay. That I'd run to him for comfort wasn't good either. Maybe on its own it would be, but not both. Not emotional comfort and physical release. It was asking too much.

Yet just standing here, my heart felt at ease and my clit swollen, as if the sight of him was enough to quench my desires.

The clang of the bar returning to the rack snapped me back to myself. Gabe bent for a towel and wiped his face.

"That looked good," I said, abandoning my lurking post. "Shouldn't you have someone here to spot you?"

One corner of his mouth lifted as his gaze drank me in from head to toe. "Probably. But I'm not going that heavy yet." He hung the towel over the bar and headed for me. "Noah will be home from training in a couple of days. I'll wait until I'm with him to go all in."

My heart pattered faster as his steps brought him close. I curled my fingers over my thumbs to keep from reaching for him and burying my head in his chest. From asking him to cradle me like the ball I wanted to curl into. Even his sweat-soaked shirt looked comforting somehow.

His smile faded as he stopped a handbreadth away and searched my face. "Everything okay?"

I clenched my teeth and shrugged, the flood of emotion from the day dangerously close to spilling over.

He nodded toward the ring behind me. "C'mon."

He led the way to the heart of the gym, then tugged the ropes apart so I could slip between them and followed me onto the mat. We sat in the middle, me cross-legged and him leaning back on his hands, his long legs splayed in front of him like he was opening himself to me.

He made it look so easy. Like the only thing he risked by trusting me with his thoughts was the time it took to share them.

We hadn't been that way growing up. He'd been in my life as long as Evan, but before the past couple of years, I wouldn't have described him as my friend.

He'd been my best friend's older brother. My childhood crush. The boy who girls at school fawned over in a way that made me feel special that he knew my name.

He'd been there but always removed—in high school when I was still in middle school. Graduated by the time I reached high school. Away at boxing camp during the summers I spent at the Hardt's. He'd been the stories Evan told me about his big brother from their calls on Skype and the weird trinkets he mailed from Thailand, Turkey, and Japan.

Yet, even then, he'd always, always made me feel safe. Where Evan had treated me like one of the boys, Gabe treated me like someone to be protected. Someone *worth* protecting.

He'd intimidated the kids at the bus stop who made fun of my braces. He'd given me hints at game night so I didn't feel lost when I was learning a new game. He'd shared the chocolate from his Halloween candy with me when Evan refused to trade.

He'd looked out for me.

Maybe that was how he felt when I'd texted him after his mom's funeral. Perhaps I'd been the safe space he needed to be broken and have it be okay.

Sitting in this boxing ring felt a little like that. Like the space within its ropes was separate from the rest of the world. Like here, it was okay to break apart, to be knocked down, to fall to your knees. Because this was where you learned to get back up.

"I miss Ardena more than I thought I would," I admitted after several moments of silence.

The words felt dangerous. A sign of weakness or a burden cast onto others no one would want to share. The kind of burden I'd trained myself out of being after my parents offloaded me to be someone else's problem.

Gabe didn't react like it was a burden. He didn't say anything at all. He just listened.

"I hadn't really viewed it as me leaving when this whole catering thing started," I went on, "but that's what it was. As much as Arden Catering is a part of Ardena, it's separate. The schedule, the kitchen, the team—it's all its own thing, and I feel like the relationships I built are fading because of it."

The more I let the words come, the more cracks formed along my shell until there were too many to hold together at once. I flung a tear from my cheek. "The thing is, I don't have that many important relationships left." My voice came out thick.

Gabe extended his arm, and I folded into his embrace as the dam of emotions broke. His hand was a shield on the back of my head as he rocked us gently side to side.

The tears hurt, like the riverbed my grief had settled beneath was being dredged up with each shuddered sob. Or maybe more like a volcano whose pressure had built too high to contain any longer. Lava scorched my throat and burned my cheeks, my tears and mascara mixing with the sweat on Gabe's shirt. I yanked off my beanie, the scratchiness of the wool suddenly too rough.

I'd learned after my grandma died, and again after Mrs. Hardt, that sometimes crying left me feeling lighter, and other times, it left me raw, like a partially healed cut that had been torn open.

That was how I felt when I could finally breathe again. Like an exposed wound. I let Gabe's hold be the thing to keep me from bleeding all over the mat.

He pressed his lips to my forehead, not caring that I used the bottom of my shirt to wipe my nose. When I'd calmed more, he said, "It was just me in the ring during a fight."

My gaze settled on the V of his collarbone as it rose and fell with the soft cadence of his voice. I felt like a bottle of honey set upside down to drain, my last drop of energy depleted. I'd have fallen asleep if it didn't mean missing out on whatever Gabe said next.

"But it never felt that way to me," he continued. "My coach, manager, cutman, training partners—they were always with me in the ring. Not during the rounds, but they were the ones who got me there. When I won, it was because of them. Not getting to be a part of that kind of team anymore was what scared me most when I got hurt."

He'd torn his rotator cuff in the High Hitter championship fight the weekend his mom had died. The two things he cared about most, both taken from him in an instant.

"Is that why you want to open a gym?" I'd figured it had always been part of his plan, a vision for down the line that moved up when the opportunity for this place arose. But maybe it was more than that.

"It's why I need it. Why I have to win this tournament. Coaching is the one way I have left I can still be in that ring, even if it's not my body on the ropes. And this ring, this gym…" He cast his gaze around the room. "It's home for me. My only one at this point."

I tightened my arm across his stomach in a slouched sort of hug. "I'm sorry about your shoulder."

He huffed out a breath. "Don't be. It's what I deserved."

"No, it's not."

His shoulders tensed. "Evan's right. I chose my career over my family and let them down."

"No, you—" My tongue tripped over the dozen ways I wanted to disagree. "It was never meant to be a choice between the two. The surgery was supposed to be straightforward. Everyone believed the worst was a long way off."

"I shouldn't have risked it. Evan—"

"Evan's upset. He's angry your mom is gone, and he's worried about your dad, about *you*." I poked his chest. "He wants to keep everyone from ever hurting again, and he knows he can't, so he's lashing out."

A muscle flexed in Gabe's jaw, his defiant gaze fastened on his lap.

"Your mom wanted you to stay for that fight," I told him. "It was all she talked about. She had Evan bring her an old pair of your boxing gloves that she planned to wear for the match and told every doctor and nurse who walked in that her son was about to be a High Hitter World Boxing champion. She didn't feel abandoned by you. She was inspired by you."

He rolled to his back and covered his face with his hands. His chest rose and fell with sharp breaths, fragments of the love and joy and comfort his mom used to bring that were left shattered in her absence.

It would pain her to see her sons like this. Hurting, not speaking, spinning in circles while waiting for the world to make sense again. She would hate it.

I hated I couldn't fix it.

"She was inspired by you too, you know." He dropped his arms to his sides and met my gaze. His eyes were red. "That Thanksgiving before she died? The last one I was home for?"

I nodded. It was the first time I'd seen him since graduating from culinary school and navigating the world as something resembling an adult. He'd texted me later that night to say how nice it was to see me.

My heart had just about exploded. Not even because his handsome features had grown more stunning as they'd matured into those of a man, like they'd been waiting since birth to reach their full potential. But because it felt like confirmation of my place within the Hardt family. A place offered by each of them in kind and not just by Evan.

We hadn't continued texting then. He'd gone into training mode for the High Hitter tournament, and I'd committed to the grind of a fine-dining kitchen. One year later was his mom's funeral.

"After you left," Gabe said, "she talked for almost an hour straight about how you were already a sous chef after just three years, and you'd graduated from culinary school at the top of your class. How she'd been there to see it and rubbed it in all her friends' faces that soon she'd have an in with a Michelin-star chef."

I snorted. "No, she didn't."

He grinned as if remembering. "She did. She had zero doubts it would happen."

"It hasn't."

"Doesn't mean it won't."

I didn't care if it did. Stars were exciting, but there were other measures of a great chef. Like the respect of your peers.

Gabe must have thought so too. "Your team still cares about you. Just because you're in a solo sport now doesn't mean they won't still be behind you in the ring. I bet if you asked, they'd all want to be."

Ah, but that was the problem: asking.

I was the person *others* asked. The person who handled things so others wouldn't have to. The one who was supposed to be solid and reliable and useful. And if I did ever ask, it was a question of how I could help.

When I'd first moved in with Nana, I'd been the one to

ask *her* for chores. She started tying my allowance to whether I played outside to make sure I still experienced being a kid. And as Jase's sous chef, I'd regularly volunteered for the extra shifts.

The one time I'd accepted help without question was immediately after Nana had died and the Hardts stepped in to help me with the million things that needed to get done. Arranging the funeral, handling the will, talking to accountants, transferring bills, notifying social security, calling banks.

A whirlwind of demands in a storm of grief, and they hadn't waited for me to ask before stepping into the eye of it with me. They'd just been there, standing in the receiving line with me at the wake and leaving food in my fridge. Sitting beside me while I met with lawyers to counter my parents' challenge on the house and helping me pack Nana's things when it was finally time to sell.

Evan had slept in a sleeping bag on my floor for a week after the funeral so I wasn't alone. I'd done the same for him after his mom.

But a little loneliness and a heavy workload weren't life and death. Neither was a creative funk. I hated the idea of bothering the guys with this, especially when they were already at full capacity with Ardena. It wasn't fair for me to ask them to take on my stuff too. Not when it wasn't anything beyond my ability to handle on my own.

"I'll figure it out," I said. "I've got more interviews lined up, so…" I tucked my knees into my chest. Nothing had been fixed, but that wasn't why I'd come. "Thank you for listening." I'd needed to release a layer of what had been building these past few months, and it was nice not to do it alone.

"Any time." He extended his palm to me, and I placed

mine in his. His thumb rubbed my wrist so gently it almost brought more tears to my eyes.

I liked this. Sharing with him in person.

We'd opened up about similar things over texts, but it had lacked this physical comfort. The connection of running my hand along the lines of his palm and tracing the veins in his forearm. Of fitting my thumb in the divot inside his elbow. Trying to connect my fingers around his bicep.

He chuckled as I failed. "What are you doing?"

I rounded my hands over the swell of his shoulder. "Exploring. Do you mind?"

His laughter was more of a sharp exhale. "No."

The hot coals of his gaze warmed me as I tucked my hair behind my ears and shifted onto my knees. I shuffled closer so I could run the backs of my fingers along his square jaw. His eyes rolled closed, his chin tipping up, and I studied each subtle movement, cataloging his every detail like he was a dish I wanted to recreate.

My fingers scraped over the sandpaper of his stubble, trailing along to gently tug on his earlobe. His ribs expanded as his breaths deepened. I traced the outer shell of his ear, then wandered both hands over his brows, easing the tension in his forehead with my thumbs.

A near-silent groan shook his chest.

His muscles grew tight, his hands in fists at his sides like my touch on his skin pained him. The growing bulge in his shorts said differently.

I did that to him. Made him hard with nothing but a few simple touches nowhere near his sex.

The power of it had my brain going fuzzy and my body

heating up, my want for him climbing with each groan he held back.

I ran my hands down the front of his chest and slid my fingers along the hem of his shirt. "Can I?"

Eyes squeezed shut, he nodded.

Dragging his shirt up his torso and over his head was like unwrapping a present. One with lean muscles that had been carved like a river through a canyon. His abs were clenched, the many ridges pronounced, highlighting the V at his waist.

I ran my thumbs over the dips peeking from his waistband, and he sucked through his teeth.

"Do you want me to stop?"

He shook his head on the mat, voice strained. "Do whatever you want to me."

The deep rasp of his words buzzed along my skin.

I licked below his navel, wanting to memorize the smooth texture of his abdomen. His taste. To map out every inch of this beautiful body he had honed from more than a decade of diligence and commitment to his sport.

His whole torso jumped beneath my tongue. I licked higher, following the line that cut through his stomach to his chest, grazing my hands over the firmness of his pecs.

When my fingers brushed over his nipples, he hissed. His pelvis rocked the smallest amount before he welded his hips to the floor, his cock straining against the fabric of his shorts.

I ran my tongue over his nipple, smiling as it drew to a peak, and let my teeth scrape the lightest bit across it.

When I switched to the other nipple, his head rolled to the side, his breaths coming in pants. Shadows jumped along his stomach as his abs expanded and contracted, his biceps bulging as he forced his body still for my enjoyment.

I almost couldn't breathe, it was so hot. The fact that he was letting me do it to him *here* on mats in the middle of the gym, nowhere close to a bed.

A groan escaped him when I hooked my fingers under the elastic of his shorts, and he lifted his hips as I tugged, letting me reveal his cock to the spotlights pinning him to the center of the ring.

"Can I—?"

"Yes," he choked out. "Anything." He threw an arm across his eyes, the other bracing the mat above his head, putting more of his flexed muscles on display.

I could hardly believe he was real. His cock jutted over his stomach, curving the slightest bit, the shaft full and thick, the head glistening. A trimmed patch of hair surrounded the base, and I ran my fingers through it before dropping my lips to the inside of his thigh.

His skin burned beneath my touch, raising my own body temperature as I licked and sucked my way higher. I shed my leather jacket and threw it aside, then straddled his knees. He peeked from under his arm, his eyes wild with need, and licked his lips like he wanted to be licking me.

I had the same idea.

Bending slowly, I kissed the very tip of him. It was more of a touch than a kiss, my lips resting on the head of his cock. Then I pulled back to circle him with my hands, exploring the soft skin of his shaft.

He was big in my palm, the way all of him was big next to me. Big and solid and warm, but never in a way I had to fear.

I played with tightening my grip, and the arm that covered his eyes shot to join the other above his head as if to anchor him in place. It didn't stop the squirming of his hips. My tongue darted out for my first taste, and my chest swelled with pride as his breaths sawed in and out with audible gasps. His sounds were like sugar in my veins, driving my tongue out again and again so I could hear more.

This kind of pleasure was new to me. Not just receiving but giving it too.

I hadn't realized I was capable of it. That my hands and lips could bring torture so sweet, it brought sweat to the skin and set the air on fire.

I smiled at what else might be possible. Like pushing him all the way over the edge and into the kind of bliss that went on for so long, up no longer had meaning.

Wrapping my lips around him, I lowered as far as I could, pausing when he neared the back of my throat. Saliva pooled on my tongue, and I swallowed on instinct, pulling a choked moan from his lips.

Keeping my hands around his base, I moved my mouth up and down, finding a natural rhythm. With each up stroke, I ran my tongue over his tip, collecting the salty taste of him and letting it fill my senses.

I wanted to know all of him—his taste, his smell, his sounds, his feel. I wanted to learn how to command his body as easily as he commanded mine.

Bolder than I'd ever been, I loosened a hand and trailed it downward over his balls. His cock jumped in my mouth.

"Yes," he groaned when I hesitated.

I rolled his balls gently, my fingers brushing the skin underneath, drawing another throb from his length.

"Fuck."

My jaw started to ache, so I freed him from my mouth

and stroked him with my hand as my tongue explored his sack. The skin was soft there too.

"God. Harder. Stroke harder."

I lifted my gaze to find him peering at me down the length of his body. His eyes burned hot and a little wild, his cheeks flushed. I tightened my grip on his shaft and sped up my strokes, and his head fell back against the mat, the ridges of his throat in sharp relief.

I grinned and returned my mouth to his shaft. This time, I tried to go deep but gagged when he reached my throat.

"Hey, easy." His abs flexed as he curled to brush the hair from my face while I caught my breath, my lips wet with saliva. "You don't need to do that."

I licked his tip. "You said anything I want."

"Yeah, but—"

"I want to try."

I never had before. Certainly never imagined I would. But his body shook beneath mine, his skin hot, pupils blown wide, and it was the most powerful I'd ever felt in my life.

I had gotten him here. I wanted to see what else I could do.

He collapsed backward, clasping his fingers like he was trying to hold himself back.

I took him into my mouth, pausing when he reached my throat, and forced my muscles to relax.

"Just—go slow," he grunted. "Go—*fuck*."

I took him to the back of my throat and held him there, breathing deeply through my nose. It wasn't comfortable, but it wasn't awful either. Feeling that much of him inside my mouth had my brain sparking and my pussy throbbing for its own taste.

Experimenting with tiny bobs of my head, I ran my fingers up his thighs and over his abs, wishing I had my press-on nails to scrape across his stomach. I tweaked his nipples instead and felt his cock swell.

"I'm gonna come," he panted.

I pulled my mouth back to his tip, moving my hand over his base.

A groan tore from his chest, and he emptied into my mouth with pulsing spurts, the taste of his precum but stronger landing on my tongue.

I swallowed it down, mesmerized by the feel of him, by the pained look of pleasure on his face, and the way, after a few seconds, his muscles unlocked all at once and seemed to sink into the mat.

I eased him from my mouth and wiped around my lips while he heaved in breaths. His hands made a scooping motion as he tried to speak.

"What?" I giggled.

He lurched forward with a grunt and pulled me on top of him. His lips landed on my cheek, then my nose, possibly looking for my mouth, but his eyes had fallen shut. I helped him out and pressed a kiss to his lips.

His tongue stroked mine as he squeezed my ass. I tried not to squirm over the sensitive skin of his cock trapped between us.

He fumbled with the waistband of my jeans. "Take," he mumbled between kisses. "These off."

"Why?" I breathed before licking into his mouth. He didn't seem to mind the taste of himself on my tongue.

"Because you're going to sit on my face and ride me until you come."

Chapter Thirteen
Gabe

"WHAT?" she said with a surprised laugh.

"Now, Aubrey." I wasn't messing around. She wasn't walking out of here without having at least two orgasms. Preferably ten, and preferably on my face. The only way it wasn't happening was if she told me she didn't want it, but from the way her breath had gone shallow and her tongue thrust into my mouth, I knew that wasn't the case.

She rose to her knees to unbutton her jeans, meeting my eyes with a self-satisfied grin she tried and failed to hide.

"All the way off," I ordered when she shimmied them down her round hips. "Underwear too."

Her gaze dropped as she obeyed, but she didn't hesitate. No, she was eager. The shy thing who had been nervous to sit next to me on her couch two nights ago had long since left the building. There certainly was nothing shy about the woman who'd just choked on my dick and gone back for more.

Jesus, I was already hard again.

When she was in only her white V-neck tee, I reached for her hands and guided her to her knees on either side of my head.

Her body was a work of art, figuratively and literally. Bright floral tattoos followed the curves of her hips and over her soft thighs. Roses and lilies bloomed across her chest with different flowers cascading down her arms, woven between other snapshots of nature. Blackberries on her forearm. A bee above her elbow. Honeycomb along the inside of her bicep.

She was a living garden for me to explore, and I was dying to get a taste of her.

Our eyes locked as she rested her weight on my chest, and a hint of shyness sneaked in behind her excitement.

It was a different kind of shyness than before. One with an undercurrent of hunger that had her shifting to get closer to my mouth. More like a reflex than true embarrassment.

That had been replaced with trust.

The honor of that trust burned in my chest. Out of all the men she could have chosen for this little experiment, all she could have turned to for comfort tonight, I was the one lying beneath her, receiving her warm gaze.

Holding that gaze, I gave her clit a playful lick. My chest was already wet with her arousal, the scent of her filling my nose, making me feral.

Her lips fell open, and I licked again, letting her become acquainted with the sensation. When her gasp turned into a full-body shiver, I planted my hands on her ass and dragged her to my mouth.

The second my tongue entered her pussy, a groan rocked

my chest. I wanted my mouth on her forever, to spend the next thousand years lapping up her arousal as she got hotter and wetter and more helpless from how good I made her feel.

I could tell the exact moment she realized it because the last of her reserve melted away, and her hips kicked into gear, grinding on my face as instinctually as she had my lap two nights ago.

"*Oh my God,*" she whispered as if tasting chocolate for the first time. I kept my hands on her ass, squeezing the fullness I loved and pressing her to my face.

A moment later, she tipped forward onto one hand while her other went for the short strands of my hair. She yanked my head to the angle she wanted and ground her clit against my nose.

Fuck. Yes.

My cock leaked onto my stomach, crying for me to reach down and jerk myself into oblivion, but I didn't want to come again. Not yet. Not if the queen riding my face decided she'd rather ride my cock instead.

My body was no longer mine. It belonged to her.

She liked my muscles? I'd never leave the gym. I'd work out day and night to give her the playground she wanted to climb. She liked giving me pleasure? I'd come as often as she wanted. It wouldn't be difficult. She sent my cock to a different level. One where it lived to serve her.

There wasn't much I trusted myself to give her. Not stability. Not love. Not the kind that could be counted on, at least.

But I sure as fuck could give her my body.

I'd go as fast or slow as she wanted. Fuck her ten times a

day in every different way she could think of or try one thing at a time until she was ready to move on to the next.

Part of me hoped she'd pick the slower route. Let me fuck her with my tongue but save my cock for later. Let this drag on as long as it could.

I didn't get to have her forever, and that was fine. How it should be.

But at least let me have her for now.

THE SHORT BURSTS of thumps against the paddles filled my head like a song, my body moving to their rhythm to guide my next jab.

Thwack-thwack. Thwack-thwack. Thwack-thwack-thwack.

"Good," Noah said before lifting the paddles again.

We circled the ring of the old gym I'd barely stepped outside the past two weeks aside from my daily runs, and finished the last of today's drills. My timing and technique were still strong, but my power had a long way to go. I rolled my left shoulder as we broke for water.

"It bothering you?" Noah asked, nodding at my healed rotator cuff. He hadn't broken a sweat all afternoon, still wearing his hoodie. Meanwhile, I'd soaked through my T-shirt, even in the chilly air. I'd almost forgotten how much easier it was on the trainer side of things. Not to mention him being a decade younger.

"Nah," I said, shaking it off. "Just a little stiff."

It was irritating more than anything. A constant reminder I wasn't the fighter I used to be.

And I'd have to be close to have any shot of winning the

money for the gym. Just because the fighters I'd be facing didn't hold titles didn't mean they weren't damn good. Diego had found the best Philly had to offer, and when it came to boxers, Philly didn't mess around. It never had.

"This dump got an ice bath you can soak it in at least?" he teased, shoving his wavy brown hair to the side. He'd already ribbed me about my sleeping cot.

"Hey, watch it. This dump is going to be the headquarters of your pro career." That was our goal for him. Compete in the Olympics, take home a medal, then turn pro.

Noah had grown up in Allentown, less than two hours from Philly, with his dad as his head coach until about a year ago when health stuff made it harder for his dad to travel as much. His dad knew Coach Peters, who I'd been assisting since I retired, which was how Noah had come to work with us in London. But he hated being so far from his dad. So when I mentioned I was planning to start something of my own back in Philly, Noah asked if I'd take him on.

It had been a good match so far. I wasn't officially his coach yet—not until after the Olympics—but I'd helped him get ready for selection camp, and if all went well, we'd be getting him ready for his first pro match in another year, right here in this ring.

Well, this ring with newer mats.

Although, I had fond memories of the current ones. I could still hear Aubrey's moans from when she'd leaned her elbows on them and rode my face through her second orgasm. It made me want to christen every mat and piece of equipment in this place with her.

She'd stopped by once in the two weeks since, and I'd set her on the weight bench and fucked her with my fingers before getting on my knees and eating her out. Letting her bask in her newly discovered love of oral sex was as fun for me as it was for her.

Noah had arrived the next day, which kicked my training way up. More sparring, more mitt work. And when I wasn't conditioning or skills training, I was watching footage of my competitors.

This old gym wasn't exactly state of the art, but it was getting the job done.

"A little paint, a few new windows, some upgraded gear," I said, "and this place will be back in fighting shape."

"Better shape than you, then?"

He laughed as he dodged the glove I tossed at his face.

"What are you gonna do when I leave again for camp in a few weeks?" he asked more seriously. "You can't spar on your own."

I couldn't. In all honesty, sparring with Noah wasn't enough either. I needed to find another heavyweight, and Noah was about two weight classes too light. But most of the boxers I knew had either moved out of the area or retired close to a decade ago.

"I'm working on a plan," I said. He didn't need to know the plan currently consisted of air. "Did your dad still want tickets?"

I had ten left to sell. My own dad had bought some for his friends, and so had Coach Lou, plus a bunch of friends from high school. I still had plenty of time to sell the rest, but I'd feel better when they were gone. Otherwise, I'd be paying for them out of pocket, and the whole point of fighting was to *win* money, not lose it.

"Oh yeah, I'll text him." He pulled his phone from his

pocket and typed out a message. "Hey, a few of my friends from high school who live here were going to check out a new bar on South Street. Wanna come?"

I climbed out of the ring and snagged the jump rope. "Can't. You may be on vacation, but I'm not. No booze while training."

"So don't drink anything. Come on, it will be fun. We went out a bunch in London, and you kept up fine, old man."

I laughed out a breath and started jumping. Somehow, London felt like three years ago and not three months. "Sorry. I have plans."

Tonight was the first night in nearly two weeks Aubrey had a break in her schedule. She'd been busy either prepping events, working events, or menu planning for the catering competition, and the couple of nights she'd been free, Evan had invited her to hang out. He still didn't know what we were doing, so she hadn't wanted to say no.

Plus, he was her best friend. She should hang out with him.

But he was working late tonight, and Aubrey would finish prep for tomorrow's event earlier than usual, thanks to the new chef she'd hired, which meant there was no way I was missing out on seeing her.

"You mean…like with a girl?" Noah asked as if that was as unlikely as me hanging on a yacht with the Phillies. I guess I hadn't dated much since he'd known me.

Or at all the past two years.

I couldn't actually remember the last woman I'd been with before Aubrey.

Which was exactly the sort of selfish shit that disqualified me from a permanent place in her life. Right along with letting her use me for my own pleasure.

"No comment," I said, my breathing heavier as I picked up my pace.

"Shit, you must like her." He slid to a seat at the edge of the ring and draped his arms over the bottom rope. "Who is she?"

I crossed the jump rope in front of my body and switched to one-legged hops. "No one."

"Yeah, right. Does she know you're into her? Or is it like a server somewhere, and you go to her restaurant every night and sit in her section, hoping she'll smile at you?"

I huffed. "Fuck off."

He kicked his legs and grinned, his cocky smirk so similar to Evan's except for the dark hair. "This is my new mission. Discover Coach's secret love."

"You're worse than my brother."

The words recoiled in my chest, leaving a sting I tried to ignore. The current status of my relationship with my brother wasn't something I liked to think about. Like how he didn't tease me like this anymore.

"If what you say about him is true, I must be doing something right. When do I get to meet the legendary Little Hardt?"

I couldn't remember which story about Evan had landed him the "legendary" title among the fighters in London. Just that I'd told a lot.

Like the time he'd climbed our elderly neighbor's tree to get their cat off their roof after it'd been stuck there for three days, and no one else the neighbor called had been able or willing to help. Or the time he'd gone to his buddy's football party in college and done a gainer off the high-dive platform into the campus pool, catching a can of soda and casually taking a sip on the way down.

I hadn't been there in person for most of them, but I'd seen the video evidence. So had Noah and the rest of the guys in London. Talking about Evan was just something I did. It hadn't hurt as much when I wasn't in the same city for him to avoid.

I was still thinking of an answer besides *probably never* when my phone buzzed on the weight bench. "Hold on," I said when I spotted Aubrey's name.

Aubrey: I have to cancel tonight. Work crisis, will explain later. I'm so sorry.

"Everything okay?" Noah asked.

I frowned at the message. "I don't know." Work crisis in a kitchen could mean anything from a burst water pipe to being in the hospital with third-degree burns and a missing finger.

I dialed her number.

I could call Evan. If she was hurt, he'd want to know. Then again, her message didn't sound like she was hurt. She'd have told me if she was, right?

The call went to voicemail, and I pocketed my phone. "Sorry, man. I have to go."

"Yeah, sure." He climbed out of the ring. "Still on for tomorrow?"

"Definitely." I grabbed my sweatshirt off the mat and jogged for the door. I didn't bother changing into pants. I'd worry about the cold after I knew Aubrey was okay.

Chapter Fourteen
Aubrey

Everything was fucked.

The chef I'd hired two days ago was a no-show. He'd done well enough during his trial shift that I was going to have him work the wedding reception with me tomorrow, but now he wasn't here, which meant I'd be working it by myself, which meant I needed to get even more prep done tonight since I wouldn't have the extra hands to handle it on-site.

Then the food delivery had gotten messed up. I'd ordered parsley but gotten cilantro, and they'd left out the artichokes entirely, meaning the braised artichoke hearts with duck jus that was the favorite of the bride's, whose two-hundred-guest wedding I was now catering alone, wasn't going to happen.

I could try getting the artichokes at a supermarket, but by the time I ran around to enough of them to get the number I needed, I wouldn't have the time to prep them and the hundred other items on my list.

It was miss out on the artichokes but have *something* or get the artichokes and sacrifice the quality of everything else. Either way, this couple would be disappointed, and everyone in attendance would likely know it.

Fuck Jeff, the fucking new hire, fuck weddings, fuck artichokes, and fuck fuck *fuck* whoever's idea it had been to package this parmesan in plastic so tight you needed a fucking chainsaw to get it open.

I shoved the tip of my knife into the corner of the plastic and pushed. It went right through, nicking the tip of my index finger on the way.

"*Fuck.*" My finger flew to my mouth, the tang of copper sharp on my tongue, and a scream lodged in my throat.

I forced my eyes closed and breathed deep through my nose. I needed to calm down and regroup before I did anything else careless that landed me more than a scratch.

The anger dissipated slightly with my next breath, making space for my eyes to burn. I squeezed them tighter and swallowed the tears of frustration. They wouldn't help now either.

Three blunt knocks pounded on the door.

When I opened my eyes, Gabe was there. He strode toward me in his gym shorts, hoodie, and sneakers, brow creased as his gaze fell to my bleeding finger.

"You're hurt," he said, reaching for me. His hands were wrapped in boxing tape.

I gaped at him. "What are you doing here?"

He gently inspected my finger. "Your text was just vague enough to be ominous. I wanted to make sure you didn't get caught in a deep-fryer explosion or something." He surveyed the small kitchen. "Do you have a first-aid kit somewhere?"

I was still stuck on the him-being-here part. "You came because of my text?"

He spotted the red plastic case on the wall and headed for it. "I tried calling, but you didn't answer. I figured I'd check in and leave once I knew everything was okay." He pulled out an antiseptic wipe, along with a bandage and finger cover. "I promise I'm not trying to pull a Ross and demand your attention at work."

My lips lifted at the *Friends* reference. His mom had always had reruns playing on their TV growing up. We'd probably seen every episode at least three times without actively trying.

The episode he referred to, Ross surprised Rachel at her office with a picnic when she had to work late on their anniversary. He'd been self-absorbed and controlling, and none of the things I thought of Gabe right now.

He'd also been Rachel's boyfriend—a detail not relevant to our situation, but my brain felt the need to point it out anyway.

"Here, sit." He unfolded the step stool I stored beneath the counter, waited for me to sit, and lifted my finger to the light, examining it closer before pressing the antiseptic wipe to the cut.

The sting hardly registered against the squeeze in my chest.

He kept his head low, his every touch careful despite the force his body was capable of. His eyes remained concentrated, framed by fine lines that crinkled when he smiled. A slight crook shadowed his nose from where he'd probably broken it, though I couldn't remember when. It must have happened after he'd gone pro.

There were faint lines around his mouth, too, that deepened when he smiled. A smile that made my heart flutter every time, especially when it was only for me.

Those smiles were softer. Slower. Like they were emerging from within rather than tacked on the surface, a sunrise of affection straight from his heart.

Or maybe that was what I wanted them to be.

He finished with the bandage and brought the wrapped finger to his lips. "A kiss makes it heal faster," he said, almost bashful. "Mom always said so."

I swallowed the lump from my throat. "I remember." It was the kind of care I'd mostly forgotten since Nana's death. "Thank you."

He brushed it off as if it'd been only my finger I thanked him for. Then he tossed the scraps of packaging into the large trash can in the corner and glanced around. "Where's your new chef?"

Right. I blew out a breath. "Not here. He never showed, and I haven't been able to reach him."

"Ah. I take it that's your crisis?"

"Part of it." He didn't need to hear the whole sob story. I'd manage from here.

Only, he didn't turn to leave. He rubbed his hands together and asked, "How can I help?"

I stared at him, dumbfounded for the second time in about ten minutes. "What?"

"Use me. I mean, if there's a way I can be helpful. You probably shouldn't trust me with a knife, but I can wash dishes or something. Unless I'd just be in your way—"

"No." My heart thumped as warmth unfurled in my body, bringing a fresh wave of energy with it. "That'd be great."

Two hours later, he got back from the supermarket with the parsley and artichokes I needed—he'd sent me pictures of everything to make sure it was right—and I'd made it a third of the way through my prep list. Then he got to work in the dish pit.

By eleven o'clock, I was finishing the last item for the night, and he was mopping the floor. I'd been here well over twelve hours, far longer than I'd imagined at the start of the day, but it was frankly a miracle I was making it out of here before midnight.

"I owe you big time," I said as I wrapped the last food tray in cellophane.

He smiled at the floor. "It was cool seeing you in your element. I mostly remember you eating lots as a kid, but not so much cooking."

"That's because your mom always stocked the best snacks." Their pantry had been a wonderland of Pop-Tarts, Dunkaroos, and all the other sugar-laden, processed junk a kid dreamed of. My grandma preferred to make things from scratch, especially the sweet stuff, so the Hardt house quickly became where I got my junk food fix. They were to blame for the Lucky Charms sitting in my cabinet.

"Chocolate still your favorite?" he asked.

I wasn't sure why my ears warmed at him knowing that. "Obviously. Chocolate is the best." And don't get me wrong, I was all for the fancy stuff. I made a dark chocolate cake with whipped ganache and tempered chocolate shards that would make Jacques Torres cry. But nothing could beat a good old-fashioned Hershey's bar.

"I don't know how you didn't get sick of it after that one

Halloween when you ate every one of our combined Snickers bars in one night."

"Excuse me, they were Snickers Minis," I said in defense. "It was a perfectly reasonable amount."

"For a kid's soccer team, maybe. I think that was the night Mom decided to make her sable cookies with chocolate instead of jam."

"Now, *they* were my favorite." I hardly cared if I came in last at every game night as long as I got to sit next to the plate of buttery cookies.

"I know. So did she. It's why she kept making them."

I always knew that was why, but hearing him say it filled my heart full with as much love as grief. Maybe they were the same thing at this point.

"She's part of the reason I became a chef," I admitted as I wiped the counter.

"Really?"

I nodded. His dad was the true cook of his family, but his mom had been the one to make me feel food as an expression of love. She and my grandma both. "Her food always felt special to me. I wanted to learn how to give that same feeling to others."

Plus, cooking was something I could control. There was an order to the kitchen I hadn't had the first seven years of my life, constantly moving with my parents. A comfort to standing beside the stove with my grandma, digging her handwritten recipes from the box she'd had for forty years, moving through the same steps she'd followed hundreds of times before to get the same delicious result.

For the most part, I still found that comfort in any

kitchen. No matter if a hotheaded chef was screaming in my face or a dozen tickets were fired at once. I'd lost sight of it these past few months but desperately wanted it back.

"What was the other part?" he asked.

I shrugged. "My grandma, mostly. And I just liked it."

"I'm sorry I wasn't there for you after your grandma died. The way you've been for me."

The heaviness of his voice had me pause with the sanitizing rag. He'd stopped mopping and stared at me with sincerity in his vibrant blue eyes.

It was true he hadn't been there for me in the same way back then—no phone calls or long messages. But I hadn't expected him to be. We weren't friends at the time. He'd been away for some training camp or international match when she died, and it wasn't like he'd been close enough with my grandma to fly all the way back for the funeral. There were other people whose absence I felt abandoned by, but his wasn't one of them.

"It's okay," I said with all the weight I could push into my voice. "You were here for me tonight."

In this silly way, Gabe showing up here reminded me of this summer when Jase had dropped everything and run from the restaurant to save Dani from what they feared had been a stalker. It had turned out to be something else, and she hadn't needed saving, but that hadn't mattered in the moment.

Jase had been there. The same way Gabe had been here tonight.

I didn't expect him to fall in love with me the way Jase did Dani or for this to mean anything beyond the boundaries we'd already laid out. But it felt good to have someone drop everything for me, even if I hadn't really needed saving either.

His mouth lifted in a weak smile, his eyes going back to the mop. Somehow, I got the feeling he didn't think it was enough.

Chapter Fifteen
Gabe

I slapped an envelope with two tickets into Noah's hand. "Tell your dad thanks again for me."

He tucked the envelope into his back pocket. "He's excited to see you in action again." Neither of them had seen me compete live, but he and his dad had watched a bunch of my fight tapes from before I retired.

"Here's hoping I don't disappoint." Boxing was—or at least used to be—the one area I usually didn't.

The slam of the front door rang across the gym, and Noah glanced out of the office to see who it was. He broke into a shit-eating grin. "Your girl is here."

I tamped down my facial expression as my heart set off at a sprint, and my shoulders snapped straight as if a rod had been shoved down my spine.

He laughed at my sudden nerves. "I knew it. You're so into this chick." He peeked toward the front again. "Holy shit, she's hot."

I pointed at the door. "You're leaving."

"What? No way. I wanna meet her."

That much couldn't be avoided at this point, but I could make it the shortest introduction possible. "You say hi, and that's it."

He beamed as Aubrey stepped into the office wearing a short ruffled skirt and leather jacket with a soft-looking sweater underneath. A small paper bag hung from her fingertips.

"Oh," she said, surprised to see Noah. "I didn't mean to interrupt."

"You're good," I said. "Noah was heading out."

He thrust his hand toward her for a shake. "I'm Noah, Gabe's fighter."

"Soon to be," I said. "Once he's done winning the Olympics." There was no keeping the pride from my voice.

"I heard about that," Aubrey said as she shook his hand. "Congratulations. I'm Aubrey."

Noah grinned. "Thanks. Maybe I'll see you around while I'm training—"

I shoved him toward the door. "You'll see *me* tomorrow at six a.m. for our run."

Aubrey suppressed her smile.

"Okay, okay," Noah said as he made his way out. He spun back to add, "Thanks again for the tickets. It was *really* nice meeting you, Aubrey." He shot her a wink and ducked around the corner.

Little shit was going to run sprints until he puked.

Aubrey turned to me. "Tickets for the tournament?"

"Yeah. You want another one?" I joked. "I've got a few left to sell."

Not that I'd let her take me up on it. I was still trying to figure out if there was a way I could convince her to let me pay for the ticket she'd already bought.

Even though I'd be lying if I said I wasn't dying to have her there. That the chance to impress her wasn't pushing me to train that little bit harder. That knowing it meant enough to her to contribute her own money didn't make me want to kiss her until our lips gave out.

"Jase might want some," she offered. "I think his brother's pretty into sports. I could ask him for you."

There she went again, caring. It melted something in my chest. "That'd be great. Thank you."

She smiled at the bag in her hands.

I sat on the edge of the desk. "How was the wedding yesterday?" The one we'd spent most of Friday night prepping for. As someone who bought my fruit and vegetables precut or frozen, I had no idea how much work went into making even the simplest ingredients taste good. I owed major props to my dad.

"It was good, all things considered. I had zero downtime and was exhausted by the end, but I think the couple was happy." She tucked a wave of dark blond hair behind her ear and extended the paper bag to me. "This is for you. As a thank-you for all your help."

I parted the bag's handles and pulled out a round plastic container filled with quinoa salad.

"I was going to make sable cookies, but I know you don't eat sugar while you're training. And then, I thought maybe steak or something more exciting, but I worried it'd get cold by the time you ate it, and since you don't have a microwave here, this seemed like a better option."

My mouth lifted higher with each word because she was right. I had an old mini fridge here that had been lying around Coach Lou's garage that I kept stocked with fruits, juices, and almond milk for my protein shakes, but that was the extent of my cooking capacity. For most of my meals, I either ate at my dad's or grabbed something at the diner a few blocks away. I could get an egg-white omelet the size of my face and a bowl of oatmeal for a steal.

I pulled off the lid and breathed in the nutty aroma layered with fresh herbs and lemon. My mouth watered. Healthy didn't always smell this good. "I'll be your dish-washer full-time if you agree to pay me in this."

Her eyes brightened and her cheeks flushed as she drank me in more fully. "I'm not sure that's a good idea."

The shift was subtle but instant. A breathlessness to her tone that pulsed in the base of my spine. I resealed the lid and set the container aside. "Why not? You don't like the idea of being my boss?"

She bit her bottom lip. My blood pumped faster.

"How about telling me what to do? Having control over me?" I rose to my feet and stalked toward her. She craned her neck to hold my gaze as I freed her lip with my thumb. "We know you like it when I give you what you want."

Her breath escaped on a sigh.

I lowered my mouth to her ear. "What do you want, Aubrey?"

Her eyes fluttered closed as her chest rose and fell in quiet pants. She gripped the hem of my long-sleeved shirt as if to steady herself before locking her heavy-lidded gaze with mine. "I want you to have sex with me."

Everything in my body tightened. "You want my mouth on you? My fingers?"

She shook her head and bit her lip again, her gaze going hazy as if she was thinking of something else. Remembering it. "I want your cock." Her gaze cleared, and she pinned me with her stare like she was pinning me to the mats. "I want you to fuck me with it."

My skin flashed hot, her eyes hard with determination as if daring me to challenge her. I had no plans to. If she said she wanted it, I believed her, and the arousal rushing through my veins had me more than ready to serve.

I stepped forward, my body meeting hers, guiding us to the wall behind her. Before she could catch her breath, I slid the leather jacket from her shoulders and hooked behind her thighs to hoist her to my waist. Her skirt rode up as she locked her ankles behind my back, and my hands settled on their favorite place in the world and gave her ass a squeeze.

Her ragged breaths weren't quiet anymore. She went for my waistband, but I caught both her wrists with my hand.

"Not so fast, greedy girl."

She whimpered.

"You'll get me," I whispered against her lips. "But you have to be patient first."

Given the painful sex with her ex, I didn't want to rush this. As comfortable as she'd become, chances were she'd still have some nerves, and the idea of her in any discomfort while I was inside her was enough to shred my stomach.

That she was initiating this, impatient for it even, was a good sign, but I wasn't willing to risk it. Not this first time.

That didn't mean I had to be gentle.

I ravished her mouth with my kiss, fusing our bodies against the wall. She dominated right back, scraping her nails over my shoulders and driving her fingers into my hair, tightening her legs around me to get the leverage she needed to grind on my dick.

I sucked on her tongue, then released her mouth and sucked on her neck, feeling her moan travel up her throat.

"Please, please—" she panted, rocking her hips.

"What?" I licked beneath her ear, then sucked the same spot. "What do you need?"

"To be filled." She groaned and flexed her thighs around my waist. "I'm so empty."

The thought of lowering her onto my cock had my abs clenching and groin aching. I'd fill her exactly how she needed as soon as I was sure she was ready for me.

I considered setting her down and sinking to my knees, filling her with my tongue the way I knew would get her off, but she seemed to like this position, me holding her with my strength, my body hers to use.

"Take off my shirt," I told her. Let her look at my muscles she liked so much.

She tugged the shirt over my head and down my arms one at a time as I alternated my hold on her, then tossed it aside and fixed her stare on my chest.

"Look your fill, baby," I coaxed.

Her lips curved as she dragged one finger up the center line of my abs at the same time I tugged her panties aside and sank one finger into her from behind.

She was soaked. A perfect, slick heat already dying to come. Her walls clamped around me like a vise as she moaned my name and rolled her hips, trying to take me deeper.

"There you go. Ride my fingers." I added another one, stretching her a little more, letting her adjust to the fullness.

She grabbed either side of my face and hauled my mouth to hers, breaking away a moment later to tear her sweater over her head, leaving her in a lacy pink bra with her skirt trapped around her waist.

Later, I'd suck on those hard nipples peeking through the lace. I'd trace my tongue over every single one of her tattoos and kiss my way over her naval. I'd get her bare and worship every inch of her until neither of us could move.

I eased a third finger inside and curled them toward my palm. Her hips bucked in response.

"Oh fuck, do that again," she gasped. "Do that again."

I repeated the steady motion, taking in her dazed expression that meant she was climbing the high to orgasm.

"*Yes.*" Her moans filled the corners of the room, making me smile at how vocal she'd become. "Keep doing that. Keep doing—*ah.*" Her voice cut off as her pussy pulsed, the rest of her muscles locking up.

I brought my lips to the curve of her shoulder, sucking gently while my fingers pumped her through it, waiting for her to come down. When she finally did, I spoke against her skin.

"Ready for my cock, greedy girl?"

She didn't wait to catch her breath before pushing and tugging at my waistband. "Please."

Her hand found my cock, and I held a groan low in my throat.

"Here." I reached into my pocket for my wallet and handed it to her. "Grab the condom for me?" I hiked her higher on my waist.

"If you need to put me down—"

"No way." I dipped my head to kiss her again before speaking the truth. "I've been dying to fuck you just like this."

"Against a wall?"

I tightened my hold "In my arms."

Her eyes softened, the green at their edges shining through their hazel depths. She plucked out the condom and tossed my wallet to join my shirt at my feet, locking her eyes with mine as she ripped open the wrapper. Her focus shifted to the condom itself, making sure the right side was up before pinching the tip. Then she rolled it down my shaft, both our breaths shortening in the process.

My dick strained from me, as if reaching for her on its own. I gave it one quick stroke to make sure the condom was good before returning my hand to her ass, moving her panties aside, and notching myself at her entrance.

I kissed her cheek. "You ready?"

She nodded.

"Tell me."

"I want you inside me," she said.

So that was what I gave her.

I lowered her onto me slowly, scanning her face for the slightest sign of pain. Her pussy was so swollen it choked off my air supply, forcing me to drag in thick breaths from how good it felt. My arms burned from moving so slowly, and probably a little from holding her this long, but I didn't care. I had the strength to manage it, and if anything, the burn heightened the pleasure. The question was whether it felt as good for her.

Her brow creased, and her mouth hung open.

"Talk to me," I groaned, sinking deeper. "How do you feel?"

She heaved out a breath and tipped her head against the wall. "Full." A laugh clenched her muscles around me, and we both moaned. "Really full. You're way bigger than my vibrator."

"Want me to stop?"

Her headshake was firm. "It's not painful. Just strange. I'm not used to feeling this much."

I buried my head in her neck, breathing in the rich coconut of her hair and licking the salt off her skin. Our bodies trapped heat between us, adding to the warmth from the space heater that was still on from overnight. "Touch your clit for me," I grumbled. "Let yourself feel even more."

Her fingers explored her entrance, feeling where I disappeared inside her and how much more I still had to give. I nipped her neck with my teeth, my hips jerking the smallest amount.

"*Oh,*" she breathed.

"Sorry." I stilled and studied her face.

"No, I-I liked it," she said, almost surprised. "Do it again."

I eased my hips forward and back with a few experimental rocks, letting her taste the friction while only giving her half my length.

Her eyes fell closed as she hummed in response. "It's never felt like this before. It's good. It's so good. Keep going."

I licked into her mouth and rocked deeper, driving into her in full, long strokes so she could savor every inch. Her fingers rubbed over her clit, drawing more wetness from her heat, soaking the base of my shaft.

"*Gabe*," she whined. Her hips were restless in my hold, her legs clasping tighter to drive her up and down, seeking whatever feeling she'd discovered. Like she'd struck oil, and now it was time to drill deep and get every drop.

"More?" I asked.

"More."

Tightening my grip on her ass, I pulled her onto my length with each thrust, grinding my pelvis against her clit in short bursts. A strap of her bra slipped off one shoulder, the cup dragging down with it, leaving her breast exposed.

I wanted to latch onto that breast with my mouth and savor it. See how tight I could get her nipple to become. I could practically feel the hard bud on my tongue.

My muscles flexed as grunts escaped me, everything about her so fucking sexy I could hardly hold myself back. Knowing she needed me to was the only thing that allowed me to maintain control.

And not for much longer if the blush on her cheeks and the fever in her eyes were anything to go by. I could already feel her pussy trembling around my shaft, the race to her orgasm rounding the final turn.

Her fingers raked through the short hair at the base of my neck as I held her down on my cock an extra few beats, grinding my pelvis against her clit when a clatter in the other room made us both freeze.

Aubrey's eyes went wide, her voice an alarmed whisper. "Did someone just walk in?"

Chapter Sixteen
Aubrey

Too many things were happening for my body to process at once. My heart rattled in my chest like a stand mixer on its highest setting, my brain on alert for whatever had made that noise. Meanwhile, everything from my chest down was still riding the edge of the orgasm Gabe's cock was about to send me flying through.

Oh my God, it was so good. Sex was so *good*.

For the first time ever, I got it. The scandals all made sense. *This* I would risk a career for, break laws for, tarnish my reputation for.

I'd been living on plain boiled potatoes, thinking they were as good as it got, and Gabe just served me french fries. The kind that are somehow both addictively crispy and well-seasoned without leaving your hands greasy. *Perfect* french fries.

I could eat him forever and never get enough.

Just make sure we're alone first, my brain whispered.

"No," Gabe assured me about the noise. "It's just the steam pipes. A few times a day, they sound like someone's taking a crowbar to a metal grate."

"I thought maybe Noah came back…"

"Nuh-uh." He kissed my mouth in this way of his that somehow used his whole body, and it short-circuited my brain with the need to fuck him more than I already was. "No one's going to walk in on us."

It was the reassurance I wanted, yet there was a tickle of something else I didn't fully understand. Something I couldn't name because I'd never encountered it before.

Gabe must have seen whatever it was in my eyes. He had no problem naming it.

"Or do you want that?" he asked, his voice all rasp and groan. "For someone to find us?"

It was as if he'd located the end of whatever string was tickling me and pulled. His words unraveled me.

"You want for them to come in and see you writhing on my cock, to see how stunning you look taking every inch of me?" He held me in place on his length as my hips moved beyond my control, not driving up or down so much as back and forth, seeking more of this sensation that was never quite enough. "For whoever it was to wish they were the one inside you, making you come? That's it. Just like that."

I was under it before I even realized what it was. One wave after another of agonizing bliss that rooted me in place and made it impossible to breathe. I thought I'd lost my vision until I realized my eyes were clamped shut, my cheek pressed against Gabe's neck with my fists on his shoulders.

He'd started to move again at some point in my ascent to another dimension, and it was another kind of pleasure entirely to watch him in this state. Sweat coated his furrowed brow, his muscles flexing with the controlled power he fed into each thrust.

Whether as remnants of my own orgasm or as encouragement of his, my pussy continued to flutter, and when I sucked on his bottom lip, his control snapped.

He whirled us from the wall to the desk behind him, setting me on its edge and fucking into me the way I'd always imagined something called fucking should be. The slaps of our skin filled my ears, the scent of arousal in the air, and I let it take me over as I pulled my bra cups aside and tugged at my nipples.

"*Aubrey—*" He choked off with a groan so loud it made me tingle, his cock swelling inside me as he filled the condom.

The next thing I knew, he was pulling out and dropping a kiss between my breasts as he hooked his fingers under my waistband. He tore my panties down my legs and sank to his knees.

"Are you—*oh.*"

He was. His tongue licked straight up my core, barely flicking my clit before trailing to where my thigh met my ass and exploring me fully.

Oh my God, oh my God, how could it feel this good?

How could I still want more?

Then again, Gabe already knew that too.

I was a greedy girl.

Chapter Seventeen
Gabe

We lay on the small cot in the corner of the office that served as my bed most nights. Aubrey's naked body was warm against mine under the blanket. I wore my boxer briefs since the weight of her head on my chest already felt too close to cheating on our deal.

She needed it. That had been an intense round of sex, and aftercare was an important part of the experience.

But that was all our deal was: me helping her experience good sex. She got to be naked afterward because it was what she wanted. Me being naked with her would be what *I* wanted, and that wasn't what this was about.

She played with the hair on my forearm. "How'd you know I'd like it?" she asked, glancing up at my face. Freckles almost too faint to see danced across her nose.

"Wall sex?"

"Well, yeah. But also the other thing."

"You mean the being watched thing?"

She nodded, a touch of pink rising to her cheeks.

I kissed the top of her head. "Just a feeling. Exhibition-ism's a pretty common fantasy."

"I'm not sure I'd want to do it for real," she said as if thinking it through. "Like, I liked when you said those things and feeling the risk of it a little, but I think someone actually watching would make me uncomfortable more than anything."

I shrugged. "So it'll stay a fantasy. They don't always have to come true. That's what makes them fun."

She shifted to see my face easier, her leg hooking over mine. "Do you have one?"

"Sure." Like hers, it would only ever exist in my imagina-tion. It was better for everyone that way.

"Will you tell me?"

I thought of telling her a different one. Something closer to what she probably expected. A threesome or bondage or something.

She sensed my hesitation. "What's wrong? Is it really weird?"

I traced the lavender stem tattooed on her arm. "I don't know. Maybe to some people." I'd never cared much whether it was.

She gazed at me, waiting. Stripped naked of more than her clothes, and she'd shed those layers with me.

I blew out a breath. "I like to imagine fucking my preg-nant wife." It wasn't a breeding thing or like I wanted to fuck every pregnant woman I saw. I wanted to fuck my wife. The woman I'd committed myself to in all ways who was offering up her body through tremendous change to bring our child into the world. Bringing her body comfort during that stage?

Bringing her pleasure? It was the most erotic thing I could imagine.

Only I didn't have a wife, and I never would.

I didn't even have a fucking bed.

Anything I had to offer a woman was strictly physical. I could fuck against a wall, haul her on my shoulders to eat her pussy, and rip off her panties with my bare hands, but I couldn't promise more than that. If I did, there was no guarantee I'd keep it.

The truth was, I didn't know how to commit myself to someone the way my parents had committed to each other. I didn't know how to fit my life together with another person's. I'd never had to try. Never had to consider how leaving for camp might affect a partner, or even a pet. Never had to think of anyone else when making decisions. And the one time I *had* needed to, I'd failed.

My mom had fucking cancer, and I chose to stay for a fight.

It shouldn't have mattered that it was the final fight of the only professional tournament of its kind, and winning would have made me the kind of money only 1 percent of boxers ever earned. It shouldn't have mattered I had peaked at exactly the right time, over ten years into my career, and was on the precipice of everything I'd worked for paying off. It shouldn't have mattered that everyone had confidence the surgery would be easy and she had at least another year before things got bad.

No justification should have been enough. The *only* decision I should have made was to drop everything and go be with my mom.

Instead, I'd welcomed the justifications. Slathered them

on my face like Vaseline so any objections from my conscience would slide right off.

It was my nature to be selfish, and at this point, chances were it was too late to change. Even Evan didn't think I could.

He'd managed to avoid me 90 percent of the time I stopped by Dad's, content not to have me in his life at all if it meant not putting up with my disappointment. I didn't want it to be true, but it was better for everyone to accept it was.

I could have a wife, a kid, a family—but only in my fantasies, where they'd never be at risk of me letting them down.

The reminder rang through me like the bell at the end of a losing round as I met Aubrey's gaze. I wanted her safe from me most of all. My arm tightened around her.

"You want kids?" she asked softly, maybe sensing the shift in my mood.

I tensed, not expecting that to be what she asked in response. Hating that my first instinct was to crack myself open further and let her all the way inside.

I needed to do the opposite. To reinforce my crumbling walls that were the only way I knew to protect her.

"Used to," I muttered like it'd been a simple matter of changing my mind. So simple it wasn't worth discussing.

I must have sold it because she didn't ask anything more. Just lay with me, existing. Letting me have this piece of her I shouldn't be allowed to have.

"A part of me always wondered why my parents had me," she said after a while. A murmured confession in a forgotten gym. The steam pipes clinked around us, keeping our words safe.

I studied her with drawn brows. "Why?"

Her shoulder dragged against my chest in a shrug. "It mostly felt like I was in the way of the life they wanted. And when they left me with my grandma, it felt like proof I was right."

I couldn't think of how anyone's life would be better without her in it. She shivered beneath the blanket, and I squeezed her close. "They did us all a favor," I told her. "You belonged here with us." I'd known that much since I was twelve, though I'd never been more grateful for it than I was now.

"One thing I know is if I ever become a mom, I want to be the kind yours was."

Just imagining it pinched my chest. She would be an incredible mom.

The kind who showed up for soccer matches and cheered her ass off no matter if her kid was the star player or the one sitting near the sideline picking grass. She'd probably invent her own games with them on car rides that would become inside jokes. She'd bake them the best snacks and know how to make anything better just by being there when they needed her. They'd be the luckiest kid in the world.

Hers and someone else's.

Thinking it was like dunking my head into the coldest ice bath.

He'd be someone she ended up with after this thing with us was over. Whose wedding I'd attend as her friend, sitting next to my dad in the front pew as I watched her promise her life to another man.

The same way I'd watch her date him and fall in love. Watch her bring him to game nights so he could get to know our family as her family. Watch her touch him and smile at him and track him with her eyes as he walked across the room.

Watch from the sidelines as he raised her kids, knowing he wasn't good enough for her. Knowing no one was.

Especially not me.

The sting of it burrowed under my skin, and I restrained my hand from stroking her belly as a different kind of longing took hold.

Not mine to want.

"You'll cook them way better dinners," I joked, mouth dry.

She snorted. "Yeah, but my flower arrangements still need work."

I ran my hand over the pink roses running beneath her collarbone and over her left shoulder. "These were my mom's favorite," I said, studying the careful shading.

"I know," she said, nearly a whisper. "I got them for her."

I swallowed the emotion from my throat. "And the lilies?" I traced my thumb to the center of her chest where orange and pink petals mirrored the roses, climbing her other shoulder.

"For Nana. Her name was Lily."

"Do they make you feel closer to them?"

Our voices were quiet, blanketed in whatever bubble we'd created.

"A little. Kind of like I always have them with me, even in a small way, you know?"

I wanted to know and didn't. Wanted my mom to still be with me, comforting me and offering her strength, even when it was the last thing I deserved.

Selfish.

"Do you think they are?" I asked anyway. "Still with us?"

She twirled her touch across the bare skin of my chest. I wanted to lift her fingers to my lips one by one. Then bring her mouth to mine for a single soft kiss. I flattened my palm over her rose tattoos instead.

She tilted her head. "I guess I believe love is a connection that goes beyond the physical, and I know I still love them even though they're no longer here. I like to think their love is still here too. That it isn't the kind of thing that fades just because their bodies are gone. And as long as our love for each other is still here, a piece of them is too."

I hoped she was right. That my mom's love still wrapped around Evan and my dad and Aubrey. That she lived on in the best parts of them.

And because of the selfish bastard I was, I hoped I got to be around to witness it. That through them, I could keep a part of her too.

Chapter Eighteen
Aubrey

CLASSIC ROCK FILLED the old warehouse-turned-shopping commons that served as the location for the ongoing charity tasting. The event was halfway through, the crowd still thickening with attendees weaving between the tables of participating restaurants. Jillian had signed Ardena up for it last year, but now that Arden Catering was operational, it made more sense for me to snag the marketing opportunity.

I let the song's rhythm guide the steady flow of my plating spoon as I topped the rows of fried oyster mushrooms and tomato béarnaise that lined Arden Catering's table with seaweed caviar.

It was a recent dish I'd come up with for the catering competition, and as far as I could tell from today's reactions, it was solid. All the dishes I'd come up with in the two weeks since the disastrous wedding-prep night were. Perfectly edible, unlike my first attempts. Skillfully prepared.

They just weren't enough to win.

Nothing on my current menu was unexpected enough. I'd incorporated some of the sustainable practices Jase had made a statement with in his menu for the symposium last year, but that alone didn't convey the kind of story the competition's event called for.

It needed drama. Passion. To inspire as much feeling through the food as the museum's art inspired in its patrons.

What I'd created was boring in comparison. Or as a local food blogger had put it in their recent post about the engagement party I catered last weekend, "Arden Catering's food lacked innovation, inspiration, or anything that hadn't already been at the table—or any table—for decades."

The words hadn't meant anything to me when Jillian had stormed into the prep kitchen yesterday, printed article in hand, and thrown it into the lit flame of a burner.

"Everything in there is horseshit. Do you hear me?" Jillian had said.

I'd been more concerned about her burning down the building than the review. Especially considering I thought the engagement party had gone well.

Curiosity more than anything prompted me to find the blog post on my phone and read it once Jillian had left. Fair criticism toward my craft only made me better, and while the blog was decently well-known in fine-dining circles, most of our clients still came from referrals, so there was little risk to the business. If it had all been horseshit like Jillian said, I would have disregarded it without losing sleep.

But while whoever wrote the blog may have thrown around a lot of commas, they knew enough about food to pinpoint what was wrong with each of my competition attempts in a single sentence.

Lacking innovation, inspiration, or anything that hadn't already been done.

They were right. And with only three weeks until the competition deadline, I didn't know how to fix it.

As if summoned by my misery, Christian emerged from the crowd and strolled to my table like this was his regular hoagie spot.

I'd spotted Pépère's van in the parking lot when I arrived, but the event space was huge, and over thirty restaurants were participating. My delusion had me convinced he and I would make it through the day without crossing paths.

Ha. As if Christian would pass on an opportunity to search me out. Especially when he had something so satisfying to rub in my face. I wanted to scrape off his smug smile with my spoon.

"Yes?" I asked as patiently as I could manage. It was by the strength of the three Advil I'd taken earlier for my period cramps that I didn't roll my eyes at his widening grin.

"I read a fascinating review recently of a new caterer in town. Arden Catering, I believe it was? I can't decide on my favorite part." He took his phone from his pocket and cleared his throat. "*'One guest described the meal as "something her grandmother would like," which isn't what you expect of an engagement party for a couple in their twenties.'*" He flashed his screen my way. "It's between that or the line about your entitled insistence to work your events alone." His gaze swept behind the table I stood at by myself. "I see he wasn't wrong on either count."

I clenched my teeth and said nothing. Better he assumed I was the only restaurant here to choose to serve hundreds of attendees solo than know how hard a time I was having finding qualified help. He'd probably send me the worst chefs he could find to waste my time. At this point, I'd probably already interviewed them.

"What, no defense for your flailing empire?" He eyed my tasting plates again. "'Cause I don't think it's working to have your food speak for itself."

Even knowing it was his goal, the words burned like the edge of a hot pan. I was saved the need to respond by two couples who approached the table.

"Welcome!" I said too eagerly. "Would you like to try our fried 'oyster' dish?"

I described the components and avoided looking at Christian. If I ignored him as if he were a bee, maybe he'd go away.

A moment later, another pair of ladies stepped behind the couples, and he did just that. I went through the rest of the event trying to forget he was ever there, offering my food to tasters with all the confidence I wished I felt.

At five o'clock, I responded to Evan's text about grabbing dinner and packed up my table.

By five forty-five, I was one of the last restaurants still loading my van, this side of the parking lot more or less empty. With all my stuff locked safely away, I grabbed the last of my trash and headed inside to pee for the first time all afternoon.

When I returned, Christian was leaning against the driver's door of my van.

I could always leave the van and walk home, I thought. It was what? Five, six miles? Sure, it would take a few hours, but I had more energy for that than dealing with him again. If I'd brought a jacket and wouldn't have frozen my ass off as soon as the sun went down, I might have seriously considered it.

I crossed my arms as I approached. "What do you want, Christian?"

He looked as smug as ever. "You never answered me before. What's your response to the article? Or are you giving up already?"

I forced back a sigh. I was too exhausted to decide if I should to scream in his face or lie on the pavement and stay there.

I'd packed and unpacked the van twice today. My back was tight from hunching over the table trying to plate perfect food for three hundred people. Having no one with me meant I never got to leave the table for a bathroom break, to try the other restaurants' dishes, or to network for Jillian (or in Christian's case, harass former coworkers). I hadn't eaten since breakfast. At this point, all I wanted was to crawl under a pile of blankets and stay there until I became one.

To make matters worse, my nostrils burned with a sudden burst of emotion, and I didn't know if it was anger or a sign that Christian was right.

Not that I was ready to give up. But that for the first time in my career, a part of me wondered if I should.

I hated that, of all people, he was the voice of those doubts in my head.

"Why do you care?" I asked. "You're the head chef of a James Beard Award-winning restaurant, remember? What does it matter to you what I do?"

It was one thing when we'd both been at Pépère, two sous chefs battling for the top spot. But I'd left. And at no point had my goal been to drag the battle along with me.

His boastful expression slid away. "Don't act like I don't know how much better than me you think you are. How you and Jase snickered behind my back and acted like I didn't deserve to be there. You two tried to push me out every chance you could."

Now, I rolled my eyes. Because yes, we did talk about him. About our multiple attempts to address his shitty behavior with him directly that went completely ignored.

There'd been one especially gross comment Jase had tried to fire him for, but the restaurant owner took Christian's side. Jase made sure I was never left alone with him after that.

"I earned my spot as executive chef," he said, a finger to his chest. "Despite what Jillian fucking Matice seemed to think when she handpicked the rest of you for her little project. And I'm going to make sure she and Jase and everyone in this city know it's *my* food they should care about. Not yours."

"Fine." It was all I had for him. That and the best of luck. I'd name him Philly's top chef right now if he'd let me get to my van so I could go home. We'd both know I was lying, but only one of us would care.

Before I could tell him as much, the door to the building swung open, and Evan stepped outside. My shoulders loosened at the same time Evan's tensed.

"What the fuck are you doing?" he aimed at Christian. They'd only met twice, but Evan had heard me vent about the other chef enough to know all he needed to about the current situation.

Going by Christian's face, the revulsion was mutual. "Just reminding Aubrey where she stands." He shot me a parting glare. "Good luck in the catering competition. You were always going to need it."

He strode for the building, ignoring Evan, who flashed

him both middle fingers. When the door clicked shut, Evan turned to assess if I was okay.

Aside from the headache pounding my skull and incessant throb of my uterus, I was peachy.

He lifted his brows. "You telling this one over takeout or drinks?"

"YOU NEED to carry pepper spray or something," Evan said as we walked into my apartment a little later, a paper bag of Indian food in hand.

"I carry a chef knife most of the time. Does that count?" I joked.

He set the food bag on my counter and pinned me with his serious face. "I don't like him cornering you like that. Not to mention, any drunk guy at a wedding or creep on the street could sneak up on you at night after an event. It's not safe."

I snatched the bag from him and pulled out containers. "All right, *Dad*, I'll be careful. Can we talk about your job now?"

We made our way to my small round table in the corner and ate while Evan told me about the rumor that the current creative director of his graphic design agency might retire next year. It meant a huge opportunity for a promotion for someone on the team.

"You thinking of trying for it? Or do you still want to start your own company?" I asked between forkfuls of chicken korma. He'd mentioned doing it more than once. Even took on some freelance projects to build a portfolio outside of his agency work.

"I'd rather the promotion. I already have good relationships with a bunch of our clients. I just want the chance to do more."

"Plus, the raise would be nice."

"I guess. I won't really need it as long as I'm living with Dad. Nothing says creative director like sleeping in your childhood bed, right?" His voice was teasing, but his eyes stayed downcast.

"Do you want your own place again?" He'd given up his Center City apartment when he moved in with his dad.

"I mean, I want one. But I don't think I should leave Dad yet. The house would be too quiet for him alone."

"Maybe Gabe could move in with him." There was an old apartment above the gym he planned to renovate once he owned the building, but he could always rent it out for the extra income if he decided to live with his dad for a while.

Evan snorted. "The guy who would rather sleep in an abandoned building than stay at home? Sure."

"You could ask him," I said. "He might surprise you."

For all the reasons Gabe preferred sleeping at the gym—reasons he hadn't said outright but I sensed were tied to his mom—he spent a huge chunk of his free time at home with his dad. Pretty much whenever he wasn't training or with me, he was there, watching whatever game was on with his dad or helping with projects around the house.

I knew Evan had noticed from how often he'd started staying late at work or grabbing dinner with me. For as much as he beat on Gabe for avoiding his family, he'd been doing a five-star job of it himself. I'd call him out for how alike he was to his brother, but he wouldn't take it as the compliment he used to when we were teens.

It didn't change that both he and Gabe cared about their dad. If their dad or Evan—especially Evan—asked Gabe to help, he'd want to do it.

"I don't want him to surprise me. I just…want him to go away."

I lowered my fork. "Do you really?"

He didn't answer. Just ripped off a piece of naan and dragged it through his sauce.

"What if you tried talking to him? Not about anything big, just…ask to see the gym or something. He'd love to show you that."

"I doubt he cares."

"You know that's not true. And I really think you'll be excited about it. It's not a lot to look at right now, but the space has so much potential. Especially when you hear what he plans for it."

He let out a breath and met my gaze, studying me as if deciding whether to say something.

"What?"

"You two are hooking up, aren't you?" It wasn't a question. Not really.

It also wasn't said with anger or disappointment. Just a need to know.

I swallowed the urge to deny it. He'd be able to tell I was lying anyway. "Yes."

He leaned back in his seat. "I thought you said you didn't have a crush on him anymore?"

"I don't. It's not like that, it's just…" Whatever word I had for it struggled to form.

"Sex?" he filled in.

I lifted a shoulder. "Yeah."

He nodded a few times, pushing his fork through the rice on his plate. "I'm guessing me saying it's a bad idea won't change anything?"

"I know why you think that, but I'm telling you, it's okay. I know what I'm doing. You don't have to worry about it."

His eyes flicked to mine, more concern lining them than I'd seen since my grandma had died. It nearly knocked me back. "I don't want you to get hurt."

"I won't," I assured him, not entirely sure it was true. But if I did get hurt, it would be my own stupid fault, which I refused to let come between Evan and his brother.

"He won't commit to you," Evan warned. "I'm not sure he can. To anyone."

I ignored the clench in my gut at the confirmation of what I'd been telling myself all along. Gabe wasn't looking for long-term. Evan knew it, and I did too.

"I know," I said.

He blew out another long sigh. "Just—promise me you'll end things before you develop feelings?"

I swallowed again, fighting to slow the heartbeat in my throat. "I will." This one was for sure a lie.

One I planned to keep telling us both.

Chapter Nineteen
Gabe

THE YOUNG WOMAN at the host stand greeted me with a smile despite my appearance better suiting a workout at the gym than a nice restaurant on Rittenhouse Square.

"We don't open for another few minutes, but do you have a reservation?" she asked. "I can grab you a water while you wait."

"I'm actually here to drop off something for Jase," I said, pulling the ticket envelope from my gym bag. "I think he knows I'm stopping by."

"I'll go check." She set aside the menus she was sorting and headed for the back of the restaurant.

It was a cool space. Lots of colors and plants that reminded me a little of Aubrey's apartment but with a fancier touch. Crystal chandeliers instead of stained glass lamps, and marble countertops instead of whatever fake stuff Aubrey's apartment had in the kitchen.

I could see her here, cooking day in and day out. Could

see why it would feel like home. Why she'd miss it. I wished I could do more to help her find whatever was missing from her catering setup to make it feel the same, but I didn't think it came down to any one thing. It seemed more mental to me, like getting psyched out by an opponent in the ring. There was only so much your coach or team could do before it was ultimately up to you to push through whatever barrier was in your way.

Aubrey was the strongest person I knew, boxer or not. She'd find her way through.

"Gabe. Hey, man." A dark-haired white guy in a chef jacket rounded the bar with the hostess and offered his hand for me to clasp. He pulled me into a loose hug, slapping me once on the back. "It's nice to finally put a face to the name."

"Same," I said, reciprocating the hug. "Wish it could have been sooner. Sorry I couldn't make it to Thanksgiving."

He waved the apology away. "I heard you're opening a boxing gym nearby?"

"That's the plan. Need to win a few fights first—which, speaking of, here are these." I handed him the envelope with the last of my tickets. "Thanks for taking these. It really helps me out."

"Happy to. A friend of mine is big into boxing, and my brother's a huge sports fan. We're excited to check it out."

"You should check out the gym, too, when it's open. I'll give you guys a discount as a thanks."

He clasped my hand again, then pointed at me as he strode for the kitchen. "You hungry? I can make you something quick before the rush starts."

"I'm good, thanks. But another time, for sure."

He gave me a nod, then tossed another over my shoulder. "Hey, Evan."

My shoulders tensed. I turned, and sure enough, there was my brother, walking into the restaurant.

His eyes swung past me to Jase. "Hey, man."

"You putting in an order with Neela?" Jase asked.

"Yeah, to go."

Jase pointed at the beer tap. "Try the Maibock while you wait. We just got it in, and I think it's your style."

My brother flashed his signature grin. "That good, huh?"

"It doesn't even need the dimples," said the South Asian bartender I assumed was Neela as Jase disappeared into the back. She smirked at Evan. "The usual for you and your old man?"

"And a Maibock while I wait, apparently."

Neela turned her attention to the computer screen behind the bar, her long dark braid hanging down her back, leaving Evan and me standing in silence.

I readjusted the strap of my gym bag on my shoulder. "You grabbing dinner for Dad?"

Hands in his pockets, he nodded. His eyes focused everywhere but on me. "You sell your tickets?"

"Jase just bought the rest."

He nodded again.

This was the least hostile he'd been toward me since I'd gotten home, and for the life of me, I couldn't think of a single thing to say. Maybe if I knew *why* he wasn't being hostile. Was he starting to forgive me? Or did he not give enough of a shit to care anymore?

I nearly jumped to attention when he cleared his throat.

"So that guy Christian who Aubrey used to work with was bugging her at the tasting event yesterday."

The fucker from our night out? "What'd he do?" My voice was as tight as my grip on my bag.

"Followed her to the parking lot and rubbed some shitty blog review in her face."

I'd tie him up by his ankles and use him as a punching bag.

"Aubrey promised to be careful around him, but I thought you'd want to know." His eyes met mine for the first time, and it was there in his gaze.

He knew.

And somehow, he wasn't screaming in my face to stay the fuck away from her or swinging at my head. Those would have been my first two guesses at his reaction to finding out I was sleeping with his best friend.

I liked this option way better.

"Thank you," I said sincerely.

His jaw flexed and stare sharpened with words he clearly wanted to say. Probably along the lines of how thoroughly he'd kill me if I hurt her in any way.

But he didn't say them. Not for my sake, I was sure, but for Aubrey's. This was him respecting her choice. Not respecting me, but not getting in my way either.

I met his glare head-on, communicating as much as I could with my own gaze.

That I wouldn't be careless with her.

That I'd do everything I could to protect her.

That if I hurt her, I'd wrap his fists for my beating myself.

"What's that guy's deal anyway?" I asked. Christian's grudge against Aubrey felt beyond your typical work rivals.

Evan scoffed. "Aubrey's a better chef, and he's never been able to handle it. He tried to take it out on her personally, and the more his attempts rolled off her shoulders, the pissier he got."

"I don't trust him around her," I said, recalling the way he'd moved in front of her at the restaurant.

"Me either," Evan said.

Our agreement hung between us like an olive branch. A single thread of connection among a pile of frayed string.

Maybe the rest could be tied back together. Or even just some. They'd never be as seamless or as strong as they were before, but that wouldn't matter. Not if it meant I could still have a little piece of my brother.

"Hey, is one of you guys swinging by the catering kitchen after this?" Jase asked as he stepped out of the kitchen again. He held up a white postage envelope. "This got mailed here by mistake, but it's for Arden Catering."

I glanced at Evan, giving him the choice. He nodded toward the bar. "I have dinner to take home."

My chest expanded in recognition of what he was giving me. Not his full trust, but a step toward it. A chance.

I'd fucking take it.

When I got to the prep kitchen, the lights were off, but I checked the door anyway. Locked. I texted Aubrey.

Me: You finish work early?

Unless she had an event on Friday, she was usually here pretty late prepping for the weekend.

Aubrey: Stayed home. Sick day.

I frowned at my phone.

Me: You need anything?

Aubrey: I'll be okay, but thanks.

Knowing her, she'd be too sick to lift her head from her pillow and would still say she didn't need help. I pocketed my phone and headed for the subway.

A half hour later, I was at her building with a plastic shopping bag full of seltzer, Gatorade, and boxed noodle soup in hand.

Me: Buzz me up?

Aubrey: Door code is 5167

I punched it into the keypad and climbed the stairs to her place. The door to her apartment was already unlocked, and I wondered if Evan and I needed to add door locking to our list of safety concerns.

"Aubs?" I set my gym bag by her front closet and the grocery bag on her kitchen counter, then made my way into her bedroom.

Tucked into a mountain of pillows, Aubrey lay in the center of her bed, curled under a mess of blankets. Her lights were off, but the setting sun cast enough of a glow through her window for me to make out her messy bun, baggy sweatshirt, and miserable expression. As much as I hated to see that last one, I couldn't help but find her adorable.

"Hey," I said softly as I approached the bed. "You down for the count?"

She made a face and groaned. "Period cramps. I'll survive." She squeezed a pillow to her belly. "It's usually only one day of wanting to rip out my uterus before it eases up."

A pinch of discomfort creased her brow, and my urge to go to her won. I kicked off my shoes and crawled into the bed behind her. "Anything I can do to help?" I asked as she settled against my chest. "I brought Gatorade and soup, but maybe you don't need those."

"No, but this is nice." She shifted the pillow in front of her to make room for my hand on her stomach. "I could have gone to work," she admitted. "Normally, I'd pop three Advil and deal with the cramps, but my next event isn't until next week, and I wasn't up for another disappointing day."

I made tiny circles against her sweatshirt with my thumb. "Evan told me about the blog review. Christian said some stuff?"

"Yeah." Her voice was flat. Void of its usual color. "Nothing that matters. It's not the kind of thing that would bug me this much if I wasn't so stuck." All the frustration and sadness she worked to hide clung to that one word. Her body sagged as if it had taken her strength with it. "I hate not knowing how to change it."

I'd been right there after every bad match. Nothing was more frustrating than feeling like all your efforts added up to nothing.

"Taking care of yourself is a good place to start." I kissed the side of her neck. "Letting me take care of you is even better."

From this angle, I could make out the edge of her smile. A small one, almost too small to see, but still there.

"Is that why you came?" she asked.

"Mostly." I trailed my hand up her forearm to play with her fingers. "Jase gave me a piece of your mail that got sent to the restaurant by mistake, but I would have dropped it in the mailbox if you were out with Evan or something."

"You said you talked to him?"

"Yeah." I flexed my hand over hers. "He knows about us."

"I know. He asked me yesterday, and I admitted it." She craned her neck to look at me. "I'm sorry. I should have told you. I know I was the one who wanted to keep it a secret, but it didn't feel right lying to him directly like that."

"No need to be sorry." I whispered against her ear, "It's whatever you want, remember?"

She nodded and squeezed my hand. I shifted to rearrange the blankets so I could get closer, and as she adjusted her hips to help, my hand brushed her chest. She hissed through her teeth.

"Shit, sorry." I moved my hand away.

"No, it didn't hurt," she said quickly. "They're just…" She motioned in the general direction of her breasts, her hard nipples visible through her sweatshirt. "Really sensitive right now. Touching them almost relieves the ache."

"Yeah?" I resettled behind her and let my hand find her breast. It was heavier than usual. When my thumb brushed her nipple, she made a noise into her pillow that sounded encouraging, so I fit the pebbled tip between two fingers and gave a gentle tug.

That got a moan.

She twisted her torso enough to grant me access to her other breast, and I moved my hand to give it the same attention. I alternated between both breasts, lightly squeezing and pulling, tweaking her nipples and massaging with various pressures.

Her sounds got louder with every touch, and soon her hand was on mine, urging my grip tighter as she worked her ass against my crotch.

Even dulled by the blankets, the sensation was enough to get me hard. Mainly because I could tell how good this felt for her.

Wanting to give her more, I pulled away and rolled her to her back, tugging down the comforter enough to remove her sweatshirt and straddle her hips. She let me do both without complaint, arching her back as I lowered my head to take the tip of one breast into my mouth.

Her long sigh filled my ears. "That feels so good. Suck on it?"

She groaned as I did.

I switched to her other breast, taking the nipple between my teeth as my fingers took over the one I just left, still wet from my tongue. I pulled on them both.

The noise she made this time was deep and guttural. Her eyes were heavy in a haze of pleasure, her head tipped back, hips rocking between my knees in nothing but a pair of plain black panties, searching for something more.

"Can you come from just this?" I asked, then swirled my

tongue over her nipple. An orgasm would help with her cramps, maybe better than Advil would.

"I don't know," she said, breathless. "I never have before, but…maybe?" Another soft moan. "*Oh*, more of that."

I sucked on her breast again, holding the suction while my tongue circled the tip, and her eyes fell closed with a sigh. I switched to her other side before drawing my mouth away.

She blinked up at me, confused as to why I'd stopped.

I dropped a kiss on her lips. "Wait right here."

As close as she was to the edge, I couldn't hold her there without knowing I could get her over the line. She needed to come, and I knew a surefire way to do it.

Chapter Twenty
Aubrey

As Gabe climbed from my bed and disappeared into the living room, my body sought to follow as if being pulled by some magnetic force. My head had gone fuzzy, and my body still floated from the way he'd played with my breasts, which throbbed where my nipples pinched tight, begging for some sort of pressure to relieve them.

I wanted his mouth back, giving that perfect warm suction as his tongue soothed the sensitive nerves. It was almost enough to make me forget my cramps. The ache had shifted into something different, my pussy swollen and wet with arousal as much as PMS.

When he came back, it was with a gym towel in hand. He crawled with it onto the bed, dropping a quick kiss on each breast before pulling my comforter the rest of the way down.

"Lift your hips," he instructed, voice soft.

I did as he said, admiring his broad frame and strong jaw, his clear blue eyes sincere in their focus.

He spread the towel across the bed beneath me, careful to lay it flat.

"What are you doing?" I asked, lowering my hips as he removed his shirt. My gaze danced over smooth skin and tight muscles.

"I want to make you feel good," he said. He pulled a condom from his shorts pocket and tossed it on the bed.

"With sex?" I asked, going breathless. My pulse pounded between my legs, the ache in my belly building.

Never in the three years of being with Patrick had the possibility crossed my mind to ask for period sex. Not even because it would have made him uncomfortable, which it absolutely would have. But because it wouldn't have helped me feel any better. It would have done the opposite, ratcheting up my nerves toward sex with insecurities around my bloated body and the potential mess.

"If you're up for it," Gabe replied. His deep voice stroked me like a touch.

Gabe wasn't Patrick. My bloated belly and disastrous hair hadn't once crossed my mind as he'd removed my sweatshirt under his caring gaze. Neither had what he might think of me. I'd been too focused on how good he made me feel.

"Okay," I answered.

He knelt over me again, dropping open-mouthed kisses to my breasts and stomach as he hooked the waistband of my period panties. I ran my fingers through his soft hair, the short golden strands nearly brown in the fading light.

Cool air touched the wetness between my legs, but the embarrassment that tried to surface failed to break through the blanket of tenderness Gabe had placed around me with his reverent kisses and careful touches.

He didn't seem to care about the blood. Not when he was stripping off his own pants with a fierceness in his eyes that warmed me like a lit burner as he took me in on the bed. His cock stood tall and hard, making my sex throb as I parted my legs in anticipation.

He rolled on the condom and settled between my legs, then sucked on my breasts, making me moan with each swirl of his tongue. I drove up my hips, seeking his erection as the pressure below my belly became almost too much to bear.

"Gabe," I moaned.

"I got you, baby. Hold on."

He notched himself at my entrance and eased inside, sliding deep with the slowest of strokes, my period slicking the way. The muscles in his neck strained as he groaned. "Fuck."

The fullness was immediate relief. I tossed my head into my pillow as my body squeezed him tight, and like when he played with my breasts, the sharp ache from my cramps swelled into an overflowing pleasure.

With small, slow grinding movements, he worked me over, stroking my clit with his thumb as he held me on his cock. It was like he was massaging me from within, seeking out the source of my cramps and soothing them over with each gentle stroke.

In an instant, an orgasm rolled over me, seeping tension from my body as my inner muscles clamped around him again and again like my vagina was trying to keep him from ever leaving.

He kept grinding, his rhythm steady, letting me have him for as long as I needed, his eyes determined as my body let go. I almost couldn't breathe, the orgasm going on and on. It was sweeter than any pleasure I'd felt, wringing out the pain of my cramps, the new ache good enough to cry.

Finally, the wave broke, and my muscles went limp. My head rolled to the side, my arms and legs bags of grain too heavy to lift.

Gabe's hips grew still, but he stayed inside me, letting me settle. He dropped to his forearms, softly sucking on my breasts, so perfect I could fall asleep.

I didn't realize my eyes had closed until his breath grazed my ear. "Be right back," he whispered and slowly pulled out.

I listened to him leave the room, my heart rate slowing. When his footsteps returned, I opened my eyes. He sauntered toward the bed, fully naked, a wet washcloth in hand, his cock still hard, though the bloody condom was gone.

Kneeling between my legs, he cleaned me gently with the warm cloth.

"What about you?" I asked, eyeing his erection. My voice had gone groggy.

He shook his head. "This was about you."

"Are you sure? I don't mind." That was possibly the greatest understatement of my life. I loved feeling him come inside me. The way his whole body went tense and his cock swelled, the rumble of his chest against mine as he groaned.

"You'd be up for hard and fast?" he asked, skeptical. "Because that's what it'd be. I don't think I could hold back enough to go slow again after watching you like that."

"Oh." My cheeks grew warm as I bit back a smile. "Probably not, then." As much as I loved seeing him lose control, my body was on sensitivity overdrive.

His mouth tipped up as he leaned in and kissed me. "Thought so. It's really okay. I'll take care of this later."

"Wait." I caught his arm as he shifted to rise from the bed. "Take care of it now." I glanced at his hard length and back to his face. "Let me watch."

His gaze turned molten as his nostrils flared, his chest rising and falling with a steadying breath. He set the washcloth aside and moved to kneel at the foot of the bed, his eyes never leaving me. Not even as he took himself in hand and gave a long, slow stroke.

Already, my clit grew swollen. The muscles of his thighs stood out, his abs and bicep flexing as he moved his palm over his cock. Everything about him screamed strength, yet it was my words that had moved him here. My pleasure he was feeding by getting himself off.

It didn't just make me feel powerful; it made me feel safe. Like I stood on the edge of a cliff about to jump, and he was the harness around my waist, allowing me the thrill of the fall while ensuring I wouldn't get hurt.

I wanted to jump with him again and again. Experience every thrill and moment of rest in his arms.

His strokes gained a rhythm, and I rubbed my legs together to quench the sweet ache that had returned. His eyes burned, jumping from the apex of my thighs to my rapidly falling chest as my breaths grew short and fast.

I trailed my fingers over my breasts, teasing my own nipples as I watched him. I bit my lip, and he grunted, his grip flying faster and harder with almost angry tugs that drove me mad with lust.

His name rose from my mouth on a moan. "*Gabe.*"

"Fuck, Aubs." He shuffled forward on the bed, straddling my hips with his strong thighs, fucking his hand directly above me.

I squirmed at the way he watched me. At how him turning me on turned him on. At the thought of him imagining it was still me he was fucking, clenching his glutes as he thrust his thick cock inside me over and over.

I pinched my nipples and arched my back, skin tingling in need of his touch.

"Come on me," I gasped. The desire gripped me almost as strongly as my last orgasm. For him to mark me, to claim me. Paint himself on my body like one of my tattoos.

He was gasping too, pushing out deep grunts with every exhale, his tempo relentless. "You want that?"

I couldn't lay still, practically thrashing my whole body with my nod. "Yes, yes, yes—"

He choked out a groan, catching himself with a hand near my shoulder as he spilled across my chest, splashing my swollen breasts with his cum.

"God…damn…" he panted, beads of sweat dripping off his forehead. I caught one with my tongue and grinned at his strained laugh.

I never knew sex could be like this. Fun and playful at the same time it was deep and intense. That it could allow me to open up in a way that made me more attuned to myself, made it easy to exist as all facets of myself at once. I'd never felt more at home in my body or at ease in my mind. Never dreamed it'd be possible to feel both those things in the presence of another person.

With Gabe, I wanted to wrap my limbs around him and bask in the magic of the glow.

I ran my hand into the hair at his forehead. "Tomorrow's my birthday," I said.

His lids grew heavy from my touch. "I know."

My heart stuttered, struggling to keep up with the warmth pouring into my chest. Our voices were whispers, like this moment was too precious to disturb.

A question sat on my tongue, big enough I almost didn't speak it. More than anything I'd asked him for, this one felt truly selfish.

But the idea of this moment ending, of going back to the deafening quiet of being alone after the fullness we'd just shared, was worse than the possibility he might say no.

My throat tightened around the words. "Will you stay the night? As my present?"

We hadn't done sleepovers. There'd been an unspoken agreement that spending the night together would go outside the bounds of the arrangement. Unless we were spending the whole time having sex, it wouldn't serve our established purpose.

And while an all-night sex-a-thon was definitely in the "yes, please" column of my Things-To-Try list, it wasn't why I asked him to stay.

Something softened in his gaze that squeezed my heart tighter. The instinct to run from it, to retract the question before he had to answer, circled my ribs, but I didn't cling to it. Not while it was just the two of us in the darkening cocoon of my bedroom and the soft space we held for each other.

A smile touched his lips. "I'll stay. But I already got you a present."

My own smile widened as he reached for the washcloth again. "You did?"

He nodded and cleaned my chest, gentle on my tender breasts.

"What is it?"

He laughed at the eagerness in my voice. "You have to wait to find out, greedy girl."

Arousal pooled in my belly at the nickname. He liked it when I was greedy. "Will you give me a hint?"

He set the washcloth on the edge of the towel before scooping me into his arms and carrying me toward the bathroom. "No, but I'll give you a shower."

Giddy energy coursed through me, guiding my tongue to his neck. "Did you bring more condoms?" I murmured.

A low chuckle rumbled in his chest. "I guess we know you're horny during your period." He took in the way I bit my finger and stared at his lips. They twitched with amusement. "Noted."

Chapter Twenty-One
Gabe

I BIT my lip against the sparks firing across my vision and straight down my spine as Aubrey's pussy clamped around my cock in her second orgasm of the morning.

I knew spending the night would be hard—sharing her bed, whispering to each other as we fell asleep, being able to feel her beside me, to hear her soft breaths as she slept. She'd asked me to stay as a birthday present to her, but I was the one getting the gift. This piece of her I shouldn't be allowed, which meant it was better if I never got it again.

But waking to her rubbing her ass against my crotch made it impossible not to want this every morning.

I'd laid the towel down, slid off her panties, and spooned her from behind, letting her sink herself onto me and take what she needed. Unlike yesterday, one orgasm didn't seem to be enough, and even after two, she was still bearing down, arching her back to grind her ass into me.

I didn't know if this was the period cramps or something else, and I didn't care. My body was hers.

As I rubbed the wildflowers tattooed on her thigh, obsessed with her smooth skin, she reached for my hip to pull me deeper.

I groaned by her ear. "You want me to thrust?" I'd been letting her guide the movement, not wanting to go too rough if she was sensitive. But the way she circled her pelvis made me think she craved friction.

She jerked her head in a nod. "Start slow, but—*God, yeah…*"

I rolled my hips in one smooth motion, pulling out and sinking to the hilt, my balls grinding against her ass while my head rubbed deep inside. I did it again and again, slow and steady, bracing my foot on the bed and holding her to me with a hand on her soft belly. Her inner muscles contracted again, and her head rolled forward on her pillow.

"There you go, sweetheart, let it come. I got you."

"Gabe. *Oh*—"

Her hand clasped my waist, pulling me so I was practically on top of her, driving her into the bed.

"God, baby." She felt unreal. Her body beneath mine seemed to glow in the bright morning light, her skin shining with sweat. I brushed her hair from the side of her face so I could watch her fall apart. Between her parted lips, deep moans, and rhythmic pulses, it was enough to send me over the edge.

When I could finally move again, I pulled out and tied off the condom, wrapping it in some tissues she kept beside her bed. Then I rolled onto my back to catch my breath, making room for her against my chest. I'd get up for a washcloth in a minute.

She didn't seem in any more of a hurry as she snuggled close, checking the towel was still in place beneath her. "Was that my present?" she asked, walking her fingers over the slick skin of my chest.

My abs contracted as my lips rose. "No. That was just fun."

Something about saying it felt wrong. Not because it wasn't true. Sex with Aubrey was always fun. More than any sex I'd had before.

But it was more than that too. Personal in a way most of the sex I'd had before hadn't been. It was the "just" that felt wrong.

Aubrey wasn't "just" anything.

She propped her chin on my chest with a glint in her eye. "So when do I get my real present?"

"Depends. What are your birthday plans?"

"Not much. I'll get drinks with Evan later. The last few years, I was always working, so that's been my go-to."

I frowned. "You don't want to do more?" It was Saturday, the weather was supposed to be perfect, and she didn't have to work. I didn't believe for a second she'd rather spend the day alone at home than do something fun.

She shrugged. "Jase and the guys are working, and so is Evan most of the day. He's trying to put himself in a good position for this promotion that might happen, and I don't want to get in the way of that."

I scrutinized her face, trying to figure out if that was what she thought she was doing when she asked others for anything—getting in the way. I knew why she might feel that way with her parents, but I never expected she'd worry about it with Evan. Especially on a day traditionally meant to celebrate her.

She deserved that celebration. Something easy and fun to let her feel special.

"We could do something," I suggested.

"Don't you train on Saturdays?"

"I'll train a few hours this morning, and then we'll do something for the rest of the day."

We'd basically handled my cardio. Even lazy morning sex got the heart rate up. Plus, Noah was packing for training camp, which meant I didn't have anyone to spar with. Until I figured that out, I could afford one light day.

And this felt more important. Making sure her day was filled with laughter, letting it be a break from the frustration and strain work had been for her lately. Letting her feel just an echo of the positive impact her existence had on others.

"I promise, you won't be in the way," I said at her look of uncertainty.

"If I say yes, will I get my present sooner?"

I smiled with feigned reluctance, the rest of me settling into a quiet glow. "Fine. You'll get it when we get to the gym."

She beamed and shot from the bed. "I'll go shower."

My laughter followed her out of the room.

Chapter Twenty-Two
Aubrey

WE GOT to the gym a little over an hour later. I'd offered to come on my own and bring Gabe's gym bag so he could run here and get started on his training, but he'd insisted he didn't need the run.

He was aware of his training needs better than I was, and with how much this tournament meant to him, there was no way he would jeopardize his chances, but I couldn't help the voice in my head telling me that was exactly what he was doing. That this one missed workout could be the difference between him getting his dream gym or not, and he'd come to regret he chose me.

I hoped that voice was wrong because the rest of me liked to be chosen. More than I'd ever be willing to admit.

Just like I never would have admitted how much I didn't want to spend my birthday alone.

I was twenty-nine. Nothing huge. Not a year worth

throwing a party for or making a big deal of. None of my birthdays since college had been. Not since Nana died.

It wasn't *because* she died I'd stopped celebrating. It had just been around the same time I'd started working in restaurants, and things like birthdays took a back seat.

But in some ways, it was easier to have work as an excuse than to think too much about how strange it would be to have a birthday dinner that didn't end with Nana's yellow cake and chocolate frosting. One she'd made from scratch with love for me. How final it would feel to know she would never give me another card with money for tattoos or tell Evan and me stories about when she was our age.

Birthdays were a celebration of life. A reminder we were still here, getting older.

Which was also a reminder of those who weren't.

Most years, it made me not want to celebrate at all. This year, it felt like maybe I should. If for no other reason than both Nana and Mrs. Hardt would want me to. That, and a birthday spent sulking alone would do nothing to help my inspirational rut.

On the stairs out front, I waited for Gabe to unlock the door. He rooted through his gym bag while focused on his phone.

"Want me to find your keys?" I offered. He'd been texting on and off all morning, much more than usual. Whatever he was messaging about must have been important.

He tucked his phone away. "Sorry, I got it."

He led me into the gym and back to the office. It wasn't as chilly inside now that the weather was warming up, but it wasn't exactly toasty either. He'd still need the space heater at night.

I bit my tongue to keep from offering my bed. Getting used to having him in my apartment in that way—to have a bedtime routine and share a morning shower, to kiss each other as we headed out the door—was too dangerous. Too much like a relationship instead of the friends with benefits this was.

I waited inside the door to the office and remembered one of those benefits in vivid detail. The time last week he'd set the desk chair in front of the full-length mirror in the corner and sat me on his cock facing away so I could see him spread my thighs with his knees while I held my suction vibe to my clit. I'd been fully naked while he'd still had his gym clothes on, his shorts scrunched down to free his length.

I'd come three times, throbbing around his fullness as he played with my breasts and shifted just enough to grind against the G-spot I used to be convinced I didn't have. When I couldn't keep the vibrator in place any longer, he held it to me as my body flew to a level I'd never reached before, and my next orgasm soaked his lap.

It had been my first time squirting. My first time using a vibrator during sex. Just like last night had been my first time trying period sex.

Gabe was giving me every new experience I could imagine, and more I never would have known to wish for. Whenever our arrangement ended, I'd have to find a way to repay him. Maybe cook him lunches for eternity or maintain flower boxes outside the gym.

Maybe both.

It still wouldn't be enough.

He reached into one of the desk drawers and withdrew a

yellow gift bag adorned with multicolored butterflies. My heart swelled so much it hurt.

I grinned and held out my hands. "Give."

Gabe rounded the desk and passed me the gift. "Don't get too excited. You might not like it."

That wasn't possible, but I didn't waste time arguing. I just tore into the glittery tissue paper and pulled out the present.

"They're more for me," he said as I examined the bright pink boxing gloves.

"Girls who box turn you on or something?" I teased.

He smirked. "You would. But these are so I can train you a little, teach you some self-defense. I'll feel better about you spending nights alone at the prep kitchen if I know you're ready with a few strong punches. That, and I figured pretending the bag is Christian's face might help you relieve some stress."

I hugged the gloves to my chest, incapable of finding the words to match the warmth brimming inside of me. He eyed me, waiting to see if I liked them, even as I strode forward and leaped into his arms.

The strength of his hold felt like coming home as I buried my face in his neck. He ran one hand up my spine to cradle my head like I was precious. Someone he wanted to protect even though we were no longer kids. Someone he wanted to teach to be strong by sharing a part of his world. The part that meant the most to him.

"Thank you," I whispered.

"Happy birthday," he said back.

I knew he'd hold me until I asked to be put down. Whatever I wanted, he'd give me.

I didn't let go just yet.

⸻

IT TURNED out pretending to punch Christian's face in *was* a great stress relief.

After wrapping my hands and helping me put on my new gloves, Gabe showed me how to punch the heavy bag. When my stance was set and I'd landed a few half-decent blows, he let me at it for real.

I barely moved it, but each pop of my glove against the bag brought satisfaction anyway, the power of my blows reverberating through my arms, making me feel alive. Powerful. Like I could take on anyone or anything that tried to mess with me and knock it on its ass.

Christian? Get the fuck out of here.

No-show new hires? Bam. Gone.

This goddamn menu that insisted on eluding me? It. Would. Not. Defeat. Me.

The anger and frustration of it welled up inside and exploded from my fists with each short burst. My heart rate rose, a flush warmed my face, and I sank into my body the way I did when I cooked and my brain almost didn't have to take part.

No wonder Gabe loved this sport.

It helped I wasn't getting punched back, but still.

After my arms tired out, I sat to the side and watched Gabe train. He switched between strength conditioning and boxing drills, some on the heavy bag I'd been punching (his hits landing significantly harder), but he also used others.

There was a teardrop-shaped bag that hung from the ceiling, a small round bag suspended in the air with ropes on top and bottom, and one that looked like someone had taped a boxing glove to the end of a spring and fastened it to a pole on the floor to make a boxing version of a jack-in-the-box. It whipped toward his head from every direction as he bobbed and weaved, popping it with punch combos that sent it flying the other way.

When he was done, we grabbed food at the nearby diner, then took the light rail all the way west to one of my favorite hidden gems—a rock garden with cobblestone paths, a few small ponds, and mini waterfalls. Even on such a beautiful day, hardly anyone was here.

We climbed the rocks near one of the ponds, explored the short hiking path covered in ivy, and spread out our sweat-shirts on the grass to lay in the sun, listening to the babbling water. I almost fell asleep with my head on Gabe's chest as he played with the ends of my hair, my skin warmed by the sun above and his body below.

I felt like a child again. Completely carefree in a way I hadn't since Evan and I explored the old creek in our neigh-borhood and the stressors of life were still too far away to touch us.

It was the best day I'd had in a while.

When it was time for me to get ready for my birthday drinks with Evan, Gabe dropped me off at my apartment and walked me to my door. I fiddled with my keys, wanting to stretch out our time together as long as I could.

Really, I wanted to kiss him. His eyes dropped to my mouth like maybe he wanted that too, but we both held back as if unsure whether it was allowed.

Today had felt like a date, but it wasn't. This was the "friends" part of friends with benefits. The part that didn't kiss each other unless it would lead to sex, and there wasn't time for that.

A kiss right now would be about nothing more than me wanting to kiss him. To feel his lips on mine and satisfy my desire to be connected to him. To show him how much today had meant to me. How much *he* meant to me.

More than he was supposed to.

More than I could ask him to accept.

Whether he knew my reason or not, he sensed I wouldn't ask for a kiss, and true to our arrangement, he let me be the one to call the shot.

"Have fun at your birthday drinks," he said. "Call me if you need anything."

I nodded, my throat tied up.

His mouth tipped into a soft smile. "See you later." He turned for the stairs and, way too quickly, was gone.

"Just for a minute," Evan said, tugging me down the sidewalk toward Ardena. "I forgot something last time I was here, and Neela said she'd hold it for me."

I stumbled behind him in my rhinestone boots and leather skirt, intentionally dragging my feet. "It's after close," I argued. "She's probably gone by now."

She probably wasn't, seeing as it wasn't even midnight, and Ardena had been busy enough on the weekends to keep the staff there well past close. But so far, my birthday had been just about perfect, and I didn't want to be reminded of how much I missed my old job by walking in there. Didn't want anything like sadness to touch the fizzy joy popping throughout my body that had nothing to do with the drinks I'd had at dinner.

Not tonight.

"Let's just check," Evan said. He yanked me through the front door, and I held my breath as the familiar colors, scents, and hum of the restaurant crashed around me.

It was quieter than I expected. Instead of the low murmur of conversation from dwindling late-night tables, the dining room itself was empty, and the conversation was concentrated around the group hanging around the far end of the bar.

Through the jumble of bodies, I spotted Jase in his chef coat, a full pint glass in hand, with Zack leaning next to him on the bar, taking a beer bottle from Neela as she laughed with the new prep chef.

A shift drink.

I jerked to a stop, slipping my arm from Evan's hold. He glanced back at me, brow creased.

"I'm going to wait outside," I said, voice already shaky. It was too much. Seeing not only the job I'd left behind but the family too.

I hadn't *lost them* lost them, but I'd lost this. The familiarity of being part of the crew. The simple knowledge I belonged instead of questioning whether I still had a place like I questioned right now. Wondering whether I'd ever be part of a shift drink again if I didn't accidentally wander into it.

I felt like an outsider, an intruder. A stranger in the place I used to call home, and I couldn't...I couldn't.

Evan's shoulders sank. "Aubrey."

"Aubrey!"

Shit.

I ducked behind Evan to wipe the stray tear from my cheek before plastering on a smile for Jase. Before I could get a word out, Zach was in front of me, clasping me in a bear hug and spinning me off my feet.

"Happy birthdaaaay," Zach said, half singing, half shouting the words.

"She's had two strawberry margaritas," Evan warned, "so the spinning might be dangerous."

"Oh, hell yeah," Zach said as he put me down. "That's my girl, hitting the party before the party."

I gave a weak chuckle as I waited for my vision to catch up with me. "Yeah, well—" The room stopped spinning, and my gaze landed on a birthday banner above the drink well. To the right of it, Luis backed out of the kitchen with a cake in hand. "Wait." My heart took off in my chest, and I glanced at Evan.

He smirked.

I took in the banner, the cake, the group of people all gathered, and gawked at him. "You did this?"

"I helped," he said, taking on a slightly reluctant tone. "It was actually Gabe's idea."

As if summoned by birthday magic, Gabe pushed through the kitchen door, wearing a dark green cargo shirt over a black tee with dark jeans and carrying a plate of chocolate-covered strawberries. His eyes caught mine across the bar, a smile bright in their depths, and the grand finale of a fireworks show went off in my chest.

"What are you drinking, birthday girl?" Neela called to me.

"I heard margaritas," Neela's girlfriend, Robin, said. "That calls for a round of tequila shots, yes?"

Zach and a bleached-haired guy with glasses I assumed was his boyfriend high-fived over Luis's head, who was already arguing with Neela about which tequila she should pour.

Evan nudged my shoulder to guide me toward the bar and into a wave of hugs. Dani hopped off her stool to give me a tight squeeze. "You look beautiful, as always," she said.

Luis acted unusually shy as I approached, gesturing to the round layered cake covered in chocolate frosting. "I've been practicing on dessert station, but this was my first time making this recipe. I hope it's okay."

Evan leaned in to whisper, "It's your grandma's yellow cake."

My jaw hung. "How?"

He half rolled his eyes. "I told Gabe where to look for the recipe in your apartment. He texted a picture."

All of Gabe's texting this morning—he'd been texting Evan? For me?

I searched for him again but found Jase first, waiting quietly at the end of the bar. He grinned. "Happy birthday, Chef."

I stepped into his hug and held it, not sure why I was suddenly ready to cry. Then he spoke his next quiet words. "We miss you, you know."

I tried to laugh, but it caught in my throat, mixing with

the tears that had risen. I squeezed Jase tighter, afraid to let go, to let him and everything here slip further from my grasp.

"Let's have fun, yeah?" Jase said into my hair.

I nodded and took one last deep breath, dabbing my cheek as I pulled away.

"Oh, Gabe, before I forget," Jase said, turning his attention to the side where Gabe lingered. "My buddy Colin boxes. He'd make a good sparring partner if you're still looking."

Gabe blinked. "Yeah. That'd be amazing."

"I'll put him in touch."

"Thanks, man."

Jase nodded, then snagged Evan's hand and pulled him in for a hug. I stepped out of the way to give them space and found myself in front of Gabe.

The rest of the room faded into the background as all my senses fixated on him. My body seemed to breathe a sigh of relief at having him so close, like his looming presence was a shelter I could rest under, a safe place to let go. And not just with sex.

"You and Evan, huh?" I asked, hooking my fingers together so I didn't reach for him. We'd touched in public before, but not around people we knew. People who would ask questions that were easier not to answer. And not when I wanted it to be real this badly. "How did that happen?"

He watched my hands, a soft smile on his lips. "Simple. We both wanted you to have a good birthday."

It wasn't just a birthday they had given me. It was a piece of myself I'd been too afraid to ask to keep. That feeling of connection with these people he'd helped bring together for me. A connection he'd known I needed.

I swallowed and met his stare. "It was one of my best," I said honestly, my heart aching with gratitude and love. For them. For him. For this place. "Thank you."

He reached out and brushed a strand of my hair. A whisper of how he'd played with it this afternoon in the garden. It was the only touch he let himself have.

"Anything you want," he murmured, "it's yours."

Chapter Twenty-Three
Gabe

COLIN'S JAB came at me straight on. I slipped it just in time, ducking to the outside and landing my own punch to his headgear. Not hard enough to do damage—we weren't going full force—but leaning into the movement and getting my timing right still invigorated me.

"Good," Colin said when the timer went off, signaling the end of that round. The word came out slightly muffled through his mouth guard. "That defensive work is solid, man. Don't stay too long on that back foot. Keep up the pressure, yeah?"

I nodded, grabbing my water through the ropes and taking a sip. We were both dripping sweat even though it was cool enough to need the space heater today. We'd been sparring for a couple of hours, this round all about drilling defense, and I was grateful for the huge amount of cardio I'd done the past two months.

Colin was a fucking awesome sparring partner. Barely an

inch shorter than me and nearly my weight, he'd been training at a boxing gym his whole adult life and was exactly the kind of body I needed to work with in the ring. We'd practiced together one other time in the week and a half since Aubrey's birthday, and I could feel my skills sharpening already.

They were almost back to what they'd been before I retired. Maybe not quite as fast, but just as smooth and every bit as strategic. With one week until the tournament, I was right where I wanted to be. Strong and getting stronger. Ready for more.

Ready to actually win this thing.

"I can't believe you were never pro," I said as we caught our breaths another minute. "You could have been if you wanted to." Probably still could. His moves weren't the most creative, but his technique was solid, and he was in absurd shape for someone who did this on the side of running his own art gallery.

He grinned, white teeth flashing against his rich brown skin. "I thought about it for a minute in uni. There was just no getting around that boxing was a passion, but art was *the* passion, you know what I mean?"

I smiled in response, his British accent putting me back in the gym in London. If I closed my eyes, I could almost be there, standing under the fluorescent lights, listening to Coach Peter's feedback, getting ready to watch the next pair of fighters spar in the ring.

I knew exactly the passion he was talking about.

"You never wished you were the one making the art?"

He shrugged. "Still getting it out in the world, aren't I? Just at a different part of the process."

I probably wouldn't have agreed before my shoulder injury. Wouldn't have imagined anything could bring the same fulfillment as being in that ring, landing and slipping punches myself. And maybe coaching wasn't the same, but as Colin said—it was still a part of the process.

My phone lit up on the side of the mat, and I spotted Aubrey's name. "I'm going to take this quick," I told Colin as I slipped off one glove.

"Go for it."

I took out my mouth guard on the way to the office and answered as I stepped inside. "Hey," I said, nearly out of breath. My heart pounded as if I'd been running.

"Hey," she greeted, her voice shining like the sun off her golden hair. "I'm heading over in a little bit. I just need to stop by the restaurant to talk to Jillian quick."

"Cool. Colin and I are almost done too."

I couldn't tell if the eagerness in my voice was all in my head or if she heard it too. If my physical desire to see her had seeped its way into my psyche. Or maybe it was the other way around—that my head couldn't get enough, and it was sending my body into overdrive.

All I knew was I wanted her here, and I'd been counting the minutes all day.

Not even for sex, just…for her smile. Her laughter. Her ability to make me laugh too. Real, genuine laughter and not the memory of it my body had tried to replicate since my mom died. The one that felt forced even when I found something funny, as if someone held a lid over my joy, preventing it from coming all the way to the surface.

Aubrey tore off that lid. She let me breathe again.

And ever since she thanked me on her birthday for giving

her the bare fucking minimum she deserved as a celebration, I'd been dying to bring her all that joy and more. Still with her calling the shots, like letting her choose to come here instead of going to her apartment.

It was better this way—easier to maintain boundaries here. Not to fall into the routine of two people who kissed each other good night, who slept in the same bed, who made love.

There was no bed for us to make love in here. No kitchen for her to cook us dinner in. No couch for us to sit on while I massaged her feet after she worked a long event. No way for me to get hooked on the familiarity of being in her life day in and day out, one small moment at a time.

"Colin still working out?" she asked, snapping me back from my impossible daydream. My fingers rubbed my chest as if working out a knot. I rolled them into a fist.

"He's awesome," I said. "I owe you for telling Jase I needed a sparring partner."

"I didn't tell him."

Wait. "You didn't?"

"No. I assumed you mentioned it to him when you were setting up for my party."

"No, I…" I shook my head. "Weird."

"I'll ask him today if I see him. I just got to Ardena."

"Sounds good. Good luck with Jillian."

She blew out a breath. "Thanks."

Back in the gym, Colin stretched in the ring.

"Question for you," I said as I climbed through the ropes. "Did Jase say anything about who told him I was looking for a sparring partner?" The only person besides Aubrey and

Noah I'd mentioned it to was my dad, and I didn't see him bringing it to Jase.

"Your brother mentioned it when he picked up his ticket."

My brain skidded to a halt as all the blood in my body tried to rush to my head. Any second, I'd wake up face down on the mat. "My brother?"

"Evan, right? Pretty blond fellow who flirts with every person he meets?"

That was definitely Evan. "What ticket?"

Colin looked at me like I should get my head checked for a concussion. "To the boxing tournament. He asked Jase to grab him one. I figured you were seeing Jase first or something, and it was easier to pass it on through him."

My legs went shaky, ready to give out. I considered sitting down, but I was pretty sure if I tried, my knees would buckle, and I'd end up sprawled on my ass. Emotionally, I was already there.

I'd assumed the extra tickets Jase bought were for his brother's friends. I never thought…

My heart pounded as too many emotions filled my chest. Evan was going to my fight. He'd found me a training partner. He…wanted me to win?

Did that mean he wanted me to stay?

I wanted him to want me to stay. I wanted him to want me as his big brother again. To be proud of me again. To think I was worth believing in again.

I wanted to call him right now and tell him how much I loved him and how much it meant that he'd be watching me from the stands.

Something told me if I did that, he wouldn't show. He

was like a wary puppy on the side of the road, and if I approached too fast, he'd run off. I had to let him come to me at his own pace. Let him see I wasn't here to hurt him. No matter how badly I'd fucked up in the past.

I faced Colin with a stronger resolve than ever. "One more round?"

His mouth curved up. "Let's go."

Chapter Twenty-Four
Aubrey

I STRAIGHTENED my shoulders and stared at the wood grain of Ardena's office door, running through what I wanted to say once more before finally knocking.

"Come in," called Jillian's stern voice, as polished and certain as she was.

Another quick breath, and I turned the handle.

Her back was to me as she adjusted one of the heavy curtains lining the wall of glass doors that led to the office's small balcony. She seemed to struggle with their height but coaxed them along rather than lose her patience.

"What can I do for you, Aubrey?" she asked without turning. The curtain ring gave way and settled where she wanted it.

"How did you know it was me?"

She waved a hand as she lowered into her plush desk chair. "Fifty-fifty chance. Only you or Jase ever seek me out.

The young men are still too intimidated to risk it." Her mouth lifted as if pleased by the idea.

It was true the best way to quiet Zach or Luis was to tell them Jillian was heading for the kitchen. The same was probably true for the new prep cook, Tyrell.

I'd finally had the chance to meet him on my birthday and could see why he fit so well with the crew. He didn't have an ego and was willing to work hard. He'd even signed my birthday card.

"My friend at Corvidea said the retirement party was a success," Jillian said, returning her focus to me. "He had wonderful things to say about the food. I'd say you've found your stride. You win this competition, and your name will be on the way to the top—"

"Jillian, I can't do this."

Her mouth snapped shut as alarm etched over her features. It seemed to deepen with each second of silence that stretched between us.

I replayed my words in my head and realized why. "I'm not quitting," I hurried to clarify.

Her shoulders lowered an inch.

"But you keep saying all these things about how great I'm doing and how successful I'm going to be, and that couldn't feel further from the truth."

She pursed her lips but didn't interject.

I swallowed against my dry mouth. "I'm struggling."

Admitting it felt like prying a knife between my ribs and popping them open like a clamshell, revealing the seeping mess I'd been trying to hold together these past months.

I hated for her, of all people, to see it. The last remaining woman in my life who I looked up to, whose strength I strived to carry. I never wanted her to see where I was weak. To be a burden she had to carry, especially when it came to her business. But it was true.

"I'm struggling to keep up with events on my own," I said. "I need a team, and I'm struggling to find one. I feel like I've searched everywhere, and without another pair of hands, I know I can't sustain this. And I've been splitting my time looking for a chef and trying to come up with a menu for the competition, but it's like without one, I can't do the other. I'm so sorry, Jillian. I don't want to let you down, but I need your help."

By the time I finished, my hands were trembling and a bitter taste lined my tongue. Somehow saying all that was more difficult than the craziest dinner service I'd ever worked. It had easily been five times scarier.

But Jillian simply smiled. "About damn time."

It was my turn to be confused. "What?"

"I was nineteen when I started my first business," she said as she wiped nonexistent wrinkles from the lap of her skirt. "You know what happened?"

"You sold it?" I guessed. Wasn't that what super-successful entrepreneurs did?

"It failed miserably. I tried to do everything on my own, refused to ask for help, and insisted the only way I could prove myself was if no one else was involved. But running a business isn't about doing everything on your own. It's about getting the right people to help you do what needs to get done." She stood and placed her hands on my shoulders. "Asking for help isn't a sign you've failed. It just means you've recognized your limits. It's what *successful* people do," she said, shaking me slightly. "I've asked a hell of a lot from you. I never expected you to do it alone."

"But *you* shouldn't be the one who has to do it," I argued.

She spun to her desk to find a pen. "Why not? It's my business. Where's the fun if I can't get my hands a little dirty?" She glanced at me from her notepad. "Figuratively, of course. I don't cook."

I cracked a smile.

"I'll make a few calls, see if we can't find a couple of promising chefs for you to interview."

Already, my chest felt lighter. I didn't even dread the idea of a few more interviews. Not if they came from Jillian.

"About the competition," she added, her face softening. "Just have fun with it. I already know what you can do. You don't need to prove it to me. Winning would merely be a bonus."

"Really?" I asked, skeptical.

She looked almost bashful. "I know you were probably annoyed I entered you, the same way Jase was annoyed I volunteered the restaurant to cater the symposium last year." She composed her face and raised her chin. "I like showing the two of you off. You'll get no apologies for it."

Well, when she put it like that.

"I'll try to let go of some of the pressure," I said.

"And you'll let me know if there's anything else I can help with." It wasn't a question.

"I will," I promised.

She nodded. "Good."

On the way out through the dining room, I popped my head into the kitchen. "Hey, Chef?"

Jase swung his gaze from the tickets to me.

"Think we could meet up next week to workshop some menu ideas for the catering competition? I'm stuck."

He grinned. "I'd love to, Chef."

I let out a breath as another weight lifted from my shoulders.

"You grabbing some food?" he asked.

I considered it. For once, the idea of being here as just another customer didn't fold my stomach into a lump of overworked dough.

But I had other plans tonight. Ones with Gabe, who I'd barely seen since my birthday, thanks to the three events I'd squeezed in the past week and a half. And with the boxing tournament next week, all Gabe's focus after tonight would be on it.

"Next time," I said to Jase, meaning it.

Maybe Gabe would want to come with me. Like after the boxing tournament, when maybe he'd be here for good.

It was a dangerous thought. One I had no business hanging on to.

I let myself have it anyway, just for a moment.

Chapter Twenty-Five
Gabe

CHEERS from the ongoing match soaked through the walls of the arena's back room where Coach Lou wrapped my hands. We sat on metal folding chairs in one corner while a few other fighters did their prefight routines on the other side. Members of their teams spoke on the phone or with each other, adding their chatter to the white noise of the crowd's hollering. I'd reached the point in the day when it all turned to silence in my head.

One hour until my first fight of the tournament.

I blocked out everything else.

It surprised me how easily my brain and body fell back into the rhythm of a fight night. The long day of waiting that gradually built to those eight rounds of pure adrenaline and physical demand.

We'd been here for hours already, mostly sitting around. After weigh-in and getting checked by the doctor, there wasn't much to do except rehydrate and fuel up. My dad had come by to give me a hug and wish me luck, and Colin and Jase's brother, Alec, had hung out for a bit while I ate.

Alec reminded me a lot of Evan. Enough that laughing with him had stung with the longing of not being able to do the same with my brother.

I tried not to let the sting linger. Tried not to focus on why Evan wasn't back here with me like he had been at the few events in Philly I'd fought in my career. Because if I did, memories of a different tournament would take hold.

With the hand Coach had already wrapped, I reached for my phone and opened Aubrey's messages. She'd had to work this morning and couldn't stop by in person to wish me luck, but she'd be here for the fight. I reread her texts from this morning, then scrolled through yesterday's messages and the ones from the day before, letting her words fend off the shadows creeping into my mind.

"Nerves?" Coach Lou asked, eyeing my bouncing foot.

I forced it still. "A few," I admitted. Not all for the fight. In some ways, that was the easy part. It was everything surrounding it that was starting to swell like skin around a fresh wound. Questions like what came next once this was over.

Coach seemed to sense it. He tapped my taped hands and nodded toward the center of the room. "Let's get you moving. Work it out in warm-up."

That was enough to bring me back to center. Focus on my body, on my form, on my fight. It had been a long time since Coach Lou was the one coaching me through it, but I was glad it was him now.

The crowd's cheers surged as a winner of the current

fight was called, leaving one more to go before it was my turn.

Boxing was what I did. Time for me to do it.

LAST ROUND, come on.

I had my opponent pinned against the ropes, struggling to keep his guard up against the barrage of punches I threw at him. My right glove connected with his face as my left came in for a hook to his ribs, forcing his torso down and leaving him open to my uppercut.

Just as it landed, the bell rang, signaling the end of the match. The ref lunged between us so the other fighter could regain his feet, then we stepped together to bump gloves and exchange a quick hug.

We'd both fought hard. I was drenched in sweat, had a few bruises that would be sore for tomorrow's fight, and felt like I could go another eight rounds right now.

God, I loved boxing. I'd missed this. Never thought I'd have it again, but here I was in the ring, coming down from a fight. Even if I lost this match, it was almost worth it just for that.

I went back to my corner of the ring while the judges deliberated and took the towel from Coach Lou to wipe my face. Aubrey screamed my name, drawing my attention to the front row, my dad and Colin on either side of her, all of them on their feet.

Joy ballooned in my chest. Having her here felt even better than I thought it would. Different from when she'd come with Evan to my beginner matches when we were kids. Like doing well for her was as important as the rest of it.

Almost enough for me not to notice the pinch in my side at my mom not being here too.

I searched for Evan, but the seat beside my dad was empty.

When I rose from my crouch as they called me to the center of the ring, I spotted him. He stood at the rear of the room near one of the exits, arms crossed over his chest, his expression blank.

Still. He was here.

I returned my attention to the ring, where the other fighter and I stood on either side of the ref. He took one of our wrists in each hand as the announcer's voice came over the speakers.

"The winner…by unanimous decision…is Gabriel Hardt!"

My shoulders dropped in relief as a familiar rush of pride surged through me. The ref raised my hand, and the other fighter stepped around to give me another hug.

"Hey, that was a good fight," I told him over the cheers. "You keep your head high and go get the next one."

He patted my shoulder in thanks, and I headed for my corner, slipping under the ropes in time to catch Aubrey as she flung herself into my arms like I'd just won the whole tournament.

"You were amazing!"

I tightened my hold on her waist, resisting the urge to spin her off her feet and claim her mouth with mine. That was probably off-limits with so many of our friends around, not to mention my dad. But her body so close as adrenaline pumped through me had me ready to do a lot more.

I dropped my chin to her ear and let my desire scrape through my voice, low enough only she could hear. "Thanks, Aubs."

I felt her shiver before she let go, her fevered stare connecting with mine a second before my dad tugged me in for his own hug.

Colin slapped my shoulder next. "Looking good, man," he said. "You must have a great sparring partner."

"Hell yes, I do."

"And hey, one down. Only three more to go."

I clasped his hand, then scanned the back wall, trying to catch Evan's eye. I found the spot where he'd been standing.

He was already gone.

Chapter Twenty-Six
Aubrey

"So he won?" Jase asked as he pulled ingredients from the box he'd brought to the prep kitchen.

"He crushed it," I said, still buzzing from the excitement of yesterday's fight. "Watching him, you'd never guess he retired." So much so a part of me wondered if maybe Gabe would decide to come out of retirement for good. He was on the older side for the sport, but nothing unheard of. As long as he was strategic with his fights and didn't push too hard, it was entirely possible he could still do it.

If the frantic sex we'd had last night at his gym was any indication, he was feeling up to it.

And boxing was his love the way cooking was mine. His heart had been broken for a while, but maybe this tournament would be what mended it.

It twisted something inside me to think about. The knowledge boxing again would make him happy the way nothing else could, and the bitterness that it would likely mean him leaving Philly again.

I was pretty sure Evan felt the same twist of emotions. The comfort of watching his brother box the way he had growing up colliding with the possibility it could take him away again. The push and pull of joy and hope, grief and spite wrestling within one heart.

"Hopefully, he'll win tonight so I can see him tomorrow," Jase said. He'd worked at the restaurant during last night's fight and had to again tonight. But Saturday's and Sunday's fights were in the afternoon, so if Gabe made it to the final, Jase could see him both days.

"Dani and Robin are going tonight?" I asked.

He nodded and blew out a laugh. "I'm pretty sure Robin is expecting something out of the WWE, so you may have to remind her not to throw any chairs into the ring."

I grinned. "I feel like she would excel at roller derby."

"I'm going to leave that one for you to bring up with her at your own risk."

"It could be fun. We could get bright wigs to wear under our helmets and have a team name like 'Crème Brû Slayers.'"

"And the part where you get tackled on rollerblades?"

Admittedly less appealing. "I'll just play the bench. Be moral support for Robin and Kelly." Those two were a dangerous combination if the few times I'd hung out with them and Dani were anything to go by.

Jase moved the empty box off the counter. "Ready to do this?"

I straightened, my eyes falling to the two cutting board stations he'd set up with identical ingredients.

"You know the drill," he said. "The guys each picked one ingredient. I had Neela pick the fourth. Appetizer or entrée?"

It was an exercise we'd started a few months before I moved to catering, one Jase got the idea for from some reality cooking competition Dani had gotten him into. Each person in the kitchen picked one ingredient, and we'd get a set amount of time to make a dish incorporating all four. Or sometimes, there was only one ingredient, and we had to make a dish incorporating it in as many different ways as possible. The tight timeframe meant no chance for overthinking. Just cooking on pure instinct.

"Appetizer," I said.

"Twenty minutes it is." He pulled out his phone and set the timer. "Ready?"

I set my knife on my cutting board and stretched my neck. "Ready."

"Go!"

We sprang into action, grabbing the ingredients lined up in front of us, peeling and chopping, dropping them into sauté pans, and snagging more items from the pantry.

The energy of having another chef in the kitchen brought more to the space than a playlist ever could. I didn't even need to see what Jase was doing. I could hear his knife making cuts, smell the onion and garlic as it hit his pan, feel his presence beside me creating without hesitation, which meant I had to do the same.

No time for thinking; just cooking on pure instinct.

What felt like twenty seconds and not twenty minutes later, his phone alarm blared, and we dropped whatever was in our hands and raised them in the air.

I looked at his plate. He looked at mine. We both grinned.

"Moment of truth," he said.

We started with his.

My favorite thing about Jase's food was how intentional it was. Nothing went on the plate without purpose. No garnish for the sake of garnish. No ten different components if the same impact could be achieved with six. When you were being forced by the exercise to use certain ingredients, it was easy to drop a shaving of one on at the end and call it a day, but Jase never did. He was mindful about his food, and it showed.

The ingredients the guys and Neela had picked were shrimp, fermented chilis, strawberries, and bacon. Jase had made strawberry carpaccio with shrimp-chili broth and bacon dust.

It was so freaking good. If I were him, I'd put it on Ardena's menu next week, no changes necessary. He was seriously the best chef I'd ever worked with.

Then it was my turn. While Jase tended to focus on how to be most efficient with the ingredients, I liked to go for the unexpected. Try out a technique that might not typically be used for something and see what it did.

"What the fuck," Jase said as he tasted it. He pointed at my dish. "That sauce is ridiculous. I never would have thought of putting hibiscus with fermented chili."

I glanced at my bacon-poached shrimp with roasted strawberries and fermented chili-hibiscus sauce, my rib cage lifting. I wouldn't put it on a menu as is, but I agreed there were special aspects to it. The kind of something that had been missing from my menu attempts so far.

"What if we used your carpaccio idea instead of

poaching the shrimp?" I suggested. "I think it'll balance better than the bacon."

"Or we could try octopus. It would elevate it slightly, which seems like what the judges are looking for."

I flipped to a new page of my notepad and scribbled our ideas, writing so fast my hand hurt.

An hour later, we'd mapped out enough for me to play with, and I felt full in a way that had nothing to do with food.

"Thanks for this," Jase said, surprising me.

"Why are you thanking me? You're the one who helped me out."

He dropped his gaze to his knife roll, almost shy. "I know, but you never ask for help. You've saved my ass a hundred times over the years, and this feels like the first chance I've had to repay you."

That couldn't be true. Could it?

"Even back at Pépère," he went on, "you never asked me to step in when Christian was being an ass or to give you the better tasks just to piss him off. Not that it would have made a difference in the long run, but it would have been something."

"You did that anyway," I said.

"Yeah, after I realized you were never going to ask. I had your back then, and I have it now. It just"—he shrugged— "feels good to know you know you can ask. Especially now that we're not in the same kitchen."

My throat tightened. "Sometimes I wish I was still your sous chef. I really liked cooking with you."

"Then we'll do more of it," he decided. "Stuff like this. Staff meals and shift drinks and team trainings." He sought my gaze.

"You're still a part of my team, Chef. An important one. And if at some point one of us isn't at Ardena any longer, you'll *still* be a part of my team. I know I'll always be able to count on you. I hope you'll give me more chances to be there for you too."

"It wasn't your job to help me," I tried to explain. It was one thing to delegate tasks to line cooks or waitstaff—that was *my* job. It wasn't asking for help when it was how things flowed in a kitchen.

But when it came to bosses and—I was starting to realize —the people I cared about, the worst thing I could think of being was a burden. What kind of boss wanted an employee who constantly needed help?

What kind of parent wanted a child who was always in the way?

What kind of friend wanted to be asked over and over for favors?

I did. It made me feel useful, assured me I had a purpose. A place.

Did other people feel the same?

"You weren't just my sous chef, Aubrey. You were my friend," Jase said. "Still are, I think."

I gave him a look like *of course*.

He smiled. "Well, I like helping my friends. Especially when they've done so much for me. Called me out on my shit and kept me from making life-altering mistakes. It's kind of the point, you know? Just because you can do it alone doesn't mean you have to. I'm glad you didn't force yourself to this time."

I didn't know what to say. He and Jillian were two people I'd gone out of my way not to inconvenience by asking for things, and now they'd both flat-out told me they'd been waiting for me to do just that. They *wanted* me to.

It was hard to doubt it when it came from both of them. When I had Gabe telling me essentially the same thing every time we were together.

To ask for what I wanted.

To say what I needed.

To allow myself the chance to be heard. I wanted to be able to do that.

And I wanted Gabe.

Not because I needed him or idolized him the way I had as a kid. But because he challenged me while still making me feel safe. He heard me before I was brave enough to say what I wanted out loud and helped me be brave enough to say it at all. To ask for help like I had with Jillian and Jase.

I owed it to myself, and to him, to be brave again.

There were three days left of the tournament that needed Gabe's focus. But after…maybe I'd try this asking thing again.

Chapter Twenty-Seven
Gabe

"Day three. You ready?" Diego asked as I went through my prefight warm-up. Coach Lou and Colin hung out in my corner, watching fight footage from yesterday.

"Hell yes. I feel good." Better than I thought I would after my first two fights in two years. Better than I thought possible.

"You look it. I still can't believe you got a knockout yesterday."

I forced down my smile. First knockout of the tournament.

Like I said, I was feeling good.

Diego ran a hand along the dark hair of the short beard he'd managed to grow since we were kids. It sharpened that pretty tan face of his. "Buzz is building, man. People are talking about you."

"Good." People talking meant high ratings for his event and free marketing for my gym. The more local boxers who knew my name and respected it, the better. "Aren't you glad I convinced you to give me a spot?"

"All right, you know what?" he said with mock reluctance. "Talk to me after you've won."

"I will," I said, grinning. I meant it, too. I was going to do this.

With my warm-up finished, I headed for Coach Lou to lace up my gloves. Colin flipped his phone screen to show me footage of my opponent.

"This Isaac Herman guy likes to play on the offensive, but his cardio's not as strong." He pointed out the other boxer's aggressive style. I'd noticed the same thing when I watched his fights last night. "Focus on slipping his punches. Let him tire himself out. Land a few good counters, and you'll be golden."

I nodded, filing the advice next to the other reminders cycling through my mind as my focus narrowed to the next twenty-four minutes. Another knockout would be sweet but unlikely. I needed to be ready for a long match, and I needed my body to outlast his.

I looked at Coach Lou. "I'm going to get us that gym."

A fresh start in a familiar place for me. The passing of a legacy for him.

I wouldn't let it be torn down and replaced with luxury condos.

His eyes filled with emotion that he cleared from his throat. "Just do your best, kid."

FIVE ROUNDS IN, and I was still feeling good. Tired, but so was the other guy.

He'd come out aggressive, just like Colin and I had predicted, but it hadn't had its intended effect. Only a few of his shots had landed, while I'd blocked or slipped the rest, and with the handful of hard, clean punches I'd gotten in each round, I was confident I was ahead in points.

Still, it wasn't this guy's first fight. He and his coach must have decided to switch tactics because we were halfway through this round, and he'd hardly made a move. He was waiting to see if I was willing to take charge or if defense was my only strength.

Smart.

Except I could already see he was itching to lunge. Whether I was good at offense didn't matter if he wasn't comfortable staying on defense.

Sure enough, the second I threw a test jab, he jumped forward with a flurry of punches I deflected with my gloves.

I lured him in again with a three-punch combo, and when his counter move came, I slipped to the side but was too slow for his second jab. It came at my exposed left shoulder, grazing the muscle when I didn't rotate in time.

I hopped back, putting space between us as I rolled out the twinge, trying not to be obvious about it. Chances were he already knew my shoulder was a weak spot. Every boxer here would have read about my rotator cuff when they did their opponent research. If he realized he'd aggravated it, it'd be blood in the water for a very hungry shark.

Rather than give him time to think about it, I went on the offensive for real. He came at me with equal aggression—a back-and-forth barrage, each landing something here or there but nothing strong enough to do real damage.

Just as I stepped in to break his momentum by wrapping him in a clinch, he threw a wide punch hard into my left shoulder.

Pain exploded up my arm and blacked out my vision. Another punch connected to my cheek, and I hit the mat.

Chapter Twenty-Eight
Aubrey

Gabe fell to one knee, catching himself on his right glove.

I stopped breathing.

The referee jumped between the two fighters to prevent Gabe from being hit while he was down and began to call the count.

Come on, come on…

I didn't care about the fight anymore or whether he won. I just wanted him to be okay.

He held still, taking careful breaths, blinking rapidly at the mat as if to clear his vision. The blow to his head had been hard, but it was the punch to his shoulder I was more worried about.

"Six!…Seven!…"

As soon as the ref called eight, Gabe rose to his feet. I let out a breath as he hopped in place and lifted his hands into position, but the stiffness of his movements cut my relief short.

At the back of the room, Evan stood with his arms locked across his chest. His eyes met mine, and the stress in his stare told me he saw it too.

Gabe was in pain.

When the bell rang to end that round, I nearly dropped to my knees in thanks.

It wasn't over, though. There were three full rounds left in the match, and if Gabe didn't fight them, he'd be out of the tournament.

He shuffled his way to the corner and sat stiffly between his childhood coach and Colin.

"Colin knows about his shoulder, right?" I asked Jase beside me.

"They talked about it before they first sparred."

Colin kneeled in front of Gabe and said something. Gabe shook his head and rolled his shoulder in response. Colin spoke again, but Gabe kept shaking his head. The whistle blew for the fighters to take their places for the next round, and I thought I might throw up as Gabe got to his feet.

"Looks like he's okay," Jase said.

I wasn't so sure. The look on Colin's face said he wasn't either. And when I glanced back at Evan, he was pacing in stiff circles, brow creased with concern.

The next three rounds were brutal.

By the end of the sixth, Jase no longer thought Gabe was okay. Gabe's movement was choppy, his punches slow. He still managed to land a few hits with his right glove, but he was clinching way more than the previous rounds, getting in close to hold the other boxer's arms at his sides in what looked like a hug rather than risk a hard jab. It was a last-resort tactic, something boxers mostly pulled when tired or desperate.

Gabe looked both.

By the last round, my nerves were strung too tight for me to cheer. My eyes stayed fixed on Gabe, every punch that came at him a strike to my heart. Dani reached behind Jase for my hand, and I squeezed it like a lifeline.

Mr. Hardt stood on my other side and was the opposite. His cheers grew louder, his shouts more forceful with each stumble Gabe took, as if he could hold up his son with his own strength of will.

Finally, *finally*, the last bell rang, and Dani's grip on my hand was what kept me from climbing into the ring. Jase, Dani, Jase's brother Alec, Mr. Hardt, and I all waited in silence while the judges tallied their final scores.

Gabe stood to the referee's right, the ref taking hold of his left glove while the announcer spoke.

"The winner by split decision is…Gabriel Hardt!"

The ref jerked Gabe's left arm in the air, and Gabe did his best to hide his grimace.

I felt no relief he'd won. I couldn't feel anything but a rising need to go to him and see that he was okay.

Only, when he stepped out of the ring, I was too afraid to touch him. Afraid I'd hurt him worse if I did. He met my eyes and held out his right arm, inviting me in.

"Your shoulder," I said, carefully avoiding his left side.

"I'm fine. Just need to ice it and get some rest. I'll be good as new tomorrow."

The thought of him fighting again shredded my stomach. He'd have to in order to win the prize money, but I didn't think I could watch eight more rounds like the past few. And if tomorrow's match looked like the last half of today's, I didn't see how he'd possibly win.

I hated thinking it. Hated doubting Gabe in any way. He had only ever believed in me, and I wanted to repay that favor, but I couldn't help the worry that filled me too.

Stepping aside so his dad could hug him next, I spotted Evan at the edge of our group. The other two nights, he'd left immediately, not bothering with congratulations or celebrations.

"He's fighting again?" he asked when I reached him. His gaze was on his brother.

"He said he is."

A muscle ticked in Evan's jaw.

For once, his anger was a comfort. A sign I wasn't crazy for thinking Gabe shouldn't do this. It offered its own kind of relief.

Because where I refused to stand in Gabe's way, Evan would have no problem doing just that.

Chapter Twenty-Nine
Gabe

THE DULL THROBBING in my shoulder was familiar enough to be déjà vu. So was the scene in front of me: my coach standing in one corner of the room while a medic poked and prodded my shoulder, the tournament promoter pacing in front of where I sat.

I knew the words he'd say before he even opened his mouth. The exact ones I'd heard two years before.

You're done.

Like hell.

Diego opened his mouth, and I cut him off before he had the chance to say it. "I'm fighting."

He set his hands on his hips and stared me down. "It's not up to you."

I stared right back. "The fuck it's not." I went to stand, and pain shot down my left arm. The medic placed a hand on my chest to keep me in the chair. I glared at him next. "I'm fine."

The medic ignored me and continued his inspection.

"That'll be up to a doctor to decide," Diego said. "And if he says you can't—"

Don't fucking say it.

"You're done."

The door to the room swung open, but I was too worked up to care who it was. "Fuck what a doctor says. I know my own body, and I'm telling you, I can fight."

"Like you did those last three rounds?" Diego countered. "Is that how you fight when you're fine?"

I had nothing to come back at him with, and we both knew it. My last three rounds tonight had been garbage. It had taken everything in me just to stay on my feet. The only reason I still won was because I'd done well enough in the first five rounds for my score to come out on top.

Barely.

"I need this, Diego," I said. "Just one more fight. It's not like I have a career left ahead of me I need to protect. If my shoulder's blown, it's blown. It doesn't matter. Me winning this does."

"What about my career, Gabe? If I let you fight while injured, I lose all credibility. Everything I've built here will crumble to nothing because no fighter will trust I have their best interest at heart enough for me to book them."

I clenched my jaw against more than one kind of pain. My breaths came heavy through my nose.

"I'm sorry, okay?" Diego said. "I get it, man, I do, but it's the doctor's call. I'll wait until the medical assessment tomorrow morning to make the official decision, but I'm letting Isaac Herman know to be ready to fight if you can't."

I kept my eyes glued to a dark splotch on the concrete

floor. Eventually, I nodded. After another tense moment, Diego turned and left.

The medic gathered his supplies. "You'll need X-rays to know for sure if it's torn. Definitely ice it tonight."

I nodded again, and he left too. The door latched shut behind him, sending a clang echoing through the silent room.

It didn't stay silent for long.

"What's your fucking problem?"

I hadn't noticed when Coach Lou left, but he must have at some point because there were only two of us here when I lifted my head.

Evan stood in well-fitted jeans and a long-sleeved shirt, his normally perfect hair scattered across his forehead. The fluorescent lights cast his chiseled features in harsh shadows, made harsher by his fists curled at his sides.

Guess he was pissed at me. No surprise there.

My voice came out hollow. "Here to yell at me again? What did I do wrong this time?"

"Let's see." His words dripped with hostility. "You were careless enough to enter into a boxing tournament when you haven't trained in two years, thanks to a career-ending injury. And now when that injury is back and probably worse than it was the first time, you're willing to risk permanent damage, for what? A few bucks?"

I forced the fingers on my left hand to move, ignoring the ache in my shoulder and growing rage in my gut. "You don't get it."

"What don't I get? That boxing is all that matters to you? That you'll choose it over everyone and everything time and time again? Trust me, I get it. I just didn't think you were stupid enough to choose it over your own well-being."

A few months ago, I would have agreed with him. Welcomed his scorn.

Not now. Not with my muscles still buzzing with too much adrenaline and my mind muddled with pain as my shoulder screamed like someone had run it through with a red-hot poker and left it there to burn. My tolerance hit its limit.

"You know what, Evan?"

"What?"

"Fuck you."

He scoffed, but I wasn't done.

"Seriously, fuck you. I've tried to be patient these past few months. I've given you space. I've let you shit on me without fucking complaint. But you act like I'm the worst thing that's ever happened to you. Like I beat you when we were kids or made it my mission to make your life miserable, and I'm sick of it. I'm sorry I left Dad after the funeral—"

"You left *me!*" The words tore from him as if they'd been ripped from his skin. As bloody and raw as the strain in his voice. "You left me when I needed you most. Mom died, and Dad was falling apart, and I needed someone to fall apart with too, only I couldn't because you were *gone*, and I had to be the one to hold everything together." He stabbed at his chest. "*I* was the one to go through Mom's things because Dad couldn't bear to step foot in their room for six months. *I* was the one to make sure Dad ate when he wouldn't cook anymore. *I* was the one who read Mom's mail and replied to the letters from her friends sending their condolences to Dad, who couldn't do more than sit in his chair with a photo of Mom in his lap.

"Mom left me, and Dad did too, and you were supposed

to be my big brother who I could count on to have my back, and you didn't even ask me how I was doing at the funeral *I* planned. You didn't call afterward like you used to. You ghosted me like I was some girl from a fucking dating app who meant nothing to you, and now you're back, making more reckless fucking decisions without thinking about how they'll impact the people around you."

Hurt poured from him like a dam that had broken, each word threatening to drown me. The weight settled onto my chest like a concrete block, pushing me below the surface one heavy truth at a time as I fought to keep my head above water.

He was right. I knew he was right. My baby brother was alone and in pain, and I'd helped put him there. I'd fucked up in more ways than I could count, and I hated myself for it to a degree I might never be able to recover from.

But I couldn't deal with it now. Not until after.

"This doesn't impact you," I gritted, my chest tight.

"It *does* impact me," he insisted, anger and heartbreak and fear tearing his voice apart. "You getting hurt impacts me. It impacts Dad. It impacts the people who care about you, you fucking asshole. You think Aubrey is okay right now?" He pointed at the wall to the arena. "You think she'll be okay watching you fight tomorrow, watching you get your face beat in while your shoulder is fucked? You think that won't affect her? That it won't crush her?"

"It shouldn't." My heart thrashed against my ribs at her name. "This has nothing to do with her."

"Really? Because I thought you were friends. Or was that nothing but a ruse to get her to sleep with you?"

Fresh anger flared in my chest, burning my throat. "Leave it alone, Evan."

"Why should I? She's my best friend, and she deserves better if this is the kind of shit you're going to put her through."

There, we agreed. They both deserved better than me. But I couldn't deal with that now either. My mind felt like it was slipping across an oiled surface toward an edge there was no coming back from, and all I could focus on was trying to claw my way to stable ground.

"You make it sound like I'm going to die," I said, grasping for any sort of ledge to hold on to. "It's just a boxing match."

"Exactly! It's just a fucking boxing match! So let it go—"

"I can't!" I shouted, not realizing I was on my feet until an agonizing heat exploded in my shoulder and wrenched me into a free fall of memories I'd tried like hell to suppress.

Every step and jab of the championship fight in Japan two years ago that injured my shoulder the first time.

Leaving the hospital after a full day of tests to a voicemail from Dad about Mom taking a turn for the worse.

Coach Peters helping me find the flight that would get me home the quickest.

Thirteen hours on a plane, my mind spinning the whole time with the urgency to *go faster*, to *get home*, to *make it to her* before it was too late.

Landing for my layover in Chicago to another voicemail that she was gone.

The blur of time that came after.

I'd sat in the terminal at my arrival gate for four hours, my phone in my hand, tears streaking my face as I missed my connecting flight. Then I missed the one I'd been rebooked on two days later because I couldn't shake the fact that going home would make it real. I'd be there, and she'd be gone, and nothing would make sense anymore, but at the airport, it was like time was suspended. I was in the moment of falling before everything hit the floor and shattered, and if I could just stay there a little longer, I wouldn't have to hear the jarring crash of the glass breaking or deal with picking up the jagged pieces.

Her funeral was the reason I got on a plane. Knowing it would matter to her I was there. That I owed it to her to honor her in at least that way.

But facing it was the hardest thing I'd ever done.

Surviving that week. Seeing her open casket. Not recognizing the face lying there, her skin too flat, her lips somehow wrong.

Everything just wrong.

I refused to let this tournament end the same way. Refused to lose boxing the way I'd lost my mom.

I couldn't control her cancer or her surgery, and I couldn't get her back, but I could control my own body. I could control this.

I *would* fight tomorrow.

I *would* win.

I would get my gym, and through it, I would hold on to this one thing I had left, and I would rip my arm clean off my body if that was what it took to do it.

"I can't," I said again, tone heavy with tears I would not let fall. "I'm sorry I wasn't there for you when Mom died. You're right. You shouldn't have had to handle it on your own. But I need this."

"More than you need me?" he asked, his voice cracking.

The weight of the ocean settled on my chest. "It doesn't have to be one or the other." I willed him to understand. "Evan—if I win, I stay."

No more goodbyes. No more missed holidays. No more piecing together snapshots of each other from secondhand accounts, trying to grasp enough of them not to feel like strangers. He had to want that too.

"What if you don't win? What then?"

I will.

It was the only answer I had, the only option I could focus on right now. The only future I could accept.

It wouldn't be enough for him.

He saw the truth of it on my face. His nostrils flared as his eyes dimmed with resignation. "Looks like I lose either way."

Chapter Thirty
Aubrey

IT WAS late by the time I left the Hardts' house. After Evan had stormed from the boxing arena's back room and informed his dad and me he'd find his own way home, Mr. Hardt and I had tried to check on Gabe ourselves, but he'd already left through a different door and taken his stuff with him.

Concern ate at me as I shot Gabe a text. All I wanted was to hunt each brother down and find some way to make it okay. One look at Mr. Hardt's face told me he wanted to do the same. But we both knew his sons. We went to his house instead.

I waited a bit for Evan, hoping to find out what he and Gabe had said to each other, but after two hours with no sign of him, I finally caught a bus back to the city.

Now, after switching to the subway that would take me closest to my apartment, my thoughts rode away with the steady rocking of the car.

Gabe would try to fight tomorrow.

I knew it as certainly as I knew sugar was sweet. Could see it in the rage on Evan's face as he'd left.

And where the idea of Gabe fighting in the championship match had sent me riding high on a sugar rush before this afternoon, now there was only dread.

Dread if he fought.

Dread if he didn't.

Dread at the realization that the chances of him getting the money he needed for his gym were essentially the same either way.

I hadn't realized how much I'd hung my hopes on him getting that prize money until now. How much I'd believed he would win. That he'd get his loan, open his gym, and stay. How fully I'd believed it would all work out despite knowing from experience how easy it was for everything to go wrong.

I hadn't even been foolish to believe it. He'd been incredible in that ring. An unstoppable force of strength, power, and grace. If it hadn't been for one unlucky punch, all those hopes would still be alive.

Instead, he'd responded to my text to say he'd rather be alone tonight, and the lump knotting my stomach grew bulkier with the weight of rejection.

I tried to shake it off.

Gabe was like Evan. Or maybe Evan was like Gabe. Either way, when they had something intense to process, they did the emotional equivalent of barricading themselves in an underground bunker.

It was why I could handle waiting for Evan to cool off instead of tracking him down. Unless he was ready to talk or stuck in a car with me with nowhere to run, he'd shut down more if I tried to push.

But with Gabe, a greedy part of me wanted to be his exception. To be the one person he let inside the bunker, who offered him what no one else could. The one who made the hurt hurt less just by being there.

I wanted him to need me. So much he never wanted to give me up.

The guilt of it shredded my stomach right alongside where his dismissal dug in its claws. Mixed with the worry rounding out my emotions, it felt like someone had split me open and poured inside the dump bucket Neela kept behind the bar to toss unfinished drinks into.

The mess sloshed around, making me sick, as I hauled my limbs up the stairs of the subway to the darkened street above.

When I reached the sidewalk, I just kind of...stood there. My body too drained to move and my brain too weary to instruct it differently. I'd planned to go home, but the idea of being in my empty apartment, dark, quiet, and solitary, was the last thing I wanted right now.

My stomach spoke up, growling in protest from not eating all afternoon. Between trekking back and forth to the suburbs and worrying about Gabe and Evan, I hadn't thought to.

Which meant I should probably eat a grain bowl or a giant salad—something substantial with a bunch of colors and nourishing stuff like protein and vitamins.

Coming up with a meal that satisfied those parameters and that I also felt like eating right now seemed about as likely as me winning a pair of custom-designed Jimmy Choos.

What I wanted was the culinary equivalent of a hug. Something comforting and sweet I could drown all my worries in, since all the worrying in the world wouldn't change things either way.

I let my legs carry me to the first place that came to mind.

The bell over the door of the Froyo shop a few blocks from my apartment rang as I walked in, and wafts of chocolate and other sweet scents filled my nose. Less than an hour till close on a chilly spring night meant I was the only customer here.

I skimmed the menu as I made my way to the front. This place offered a wide variety, like artisanal ice cream and water ice, which was probably why they hadn't shut down like a lot of other Froyo spots in town.

But I didn't need fancy tonight. I craved something simple and sweet under a mound of candy, cookies, and fruit. And if I could get it without having to decide which of those toppings I ended up with, even better.

I took two twenties from my wallet. "This is probably a weird request," I said to the lone worker, whose long box braids were tied in an intricate knot held back by a brightly patterned headband. It did way more for her cool brown skin than the black corporate T-shirt she had to wear. If I had to guess, she was in college, maybe a little older. I slid one bill across the counter. "If I gave you this and asked you to make me a large Froyo with as many toppings as it would get me in whatever flavor combo you think is best, is that something you'd be up for?"

One dark eyebrow rose above her wire-rimmed glasses. She glanced at the twenty and back at me. I tucked the other twenty into the tip jar.

She shrugged as she put the first twenty in the register and reached for a large cup.

I expected her to dump some vanilla frozen yogurt in the bottom, walk down the row of toppings, grab a spoonful of each, and call it a day. Which—for the record—I'd have been good with. Whatever ended up in that cup worked for me as long as it was more sugar than anything else, and I didn't have to make it myself.

So when she set the cup to the side and headed for the topping bins first, armed with a plastic tray of empty to-go sauce containers, I got curious.

After a moment of contemplation, she filled each sauce container, nine of them total, with a different topping and brought them behind the counter. Then she grabbed the large cup and went to the Froyo machines.

She picked one flavor, filled the cup a fraction of the way, brought it back, and carefully arranged a layer of toppings. Then she set the cup on the scale, checked the weight, and went for more Froyo. This time, she chose a different flavor, still only adding a little bit, before bringing it back and selecting a different set of toppings.

She went through the routine twice more, creating a parfait-style concoction I imagined Jase would make if he ever came here.

When the cup was overflowing and the scale read a few cents shy of twenty dollars, she went for a small cutting board and paring knife, grabbed a strawberry from a fridge behind the counter, and sliced it in a perfect fan before placing it on top of her creation. She stuck a spoon into the cup, slid a rainbow gummy ring over the handle, and handed the whole thing to me.

"You ever work in a restaurant before?" I asked as I took it. She moved like she had. Gathering the ingredients she needed beforehand, being precise and methodical, cleaning her space as she went.

She blinked at the question. "Yeah. I do now, just…as a dishwasher. They haven't let me cook yet."

"Do you want to cook?" I pulled the spoon from the top layer, leaving the gummy ring on the handle, and took a bite. Mmm. Taro Froyo with coconut flakes and white chocolate chips.

Her guarded expression eased slightly when it was clear I enjoyed what she'd made. "I mean, yeah."

"But most restaurants want you to stage for free first, and you can't afford to lose a month's income, right?"

A mix of surprise and suspicion knotted her brows. "Right. I work here because dishwasher pay sucks enough on its own."

I nodded. *Been there.*

"Do me a favor," I said, taking another quick bite before setting the cup down to grab a napkin and scrawl my email on it with the register pen. "Send me your résumé. I'm looking for a chef to join my team, and the pay is way better than a dishwasher. No free labor required."

She scanned the email address. "Ardena?" Her brows rose. "The restaurant on Rittenhouse?"

I smiled. She wasn't washing dishes at McDonald's if she got that excited about Ardena.

"Sort of. The job is with our new catering division. Similar food, high-end events, lots of opportunity to be creative. Think about it." I ate another scoop of frozen yogurt, this one coffee with mini marshmallows, walnuts, and dark chocolate chunks. "And thank you," I mumbled, mouth still full of the delicious bite. "This is perfect."

The corners of her mouth lifted with the makings of a smile as I turned for the door.

Maybe nothing would come of it. She might not apply for the job, and Gabe still was or wasn't going to fight tomorrow. Evan was still MIA, and no amount of gummy rings would fix the fracture between him and his brother.

Nothing was certain. All I'd gained was temporary relief from my wallowing in the form of a sweet treat and the ultimate brain freeze.

Yet it was something. The tiniest flower emerging from a busted-up sidewalk, and if nothing else, I'd let that sliver of hope get me through tonight.

There was no question that whichever way tomorrow went, Froyo wouldn't be enough.

Chapter Thirty-One
Gabe

I KNEW before the doctor said anything. Had known since the moment I woke up this morning after a shit night's sleep, unable to lift my arm.

I wasn't fighting today.

Not today or ever again.

My go in the tournament was finished. Coach's gym—my gym—was gone. I didn't have the money to get the loan, and Coach Lou couldn't push off the developers any longer. Not if he wanted his retirement.

Everything I had trained for since I was fourteen, my life's work, my *life*, was coming to an end in this room, and all I felt was numb.

The doctor had me hold my left elbow at my hip and raise my fist to a ninety-degree angle, then he nudged the outside of my wrist, and that numbness sparked into electric pain that radiated from my shoulder to my fist. I clenched my teeth as my arm gave out, too weak to resist the doctor's slight pressure.

Diego's head dropped where he stood behind the doctor. He pushed aside his suit jacket to rest his hands on his hips. "Gabe…"

"I know," I said, voice flat.

He'd been right yesterday. If he let me in the ring, no coach would let his fighter book with him again. Not to mention it would be a shit performance. People didn't turn on the TV to watch a guy with one functioning arm get knocked out in the first round. Not during a championship fight.

The doctor removed his exam gloves. "You'll want to go to the hospital for X-rays. You may need surgery if it's a complete tear, but you'll need treatment either way."

I nodded. I knew the drill.

He walked to the other side of the room to examine the next fighter, and I lowered into a chair. That simple motion was enough to pull an ache from my shoulder.

Diego watched, face pained. "You fought a hell of a tournament."

It didn't feel like it. It felt like I'd given everything I had and it wasn't enough. Like I'd failed to do the one thing I'd sacrificed everything for.

Again.

Heat crept up my neck as my chest tightened, the air suddenly too thick to inhale. I closed my eyes to block out the pressure, but I couldn't block out the images.

My mom at my first boxing match. My mom's open casket. The hug she'd given me the last time I was home. The cake she'd baked the first time I won a title belt. The brightness in her voice the last time we spoke on the phone, right before her surgery, when we all thought everything would be okay.

With each memory came a sharp stab, deeper and more painful than anything my shoulder had brought.

It was like I'd been running from it all since she'd died, the despair and the grief and the reminders she was really gone, and now it was all crashing on top of me, burying me under its weight.

Mom was gone.

Boxing was gone.

What did I have left?

Aubrey's face flashed across my mind. Her big hazel eyes and bigger, sweeter smile.

God, I'd wanted her with me last night. Had wanted to cradle my arm to my chest, curl against her body, and stop time so I could stay there forever. Just her and me, and nothing else in the world.

But the idea of her seeing me like this, for her to witness my failure up close—I couldn't stand to see the pity in her eyes.

Or worse, the pain.

Evan was right—it would hurt her to watch me fight like this. Hurt her to know that even now, for all the agony I was in and as pathetic a showing as it would be, if they let me, I'd still fight. Her pain wouldn't be enough to stop me, which told me everything I needed to know about me. Everything I already knew.

She was better off without me.

"You going to stick around for a bit?" Diego asked. "I can

introduce you to some people if you want. You can capitalize on all that talk you've been getting."

I squeezed my eyes shut a few more seconds before I gazed up at my old friend, amazed my head would lift. It was like my energy had been sapped from me, my body practically sinking into the chair. "No. I should probably go to the hospital."

"You need a ride? I can find someone to take you."

It was a good question. One I should have been able to answer. Yet even that decision felt like too much.

"I can drive him."

A tall Black man I hadn't noticed in my misery stepped away from the wall to join Diego. He had a shaved head and trimmed beard, and the way he carried his broad build told me he'd thrown around in the ring before.

"Sorry to interrupt," he said, then addressed me. "I was hoping to chat for a bit. I'm happy to drive you to the hospital if you're willing to hear me out on the way."

I glanced at Diego, who shook his head. This wasn't one of his contacts.

My brain itched like I'd seen him before. His plain white polo and black pants did nothing to clue me in.

"I'm sorry, but who are you?" I asked.

If he was offended, he didn't show it. Just gave an amused smirk. "We didn't get to meet at selection camp. I'm Joe Dotson, head coach of the US Olympic boxing team. I wondered if you might be interested in a job."

Chapter Thirty-Two
Aubrey

THE FIRST PIECE of cooking advice Nana ever gave me was to always use a bigger mixing bowl than you think you'll need. As I got older, I began applying that advice to life.

Give yourself more time than you think you'll need. More space. More patience. More rest. No sense in creating a mess of things by trying to force it when giving yourself a little more of what you need from the start could avoid the headache.

And if you didn't have a bigger bowl, it probably meant you needed to cut the recipe or whatever else you were trying to manage in half.

This morning at the arena, when Gabe's promoter friend came out of the back room and told us an Olympic coach had offered Gabe a job, I realized I'd used too small a bowl for my feelings.

After New Year's, I'd thought I could contain those feelings to the same volume they'd been in high school—more of the idea of love than anything tangible or sticky.

But this recipe was far more complex than any I'd contemplated back then. Here I was with my feelings overflowing the rim, dripping down the sides and pooling on the counter, because not only was Gabe not able to fight in the tournament—he was probably leaving again. For good.

None of it should have shocked me. Even before he got hurt, there was always a chance he'd lose the tournament. A chance he'd need to find an opportunity somewhere else.

It was one of the reasons what we'd been doing felt safe. Because he was always going to leave, the way he always had. Here for short bursts, then off on another boxing adventure, doing what he loved. He wouldn't be leaving *me*; he'd just be leaving.

Yet as soon as Diego had said it, I'd turned to Evan and seen the same overflow of emotions in his eyes he no doubt saw in mine. Our hope bursting and hearts breaking.

Because deep down, even if Gabe couldn't fight, we'd still hoped he would stay.

Back at my apartment, I skimmed through my streaming services, trying to find something that would hold my scattered attention enough to keep me from checking my phone every thirty seconds. It was almost seven, and I'd heard nothing from Gabe.

Diego had said he'd gone to the hospital, but there'd been no text. No call. No word about his shoulder or mention of the job. No form of communication at all since his message the day before saying he wanted to be alone.

Was he okay? In shock? Devastated about the gym?

Ecstatic about the job offer? Bleeding out in a dark alley after being mugged on the street?

I could text him and ask. See if he wanted to talk.

But what if that made it worse? What if he felt like I was hovering and making this about me instead of giving him the space he needed?

He knew where I was if he wanted me. Had known he could reach out since way before New Year's, and I hadn't had to chase him down for it to happen. No point in that changing just because we'd slept together.

Something snagged in my chest, and I slammed whatever door tried to open firmly shut. There'd be no thinking about what might have been or revisiting memories and wishing for more. No feeling bad for myself when this was what I'd signed up for from the start—casual and temporary.

I abandoned the streaming services and sprawled across my couch, clicking into my email on my phone. I paused when I spotted the new sous-chef application in my inbox.

It was the worker from the Froyo shop. Mackenzie Bishop. Not only did she—or rather they—actually apply, but their experience was solid. They didn't have a lot of it, still fairly new out of culinary school, but that they'd been to culinary school at all was a pleasant surprise, and in some ways, the lack of experience was better. Made them a fresher slate, still willing to learn.

I hit send on my reply to schedule an interview as a knock came at my door. My neighbor must have gotten more of my mail. That, or my landlord wanted to inform me about upcoming building maintenance.

I pulled out my hair tie and combed my fingers through

the strands in an attempt to look presentable in my pink pineapple pajama pants. Not that anyone would judge me for them on a Sunday evening, but I also wasn't wearing a bra, and I didn't know how obvious that was through this shirt.

Except it wasn't my landlord I saw through the peephole. My pulse skidded as I swung the door open.

Gabe filled the doorway, his hunched shoulders making him seem smaller than usual. Defeated. Like someone had punctured him with a thumbtack, and all his air had seeped out.

My heart thumped faster as I stepped aside. "Do you want to come in?"

He drank me in with his darkened gaze before nodding, his silence following him across the threshold like a presence I wished I could lock out. It loomed behind us as we made our way to the living room.

"Can I get you anything?" I asked, no longer able to stand it. "Water? Have you eaten?"

"At the hospital," he said, his voice a low rasp. It folded around me the way I wanted to wrap my arms around him. "I meant to text you while I was there, but my phone died. I guess I forgot to charge it last night." He sounded as beaten as his body must have been. Too drained to feel much of anything.

"It's okay," I said as I sat, focusing on the fact that he was here. That mattered most to me right now.

He dropped to the opposite cushion like he could no longer carry his weight, his elbows crashing to his knees.

I thought back to the last time we sat on this couch, the night I asked him to have sex with me. My nerves had been a living thing under my skin, warring with my desire, and he'd comforted them both. Allowed me to feel them fully. Eased me into asking for what I wanted.

It was my turn to comfort him.

"Is your shoulder okay?"

He stared at the vase of tulips on my coffee table. I wasn't sure he actually saw them.

"They're recommending surgery," he finally said. "Not right away. Coach Dotson has a guy he's going to put me in touch with. A shoulder specialist he says is good."

"Coach Dotson is who drove you to the hospital? The Olympic coach?" I ignored the wooden skewer lodged in my chest.

He nodded, still looking at the flowers. That I couldn't see his eyes bothered me as much as his silence had.

"I heard he offered you a job." No point avoiding it. My pitch was shaky, but it came out neutral enough.

"Full-time assistant coach. I'd work with him in the central office. Help oversee training camps and selections."

I swallowed. "The central office...is in Colorado?" That was where the selection camp had been.

He nodded.

"That's an incredible opportunity, right?"

His brows rose in disbelief, as if words alone couldn't describe it. "It's a dream job."

The ache in my chest caught in my throat, making it harder to breathe. I'd already known what this job meant for him, but hearing the words made it worse. Made it *real*. Enough that my heart cracked at the confirmation of what else I'd known since Diego stepped out of the arena's back room.

This was goodbye.

Not just an end to whatever the past two months had been but an end to having Gabe physically in my life. To seeing him at game nights and grabbing coffee on the museum steps. To being able to hug him when I needed and taking comfort in the familiar fresh scent of his deodorant mixed with the salty musk of his sweat.

Yet I couldn't not be happy for him. Happy something good had come from all this pain.

Except he didn't sound excited.

He blew out a long breath and buried his head in his hands. "What does it mean if I don't think I deserve it?"

My heart broke more at the doubt in his voice, at the jagged notes of confusion and weariness. "It means you gave all of yourself to something that didn't work out, and that defeat makes it hard for you to accept how amazing you are."

He scoffed. "I'm not. Just ask Evan."

"What happened between you two yesterday?"

Gabe kept his eyes on the floor, like he didn't want to look at me while he remembered. "We both said some things… some that needed to be said. A lot I wish I hadn't."

My curiosity swelled like a tidal wave, a hundred questions circling my mind, but I bit my tongue and focused on him.

"I don't know how I got here," he said, grief scraping the words from his chest. "It's like I stepped into the ring at High Hitter two years ago and was knocked into another life. Some alternate universe where nothing makes sense. And each time I try to get back to a place I recognize, something else happens that smacks me sideways and takes me further from where I'm meant to be."

I knew that off-kilter sensation. Like being tossed in a

dryer set to high. Some days, I was still trying to regain my balance.

He shook his head. "This job wasn't the plan. It wasn't even a possibility. I was never supposed to be an Olympic coach, so how do I say yes when it never should have been?"

"Because things that shouldn't be happen all the time. Cancer. Car accidents. Natural disasters. The kind too unlikely to believe. Saying yes to the good things is how we keep living."

"I haven't done a good job of that lately."

"You haven't stopped trying either." Sometimes trying looked like training for a boxing tournament. Sometimes it was simply replying to a text.

It all counted. Even when it didn't work out the way you hoped.

"I'm sorry about your gym," I said softly, wishing I had better comfort to offer. "I know how much you wanted it."

He stared blankly at the tulips. "I wanted to fix things with Evan too. Earn back his trust. I thought…" His mouth pulled tight. "I don't know. I thought maybe I could fix it with the gym. But I don't know what happens to that now."

The longing in his voice was almost too much to bear. "Evan will be happy for you."

He scoffed harder this time.

"Hey." I scooched closer and almost reached for his chin but stopped myself, unsure if I could still touch him like I would have before. If we were still us or had crossed over into whatever we became next. "Look at me."

He tilted his head, his eyes finally meeting mine. Their stunning blue was clouded with uncertainty.

"Evan *will* be happy for you," I said, tone firm. I didn't

need to know what they'd said to each other to know it was true. "Because even if he hated you, he'd still want you to be happy. He knows how hard you've worked. How much you deserve this. And you *do* deserve it. Just like you deserved to win High Hitter, and this tournament, and to have a gym of your own. You deserve a job doing what you love."

His hand shot out for mine and squeezed tight.

I squeezed back, wanting to hang on to whatever piece of him I could. "And you can still rebuild your relationship with Evan from Colorado. He might even be more open to it that way. You can call and text. Go back to regular video calls. Show him you still want to be there for him even if you can't be *here*." My throat constricted on the last word.

"I'd be leaving you behind too," he said softly. Too softly for me to identify the emotion in his voice.

Knowing him, he hated being the one to call things off. Hated having to say no to me when he'd tried so hard to always say yes. From the start, he'd wanted to go by my terms, and he would have wanted to end on them too. But it was what it was.

I forced a shaky smile. "It's not like it's goodbye. We'll still be friends."

He squeezed my hand again. "That's what you want?"

My heart was being shoved through a garlic press. I couldn't speak for a moment, my throat too clogged with words I wished I could say. Words like *I want you. I love you. Stay.*

Words I'd planned to say to him at one point but no longer would. The same words I'd wished to say more than once in my life.

To my parents, who wouldn't have stayed no matter how hard I begged.

To Nana, who would have stayed if it was within her power not to grow old.

To Mrs. Hardt, who would have stayed for her husband and sons as much as for me.

Gabe would want to stay too, if only to give me what I wanted. But it wasn't what *he* wanted, and I refused to put him in the position of having to let me down. Of thinking he wasn't worthy of his dream because it might make me unhappy. As if my happiness meant more than his.

It didn't. Not to me. And if he wouldn't protect it, I would.

I met his eyes. "I want *your* dreams to come true." He'd already given me more than one of mine.

His gaze softened, clinging to mine as his grip on my hand tightened. It almost looked like he was fighting against himself until something gave way, and he pulled me forward to capture my lips with his.

It was hard and consuming, a desperate kiss made of want and need, and I kissed him back like I'd die if I didn't, my free hand finding his good shoulder to hold on to as my heart flew high and fast.

His kisses turned staggered, his mouth leaving then returning, as if he was still at war with himself.

"Can I?" he breathed between presses of his lips, his large hand cradling my cheek.

I couldn't speak, my voice gone with my heart, so I clasped him tighter, my fingers twisting in the collar of his shirt, and nodded against his mouth. I wanted him to kiss me more than anything.

I wanted him to kiss me forever.

And if I couldn't have that, I would at least have this. One last moment with him in this way. One more chance for my body to say what the rest of me wouldn't.

I want you. I love you. Stay.

And then, I'd let him go.

Chapter Thirty-Three
Gabe

Aubrey nodded against my lips, and this time, I didn't pull away. I kissed her like I needed her lips on mine to breathe. Like my very existence depended on the feel of her mouth, the softness of her cheek beneath my hand, on being as close to her as I could.

I released her hand to cup both sides of her face, and the shift of my torso made my shoulder groan. I ignored it and drew her closer.

In some ways, I welcomed the pain. Needed it as a reminder of why I didn't get to keep her in my arms. I'd only end up breaking her the way I broke everything. Taking from her the way I took from everyone close to me, never considering how it might hurt them.

I'd hurt her worse if I stayed. I wouldn't mean to, but I would.

If my mom's death had taught me anything, it was that I was selfish, and without trying, that selfishness would lead me to let the people who cared about me down. Better I stayed away than let them care about me at all. Better I loved them from afar than do more damage than I already had.

Aubrey's fingers threaded my hair, and I parted her lips with my tongue.

One last time. One last time I would be selfish with her. One last time I would take as much of her as she was willing to give me.

I hadn't waited for her to take the lead, too afraid she wouldn't. Too afraid she'd say we were friends and I would have to go back to the way we were before New Year's like I promised her I would.

I wasn't ready. Not to go back to wanting her from afar like I had since the Thanksgiving before my mom died. Not to give up the taste of her on my tongue and the heady scent of her coconut shampoo or the unrestrained trust she handed me every time I touched her.

Even now, she inched forward on the couch, trying to get closer as if being with me made her feel as whole as being with her did me.

I scooped her onto my lap, and she squeaked as I stood, wrapping her legs around my waist as I trailed kisses down her neck.

"Your shoulder," she said, barely grazing my left arm with her fingers.

"It's okay." I sucked below her ear and strode for her bedroom, the pain in my shoulder dulling against my need for her.

She pressed soft kisses along my shoulder as if to make it better. If anyone's touch could, it would be hers.

I eased us onto her bed, bracing myself over her on my

right arm, and kissed her again. Her hands snaked around my torso, pulling more of my weight onto her, connecting us from chests to hips. I was hard, my erection nestled between her thighs, but even that felt secondary to kissing her. Holding her. Existing here with her.

"Let me feel your skin?" I murmured against her lips.

Her nod was instant, her hands already peeling off my T-shirt.

I sat back to pull it over my head, then ran my hands along the soft rise of her stomach, lifting her shirt's hem as I went, revealing each of her tattoos. She arched her back so I could free her from it completely, no bra in sight.

"You're beautiful," I said as I drew my thumb across one breast. My tongue followed, swirling over her nipple before switching to the other, her chest rising and falling with quickened breaths.

She scraped her fingers lightly over my scalp, sending a shiver down my spine that tightened my balls and made my cock throb.

Moving lower, I kissed the vines and butterflies tattooed along her ribs, then dragged my lips across her belly to reach the daisies on her hip. I worked the waistband of her pants down, kissing each inch of newly discovered skin, sucking briefly on her clit, committing every part of her to memory.

Only when I had her completely naked did I bother with my own pants. I almost kept my head between her legs all night, not wanting to give up her taste or her wetness on my tongue, but I needed the feel of her body against mine more.

Her eyes devoured me as she slid her gaze over my torso and below my waist before quickly bringing it back to mine.

We stayed there for a moment, watching each other. Both

fully bare and at our most vulnerable. Both not hiding, letting the other see.

Being seen by her was better than any sex. And sex with her...

I couldn't wait anymore. I lowered myself to her, my eyes falling closed at her softness. Her smooth skin. The warmth of her body and the clasp of her thighs. I opened my eyes and looked into her hazel gaze, rocking my hips to feel more of her.

My length slid over her clit, and we both groaned. I did it again, raising goose bumps along my skin.

"You still have those condoms I gave you?" I whispered against her lips. She'd wanted a few on hand in case I ever forgot one or we needed extra. Her tongue slid into my mouth as my cock slid along her slit. My body shuddered. I wanted to bury myself in her heat and never leave.

"Yeah, but—" She moaned, rocking her hips to meet mine. "Not yet. Keep doing this. God, you feel so good."

Fuck, so did she. I dropped my head to the mattress alongside her cheek and drew back my hips, rocking forward in one long glide, letting her feel all of me. My cock was coated in her arousal, our bodies growing sticky with sweat, and for a moment, I imagined what it would be like to slip inside her bare. To have absolutely nothing between us. To empty myself in her and give her all of me in a way I hadn't with anyone else.

It was enough to let myself imagine other things. That I'd won the tournament and gotten my gym. That my dad and Evan both had been in the front row, celebrating with me. That when Aubrey jumped into my arms to congratulate me,

I'd kissed her like I was kissing her now. With my whole body. Unrestrained. Not hiding any of how I felt for her.

I let myself imagine one day being married. Let myself imagine Aubrey being that wife. That I was making love to her as her husband. Her partner. That we were sharing a life together. Raising kids together. Chasing the things we both wanted, together.

Teammates.

Life mates.

Two people who belonged to each other.

Who loved each other.

"Aubrey." A low groan escaped me as my muscles strained, my rhythm picking up. I'd have to stop soon or I'd come. But the way her hips were circling and her breath had caught told me she was on the verge herself. "Breathe, baby. Breathe into it."

"Gabe," she whimpered.

"I got you." I kept up my rhythm, sliding against her clit with long, steady strokes. "Let it go. That's it. That's it."

Her head flew back, eyes squeezed shut as her body convulsed as if the pleasure jumped through her like electricity. I focused on her face, memorizing the flush that stained her cheeks and the way her lips fell apart. When her muscles relaxed, I kissed her neck and behind her ear.

"Condoms are in the nightstand," she whispered, voice shaky.

I pulled back to meet her gaze. Her eyes were shiny. "You okay to keep going?"

"Please don't stop."

I wouldn't. Not until she told me to. That or we couldn't

stay awake any longer. If this was my last night with her, I would make it last as close to forever as I could.

I got up and rounded the bed, grabbing all three condoms from the nightstand. When I returned to kneel between her legs, she plucked one from my hand.

"Let me," she said.

Her hands were steady as she opened the wrapper and placed the condom on my tip. We held each other's gazes as she rolled it over my length, just like she had the first time we'd had sex. My cock jumped in her hand.

I'd never wanted a woman the way I wanted her. I braced myself on my right forearm and let her line me up at her entrance.

"Ready?" I breathed, brushing her hair from her forehead.

"Ready."

I eased my hips forward, her clasp around me unreal. So warm. So wet. Her body opened for me like it was welcoming me home.

I cupped her cheek. "You're amazing," I whispered, wishing I could give her more. Be more. Be everything she deserved.

Tears welled in her eyes, one escaping down her cheek. I wiped it away with my thumb as my own eyes burned.

Her lips lifted into a shaky smile. "Kiss me."

I dragged my thumb over her bottom lip as more of her tears fell. Then I held her gaze as I pressed my mouth to hers, matching the tempo of our bodies coming together in the gentlest of waves. Our stares stayed connected, mouths tangled, hips rocking, neither of us looking away as something too big to name built between us.

When her next orgasm hit, she melted into it, moaning as if taken by surprise. The way her inner muscles contracted around me and the way she breathed my name like a chant had my hips pumping faster, chasing her pleasure with my own. When it had strung me up tight enough to cut off my breath, I gave a final thrust and let go, pulsing my release into the condom, the feeling so good I thought I might die.

Her arms around me, holding me to her as she buried her face in the crook of my neck, was the first thing I registered when my thoughts came back online. The ache in my left shoulder from collapsing my weight onto it was the second.

I shifted to check on her, but her hold on me tightened. "Not yet," she mumbled against my skin. Her voice was thick with emotion. "Just...don't go yet."

Letting more of my weight settle over her, I lowered my forehead to her mane of blond waves. The scent of coconut and *her* washed over me, easing my muscles.

I'd stay.

Despite everything in me that wanted the best for her screaming it was wrong, if she asked me to stay, I would. If she told me it was what she wanted, what she needed, I didn't think I would be strong enough to deny her. Not when it was what I wanted too.

But she wasn't asking me that. She probably knew as well as I did what a terrible idea it would be.

All she was asking for was right now. One more moment of comfort in each other's arms before returning to a sensible path.

I ignored my aching shoulder, not caring about it at the moment, though I'd need to take care of the condom soon.

But for a minute, I'd savor holding her and pretending she was mine.

Pretending I was hers too.

Chapter Thirty-Four
Aubrey

I WIPED the edge of a dessert plate with my towel, letting the precise movement soothe my mind. For the first time I could remember, cooking in the catering prep kitchen brought me a kind of peace. Almost like something had settled that allowed the space to feel more like home. Or the start of one, at least.

The five dishes Jase and I had brainstormed for the catering competition sat completed on the counter, and they felt better too. Not quite perfect, but something I was proud of. And grateful to be able to sink myself into after last night with Gabe.

If I thought about it too much, I'd end up crying again, and it wasn't something I wanted to cry over. Crying made it seem sad, like something else to mourn, when what Gabe and I had shared these past few months was something I wanted to celebrate. To think back on and smile. To remember the confidence he helped me feel and the boldness I'd found, the freedom it had given me. To have experienced that level of passion safely, in a way that nothing had been taken from me that I wasn't ready to give.

It had been perfect. Especially last night.

Right now, there were also just tears. So many of them sitting below the surface, ready to pour out of me at the slightest nudge, like a giant Jenga tower of emotions balanced on a single block I was desperately trying to keep standing.

I would have to see Gabe again before he left for Colorado, and no doubt at several points in the future, and I couldn't be a weepy mess in front of him. He couldn't know how hard it was for me to say goodbye or realize I ached for him in any way beyond the physical. I wouldn't let him take on that guilt or feel like he didn't deserve to choose his own path forward because of me. I would be fine.

I was lucky enough to have experienced more than one kind of passion in life, and the satisfaction I got from my job would be more than enough to make me happy. Even if sometimes that work had to happen alone like it did this morning. That didn't mean *I* was alone. And unlike a few months ago, it felt true.

The thud of a knock on the door rang through the space, and I checked my phone for the time.

Five minutes early. Off to a good start.

I pushed open the back door to let in the young chef.

Their braids today were pulled up in another patterned headband, but instead of the Froyo tee, they wore the standard chef uniform—a plain white T-shirt and loose black chef pants. The large teal cloud-shaped hoops they'd added to the outfit gave the vibe they would rock some stellar press-on nails when they weren't working.

"Mackenzie Bishop?" I confirmed as they stepped inside. "I'm Aubrey Witter. Nice to officially meet you."

They shook my hand. "Mack is fine." Their nails were clean and unpolished. Another good sign.

"Mack. Got it. I go by she/her pronouns. Your résumé said you use she/they. Do you have a preference?"

They adjusted the strap of their bag on their shoulder. "Not really. I usually go by she/her at work."

"Is that what you want to go by here?"

She nodded.

"She/her it is. Let me know if that changes, all right?"

Another nod.

"You can hang your bag there." I pointed at the coat hooks on the wall behind the door. "Grab your apron if you have one. We'll do some cooking later. For now, why don't you tell me a little about yourself? What made you want to be a chef?"

We talked for a bit while I got a feel for her. She'd grown up in Philly with both parents and a younger sister. Her parents kept their meals pretty basic growing up, and after seeing food posts on social media and watching a bunch of cooking videos online, she took it upon herself to experiment with the kind of food she'd been curious to try. That led her to culinary school and, after a year of washing dishes and serving frozen yogurt while she waited for her shot, here.

"You don't want to stick with a traditional restaurant?" I asked. "This won't be as structured. The schedule will be all over the place, depending on the event."

She shrugged. "I'm more interested in the food than the schedule. And I don't think I'm really a fan of big kitchens. Something small like this seems cool."

"Okay, well…" I gestured to the lineup of plates on the counter. "Here's a peek at the food. Have a taste and tell me what you think."

Her eyes brightened as she took in the dishes, and excitement sparked in my belly. I wrestled it down, not wanting to get ahead of myself. There were still a thousand reasons she could end up not working out.

I passed her a silverware roll and stepped aside so the countertop was hers to explore. She took a moment to look at the dishes together, then homed in on the hors d'oeuvre, leaning closer to examine it from all angles. After a couple of deep breaths to capture the aroma, she gathered a bite with her fork and had her first taste.

Nothing on her face gave her away. She could have loved it or hated it, but after a few seconds studying the bite, she moved on to the appetizer and repeated the same steps.

My nerves disintegrated into Pop Rocks bursting throughout my body. It didn't matter what she said about the dishes; she was hired. Everything I needed to know was in how she approached the food. Like she respected it. Like she was trying to learn from it. Like she wanted to give it her best.

I could help her reach her best. The same way Jase helped me.

He could help her too. Between her and the guys, we could foster a whole new set of chefs, bring new voices to Ardena. And I could already tell she'd make me better too.

When she'd finished her bite of the dessert, she lowered the fork and turned to me. I gave a nod of encouragement.

"It's…" She appraised the dishes again, a faint smile tugging her lips. "Really good. The progression is awesome. Everything makes sense, and the presentation is gorgeous…"

I tried not to smile at the note of something else in her voice. "But?"

Her gaze lingered on the entrée as she fought her hesitation, no doubt a holdover from whatever kitchen she'd apprenticed in during culinary school that probably drilled the expectation of never questioning the head chef. We'd work through that real quick.

She finally let the words free. "The rhubarb-glazed squab…I'd use duck instead."

I nodded in concession and gestured at the counter. "Let's try it."

She beamed and reached for her apron as I went to grab the duck still in the walk-in from recipe testing earlier in the week.

Her knife skills proved to be as clean as I expected from someone who went to culinary school, and she asked the kinds of questions only someone with a strong understanding of flavor profiles and cooking techniques would. She even plated the dish to be nearly identical to the original, committing to her placement of components rather than giving her hands the chance to shake.

When it was time to taste the updated version, I let her go first, then followed her steps of smelling the dish before taking a careful bite.

She sought out my reaction, but I made her go first.

Her opinion came out quicker this time. "The texture's not as good."

"No. That's why we ended up going with squab. But this has a richer flavor. It might be worth trying to combine the two."

"You mean like rendering the duck fat and using it to

cook the squab?"

"That could work. There's a risk it will be too busy, but we won't know until we taste it. You want to come back tomorrow and give it a try?"

She grinned. "Really?"

I grinned back. "This week is all about fine-tuning this tasting menu to submit by Friday's competition deadline. Then we're back to events. If you're still interested, I'd love you to join me for both."

"I'm so in."

A wedge of frustration that had been jammed between my ribs for weeks dissolved as another piece of the catering puzzle settled, and an eagerness for tomorrow shimmered throughout the kitchen.

"Here," I said, digging my phone out of my apron pocket. "I'll email you the paperwork Jillian will need so you can bring it back tomorrow."

A text message popped on my screen before I had the chance. I read it and froze.

"Is…everything okay?" Mack asked when I didn't move.

It took me longer than it should have to process her question. Then longer still to answer it. As soon as I could, my body snapped into action.

"No." I ripped off my apron and spun to find my bag. "I'm going to have Jillian email you the forms instead. I'm so sorry, but I have to go. Don't worry about locking up." I'd ask Jillian to handle that too. She'd have one of the guys run over if she couldn't do it.

"Sure, no worries," Mack said as I rushed by.

I attempted another smile, hoping to whatever goddess

ruled the kitchen that I hadn't just lost the perfect sous chef for my team, but I couldn't worry about it now. I pushed through the door and took off for the subway, dialing Evan's number on the way.

Chapter Thirty-Five
Gabe

IT HAD BEEN one gray-as-fuck day, the sky dreary and dark, a perfect match for my mood. Even rain would have been better than the endless clouds. They made it impossible to escape the gloom that had shrouded me since I left Aubrey's apartment early this morning.

I'd planned to leave earlier and not stay the night, but every time I told myself it would be the last kiss, one kiss turned into two, which turned into more, our hands roaming, mouths seeking, bodies joining together in pleasure so strong, it drowned me.

I was still drowning.

Last night may have been our last together, but I'd been over my head in my feelings for Aubrey since the moment she first kissed me, and none of me wanted to come up for air. I'd rather my lungs burned forever surrounded by the thought of her than take another breath without her at the forefront of my mind. It didn't matter whether I was in Philly or Colorado.

Letting her go was what I'd do to protect her.

Hanging on to the contentment she'd poured into my heart was what I'd do for me.

Even now, as I stepped out of the subway to meet Coach Dotson at the bar of his Center City hotel to discuss the job offer, I carried her with me. I wished I had something more concrete, a picture of us or a trinket of hers, but everything she'd given me had been from within.

Maybe I could get a picture with her before I left. I could ask my dad to have us take it so seemed like his idea.

Or maybe it would be okay if I asked. Friends took pictures together. They were allowed to hang on to memories of each other. To miss each other.

My phone buzzed in my pocket, which meant my reception had returned. Service had gotten better on the subway, but there were still dead zones, and it always took my phone a few minutes to bounce back.

I expected a text from Coach Dotson letting me know he'd be a few minutes late, but it was a voicemail.

From Evan.

He hadn't called me once in the months I'd been back. Not to mention, I didn't think he was speaking to me after our fight at the tournament.

My heart sped up as I played the message.

"Gabe—" His voice was panicked, the muffled yell of sirens screaming in the background. *"Dad had a heart attack. He was awake in the ambulance, but they just took him inside, and I don't know what's going on. We're at Philly Memorial. We were in the city for*

dinner, and he was fine, and then he collapsed and—I-I don't know when you'll get this. Just call me."

The line clicked dead, and for the second time in my life, the world around me skidded to a halt.

The phone's weight in my hand was all I could process as my heart beat faster and faster. Its pounding filled my ears like gloves on a bag, the punches too quick to keep up with, as if each attempt to make sense of the message got knocked down before it could reach me. A buzz built in my head—

And then, the world slammed back into motion. Car horns blared at a nearby intersection, and the first drops of rain splashed cold on my face. A bus rumbled past, its brakes squeaking as it slowed, exhaust fumes fogging my nose.

My vision came into focus on the building across the sidewalk where a hotel's logo was fixed on the brick.

The hotel that held the man in charge of my future.

I stared at the logo a few seconds longer as my pulse pummeled my ribs, my throat, my ears. Almost at once, the racing dropped to a perfect calm, my body taking charge of the shock and putting my mind back into the driver's seat.

I took a deep breath, forcing air into my lungs. More rain splashed my face.

Another breath, a final glance.

Then I turned the other way and ran.

Five minutes later, I burst through the emergency entrance of Philadelphia Memorial Hospital, drenched in rain and sweat. My shoulder screamed at how hard I'd sprinted, and I was still catching my breath when I stepped off the elevator to the cardiology unit and crossed into the waiting room.

Evan paced between two rows of chairs. He spun at the far end, saw me, and stopped short. His face was a wall of stone.

"He's in surgery," he said, voice rigid.

The words hit me like a battering ram—a single strike straight to my core.

They should have been reinforcement. Surgery meant Dad was getting help. It meant there was something they could do. That he'd gotten here in time.

Instead, those three words knocked me right back to Mom. To the standard procedure meant to buy her more time that became the start to an end none of us were ready for.

To an airport terminal and a shitty hotel, its thin walls the only thing standing between me and devastation.

My hands shook, my body getting ready to pull up the same defenses. One look at Evan told me he was doing the same.

Except where I'd barricaded myself from the worst of the storm, he'd been caught dead in its center. Both times.

As hard as I gritted my teeth against the familiar terror, the onslaught of worry and helplessness and straight-up fear, it had to be worse for him. He'd sat in this very hospital while our mom got sicker and witnessed her fade. Had watched our dad collapse in front of him and get rushed away on a stretcher.

He'd faced it. Carried what I hadn't.

I wouldn't let him face it alone again.

I met his gaze, his blue eyes as gruesome as the downpour

beyond the wall of windows at our side. "What do you need?" I asked.

His nostrils flared, and his jaw flexed.

Then his wall of stone crumbled.

I reached him in five steps and caught him as he collapsed in my arms. His hands clung to the back of my shirt, twisting it in his fists as his tears soaked my already wet collar. I held him to me while sobs rattled his body, letting him fall apart. My own tears filled my throat.

We both needed our dad to come out of surgery.

We both needed him to be okay.

We both needed not to face another goodbye.

We both needed each other too.

I didn't know how many of those we would walk away with at the end of this. But I would stand here, holding us up until I couldn't stand anymore.

Chapter Thirty-Six
Aubrey

It took me twenty minutes to get to the hospital. I'd considered taking a cab, but the rush-hour traffic meant driving would take as long as the subway, and sprinting through the stations at least made it feel like I was getting there faster. I tried calling Evan on the way, but he didn't answer, leaving me with nothing but his single text to go on.

Evan: Dad had a heart attack. At Philly Memorial

I could strangle him. He'd always been brief in text, but he could have at least let me know how bad it was, his dad's current status—*something*.

Beneath the fright, I recognized he probably didn't know much more than I did and was dealing with doctors and paperwork and shock, all while trying not to have a panic attack from being back in the hospital where his mom had died. It was why I hadn't kept calling. The best way for me to figure out what was going on was to get there.

I did try calling Gabe, but his phone went to voicemail too, and I didn't want to leave a message about this. Not until I had more information.

It turned out I didn't need to. He was already in the waiting room when I found the right one, with Evan slouched in the chair beside him.

The picture tugged at my heart, throwing me back to theme park trips and visits to the museum growing up when they would sit side by side on a bench just like that. Except those times, Evan had usually beamed up at his big brother, laughing at something Gabe said.

Now, they both looked drained. Two worn rags with every drop wrung out.

They lifted their heads as I approached. Evan's eyes were red and puffy.

"How is he?" I asked, bracing for the worst.

"In surgery," Evan said. "No word yet how it's going."

Surgery. A thousand thoughts had to be running through his head from that one word. At least that many ran through mine, few of them comforting.

Before I could think of what to say, Gabe took Evan's hand in his and squeezed it. More surprising still was Evan squeezed it back.

I sought Gabe's eyes, no clue what I would see there. Between the tournament, his shoulder, the coaching offer, and last night—so much had happened in so short a time, I wouldn't blame him for shutting down completely.

But he hadn't. His gaze shone clearly with warmth, fear,

and above all, determination. The kind he wore into a fight, ready to withstand any swing that came his way.

I reached for his left hand with my right and Evan's right with my left, connecting us in a circle. They clasped my hands back, grounding us together in a way that felt like if we could just hold on, everything would be okay.

I poured every ounce of love, strength, and hope I had into those bonds. Then all we could do was wait.

AN HOUR LATER, Evan was passed out on Gabe's right shoulder, and I had taken the seat on Gabe's left. Still no word on their dad. None of us had said anything since we'd joined hands earlier, finding a strange comfort in the silence, but it was taking everything in me not to break that silence now.

Normally, I had no problem not talking, especially when things were intense. But sitting next to Gabe, all I could think was how I probably wouldn't have many more opportunities to spend with him in person, and I didn't want to waste it.

I also didn't want to throw him off if *he* preferred the silence. He saved me from having to guess.

"I've been trying to decide what my mom would be doing if she were here," he said quietly, his focus directed out at the room. "I've narrowed it down to yoga by the window or holding that woman's hands and telling her everything will be okay."

I followed the shift of his gaze to the family in the row of chairs perpendicular to ours, a woman in probably her late sixties holding a fist to her mouth while tears wet her cheeks.

Three younger adults—her kids, I guessed—sat shell-shocked around her.

Immediately, my brain filled in the image of Mrs. Hardt kneeling in front of her, holding the woman's hands between hers, murmuring words of encouragement. To hold on to hope. That doctors could do miracles these days. That her husband or mother or sister—whoever it was—would pull through and be bitching about the hospital food in no time. It was in her nature to put others at ease and prop them up when they were ready to fall down—like a dowel propped up a plant whose leaves had grown too heavy for its stem.

"She was always solid in a crisis," I said. My lips rose. "Remember when Evan flipped his bike and broke his arm, and I went screaming down the street to call nine-one-one?"

Gabe broke into a grin. "Didn't you actually scream nine-*nine*-one?"

I laughed, remembering. "Yeah. Your mom came outside, calmly jogged to Evan, moved his bike onto the lawn, and carried him to the car. I was melting down because I thought his arm was going to need to be cut off, and she didn't even blink."

She'd been my superhero. And when she got sick, she'd been stronger than all of us.

I tried to carry some of her strength now. Gabe seemed to be doing the same. Maybe between the two of us, we could offer a fraction of her comfort to each other.

My phone buzzed in my bag, and I dug it out to find a message from Jillian.

Jillian: Looks like a keeper.

Two photos were attached to her message: one of a spotless prep kitchen and one of Mack's completed paperwork.

Me: She cleaned the kitchen?

I figured she'd just leave, and if I was lucky, she might come back.

Jillian: Was mopping the floor when Luis got there. I added the time to her payroll.

My shoulders sagged in relief.

Me: Thank you

Jillian: Go be with your family.

I didn't have to tell her that was what the Hardts were to me.

"Everything okay with work?" Gabe asked. "You didn't leave an event, did you?"

"No." I showed him the pictures. "I finally have the start to my team."

It brought back the buzz of excitement I'd had when plans for the catering division were first underway. I'd missed that buzz. Missed looking forward to being in the kitchen.

Allowing myself to open up to Jillian had helped. It made me feel like she really was on my team, a partner, even though I technically worked for her. She and Jase had that sort of dynamic at Ardena, but it had taken this long for me to embrace that I got to have it now too. Almost like I'd been stuck in my sous-chef mentality and had finally stepped into the role of head chef for real.

I looked at Gabe. "Thank you for helping me with all this. You really kept me going."

Professionally, these had been the toughest months of my life. Tougher even than after my grandma and Mrs. Hardt had died.

Back then, work had been a refuge from the grief. Something I could sink into the tempo of since I wasn't the one leading the ship. Every little decision hadn't come down to me. I just did what I was told, even if the one giving the orders was an egotistical prick.

This was the first time I'd had to navigate things on my own, and in what had sometimes felt like floating alone at sea, Gabe had been my inflatable raft.

He gave me a doubtful look. "I didn't do anything."

"Yes, you did. You helped me prep for that wedding when the guy I hired bailed. You went with me to get menu inspiration and had my back with Christian. You let me vent and made it okay that I missed my old job. You reminded me I still had a team."

He'd given me the courage to go to Jillian and Jase for help when, before, I would have rather muscled through the frustration on my own for fear of being a burden.

I never felt like one with Gabe. He'd made me feel safe to voice my wants and needs. To let myself have them in the first place.

He squirmed in his chair as I rattled off the list but didn't argue against it. Which was good. In the same way I needed to let myself accept it was okay to sometimes take from others, he needed to accept he was capable of giving.

Not just capable. Exceptional.

There wasn't a doubt in my mind how much of himself he would give to his fighters as a coach in Colorado. Envy rooted deep in my chest at how lucky they were.

I was about to ask about the job, since he'd probably gotten more details by now, but a man in dark green scrubs walked into the waiting room.

Gabe and I lurched to our feet as he headed our way, startling Evan from his sleep. He blinked a few times, saw the doctor coming, and jumped to his feet beside us.

The doctor greeted us. "I'm Dr. Cho," he said, shaking our hands in turn. "I'm the surgeon on your father's case. He's doing well."

Our collective breaths released.

"He was lucky. We had to place three stents in his heart to open the blockages, but so far, they seem to be holding, and his blood flow has improved. I'd like to keep him for a couple of days to monitor him closely, but I have every reason to believe he'll be fine."

"When can we see him?" Evan asked.

"We had to put him under general anesthesia, so it will be an hour or two before he's awake and settled in his room. A nurse will come get you as soon as he is. I'll check on him regularly throughout the night and will be around tomorrow to talk through any questions."

"Thank you," Gabe said.

We shook his hand again and watched him leave.

Evan scrubbed his hands over his face. "I need a sedative."

"We all need food," I said. "We should see what the cafeteria has."

"Maybe one of us should stay here, just in case?" Evan said. "Actually, let me run to the bathroom quick, then whoever wants to go to the cafeteria first can."

He headed down the hallway for the bathroom, seeming less shaken than before. I doubted he'd actually relax until he was by his dad's side with his dad awake and talking.

Gabe stared out the window.

"You okay?" I grazed his pinky with mine. The faint touch zinged up my arm, and I curled my hand in on itself to stop from lacing my fingers with his.

He blinked as if coming out of a daze. When his eyes found mine, they were impossible to read. "Can I hold you?"

The question caught me by surprise, twisting my heart, but I recovered quickly. "Of course."

He could always hold me. Always.

I stepped into his arms, melting under their solid warmth and inhaling the smell of rain that clung to his shirt. I savored the moment, knowing it would be one of the last I'd get in his embrace.

It didn't stop me from noticing he hadn't answered my question.

Chapter Thirty-Seven
Gabe

THERE WAS a stillness to the morning I'd always liked. Those few hours of lag between the sun peeking over the clouds and the rest of the world waking when it was too quiet for even my thoughts to interrupt.

This morning's sunrise was masked with clouds, the ground still damp from the rain. An orange glow had broken through the gray blanket, slowly burning away the veil to let the first glimpses of daylight through.

I watched with the cold stone of my mom's grave against my back, an early blossom from her rose garden between my fingers.

It had been a late night at the hospital, mostly watching Dad sleep. The anesthesia had worn off, but it turned out emergency heart surgery did a number on the body. The doctor assured us it was normal and would likely take a few weeks for his energy to fully recover. When it was time to leave, I'd driven Evan home in his car.

Neither of us had said much on the drive. The same was true once we got home. I'd hung out in the kitchen until he'd gone to bed in case he needed anything, then I'd gone to bed myself.

After as little sleep as I expected, I'd walked to the cemetery. The towel I sat on protected my jeans from getting wet, but I welcomed the early morning chill. It sharpened things. Reminded me what was real.

My mom's gravestone behind me.

That my mom was actually dead.

That my dad had almost died too.

All of it felt wrong. Like the world had been flipped upside down and no one else noticed we were walking on the ceiling. If it weren't for the sharp sting of cold against my cheeks, I'd be sure this was some fucked-up dream. No matter how much time passed, a part of me still expected to wake up.

Yet oddly, being in the hospital yesterday had made the truth of it easier to accept. Like I was finally walking the steps I'd been meant to take when my mom got sick, and now that they were behind me, I felt closer to her somehow. Almost as if I'd finally been able to put down enough of the shame I'd been carrying by not being there with her that she could fit her arms around me again.

It was like Aubrey had said—love remained after a person passed. I did believe it. I'd just struggled to feel it with my mom.

Ever since she died, there'd been this distance. I had memories of her, but her love—the love I'd always, always known from my mom no matter how many miles separated us—felt out of reach. Like not only did I have to watch the game on TV instead of being in the stands, but then the TV had been locked away in a separate room so all I could hear were muffled sounds.

My dad, Evan, Aubrey—in my head, they were all in the room with the TV, watching the game loud and clear, getting to experience the rush of the plays and the energy of the crowd. None of us got to experience it in person anymore, but I felt like the only one shut out completely.

Why else if not that my mom was mad at me?

Why else if not that I didn't deserve it?

Yesterday at the hospital, it was like the door had been cracked open. I'd heard the game again. I'd felt her there. And it felt like she was telling me we were okay.

Maybe she had forgiven me. Or maybe she'd never felt there was anything to forgive.

Maybe I was the one who needed to forgive myself.

Here, with her, felt like the place to try.

I couldn't say how much progress I'd made, but it felt good to sit with her in the quiet. To feel her again, even if it was all in my head.

I told her about London. How I hadn't minded the weather but had missed good Mexican food. Nothing had come close to the family-owned restaurant in the strip mall here by our house.

I told her about assistant training for Coach Peters. How I'd worried I'd be too bitter about giving up competing to do it well, but it had given me as much satisfaction, if not more. How Noah had made the Olympic team, and I might have been happier for him than I ever had been from one of my own victories.

I told her about my ideas for Coach Lou's gym. How I'd

planned to coach Noah when he went pro, and about the amateur and pro rosters I'd wanted to build. The kids' summer camp I'd envisioned my pro boxers teaching at.

I told her about Aubrey.

How she'd been a light in the darkness for me the first six months after the funeral. Before that, even.

She'd been the one to pick me up from the airport when I'd finally landed in Philly. My dad and Evan were dealing with the funeral arrangements and things like neighbors stopping by with food, and instead of whisking me away and tossing me into the fray, she'd stood with me in baggage claim long after I'd gotten my bags and hugged me. The same way she'd hugged me yesterday at the hospital when I'd asked.

No words. No accusations. No attempts to make anything better. She was just there. The ropes for me to fall onto, holding me up. Holding Evan and my dad up too.

Even once I'd run back to London after the funeral, she'd been there. Mostly in brief texts she'd send every so often. Nothing pestering, but enough to know I hadn't been forgotten.

There'd been one match—my last before retiring—that had been especially rough. I'd blamed my shoulder, but that wasn't it. Physical therapy had done its job, and physically, I was fine.

Mentally, I'd unraveled.

I retreated to my hotel room, wanting to cry but not able to even do that. So I texted her. Three words I hadn't felt allowed to admit.

"I miss her."

With the time difference, I figured she'd be at work and wouldn't have the chance to reply, but she did right away.

It allowed me to breathe again. And the conversation never stopped.

We didn't always reply to each other immediately. If I was traveling for one of my fighter's matches or she was busy with work, we'd go several days between messages, sometimes weeks. But the conversation was always open, reminding me I wasn't alone. Even when I felt like I should have been.

Her leaving the door open like that was a big part of why I'd been brave enough to come home. Knowing there would be at least one person here who didn't hate me, myself included.

Seeing her in the kitchen on New Year's…my nerves had been unreal. When I looked back, the excitement at seeing her wasn't new. As kids, she had always lifted my mood.

Being around her was like basking in the sun. Being *with* her…it was like being lit by the sun from within. A burning star that could never be extinguished.

A different kind of warmth filled my chest at the thought of Mom smiling as I talked about Aubrey. I could picture the glint in her eye, like she'd known all along.

Maybe she had. Maybe when she'd boasted to me about Aubrey that Thanksgiving, she'd been planting a seed. I'd never know. Right now, I wasn't sure it mattered. I still had a job offer on the table from Coach Dotson.

It felt wrong to think about with Dad still in the hospital, but I'd need to decide eventually. Sooner rather than later.

Across the headstone-covered field, another factor in that decision trod down the path toward Mom's grave. He walked with his hands in his pockets, so much more grown up from the kid he still was in my head. More grown up than me in a lot of ways. It had been especially true these past two years.

Evan's steps slowed as he reached Mom's row. He stopped a few feet away, studying her headstone, partially obscured by my torso. "Mind if I join you?"

I scooted over so there was room for him on the towel. He sat beside me with his back against the other half of Mom's grave.

We'd need to leave for the hospital soon. Hopefully, the rest of Dad's night had gone well. For now, we stared out at the rows of memorial stones in silence, an easiness in the space between us that had been missing for a while.

Evan picked at a clump of grass by his knee. "This is the first time I've been here since the funeral," he admitted.

That was unexpected. I figured he tagged along for a good number of Dad's Saturday morning visits.

"I know," he said, taking in my expression. "You're not the only one who's been avoiding shit."

"What have you been avoiding?"

For me, it had been that Mom was really gone. The longer I'd stayed away, the more it had morphed into shame. Knowing what Evan and Dad must have thought of me and not being able to face it. To face Mom. Or myself.

No way Evan held that shame. He'd been here when both our parents needed him most. Had stood strong when all I could do was crumble.

He peered at the headstone in front of him. "Anger mostly. At Mom."

"What for?" They'd been on good terms when she died. I was certain of it.

"For dying." He laughed once under his breath and threw the loose blades of grass. "Can you believe that?"

"Yes." I'd had moments of anger too. Just another form of the same pain coming to the surface.

"It's not like she chose to get cancer and die," he said, still looking out at the cemetery as if he were talking to the graves instead of me. "But she was supposed to hang on. *God*, I was so sure she'd beat it. If anyone could, it'd be her. At the very least, she was supposed to give us more time, but she didn't. She was always so strong for everyone else, but when it came time to fight for herself, it felt like she just gave up. And I know, *I know*, it's stupid to feel that way. I know it's not what happened. But every time I think of her, I can't help but wonder why she didn't fight harder. Why was she so quick to let go? Why was she okay with leaving us?"

I had no answer for him. I could only be glad she'd been so at peace with what her life had been that she'd been able to let it go without regrets.

"And then, *I* left you," I said, realizing how much that must have stung when he'd already felt abandoned by our mom.

"Yeah."

I had this picture in my mind of Evan at the funeral, his face twisted in anger. He'd simmered with it the whole service, his cold shoulder feeling personal at the time. He, more than my dad, became a reminder of my shame, and I hadn't wanted to face it, even over the phone.

Only now did it occur to me his anger might not have been about me that day. That maybe if I'd reached out, I could have helped him through it sooner.

"I should have called," I said. Being here in person had been beyond my capability, but I could have checked in. Should have.

"If I'm honest, I'm not sure it would have made a difference," he said. "It was easier for me to hate you than be angry with her."

I glanced at him from the corner of my eye. "Does that mean you don't hate me anymore?"

He sighed, long and deep. "It means I'm tired of being angry, and I miss my big brother."

I ignored the ache in my left arm and looped it around him. He lowered his head to my shoulder.

"I missed you too, baby bro," I said into his hair. More of his weight rested on me as if he didn't have to carry it alone any longer. It meant everything that he trusted me with it again.

As if the clouds agreed, they parted enough for a few rays of sun to shine through, officially banishing the gray. Or maybe that was Mom looking in, telling us she was here.

"I want you to know I'm excited for you," Evan said. "For your job in Colorado. I won't be mad when you go. I mean, at least we'll be in the same country this time," he teased.

"If I go."

He pulled back and looked at me.

"I haven't accepted the job yet," I explained. "I was on my way to talk through the details with Coach Dotson when I got your message about Dad."

"Wait, so…are you thinking you might not take it?"

I shifted on the towel, rolling out my shoulder to hide my unease. I didn't know what I was thinking. Other than I'd be a moron not to take it. Even if the pay was shit, it'd be the perfect job for me. I didn't need much money to be happy; just enough to get by comfortably. Boxing was the thing I needed most.

Or it used to be. Now I kept going back to how nice it had been to be close to my family again. To see my dad multiple times a week. To have the option to catch up with my brother in person rather than video chat, even if he was too pissed to speak to me.

Thinking of leaving again put a sting in my chest that hadn't been there the previous times I left.

"Because of Aubrey?" Evan asked. I might have been mistaken, but he sounded almost hopeful.

"No," I said quickly. Probably too quickly. "We're back to just friends." It tasted like a lie. Not because I wasn't her friend—I always would be.

But she would always be more to me. The person I wanted in all ways. Ached for so much I sometimes couldn't breathe. Loved in a way I hadn't believed I was capable of.

If I was the rose in my grasp, she was the sun brightening my world, shining the light that inspired me to grow. The thought of being near her made me want to both stake my feet in the ground so nothing could tear us apart and fling myself as far away as fucking possible before I did real damage.

Already, I'd fucked up. Stressed her out with the tournament drama and my shoulder. She didn't need more.

"So what, then?" Evan asked.

I let out a sigh. "Dad's heart attack, for one thing. We don't know what kind of rehab he'll need, and handling that shouldn't all fall on you."

"Look, I appreciate that. I do," he said. "But I'm already living with him. It's not like I have to uproot my life again to keep an eye on things. And this is the Olympic team we're talking about."

It *was* the Olympic team. So why did going feel more like a penance than the dream it should have been?

"I guess I've still been thinking about my own gym," I admitted. "Not Coach Lou's. That's not an option anymore. But maybe finding somewhere else. A place that could be all mine." I saw the vision I described to my mom—the career plan Noah and I had sketched out for him. The fellowships I'd foster within the community. The sanctuary I'd create for anyone who wanted one.

That was my true dream. To lay down roots. Buy actual furniture and let myself settle. To build a home.

The job in Colorado would give me a chance to do all that, just with my roots planted in Colorado instead of Philly.

A faint voice in my head warned that was still the better choice. Not for me, but for my family. That they were safer from me if I was a good distance away. Like Evan had said, at least this time it would be the same country.

Maybe that was the happy middle. I'd get to be closer but not too close. Get some of what I wanted but not all.

Not more than I deserved.

"When do you have to decide by?" Evan asked.

"Coach Dotson and I rescheduled our meeting for tomorrow." He'd been super understanding about my dad being in the hospital and had enough business in the city to extend his trip a few days.

His reaction made the job look sweeter. A boss who cared about people as much as productivity wasn't easy to find.

And still, I hesitated. Whether because I was convinced I didn't deserve something good or just the opposite, I was no longer sure, but I was done trying to figure it out. For today, all I wanted was to be with our dad and not think about it.

Tomorrow would come soon enough.

Chapter Thirty-Eight
Aubrey

I STOOD along the wall of windows in the hospital waiting room with my phone to my ear, as out of the way as I could get not to disturb others.

"I know that explanation might not be enough," the soon-to-be bride said on the other end of the line, "but you're our first catering choice, and I at least had to try." It had been her engagement party the food blogger had written that negative review about. It turned out the food blogger was her cousin.

She'd invited him as family, not thinking he'd use the party for his blog. It was only after her maid of honor called her, furious at how he'd taken her comment about her grandmother out of context, that the bride had learned about the article at all.

Apparently, the maid of honor's grandmother had been a professional chef who usually hated catered events because she found the food either bland, cold, overcooked, all of the above, or simply a variation of the same four dishes there seemed to be at every wedding. The blogger overheard her say the food was something her grandmother would love and, without knowing the full story, took it and ran.

Now the bride was mortified, especially since she and her fiancé had their hearts set on Arden Catering for the reception.

"My cousin will *not* be attending," she assured me. Someone said something in the background, and she huffed. "Fine, but he's not eating the food. He can have microwaved chicken nuggets at the kids' table and blog about that."

"I'll have to double-check the calendar to confirm, but I don't believe we have any other events scheduled for that week," I told her. "We'd be happy to cater your wedding. I'm honestly thrilled you reached back out."

I wouldn't even care if her cousin blogged about it again. It'd be nice to have the chance to change his opinion. Maybe redeem myself and Arden Catering.

The bride let out an audible sigh. "Really? I can't tell you how much that would mean to us."

"Really." Knowing how much they liked the food was satisfying enough. And now that I had Mack on the team, we'd be able to go all out to make it a truly special day. "Let me check the calendar, and I'll confirm with you by the end of the week. After that, we can talk details."

"Aubrey, thank you," she said. "This is such a huge relief."

Evan appeared at my side and leaned against the window.

"You're welcome," I said. "Talk soon."

"Good news?" Evan asked as I hung up.

"Validation, mostly." I told him about the blogger mix-up.

He rolled his eyes. "This is why I hate weddings."

"Food bloggers?"

"A bunch of extended family doing ridiculous shit."

I chuckled. "But they give you money."

"If you're lucky. One of my friend's brothers got a used handheld mixer with food still crusted on it."

My eyes widened. "No."

"That's what he said."

"Maybe it was a family heirloom. Or like a magic object that grants you a wish after you eat whatever you make with it."

"Or people are cheap and fucking gross, and I'm never getting married."

I pouted. "But then, you'll miss out on all the epic catering I'll do with my awesome new team. Mack and I just perfected some of my favorite dishes I've ever cooked."

We'd fine-tuned the last details of the competition menu this morning, then gone to Ardena to plate fresh versions and photograph them in the dining room. Jase and the guys gave their input on the photos, and I was glad to see how comfortable Mack seemed around them. Hopefully, we could work out a regular staff meal or shift-drink combo like Jase suggested to make this dynamic the norm.

Now, all that was left for the competition was to finalize the written portion, which Dani had offered to proofread for me tonight. I'd submit everything tomorrow, one day before the deadline, and I could honestly say it didn't matter to me if we won. I wanted us to and hoped we would, but I didn't need the award recognition to know the value I brought to Arden Catering and the Ardena brand.

In many ways, the competition pushed me to accept that value by reminding me what I was capable of. Dealing with such a shitstorm of a time finding a sous chef helped too. Not only by forcing me to take on so much by myself and prove I could do it but also by reminding me of the things outside of cooking I brought to this position.

Like showing up on time. Keeping my word. Finding creative solutions. Trusting my instincts.

I used to believe never needing help was what made me valuable, but it wasn't. If anything, what I brought to the table had been in *spite* of not asking for help. It was time to see how much more I could learn by doing the opposite.

"Guess I'll just have to settle for your holiday party food," Evan said.

I accepted defeat. "Fine. Your dad still napping?" He had been when I'd texted Evan on my way to the hospital. The call from the bride-to-be had come as I'd gotten off the elevator.

"He just woke up. The nurse brought him dinner, so I figured I'd grab some food too."

"Isn't the cafeteria closed?"

"Yeah. I'm going off campus."

I raised my brows, shocked he felt comfortable leaving for that long.

He shrugged. "Gabe's with him."

A flurry of emotion swirled in my chest. I didn't mention that only a few days ago, Gabe being around would have put Evan *more* on guard, not less. It was a relief to see his face free from the anger it had been lined with for so long. To hear love for his brother when he said Gabe's name.

It also made it that much harder not to seek Gabe out, to be in his physical proximity while I still could. To catch his smile grow as I walked into the room and feel my body settle in the cradle of his arms.

Already, I missed him. The sturdiness of his presence and the gentleness of his heart. The way he steadied me by just being near.

I could use some of that steadiness. We hadn't texted the past two days due to everything with his dad, and in some ways, it felt like the distance to Colorado was slipping between us even before he left for his new job.

Maybe it was easier that way—to simply let what we'd shared these months fade rather than endure the heartache of another goodbye. To fall back into the sporadic rhythm of texting how we had when he'd been in London, still connected to each other but not as present.

Or maybe, the cord between us would keep stretching until it eventually snapped.

"I'll go with you," I said to Evan, not ready to face either option. Plus, my lunch had been nothing but a few tastes of the competition's dishes, and that had been hours ago.

We took a few steps toward the elevators before Evan spoke. "About Gabe."

"You can save your I told you so," I said before he could pry open the can of emotions I'd just managed to contain. "I already told him to take the job."

I got why Evan had been worried about Gabe abandoning me the way he'd felt abandoned after everything with their mom. The way I had felt abandoned in my past too.

But this wasn't that. Gabe had never promised me anything more, and I'd never asked him to. I'd specifically *not* asked him to, and I was glad I hadn't forced myself between him and his dream.

"That's not what I was going to say. I think you should tell him how you feel."

My heart jumped as I stamped the "down" button for the elevator. I crossed my arms. "What do you mean?"

"I mean you should drop this 'it's only sex' act and tell him you have real feelings for him. And before you say anything," he added when I opened my mouth to protest, "let's pretend like I've been your best friend for over twenty years and know you well enough to tell when you're lying. Even to yourself."

The elevator doors opened, and we stepped on. Evan pushed the button for the ground floor.

"Why the sudden change of heart?" I asked, not bothering to deny how well he knew me. "Aren't you the one who was convinced he'd leave? Now you think I should, what? Ask him to stay when he just got offered his dream job?"

"Yes," he said simply.

I adjusted my balance as the elevator lurched into motion.

"So are you going to do it?"

I huffed. "No way."

"Why not?"

My shoulders tensed as if to block out the suggestion. "Because this job is everything he wants. It wouldn't be fair for me to ask him to give it up after what he's dealt with in his career."

Evan opened his mouth—

"And no avoiding the question," I said, cutting him off this time. "Why the change of heart?"

He heaved a sigh and leaned against the stainless steel wall. "Everything that happened yesterday sort of forced me to realize the anger I was hanging on to wasn't all about Gabe. You were right. I wasn't being fair to him."

His eyes flashed with an apology, and I nodded in acceptance. I cared more that he seemed interested in a relationship with his brother again than I did about being right.

"But you're wrong about this being his dream job," he said.

I scowled at him. "*He* called it his dream job."

"He may have used those words, but it's not everything he wants. Otherwise, he wouldn't have he told me this morning that he doesn't know if he's going to take it."

My stomach flipped the same moment the elevator jolted to a stop. The doors opened, and Evan strode for the hospital's main entrance

"You guys talked?" I asked, hurrying after him.

"We did." He said it as if it felt good. Like they had found a way to move forward that brought relief. "I think he wants to stay but doesn't know if he should. And I think you're part of the reason why."

My pulse was a fluttering mess. "He said that?"

"No," Evan said as we crossed toward 10th Street. There was a comfort-food café we both liked that had a buffalo chicken mac and cheese I would shave my head for right now. "He said you were just friends, but I can tell when he's lying as easily as I can with you. *Especially* to himself."

I chewed on my bottom lip, barely avoiding collision with a trash can as I stepped around a flock of pigeons pecking at a scrap of food.

"Why would that be a bad thing?" Evan asked, taking in my expression.

I tried to make sense of the gnawing doubt in my belly. It

wouldn't be bad if Gabe wanted to stay. It would be amazing. Exactly what I hoped for.

But Gabe's nature had always been to explore. To spread his wings and fly as far as the wind took him. It was one of the reasons boxing had suited him so well.

He reminded me of my parents in that way. The air force had provided them the opportunity to see the world as much as it gave them a job.

I had made that opportunity more difficult. Had added stress and limitations to perks that already came with the strict conditions of military life. I'd required them to sacrifice more than they'd been willing to give in order to meet my needs, and I didn't want to put the same stress and limitations on Gabe.

I didn't want to be the weight tying him down. The burden that held him back.

My answer was salt on my tongue. "Because what if he ends up regretting not taking the job, and I'm the reason he didn't?"

Evan's expression softened with understanding. "Those are your fears, A. They're not the truth."

"How do you know?"

They'd been true for my parents, who hadn't even needed to give up their jobs for it to happen.

He didn't have to think about it. "Because since he got home, the only thing Gabe has wanted more than his gym is to be close to you. I avoided him every chance I could, and I still saw it clear as day. His first night back, I told him to stay away from you, and didn't. He was willing for me to stay pissed at him in order to have you in his life, and if he wouldn't resent you for that, no way would he resent you over a job. I don't care how good it is."

My chest burned. I wanted to believe it more than I wanted to cook anything again. But my body wouldn't let go of the fear.

"Look," Evan said, stopping in front of the café. "Maybe you're right and this is his dream job. But that doesn't change the fact that neither of you seem to know how the other feels, which really seems like a conversation you should have before one of you decides to move across the country. Especially given the way you light each other up. I didn't realize it until your birthday, but he helps you be a brighter version of yourself—maybe the happiest I've seen you. And you do the same for him. From where I'm standing, the worst-case scenario isn't that you tell him and he leaves. It's that he leaves when what you both really wanted was for him to stay. So think about it."

He left me to do just that as he held the door open for an older couple on their way out. I followed him to the counter to put in our to-go order, and the bartender poured us waters. The sharp bite of cold liquid grounded me as I processed what Evan had said.

I believed Gabe cared about me. I believed I made him happy. And it wasn't like I wanted him to choose me *over* boxing. If there was a way I could make his dreams come true that allowed him to stay in Philly, I'd do it in a heartbeat.

Plus, his family was here. His home. Gabe could have chosen to open his own gym anywhere in the world or stayed with the boxing community he already had in London, but he chose to come back to Philly. Before anything physical had happened between us.

That possibility made it easier to accept—that instead of staying for me, he might not have wanted to go in the first place. That I wasn't the only reason.

Even though a different, equally confusing part of me wanted to be. The part that glowed at recalling how, unlike my parents, Gabe had gone out of his way to spend time with me. How he'd come to the prep kitchen the night all hell had broken loose, and checked on me when I was on my period. How he'd put together the surprise for my birthday so I wouldn't feel alone.

My parents had never done anything like that, even before they'd left me with Nana. As far back as I could remember, it only ever felt like they'd resented me for needing them.

My mind turned to Jillian and Jase. I'd worried about them resenting me in a similar way, and all along, they'd been wishing I would lean on them more.

Gabe had only ever wanted me to lean on him too.

I *wanted* to lean on him now. Wanted the courage to ask him to stay. Courage I hadn't needed to tell him to go because I'd been telling myself all along he might do just that.

If I never told him how I felt, I never had to risk his rejection. The knowledge that he didn't choose something better; he just didn't want me.

The way my parents hadn't wanted me.

I stared at the black marble of the bar as my fingers went numb against my water glass.

All these years, I'd told myself I'd been too much for my parents, but when it came down to it…I hadn't been enough.

Not enough to raise or love.

Not enough to bother knowing.

And in every relationship since, I'd feared the same. That I wouldn't be enough for them unless I was everything they needed. It was true at work and with Patrick. Even with Nana.

I'd done everything I could to make sure I was enough for people to keep me in their lives, and despite everyone who'd told me differently, here I was still terrified of the same with Gabe.

Not that I would weigh him down but that I wouldn't fill him up the way boxing did; the way this job could. That no matter what I did or how much I offered, it wouldn't be enough for him to want *me*.

The air was suddenly too hot and freezing cold all at once. I felt one nudge away from collapsing like an under-cooked soufflé, exhausted from measuring myself against an invisible line my parents had drawn in my heart when they dropped me at my grandma's and walked away.

I didn't want to live by that line anymore.

I wanted to be capable of believing Gabe wanted me back. To trust that the people in my life chose to be there because of who I was more than what I did for them.

And by not telling Gabe how I felt, I was robbing him of the chance to make that choice for himself.

Evan was right.

He sat quietly beside me while my thoughts spun.

"It won't be weird for you if I tell him?" I asked. He'd known about Gabe and me hooking up, but if he was right about how Gabe felt, this would be different.

"You know back in high school when you were obsessed with him even though you pretended you weren't?" he asked.

"I was not obsessed."

He smirked. "Your subtle way of asking about him the mornings after you knew I had a video chat with him wasn't so subtle."

I threw my crumpled straw wrapper at his forehead.

"My point," he said all smug, "was that I also secretly hoped you and Gabe would get together for real one day. In a fairy tale, never going to happen, but it'd be cool if it did kind of way."

"Really?" I figured my crush had bored him more than anything.

He nudged his shoulder into mine. "It'd be nice to get to call you my sister. You know, for real."

It was a small thing to want. Only a word. One that changed nothing about who we were to each other and added no real value to our friendship. Yet its meaning melted the worst edges of my fear and filled me with the same affection his voice carried as he said it. An overflow of gratitude and love that worked its way into my throat. "It would."

"Does this mean you're going to tell him?"

I traced my thumb through the condensation on my water glass and took a steadying breath. "It means I'm going to try."

"Don't wait too long," Evan warned. "He meets with that Olympic coach again tomorrow."

My stomach clenched as I forced in another breath.

Gabe could still choose Colorado. And if he did, I wouldn't hold it against him.

I *would* hold it against myself if I didn't ask for what I wanted one last time. Especially from the person who'd helped me feel brave enough to ask in the first place.

Anything you want, I heard Gabe say.

It was time I found out if he wanted it too.

Chapter Thirty-Nine
Gabe

DAD'S HOSPITAL room was cramped. His bed filled most of the space, the head currently raised so he could sit and eat comfortably from the tray the nurse had situated over his lap.

The same nurse had brought in an extra chair so Evan and I both had a place to sit, which we'd squeezed along the wall in front of the narrow window to make sure the staff still had room to do what they needed to do. Right now, it was just Dad and me, which meant I could stretch my legs in front of me as I sat.

Dad seemed okay, considering. His skin had more color than yesterday, his appetite was strong, and he was on a first-name basis with every nurse on the floor. He'd said he felt a little sore but otherwise fine. So far, the doctor liked what he saw from his post-op tests and felt good about releasing him tomorrow.

A tomorrow that sped at me like a bull.

I still hadn't decided about the job.

Usually, one gut check and my decisions were made, but at some point in the past few days, my gut had been turned into a speed bag, and it was too busy jerking all over the place to be of any use.

My nerves were equally out of control, and not like my prefight jitters that were more anticipation and adrenaline—a steady build that hyped my mind and body for the match. This was me ready to jump out of my skin.

Not thinking about it hadn't worked either. Not when Dad told every hospital staff member who walked into his room that I was going to be an Olympic coach.

It felt like his way of telling me I should go. The same way Aubrey had told me to go. And Evan.

The decision seemed straightforward to everyone else, so why couldn't I make it?

"I think the food got better here in the past few years," Dad said, scraping the last traces of his mashed potatoes onto his fork. "Your mother could hardly eat it, it was so bland. But that was delicious."

Mom had hardly eaten because her stomach pain had been unbearable whenever she did. There were pictures of her in the months leading up to her diagnosis that showed how thin she had become. I'd been spared the worst of it by being away. Mom had insisted on exclusively phone calls once she was in the hospital. No video calls. No mention of her pain. She only wanted to talk about me. The little I knew had come from Evan, who filled me in after Mom got too tired and needed to pass the phone off to rest.

If it was less painful for Dad to remember her not eating because of the lousy food, I couldn't blame him for it. I certainly wouldn't correct him.

"We'll have to start cooking more at home again," I said. "All that takeout isn't good for your heart."

He grunted. "I'm sure Evan's already worked out a keto-genic, hypno-vegetarian, paleontolic something."

"You mean paleo? What's hypno-vegetarian?"

He waved a hand and pushed his empty tray aside. "You know what I mean."

I chuckled. "Healthy? Yeah, Evan's probably going to have a few meals in mind. I'm sure he'll let you throw in a chunk or two of butter if you decide to help."

He glanced at the framed picture of Mom propped beside his bed. "She was the reason I learned to cook in the first place. I ever tell you that?"

I shook my head.

"On our first date, she said she'd never marry a man who didn't cook because she once managed to burn salad and wasn't looking to starve for the rest of her life. The next day, I bought a copy of the *Better Homes & Gardens* cookbook and started practicing. For our second date, I cooked her dinner at my apartment, complete with an appetizer and dessert. She rated it a B plus and said I could earn extra credit by cooking something else for her the next night."

He laughed softly, his eyes still on her picture. "That next night was the first time she watched me cook. The first time she leaned over my shoulder and asked what I was doing. I made up half my replies. My heart pounded the whole time."

It was the most I'd heard him talk about her since she'd died. The first time I felt allowed to ask him to.

"Is that why you started making grilled lettuce? Because she once burned salad?"

His laughter came deep from his belly. "Yeah. She liked that one."

"She called you a fucker every time you made it."

"That's how I knew she liked it. And there was never a crumb of it left on her plate."

He transformed when he talked about her like this. His face looked ten years younger, and I was suddenly staring at my dad again. The bold, loud man who filled the rooms he walked into with his joy.

I hadn't seen him much since I'd been home. Mostly just the shadow of the man he seemed too tired to be.

I was afraid I'd go to Colorado and come back to even more of him missing. That his shadow would shrink to little more than a speck, haunting the home he'd once shared with Mom. Maybe he could tell.

"I'll cook more," he promised. "She'd want me to take better care of myself."

"She would," I agreed.

"Is that what you're worried about?"

"What do you mean?"

"You haven't sat still since you got here this morning. I know there's a lot on your plate, and I want to make sure I'm not part of it. You shouldn't pass on this job because of me."

I rubbed the ache from my brow. I was getting really sick of people telling me I should leave. "Dad, you're in the hospital from a heart attack. Of course, I'm worried."

"I get that, and I won't tell you not to be. But I will tell you that I'll be fine. I mean it, I'll be okay."

"I've been told that before."

"I know you have." He sank against his pillows as if the past's weight came down on him again. "I know."

My gaze wandered to the plastic hand sanitizer dispenser by the door. The rounded edge caught the glare from the overhead lights, the sticker on the front faded. I thought of the coaching job and back to Mom.

"You know, I'm actually glad I lost that championship fight two years ago. Because winning might have felt like a justification for staying, and there wasn't one. Nothing should have prevented me from being here."

"Your mom didn't feel that way."

Aubrey had said the same, yet it didn't ease the fracture inside me. The one that felt like my heart had been split down the middle and hollowed out so it had nothing left to pump but air.

"I wish she had," I said, finally naming the pain. "I wish she'd told me to give it all up. Because none of it mattered. I didn't need another title or millions in prize money. I needed—" I caught the rush of emotion in my throat. "I needed to be here. And if she had told me to give it up and come home, I would have. And I could have said goodbye."

"You know why she didn't?"

I shook my head, not trusting myself to speak.

"Because she loved you."

My nostrils burned as the words pierced the bottom of whatever bag I'd been piling my mess into since the moment Mom died, and all of it spilled out around me—pain, guilt, regret.

Relief.

At the reassurance Mom loved me. That she hadn't been angry with me. That I was still her son the way I always had been, even now, after I let her and our family down. I'd known it on some level, but hearing it from my dad, who knew her heart better than his own, meant it had to be true.

I swiped my nose with the back of my hand, catching a runaway tear with my sleeve.

Dad reached over the bed's railing. "Come here, son. Come here."

I coughed out more tears, unaware so many had been ready to fall. They came hard and fast as I scooted forward to clasp Dad's hand with my own. His grip was firm. Stronger than I expected it to be.

He squeezed my hand. "Your mom never wanted to be the reason you gave up your dream. Just like I don't want to be the reason you give up this job. We love you so much, Gabe. You and Evan are the two things we're most proud of in our lives. Not because of your accomplishments but because you've found something you love, and you lead your life being happy doing it. Your joy is our pride. Your joy mattered more to your mom than goodbye. And I know that was probably selfish of her, but she had no problem being selfish when it came to you kids."

"I hate that I didn't get to say goodbye," I choked out.

"I know," he said, voice steady. "But no goodbye would have made it feel okay."

More tears came as the realization struck. That no matter the circumstances, her death was always going to be unbearable. It was always going to feel like *this*.

It didn't excuse the rest. "I was selfish to leave after the funeral."

"Maybe." He shrugged it off. "She taught you kids to be selfish once in a while. It isn't always the worst thing to be. Sometimes it's even important."

I sniffed as the tears slowed, Dad's grip an anchor for my emotions. A whole bunch of them swirled, but after a few more breaths, they mostly melted into sadness, the guilt and shame buckling under the enormity of how much I missed my mom. Almost like those other emotions had been trying to protect me from feeling it all at once.

Like Evan's anger. The same pain expressing itself in a different way. One that was easier to bear than pure grief.

I was done curbing the pain.

There was freedom in embracing the sadness for what it was instead of masking it in another emotion. An honesty that was its own kind of relief. It created space in my chest for what might have been the forgiveness toward myself I'd started to accept at Mom's grave. Forgiveness that grew stronger now.

Or maybe that was the comfort of knowing I got my selfishness from my mom. That we were all just human. That maybe I no longer needed to punish myself for decisions none of us could change.

Maybe the decision I made next didn't have to make up for the past.

"Will you tell me more stories about her?"

"Gladly—Oh, Wendy." His voice got brighter as a dark-haired nurse strode in. "You want to hear about the time my wife dragged me skydiving for our two-year dating anniversary? I'll let you guess which one of us vomited."

She chuckled and picked up his empty tray, her smile warm in the cool room. Something told me she'd worked as a nurse long enough to have heard it all. "Did you at least make it to the ground before hurling?"

He smirked. "Barely."

"Mom saw?" I asked, amused.

"She had an aerial view."

"Lucky woman," the nurse said, her dark eyes sparkling. "A man willing to vomit for her must love her indeed."

"I sure did," Dad said. He gazed at her photo. "Sure do."

The nurse's smile softened. Her eyes slid to mine before she nodded and slipped from the room.

"So Mom dragged you onto that plane or what?"

Dad was halfway through the story when Evan returned with his takeout. Aubrey walked in behind him. I straightened in the stiff chair as her gaze landed on me.

She smiled, a little shy but still fucking radiant with her blond hair and earthy gaze, and handed me a burger. She must have figured I hadn't eaten. Or known I'd be hungry regardless.

Both were true. And now that I didn't have training to worry about, I could eat the burger without consequence. Silver linings and all that.

We rearranged the chairs so Aubrey could perch on the windowsill between Evan and me while Dad finished the story.

"She said that was the day she knew she wanted to marry me. She'd already had the feeling, but that sealed the deal."

"Because you puked all over your skydiving instructor?" Evan teased.

Dad shrugged. "Hey, I didn't question it. I was just glad it did the trick."

"What was your wedding like?" Aubrey asked.

She scooped a forkful of mac and cheese into her mouth, eyes bright with curiosity for this peek at my parents we hadn't seen much of. Especially not from my Dad.

It was right, her being here. The way boxing had always felt right.

That this job offer didn't bring me the same assuredness told me more than I needed to know.

Dad went on to share his and Mom's wedding story, which reminded Evan of the time she'd tried to plan a surprise party for my sweet sixteen but waited too long, so the only place available to book it was Chuck E. Cheese. I'd forgotten all about it until he brought it up. Then I couldn't stop laughing.

One after another, we recalled stories about Mom. Some ridiculous, some endearing. Some we each remembered different aspects of and had to piece together as a group.

Talking about her like this—remembering her out loud and together—felt good. Like a balm to the places inside us she'd been ripped from that had since been bleeding.

Those pieces of us would always be missing. But the happiness of these memories, and the sadness they brought too, was somehow a comfort. A reminder I still carried her with me, both as love and as grief.

Different emotions for the same pain, the same joy. Which was which no longer mattered.

A few hours must have passed. It had long since grown dark outside, and the night nurse would be in soon to check on Dad. He'd drifted asleep while Evan and Aubrey had worked out whether my mom ever went trick-or-treating with them as Captain Jack Sparrow from the *Pirates of the Caribbean* movies. It sounded like something she'd do, but I couldn't remember.

Now Evan slept too, his chin tucked to his chest where he slouched in his chair. I'd drive him home soon, but not yet.

Aubrey shifted along the windowsill, the glow from the dimmed ceiling lights casting her hair in a caramel shine. No wonder she wasn't asleep. Her ass was probably numb from sitting on the narrow metal ledge.

I could offer her the comfort of Evan's car as I drove her to her apartment, but that would mean saying good night—something I had no interest in doing. For once, everything felt at peace. With Evan, with my dad, with my mom. I wanted to stay in this peacefulness a bit longer, and I wanted to share it with her.

I caught her eye as she leaned against the corner of the window. "You could sit here," I said, gesturing to my seat.

She made a face like I shouldn't worry about it. "You're way too big to fit on this ledge."

My heart thumped against my sternum. "We could share."

Her face went blank the way it did when she was trying to play it cool, but the pink in her cheeks gave her away. "You mean…like I sit on your lap?"

"Yeah." I cleared my throat. She wasn't the only one trying to play it cool.

I knew we weren't what we had been anymore. And I didn't know if it was possible to be that again. To be more than that. But I wanted her close anyway. Wanted her comfortable and safe in my arms.

Maybe she wanted it too because she hopped from the window and took careful steps past Evan's chair.

My hand shook as I grasped the tips of her fingers and guided her to my lap. She rested her head on my chest, the scent of coconut flooding my nose, and her ear settled over my rattling heart.

With her hand still in mine, her body released its weight like it knew it could in my hold. Or maybe this felt as right to her as it did to me. I played with the ends of her hair, loving its silky texture.

"Tonight was good," she said, her soft voice a soothing melody in the quiet.

My lips rose. "Yeah, it was." Maybe it was her body heat, but I felt warm all over, like being bundled in blankets on a cold winter morning. I'd stay like this forever if I could.

"Thank you for this," she murmured, her words growing hazy. Her eyes had fallen closed. "You're always taking care of me."

My impulse was to eject the thanks like a crinkled bill from a vending machine.

Taking care of her hadn't been conscious. Those things she'd thanked me for yesterday, having her here with me now —all of it had been for me as much as her. Had fed this need I had to watch her back and make sure she was okay. To be near her, have more of her. To satisfy the selfish part of myself I hadn't found a way to deny when it came to her.

But what if it went beyond that? What if as much as I shared my mom's selfishness, I shared some of the care she had for those she loved. The part that made her willing to drive eight hours for a single boxing match or stay up all night when Evan or I were sick. The part that made her willing to suffer any discomfort if it meant her kids were happy.

Mom had both. Maybe I did too.

It had me thinking more about Dad's words from earlier.

There was more than one way to lead my life with joy. More than one way to find my center. And as much as Dad hadn't wanted me to turn down the job for him, I got to decide what was right for me.

It hadn't been a decision the last time I left. More like the jerking back of my hand from a fire after being burned. I hadn't thought about it, had hardly been in control, desperate for the only way I'd known to keep functioning after losing Mom.

For the first time in two years, my mind was clear.

I settled into the chair, savoring Aubrey's weight as her chest rose and fell with the steady breaths of sleep. I pressed a kiss to her forehead.

Over her shoulder, Dad cracked his eyes open. His gaze went to Aubrey cradled in my arms, then to my face, his eyes meeting mine. A soft smile touched his lips.

I smiled back, surrounded by a comfort that felt a lot like Mom's embrace.

He nodded once, then closed his eyes and went back to sleep. I sank into the peacefulness of the room.

Maybe it was selfish to love Aubrey the way I did.

But maybe, this time, that was okay.

Chapter Fourty
Aubrey

I CHECKED my phone for the time and picked up my pace to a jog. Sweat already clung to the back of my white T-shirt, thanks to the sun beating down on a freakishly warm day for the second week in May. I would be a sweaty mess by the time I made it to the gym, but I didn't have time to worry about it.

I hadn't had time to change my chef clothes either. Or make sable cookies to arm myself with or do any of the other dozen things I'd wanted to prepare for this conversation with Gabe. Not once his earlier text had come through:

Gabe: Meeting Coach D in a little bit. You around after?

That "after" was chasing me with a rusty knife, pushing my legs faster. I needed to talk to Gabe *before* he met with Coach Dotson.

I'd hoped Mr. Hardt's doctors might drag their feet with

his discharge so I could catch Gabe at the hospital, but his dad had been released this morning while Mack and I were pressing submit on our competition entry.

I still might have made it if it weren't for the internet at the catering kitchen picking today of all days to crap out. We'd been halfway through the online form before having to rush to Ardena and fill the whole thing out again, costing me an hour.

Now, I ran down Girard Ave from where I'd parked the catering van four blocks away—because *of course* there'd been no parking spots closer—and prayed to whatever goddess granted luck Gabe was still at the gym.

I was sucking down air by the time I reached the steps, right as the door swung open and Gabe's impressive form filled the entryway.

"Aubrey? What are you—"

"Don't take the job," I blurted, still struggling to calm my lungs so the words came out somewhat normal. At least I'd caught him in time.

It might have been surprise that flashed across his face, but it was hard to tell with the the cramp stabbing my side like a carving fork. Gabe stepped back to hold the door open. "Here, come inside."

I shuffled into the space that had become my own kind of sanctuary these past months, the familiar punching bags and weight racks helping to even out my breathing.

Gabe lowered his gym bag to the floor. "What's going on?"

The air seemed to suck from the room as he trained his focus on me, my words no longer wanting to come out. Not now that my initial panic had subsided, and I registered the frizzy mess my hair had become. My armpits were damp with sweat, and I had at least three new stains on my chef pants from this morning.

It triggered a new kind of panic. One that squeezed the sides of my lungs so it felt like I was breathing through a straw.

More than with Jillian or Jase, my body resisted opening in this way for fear of coming up short. Of losing this person who for so long had been a touchpoint but now felt structural to my life. As if he were a support beam or staircase that helped me access parts of myself I hadn't known how to fully reach.

What I said next might change that. Maybe not so much that I lost him completely, but enough to form a wall between us. One of measured pleasantries and polite interactions that scraped my skin raw with each awkward smile.

In the dim shadows, his gaze was a spotlight, leaving me with nothing to hide behind and nothing to offer. Nothing but myself.

I almost offered more. Money to help him buy his own gym. Specifically, the money I'd gotten from my grandma's house.

It wasn't a ton in the grand scheme of things, but Patrick had helped me invest it after the sale, so it was more now than it had been. Enough to get Gabe a bank loan or possibly buy a place outright if he got a good deal.

But the idea sounded a lot like the voice in my head I'd clung to all those years telling me the only way anyone would care about me was if I offered something else. Something more. And I didn't want Gabe to stay because of the gym. I wanted to be enough without anything else.

The more I challenged that voice, the more I believed I was.

Even if Gabe said no and moved to Colorado and we went back to being just friends, or whatever version of Evan's-best-friend-slash-big-brother we became, I was enough to ask for this.

I was enough to be okay, no matter the outcome.

Knowing it freed my lungs to take a full breath and steady my voice. "Don't go to Colorado. Stay. I know this is your dream job, and I meant every word I said about you deserving it. You deserve happiness. So if this job is really what will give it to you, then I want you to take it. But I also just want you."

His eyes flared with emotion as his chest expanded, and my words poured out faster.

"I want to sleep with the weight of your arm around me and wake with you warm in my bed. I want to eat breakfast together and for you to turn me into a morning person. I want to unwind with you on the couch after an event and laugh about the wedding speeches, and I want to watch you light up as you talk about Noah's improved speed. I want to chase our dreams together and explore more than just sex. I want to build a future with you. And I know you're meeting with Coach Dotson soon, and I'll understand if you still accept—"

His hand found my cheek as his mouth pressed to mine, dissolving the words from my lips. The tenderness of it stopped my breath as much as the kiss itself. How he lavished my lips with sweet presses as if sampling me, in no rush to stop. I rose onto my toes to get closer, equally desperate for him.

He broke the kiss and pressed his forehead to mine. "I turned down the job."

My pulse jumped. "What?"

"I called Coach Dotson this morning. We're meeting in a little bit to talk strategy for Noah, but I told him I can't accept the job. That my family is here, and so is the woman I love, and this is where I want to be."

I tried to contain my smile and failed miserably. "Love?"

He released a laugh. "Yeah. I've been stumbling around for weeks trying to convince myself otherwise because I thought it was better for you that way. That my kind of love would only hurt you, but all I've done is fall harder." He stroked my cheek. "I love you. Completely. From your never-ending shoe collection to the way you talk to your plants when you water them, and how you'll ask for to-go containers even if you don't plan to eat the leftovers because you want the chef to think you liked it. I love how strong you are in the way you lead your life but that you never let that strength harden you or shy away from how you feel.

"And I should have told you sooner. Should have said it last night, or at your apartment after the tournament, or on your birthday. I should have admitted it to both of us a long time ago. Just like I should have admitted you're the reason I came back to Philly in the first place." He ran his thumb along my jaw. "You reminded me what home could feel like. Made me want one for real. I just didn't trust myself to have one the way I wanted. To have *you* the way I wanted. Not after everything with Mom."

My heart squeezed, too full to maneuver around the swell of emotion overflowing my chest. In a different way, I hadn't trusted myself either. Maybe we'd both struggled to feel like enough.

"You do now?" I asked.

"I'm working on it. I actually asked Jase about seeing if his therapist recommends any grief counselors. I realized none of my family has really dealt with my mom's death. We've been going through the motions, mostly trying to avoid the pain, but that doesn't feel like enough anymore. He sent me the link to a support group I'm going to try."

Hearing it brought tears to my eyes. That he'd reached a place where he was ready to face the blame he'd placed on his shoulders surrounding her death. That he was ready to try to find peace with himself.

He cupped the back of my neck and brought me closer. "I want us all to be okay, and I don't want to run from myself anymore. I especially don't want to run from you."

I gripped his broad shoulders, drawing reassurance from his steadiness. "I don't want to run from you either. Whatever kind of love you think yours is, it's the most generous and considerate I've ever known, and all I want is to love you back for as long as I can. Because I love you too."

Not the way I did when I was ten and dreaming of a bubbly, pink, perfect picture of a princess and her hero where they were always happy and nothing bad ever happened.

This love knew sorrow and doubt. It knew vulnerability, longing, and heartbreak. It was the safe space to hold each other in and find our way through.

And it was better than anything I'd imagined as a kid.

"Then it sounds like we want the same thing," he said before dropping his lips to mine.

I wrapped my arms around his neck and tried to kiss him

back, but my smile got in the way. His grin matched mine as we broke into laughter.

"What about this place?" I asked, scanning the room. "Are you saying goodbye?"

"Yup." He nudged his gym bag with his foot. "I grabbed my stuff. The rest will be cleared out once the sale is finalized. Probably another month or two."

"Coach Lou accepted the offer from that developer?"

"Yesterday. Got an extra ten grand out of them because they worried he'd hang onto it longer to see if the value would go up."

I rubbed his chest, imagining the ache he must feel at having to let this place go. "I'm sorry. I know how much you wanted it."

"It's okay. Coach got more out of it than I could have given him, even if I won the prize money. He deserves to cash out and relax." His hand covered mine and held it over his heart. "I'll have other chances. Find another building I can afford, and if it does well, I'll upscale when the time is right."

I rose to my toes and kissed him again, loving I could just because I wanted to. "Well, in the meantime, my bed is big enough for us both if you need a place to sleep."

He grinned against my lips. "God, that sounds good." His hands slid to my ass where he gave a teasing squeeze, and I wondered if we had time for one last go on the mats as a final send-off to this place.

A buzz came from his bag.

"That's probably Coach Dotson," he murmured. "He was going to let me know when his meeting finished."

I forced my feet flat. "I can give you a ride. I have to bring the van back to the kitchen."

He clasped my hand, and we meandered toward the front door. "Want to come to my dad's house for dinner after? Evan and my dad are cooking." He flashed his brows. "We can make out in my room until it's ready."

I laughed, joy reverberating up my arm from where our hands were joined and bursting through me like bubbles. "You're about to make all my high school fantasies come true."

"Good. When we're done with those, we'll get back to your current fantasies." He squeezed my hand. "Same rules apply. You tell me what you want, and I'll give it to you."

Heat flashed low in my belly. "Okay, but only if it goes both ways. I want to give you what you want too."

He leaned down to kiss to my lips, then moved his mouth to my ear and whispered, "Anything you want, greedy girl. It's yours."

Epilogue
Aubrey

Eight Months Later

"*YES*," I gasped. My hand tightened in Gabe's hair, the strands long enough for me to tug on now, and I stifled a moan as his tongue swirled my clit. My other hand clenched the edge of the bathroom counter so hard I worried it might snap, but loosening my grip wasn't an option. Not with pleasure gripping my muscles as my orgasm hurdled toward me like a speeding train.

Sounds from the party we'd snuck away from reached us through the kitchen on the other side of the wall. Gabe had barely been on his knees for more than a minute, but I didn't need much longer. It turned out sex in a public bathroom was a major turn-on for me.

He slid one finger inside me as his lips latched onto my clit—

"Oh *shit*, I'm coming—" I slapped a hand over my mouth as my back arched and my hips jerked, his hand on my thigh the only thing keeping me from slipping into the sink once the orgasm locked me in its hold. I tried to catch my moan in my throat as it broke, and a low, deep hum radiated from my chest, the residual pleasure washing over me like a warm shower.

"I want you inside me," I mumbled, the glass of the mirror cool against the back of my head. Gabe kissed the inside of my thigh.

He got to his feet with a pleased smirk on his lips, the bulge in his dark jeans unmistakable, but he didn't reach for his zipper. Instead, he slid my chef pants back up to my waist and dropped a kiss on my lips. "No time, greedy girl. You have to get back to work."

I pouted, but he was right. It was less than ten minutes to midnight, and Jillian expected me to make an appearance. Even though it would be so easy for him to hike me onto his hips and sink me onto him. Thanks to that specialist Coach Dotson recommended, Gabe's shoulder could handle it with no problem. He hadn't even needed surgery since he'd retired from fighting for good.

He kissed me again. "Later," he whispered as if he'd read my mind. "You can ride my cock slow and deep the rest of the night once we get home."

A whimper escaped my lips, and I licked into his mouth, tasting myself on his tongue before managing to pull back. "I'm going to hold you to that."

He grinned. "Promise?"

I shoved him away before I jumped him right here, and turned to adjust my chef cap in the mirror. My long ponytail was secure in its braid, my appearance no worse for wear. The flush in my cheeks could be explained by the "fresh air" Gabe and I had told my staff we were getting on the balcony. An excuse they may not have bought.

Once cleaned up, we exited the staff bathroom and headed down the short hallway that connected to the kitchen.

"How we looking?" I asked Mack as they finished garnishing the last tray of baked chocolate custards with hazelnuts and brown sugar fluff. We'd been in good shape when I stepped out, with only desserts left to finish before the ball drop.

"Good," Mack said. "Sydney is getting a jump on clean up, and I'll be done with this in a minute."

"Once you're done, go enjoy the party, okay?" I glanced at Sydney, where she loaded one of the dishwashers. "Same for you, Syd. Finish that load, then the night is yours."

"Heard, Chef."

"Great job tonight. Both of you."

We'd been the definition of a well-oiled machine. Three little bees running the beehive in perfect sync.

Mack and I had fallen into a rhythm as soon as they'd started—one they'd been comfortable enough to switch to they/them pronouns in after only a few weeks—and business had been so good, we'd brought on Sydney as a line cook a few months later with help from Jillian. Syd was even younger than Mack and had never been to culinary school, but the drive and raw talent were there, and Mack had been as eager as I was to take her under their wing.

It was my first time working in a kitchen without a single

male chef, and while that hadn't been an intentional decision, it was a cool shift in dynamic from what I'd experienced so far in my career. Made better by the fact that I still got to see my boys regularly.

Both sides of Ardena's operation got together for a weekly staff meal and monthly shift drink, and this year, we had our first staff holiday party. It was a potluck at Ardena's, and the winner of the favorite dish of the night got a hundred-dollar gift card from Jillian, though the real incentive was trying to beat Jase. He'd technically won the most votes but had declared himself ineligible to win, so the prize went to Luis with his upgraded spin on his mom's pork tamales.

I'd left that night with both my stomach and my heart full, a feeling I'd had a lot lately. In no small part due to the breathtaking man waiting for me near the door.

Gabe gave me an easy smile. "Ready?"

I took his hand as he pushed us through to the event hall. Live music and the sounds of celebration rushed my ears as energy from the party bubbled inside me like water overflowing a pot.

After last year's success, Jillian's party had become *the* New Year's Eve party in Philly. She took the reputation seriously. Not only had her replica Millenium Times Square ball returned in all its glory, but professional acrobats swung from the ceiling and performed jaw-dropping stunts on the stage. I had no idea how she'd keep upping herself year after year, but I looked forward to finding out.

I spotted her along the stage and made my way to her and the gentleman she talked with. Gabe let go of my hand and fell behind to let me network.

Jillian opened her arms to me. "The chef of the hour, as

promised. John Patel, this is Aubrey Witter, the head chef of Arden Catering."

I shook his hand.

"John's daughter is getting married to a professional football player next year," Jillian explained. "They're expecting quite a few guests and will need a caterer up to the task."

A year ago, I would have dreaded the idea. One more mammoth event to manage on my own. Now? "Our team's one of the best," I said. "We'd be happy to make your daughter's wedding everything she hopes for and more."

"You saw the *Philadelphia Food Journal* article, right?" Jillian asked him.

It would have been impressive if he hadn't, seeing as Jillian had blown up a copy and hung it on either side of the party's entrance. The headline was practically legible from the ground floor. How she'd gotten it in advance, I had no idea, since the magazine issue wasn't officially available for a few more days, but every guest's swag bag tonight had a copy.

It was the issue featuring the art museum's seventy-fifth-anniversary celebration that had taken place earlier this month, highlighting the winner of the catering competition whose food was the star of the show.

We had not been that winner.

While we did make it into the final round and got to serve our food to the judges, one of the bigger and more well-known restaurants ended up winning the whole thing. Jillian heard it was because they liked the idea of another longtime Philly establishment being a part of celebrating the local institution, a touch we couldn't offer yet as a start-up.

I was fine with it, especially since Pépère wasn't the

winner. Christian's menu submission hadn't even landed them a spot in the final round.

Meanwhile, Arden Catering got featured in the magazine as an honorable mention. It wasn't something the magazine planned to offer, but the judges loved our menu so much they decided to add it to the mix. I had no idea what it would mean for business, but my guess was we'd need to hire another chef soon.

After another minute of Jillian talking me up, I politely excused myself, and Gabe and I weaved through the crowd to our friends. We were down to three minutes until midnight, and most of the group was together in a cluster on the edge of the dance floor, ready to ring in the New Year.

"They're here," Dani said, beaming as brightly as the engagement ring on her finger. "We can ask them."

I hugged her first, then Jase. I'd seen them a week ago at the staff holiday party, but we'd missed our Monday night get-together so I could prep for tonight. Most weeks, the four of us did dinner together, either out at a restaurant or at one of our apartments, but sometimes we went dancing or had a game night with Evan. And on the weeks it couldn't happen, Dani and I tried to plan something with the girls instead. "Ask us what?"

"Okay," Neela said, her arm around Robin's waist. "Would you rather get ten million dollars or never have to eat ever again?"

I scrunched my brow and looked at Jase. "Ten million dollars."

He tipped his head. "That's what I said."

"Zach said never eat again," Robin informed us.

All eyes went to Zach, who tried to use his much shorter

boyfriend as a shield. "It would save me time, okay? I'd still eat when I wanted to."

"I'm with Zach," Gabe said. "I'd get way more done if I didn't have to think about food."

"Yes," I said, "but Zach's literal job is to think about food." He'd officially become Ardena's sous chef six months ago and was crushing it.

"Speaking of jobs," Jase said to Gabe. "The gym opens in what, ten days?"

"Eleven," Gabe said with a grin. "I saw you and Colin on the registration list."

"Hell yeah. You're close enough to where Colin works that you may poach him from his current gym for good."

Gabe had found a building in Queen Village for his boxing gym, just a few blocks south of Colin's art gallery. It had been in need of major repairs, but since Gabe needed to gut it anyway to turn it into a boxing gym, that hadn't been a problem. And since he was still living with his dad and Evan at his dad's house (when he wasn't staying with me), he had a second stream of income renting out the apartment up top.

At least, he would once Noah began making professional money. He'd won the silver medal in his weight class at the Olympics over the summer with Gabe in the crowd cheering for him right next to Noah's dad. Now, Noah was transitioning to professional boxing with Gabe as his coach. He'd moved into the apartment above the gym, which Gabe was letting him stay in for free until he had more steady earnings.

Given how quickly sign-ups for the gym's public classes had filled, I wasn't too worried about Gabe needing that extra income for the gym to stay afloat. Even with the two assistant coaches he'd hired.

Evan wandered up beside me, hands in his pockets and a scowl on his face.

"What?" I asked. I followed his glare to a pretty brunette with fair skin and a French-style bob that looked chic against her sharp features. Maybe she'd tell me where she got her hair done.

She flipped Evan off.

Or maybe not.

"Get rejected?" I asked.

Evan scoffed. "Please, I work with her. I have no clue why she's here, seeing as her idea of fun is staking out the office refrigerator to snap at anyone who dares breathe near her precious grain bowl. I assumed being in a room full of humans having an actual good time would be her worst nightmare. But I guess ruining my night makes up for it."

"How'd she ruin it?"

"I was having a perfectly lovely conversation with her friend until she butted in."

Ah. That explained the lack of lady on his arm. "Sorry. I promise a New Year's kiss isn't everything."

He broke his glare with a roll of his eyes. "Whatever." Something caught his attention behind me. "Dad made it?"

Gabe's head whipped around. "Where?"

Evan pointed across the room to the main stairs, where Mr. Hardt stood in a royal-blue dress shirt. Beside him was a woman about his age, her long dark hair flowing in an elegant wave over one shoulder.

My jaw dropped.

"Did he bring a date?" Gabe asked. The three of us exchanged glances, similar levels of shock on our faces.

"This is good, right?" I asked.

"I think so?" Evan said. "Do we know who she is?"

"He hasn't mentioned anyone." Gabe leaned to the side, trying to get a better view. "She looks kind of familiar."

I agreed, but before I could place her, the music cut off, and Jillian's voice radiated from the speakers. "One minute to go!"

Gabe crossed my arms in front of me, bringing my back to his front so we could both watch the ball light up. With thirty seconds to go, it started its descent, raising cheers from the crowd. At ten seconds, the whole room counted down. I joined them, my chest buzzing with more than just excitement.

I took in my friends around me, some that I'd had for a while and others I'd never expected.

Like Dani, who I now counted as one of my closest friends. My first real female friend, but no longer my only one.

Jase and the guys, who had always been my work friends but I now knew were more. Family in the truest sense of the word. One that continued to grow with Mack and Syd.

Evan, my soul brother, standing shoulder to shoulder with *his* brother, more whole than I feared he'd be able to be after his mom died. Gabe and Evan had been going to the support group Jase's therapist recommended, and it had gone a long way toward healing deeper wounds.

I hadn't considered myself lonely before, but standing here now, it was clear I had been. The connections I'd limited myself to had been nowhere near enough.

The countdown hit the final second, and the ball reached the stage, its lights sparkling as confetti rained from the ceiling.

Gabe spun me from our hold and dipped me into a kiss, making me squawk, then laugh, then finally kiss him back. It was sweet and a little dirty, his tongue dipping between my lips at the end. A hint of what would come later.

He drew me to my feet and clasped his arms around my back, keeping me close. "Happy New Year, baby."

I'd told Evan the truth before—it wasn't the kiss that mattered.

It was the look in Gabe's eye just now. The familiar press of his lips against mine. The safety I felt in his arms.

It was knowing I got to spend the next year with him. And hopefully the one after that, and after that. It was knowing he would put as much of himself into making me happy as he would making his own dreams come true.

Knowing *I* could make him as happy.

That if we strove for them together, the things we wanted were never out of reach. That as much as we'd lost, there was still a whole life of hope, beauty, and possibility for us to live.

I pressed another kiss to his lips, seeing that possibility reflected in his eyes. "Desserts first," I told him since I had a job to finish. "But then I want to dance with you."

"Well, then," he said, mouth lifting. He took my hand and led us toward the kitchen.

Thank you for reading *Ours to Lose*! If you enjoyed it, please consider leaving a review. Even a short line or two is a huge help!

Want more sweet (and spicy) moments between Aubrey and Gabe?

Join my newsletter to receive their bonus epilogue!

laceyburke.com/ours-to-lose-bonus-epilogue

Acknowledgments

There are times writing a book feels like pouring water from a bottomless pitcher, the characters and dialogue flowing onto the page and bringing it to life, and other times it feels more like trying to shake out the last drop of seltzer that's stuck behind the metal lip of the can. This book had moments of both, as well as a few where it felt like the water was buried beneath six feet of mud, and I had to dredge it up with my bare hands, one grueling heap at a time.

I have more than one person to thank for helping me push through the muddiest parts.

Steph, for reading the draft in its sloppiest form and still finding things to love about it. Nicole, for pushing my writing to the next level and letting me brain dump ridiculously long emails when I was spiraling through edits. Drew, who I can count on to catch those pesky typos that survived a dozen previous read throughs.

Thank you to my family, whose love and support continue to mean the world to me.

And thank you to every single reader who has read, shared, posted about, and reviewed my books or supported me in any way. I can't express what it means to have the stories I feel moved to share resonate as deeply with you. Thank you.

About the Author

Lacey Burke is a contemporary romance author who's lived all over the place but finds herself most often in Vermont. She loves writing relatable characters finding their happily ever afters and all the emotional twists, turns, and climbs that come with them.

www.laceyburke.com
lacey@laceyburke.com

* 9 7 8 1 9 6 4 9 7 3 0 1 2 *